INSANELY

SANE

JASMINE SHOUSE

INCLUDES CONTENT PERFECT
FOR THE CLASSROOM
AND BOOK CLUBS

DISCUSSION QUESTIONS
MENTAL HEALTH RESOURCES
MINDFULNESS EXERCISES

This is a work of fiction. Unless otherwise indicated, all the names, characters, businesses, places, events and incidents in this book are either the product of the author's imagination or used in a fictitious manner. Any resemblance to actual persons, living or dead, or actual events is purely coincidental.

Text copyright © 2022 by Jasmine Shouse
All Rights Reserved. Printed in the United States of America

Published by Motina Books, LLC, Van Alstyne, Texas
www.MotinaBooks.com

Library of Congress Cataloguing-in-Publication Data:
Names: Shouse, Jasmine
Title: Insanely Sane
Description: First Edition. | Van Alstyne: Motina Books, 2022

Identifiers:
LCCN: 2022944852

ISBN-13: 978-1-945060-63-2 (paperback)
ISBN-13: 978-1-945060-50-2 (e-book)
ISBN-13: 978-1-945060-65-6 (hardcover)

Subjects: BISAC:
YOUNG ADULT FICTION / Social Themes / Mental Illness

Cover Design: Diane Windsor
Interior Design: Diane Windsor

DEDICATION

To the ones who hurt and go unheard. To the misdiagnosed and mistreated. To the ones who face the day no matter how difficult it seems. To the ones who don't give up the fight and the ones who lost their war.

I believe you.

And to my husband and friends who never gave up on me.

AUTHOR'S NOTE

Healing from trauma isn't linear. There's no magic button that restores you back to a previous version of yourself. Transitioning from survival mode to healing and recovery doesn't stop at the end of the story. The characters in Insanely Sane don't have neat and clean endings because that's not how healing works. It's an ongoing process that can have tons of relapses. But healing is possible.
If you find yourself in a troubled state while reading this book, please practice positive self-care.

Praise for *Insanely Sane*

"An insightful, hard-hitting, and tender tale of converging mental health journeys."

—*Kirkus Reviews*

"With a depth of compassion, Ms. Shouse has created a story of despair and repair with finely drawn characters, each young adult striving to fit into their respective rejecting social/familial circle. The story is rich in feeling and detail and reminds us we are each uniquely different and yet universally the same."

—Parris Afton Bonds, New York Times Bestselling Author

"Insanely Sane is excellent, and I thoroughly enjoyed every page. Together, and with the help of the wonderfully supportive staff at Pleasant Valley, these ten patients slowly revealed the traumas of their past, their fears for the future, and the uncertainty of returning to life outside the walls of the treatment center. Tobias listened as each and every one of those struggling teens revealed their stories despite the fear of being judged. Inside and outside group therapy sessions, friendships were formed as dark secrets were slowly revealed, and the teens learned there was only one thing they could always rely on—each other."

—Sarah McKnight, Author of *Life Support*

TRIGGER WARNING

This story contains content that may be troubling to some, including, but not limited to:

suicide/self-harm,
addiction,
abduction,
child abuse,
homophobia,
misdiagnosis,
death,
violence,
arson/fire,
sexual assault,
childhood trauma,
neglect,
& more.

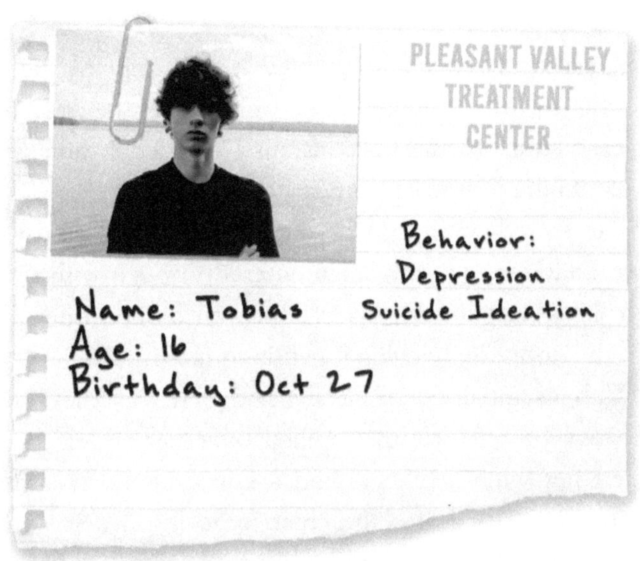

TOBIAS

The walls were sick. Not white. Sick. Like someone mixed a ton of white paint with a bucket of vomit. Each of the tiny room's walls were bare except for the lone opposite the dark door which had slammed shut behind the attendant. That wall sported one of those cheesy motivational sayings written in a loopy brown script.

Great. Puke and shit. Exactly what I wanted to see in a hospital.

I crossed my leg so that one ankle sat on top of the other knee and started bouncing it. There was no clock, and the lady at the front desk took my cell phone, so I had no way of telling the time. I slumped back against the leather couch where I sat. My fingers found their way under the bandage on my forearm and absently scratched until red blotted the gauze.

For a brief second I regretted it, realizing for the first time that I probably wouldn't be walking out the front door any time soon. In the next instant I decided I didn't care. My hand fell into my lap, and my eyes closed.

The sound of the door jangling jolted me awake, my entire body tensing. A woman entered through with a large set of keys dangling from a black lanyard. She turned away from the door after closing it gently to face me.

With a sympathetic smile she said, "Hi, I'm Riley." Riley had wavy brown hair that spilled over her shoulders and framed her wide face. She had a curvy figure, not overly plump, that settled into the chair opposite me. She pulled one foot out of her shoe and tucked it underneath her then rested her clipboard on it. "I'm going to be one of your therapists. I just need some info from you so we can get you checked in." Her voice was kind and gentle, like she was speaking to a spooked horse.

Tears pricked at my eyes, unbidden. *Way to go, loser,* I thought. *Can't even handle five minutes in this place before I lose my shit.* My fingernails automatically dug into my palm until I could focus on answering.

I reluctantly answered Riley's questions about where I lived, my cell phone number, and my school information. Finally she put her pen down and caught my eye. "Why are you here?" she asked, still in that soothing voice.

What kind of idiotic question was that? Did she not see the bloody bandage on my arm? Could she not read the notes from the hospital visits? I opened my mouth to say as much, but something about the intensity of her gaze prevented my smartass comment from coming out.

"I want to die," I said flatly. I glanced down at my

hands. The fingernails on my left hand had dried blood under them. The honesty of my words deflated me.

"Thank you for being truthful, Tobias," she said so sincerely that it made me look at her. Her pale lips parted in a sad smile as she stood. "Come with me. You can rest soon."

She opened the door for me. I looked down the hallway towards the front door, debating on making a break for it. Riley paused, waiting for me without saying a word. I sighed for show and followed her in the opposite direction.

We entered an examining room where I was questioned by a man in scrubs about my name, birthday, and why I was there. He had me pull off my shirt and roll up my pant legs. "Checking for cuts and bruises," he explained in a way that made it clear he'd rather be doing something else.

"You mean besides the obvious ones?" I said, holding out my arm.

The guy flashed me the briefest of grins before taking a hold of my arm and unwrapping the bandage. I grimaced as it came away, reopening the scab. My eyes stayed on the crimson blood starting to pool at the opening before it was covered by a new wad of gauze. I blinked and looked away, feeling the heat of shame creep up my neck.

"Do you feel safe?" The man asked as he finished redressing my self-inflicted wound.

I stared at him. "Uh, what?"

"Do you feel like you're going to try to hurt yourself or others?"

"No," I said after a moment.

"Then you're safe. All done." He turned away to write in a binder while I put on my shirt. "The doctor will meet with you in the morning. Do you have any questions?"

Only about a million.

"No," I said.

Riley was waiting for me when I left the examining room. She led me down two more hallways until we reached a door that showed the last of the day's sunlight coming through the glass. Riley swiped her badge against a black reader on the wall to unlock the door.

The warm air washed over me, welcome after the coldness of the building. I'd heard that hospitals were kept super cold to slow the spread of infections, but it made me wonder why a place like Pleasant Valley Treatment Center would worry about that. It's not like crazy was communicable.

A cement path branching out to other walkways led to buildings around the compound. Each building seemed to be labeled with the name of some type of tree. We passed by Elm, Aspen, and Oak before Riley turned and gestured me to follow her to a squat reddish-brown building aptly named Sequoia. She used her badge to unlock the tinted glass door which led to yet another heavy wooden door. This time she inserted a key from her lanyard into a lock on the wall, not on the door. The door swung open.

Holy Susanna Kaysen, I thought as I followed Riley into the ward. A gangly woman with ragged hair and a glassy look in her eyes sat on a tan leather couch and glanced at us as we walked past. Behind the counter stood a large woman with dark skin and bright pink hair. She smiled as Riley approached. "New check in?" Her voice was husky and matronly.

Riley placed a binder on the counter, the same one the guy who had examined me used. I hadn't realized she took it. The three-inch binder had my first name printed along the spine. It hit me again that I would not be leaving any time soon. She put a bag alongside it that had a biohazard mark on the outside.

"Tobias?" the pink-haired woman asked. She repeated the question I clearly didn't hear the first time. "How old are you?"

"Seventeen," I said.

The lady looked at Riley. "He can't stay, you know."

"He can't go to Maple yet. He needs to be kept under observation before we can give him a room there."

I shifted uncomfortably and kept my eyes on the floor. They reminded me of my parents, arguing about whose turn it was for custody.

Riley's hand touched my shoulder. I didn't look up at her. "It's only for a little while. I'll come and see you tomorrow, okay?"

I nodded. I wanted to look nonchalant, like I didn't care if she came or not. But when she lifted her hand and started to walk back the way we'd come, my eyes followed, begging her silently not to leave. She didn't look back.

"Come on, shug," Pinky said. I missed it when she said her name. "Let's get you set up in a room." She walked out from behind the desk. "Do you have any belongings with you?"

I shook my head. "Just my cell phone and these clothes." I resisted the urge to scratch at my arm.

"Don't worry, we'll scrounge up something for you." She walked past a large room with a few round tables and mismatched chairs where a few other patients lounged about. A couple of them watched TV while another colored. On the other side was a series of tan doors that stood open, revealing matching rooms. Pinky stopped at the end of the hall and opened the door. I walked inside.

"You won't have a roommate here unless another young'un comes in while you're here. But they'll probably move you soon. At Maple, you're like to have a roommate."

I examined the room while she spoke. There was a bed in two of the corners, one by the window, and a door in the third that presumably led to the bathroom. Well, it was almost a door. There were big gaps at the top and bottom. A large set of shelves stood along one wall. There was nothing else in the room. No pictures, no desk, not even sheets.

"Dinner's already over," Pinky continued, "but we'll have evening snack out in about an hour or so."

My stomach growled at the mention of food. I nodded.

"Is there anything I can get you?"

"Uh, could I get maybe a blanket and pillow? And something to write with? Please," I added. It'd do me no good to piss off the staff if I ever wanted to get out of this place.

Pinky graced me with a wide, gap-toothed smile. "Sure thing." I could hear her steps on the tile heading away from the room.

I heaved a sigh and sat on the bed nearest the window. It sank with a disturbing squishy sound. The mattress was situated on a heavy wooden frame. Everything in the room was designed to prevent suicide attempts. I bit my cheeks to fend off the emotions threatening to overwhelm me. A knock at the door interrupted my thoughts. Pinky had returned with a couple of thick blue blankets in her arms and a notebook balanced precariously on top.

"Can't give you a pillow because of safety reasons, but you can use one of these blankets instead. The other one's to cover up." She dropped the bundle onto the bed. "And there's a notebook for you too. I found some paper scrubs so you can change if you'd like."

"Thank you," I managed to say.

"I'll leave you to get settled in then," Pinky said. "Let us know if there's anything else."

"What about a pen or pencil?" I asked while inspecting the flimsy scrubs.

"Crayons are in the main room if you want to write or color," she replied.

I couldn't help it. My mouth fell open. "Crayons? Are you serious?"

Pinky's expression hardened. "Yes, we take safety very seriously."

I took the hint and nodded to show her that I understood. I hadn't even wanted to do any damage, just actually write, but I got it. I knew there could be people here who would use a pencil to hurt themselves. Hell, I was one of them.

After Pinky left, I spread out one of the blankets on the bed then folded the other to use as a makeshift pillow. I kicked off my shoes, tied with zipties in place of laces, and lay on the bed again.

How much more of a failure can I be? I couldn't even kill myself right, I thought. My arm started itching again. I considered how good it would feel to take the bandages off and scratch until the pain was the only thing I could focus on. With another sigh, I sat up and headed out to mingle with the other crazies.

A few more had drifted in while I was setting up my room. A man and two women lingered by a wall made of glass that I had somehow missed earlier. The women seemed young, maybe a few years older than me. One of them, rail thin with stringy blonde hair, bounced on the balls of her feet. She kept glancing outside, her eyes sliding back and forth from the desk.

"Can we go smoke yet?" she squeaked.

Pinky glanced at the clock on the wall behind the desk. "I suppose so." She made her way to a keyhole on the wall, winding around scattered chairs as others in the room rushed to the glass.

I took the chance to examine the room more closely. A stack of books lay on one of the tables next to some sheets of paper that looked like they had word searches and coloring pages. Beside those sat a plastic bin full of crayons. Another table held the remains of what was once a checkers set. A small TV attached to the wall played a game show. That was it.

Taking a closer look at the books revealed only one even remotely interesting, but it was the third in a series with neither of the first two anywhere to be found.

"Maybe I succeeded after all," I muttered, "because this feels like my personal hell."

"Why are you here?" It felt like the billionth time someone had asked that question in the past few days. This time the question was posed by Dr. Larson, who spoke with a trace of an accent. German or Russian maybe. I wasn't very good at accents.

I stopped tracing the wood patterns on the desk to look up at the bearded face of my newly assigned psychiatrist. He had brown hair cut just above his ears and eyes the same color that were filled with patience and feigned understanding.

I hated that look. I wanted to do everything in my power to make that look go away.

My eyebrows raised, and my lips curled into a smirk. I stared at him for a few moments, contemplating whether or not I should answer. But that would defeat the purpose of my silent defiance, so I decided against it.

Dr. Larson consulted the binder in front of him—my binder. "You were admitted three days ago for suicidal behavior," he said as though to remind me. "Since then, you've been withdrawn from others and disinterested in groups." He raised his head, and I was sure he noticed the mystified look on my face.

Before I could stop myself, I spluttered, "I'm not like those people. I'm not a druggie or anything. I'm probably the youngest one in there, so how can you think I'm going to be going around and making friends?"

The doctor smiled slightly. "Perhaps it has not been easy these few days, but you have not shown any reason to think you may still be a danger to yourself, so I am recommending you be relocated to the Maple unit."

Relief spread through me, though I tried not to let it show on my face. We weren't allowed to lock our doors in Sequoia, and it was really hard trying to sleep knowing that the guy next door could come in at any time. Even with the staff manning the desk all the time, they weren't always paying attention, and it would take longer for them to get to my room than the guy would need.

"How long do I have to stay here?" I asked, forcing my voice to sound bored.

Dr. Larson gave me another of his piercing looks. "That depends on you. If you wanted, you could leave right now." I sat up from my slouched position. "Of course, that would be against the doctor's recommendation which would then leave you to face what awaits you out there. Otherwise, a typical program for youths is about 90 days."

"So glad I have a choice," I muttered and slumped back in the chair.

I left the doctor's office a short while later, taking a seat in one of the chairs to wait for the escorting staff to bring me back to Sequoia, hopefully for the last time. I shivered slightly and wished I had a hoodie because the doctor's office was even colder than the ward. My head bumped up against the wall. *Great,* I thought, *only three more months of this.*

"Tobias?" A high-pitched voice called out. I raised my hand half-heartedly and stood. The woman standing before me was about two heads shorter than me. She was cute, though, with warm, light brown skin and bright brown curls pulled up into pigtails. Her glasses were huge, and her smile was bigger.

"I'm Tobias," I said then mentally kicked myself. She obviously knew that already.

"My name is Iesha. I'm one of the nurses in Maple unit. We'll go get your stuff from Sequoia then I'll take you over there."

I realized too late that the paper scrubs did little to offer discretion, but if Iesha noticed, she mercifully said nothing.

She chattered all the way back to Sequoia, and I found myself telling her my annoyance at the lack of any decent reading material. For the first time in days, I felt almost human again.

When we reached my room, Iesha waited outside with the door cracked since we weren't allowed to have it closed all the way. I changed back into my jeans and t-shirt that I wore when I arrived, discarding the paper scrubs in the trash. I grabbed my notebook and the sharpest crayon I could find. By the time I exited the room, Iesha had the bucket that held the hygiene products given to me and the bag that held my medication, wallet, and cell phone.

"All set?" she asked in that same perky voice.

I nodded, eager to be away from the deathly despair that clung to Sequoia.

She led me back to the cement pathway outside, and I was reminded that I hadn't even stepped out of the building since entering the ward. Breathing in the fresh air felt like stepping into a warm shower on a winter day. Iesha and I walked further into the compound to the far side from the front entrance. The building looked almost hexagonal with brown and green paint that nearly blended in with the trees towering overhead.

Another badge reader and wall lock later, and we were in Maple. The hall we entered was lined with a dozen rooms, six on each side, that led to two common rooms with a staff desk that spanned the wall across both rooms. As we approached the desk, I could see the same round tables. At least the chairs matched in that room, though. There were also a few leather lounge chairs facing a wall that had a TV mounted. A door led out to a paved courtyard.

Two more nurses stood behind the desk, both men. One was light-skinned and wore glasses like Iesha's, but they looked more like owl eyes on him. What was left of his greying brown hair was combed over. The other was tan nearly to the point of burnt and had dirty blonde hair with frosted tips. They both greeted me, and I grimaced in return.

Iesha placed my hygiene bucket and bags on the counter. She pulled some papers out of the pocket of her scrubs. "These are his transfer orders."

I tuned them out and peeked around the corner at the other room. It had another TV and the same leather lounge chairs but a lot more of them. There was also a kitchenette along one of the walls. I caught sight of the coffee dispensing machine and let out a small happy sigh. As my eyes continued to roam, I noticed a couple of very tall bookshelves. One was stacked with board and card games, but the other had a decent number of books, though I couldn't read the titles from where I stood.

"Here's your welcome bag," one of the men said, pulling my attention away. The one with a combover handed me a black nylon bag. I glimpsed inside to see a few thin books, a water bottle, and a coffee mug.

"Already more welcoming than Sequoia," I said with a grin.

"We get that a lot," he chuckled. "I'm Troy, and this is Kal. Schedule is on the wall. You'll get to meet the others when they come back from lunch. Iesha, do you want to show him to his new room?"

I followed her past the room with the bookcase to the other hall with another dozen rooms. "How many are in each room?" I asked Iesha.

"Only two per room," she chirped. "We're rarely at capacity, though. Boys are on this side, and the girls are down the other hall."

"Co-ed?" I raised an eyebrow. "Is that really smart with all the hormones running wild at this age?"

"Between the cameras and the age range, it's actually not that big of an issue," Iesha said, completely missing or ignoring the humor in my voice. "Here we are." She stopped at the third door down on the left. The door was already cracked, but she knocked anyway.

No one answered so she pushed open the door. The room had two beds on the same wooden frames, but they were positioned with the heads against one wall. Light wooden nightstands stood between them. One was bare, but the other had a smattering of books and papers and a painted mask. Some of the shelves held clothes while others were empty. A built-in desk sat between the bathroom and the shelves.

The biggest difference between this room and the one I occupied in Sequoia was the window. The wall opposite the door held a full panel window that, while covered with slatted blinds, offered a glimpse outside to the walled courtyard.

Iesha didn't follow me into the room. She said from the doorway as I inspected my new surroundings, "You can join the others with the next group after lunch. They'll meet out in the common room. Your hygiene stuff will be kept at the desk, but you can have it whenever there isn't a group going on. There's a schedule posted near the desk. If you have any questions, just come ask us." She gave me a warm smile before walking away.

I walked over to the bare bed and set the nylon bag on it. After I withdrew the water bottle and coffee cup, placing them on my new nightstand, I emptied the rest of the bag's contents. The books turned out to be self-improvement workbooks and journals. I rolled my eyes and made to move the bag but there seemed to be more in it.

My hand felt around inside the bag and came out with a small tub of putty and a smooth rock. The last thing caused the corner of my mouth to tug up in a half grin.

"Maybe this ward won't be so bad," I muttered aloud as I grasped a pair of pens.

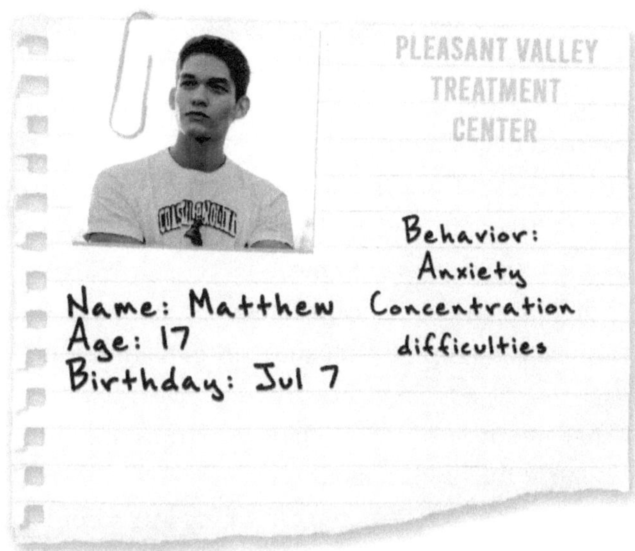

MATTHEW

"Hey, man, if you take the rest of the fish, we're going to have words!" Renee called.

I turned around and grinned at the girl a few places behind me in line. "Oh, you know I'm taking all of it," I said.

Her pale mouth pouted, but her gray eyes still held a smile. She broke eye contact after a moment, and I turned back to the lunch line.

"Good afternoon, Ms. Dora," I said to the portly Hispanic woman behind the counter.

"What'll it be?" She tried to keep her voice stern.

I paused to look down the line of food displayed. The chicken always managed to taste dry even when heaped with sauce. The rice usually wasn't too bad, and the veggies were okay with a packet of salt. But the fish was always on point, even if it didn't much look like fish. "Give me as much fish as you can while leaving enough for my red-headed friend back there."

Ms. Dora smiled and piled three of the five remaining chunks of fish onto a plate. She added a scoop of veggies and handed the plate over to me.

"You're my hero," I heard Renee say as I moved down the line to pick up a container of two chocolate chip cookies.

"That was nice of you," Darla purred as she sidled up next to me at the drink dispenser.

I shrugged, unscrewing the cap of my water bottle to fill it with Pepsi. I tried to keep my expression neutral while my neck and face started to heat up. There was no denying Darla was hot, but I'd been around her too long to fall for her tricks.

"The kid could use a break," I said quietly. "She had a rough morning."

"Yeah, she did." Darla's voice lost its sultry sound. "If he tries to show up here again, it'll be his funeral."

Nodding in agreement while knowing full well she wouldn't do anything, I took my tray and moved away from the line to find a table in the cafeteria that often doubled as a group room for the older patients. We were encouraged to eat quickly since one of the older groups was scheduled to follow us, but they weren't allowed to enter until we were out of the door. That suited me just fine. Though the military unit wasn't bad when it was their turn, some of the other patients gave me the creeps the way they stared at us when we passed.

I joined Kate and Ciro at the table nearest the door.

Kate scowled at the food. "Nothing here is ever edible," she complained loudly. "We're better off sticking to the cereal and cookies."

Ciro didn't seem to be listening. He stared off into the distance at nothing in particular, absently twisting a plastic fork in the mess of chicken and veggies on his plate. Even the sound of my chair scraping against the tile didn't stir him from his reverie.

"You good, man?" I asked him.

"He's been like this ever since he got back from seeing Michelle," Kate said, the slightest hint of concern crossing her pale face.

"Ah," I said as if that explained everything. Which, to me, it did. Ciro and I shared the same therapist. Michelle was uncannily good at her job, so I actually understood that lost feeling that sometimes followed sessions with her.

"We talked to my mom," Ciro murmured. I barely heard him over the commotion of the cafeteria.

Kate and I exchanged a glance. "Uh, you said you didn't have a mother," I said after a moment. "I know we're all some kind of crazy in here but are you having a psychotic break?"

Ciro stirred in his seat, and his bright blue eyes looked at me as though seeing me for the first time. His honeyed skin reddened slightly. "I didn't mean she was dead. Just dead to me. At the time. But now..." he trailed off, lowering his head to look at the plate in front of him. "What even IS this stuff?"

I couldn't help it. I started laughing. Kate joined in, and, after another blush, Ciro did too.

We finished the edible parts of the meal and put the trays on the dirty rack before joining the line of others in

Maple who were waiting to return to the ward. Ciro, no longer in his catatonic state, made no mention of his mother again, and we let the topic go. Voices gradually grew louder in the echoey room as more people finished their food until soon we were shouting and jostling each other.

A piercing whistle sliced through the room, quieting us immediately. "Line up and count off as you go through the door," commanded Maria, the nurse who accompanied us to lunch.

"Six," I muttered as I passed, feeling the familiar tingle of embarrassment creep up my spine. Three weeks already, and it still made me feel like a little kid.

When we returned to Maple, everyone splintered off to go to the courtyard or to their rooms for a few minutes of peace before the next group.

"Hey, Matthew," Kate said, pausing at the desk, "Looks like you have a new roommate." She pointed at the whiteboard that listed our names. Next to mine, Troy had written the name Tobias.

With a shrug, I turned away from it. In spite of myself, I felt a prick of curiosity. I was the most recent addition to the ward, and that had been three weeks ago. I wondered how the new guy would fit in—if he would fit in. "I hope they didn't stick me with one of the kids," I muttered.

The door to my room was barely open when I walked up to it. Kate and Darla hovered near their door across the hall, eyes on me. "Obvious much?" I teased them. Darla stuck out her tongue while Kate rolled her eyes.

I tapped the door twice with my knuckles and paused for a moment before entering. The guy at the window turned his head and gave me a slight nod before returning his gaze outside. His hair was a dark brown mess of curls cut just shy of his ears. He kept tossing his head to get the hair out of his eyes as he bent over the notebook perched on long legs he had propped onto the windowsill.

"Hey," I said, "I'm your roommate."

"Figured as much," he answered. "They said we aren't allowed in rooms that aren't our own."

"Yeah." I chewed on my lip for a moment, but Tobias didn't seem interested in saying anything else. "Group's starting in ten minutes," I said, wanting to fill the silence.

No reaction. What a chatterbox.

I grabbed my own notebook and a pen off of my nightstand and retreated to the hall. Kate and Darla ambushed me almost immediately.

"So?" Kate asked.

"What's he like?" Darla supplied, one of her fingers finding her hair and twisting a strand.

"A real conversationalist." I walked past them and dropped into a chair in the common room. Swinging my legs over one of the armchairs, I settled in to wait. The others trickled in slowly as the minutes passed. Renee took the seat next to mine and tucked her legs up under her small frame.

"Are you okay?" she asked in her usual whisper. "I saw you had a new roommate."

That was the problem with living in close quarters with the same people who you did literally everything but shower with—nothing felt private. "Why wouldn't I be okay?" I couldn't twist my head far enough around to see more than a sliver of her profile.

"I don't know." She seemed to be chewing over her answer. "New people can be scary."

I chuckled. "Yeah, they can be."

One of the intern therapists walked into the room carrying a stack of papers. She seemed a bit frazzled as she headed towards a chair placed under the TV where all the group facilitators seemed to favor. "Sorry I'm late, everyone. My last group ran long."

Several of us chorused that it was fine. Movement caught my eye, and I saw Tobias coming down the hallway. He passed by without looking at me, heading for the back of the group.

"To start off," the intern said, "we'll go around and say your name and how you're feeling and if you're feeling safe for group." She adjusted the headband holding back her black hair before continuing. "I'm Amy, and I'm safe. I'm feeling rushed." She allowed a sheepish smile before looking to her left.

"I'm Ciro. Safe and feeling..." He paused and looked puzzled. "Conflicted."

"Meera. Safe. Tired," said the girl next to him.

Amy's eyes landed on me. "Matthew. Safe. Anxious." The words were automatic, unchanged since the day I arrived.

"My name is Renee. I'm safe, and I feel concerned."

The check-in continued in the same fashion down the line with Kate, Darla, James, and the one we called Bullfrog. Then it was the new guy's turn.

My resolve not to look at him broke, and I found myself turning around. "Tobias," he said through a grimace. "Safe, I guess. On edge."

"Welcome, Tobias," Amy said with a smile before the next person could speak. "Have you met everyone yet?"

He shook his head. "Just got here during lunch."

"Oh, okay. I get that it can be overwhelming at first, but

everyone here is very welcoming." She beamed around the room, and I felt a slight twist of guilt in my stomach.

When everyone had checked in, Amy moved around the room, handing out the papers she brought. A quick glance at it almost brought a groan out. "We're going to be talking today about mindfulness," Amy said with much more brightness than was warranted. This was one of the lessons that already felt beaten into our heads, and I did not look forward to another hour of sitting quietly and listening to meditation sounds.

It seemed I did a better job of concealing my annoyance than most, judging by the faltering smile on Amy's face. "Not your favorite topic." The way she said it was more of a statement than a question.

"Can we talk about something we haven't discussed a dozen times already?" Kate said, her arms crossed.

"What are some ways you can practice mindfulness?"

"Meditation," Renee answered dutifully.

"True. What else?"

The silence was deafening.

A sly grin spread across Amy's face. "Really? I thought you were experts already. Kate?"

Kate's face flushed, but she said nothing.

"So let's backtrack. Mindfulness is more than meditation. It's being fully aware and present in the moment. Understanding what you are thinking or feeling but *without* judging them." Amy held out her sun-tanned arm with several bracelets hanging from her wrist. "Each of these bracelets has a different touch to them. They're made from different materials." She reached out with her other hand to grab a silvery bangle. "In practicing mindfulness, I focus my attention on this one, noting if it is smooth or rough or where the metal joins together.

"Some of you still look lost," she smirked. "How about this. Think about the best dessert you have ever had in your life. When you bit into it, was it sweet? Crunchy? How about the flavor?"

My mouth started salivating at the thought of cheese-cake.

"When you are taking in the sensation of something, whether it be food or the way your body is feeling, and you are not judging but rather experiencing that sensation, that is mindfulness. It does not have to be meditation." Amy held up a sheet of paper. "I want you to pick up an object. It could be a book or a pen, something you can hold in your hand."

I pulled a rock out of my pocket and held it.

"Now examine it," Amy continued. "Describe it. Don't say whether it is good or bad or evil, just note what it is or isn't. Matthew, describe your object."

Feeling stupid, I stared at the rock in my hand and considered it. "Gray. Smooth but angular, not round. Cool to touch. There are flecks of other colors, yellow and red."

"Good." Amy smiled warmly. "This is a form of mindfulness. Being fully aware of what you are experiencing in the moment. No meditation required." Her lips quirked up into a grin.

"Like cutting." The words escaped my mouth before I realized the thought had even formed.

Amy's smile and the quiet chatter from the others faltered and died.

I bit the inside of my cheek and sent her a weak smile. "Sorry, Ms. Amy. My filter is broken."

Instead of the expected admonishment, Amy tilted her

head slightly and considered my words. "Actually," she said slowly, "there would be an element of mindfulness in that, albeit not exactly a healthy one." One by one, the group's gaze shifted from me to her. "Could you explain more of what you mean?"

My eyes dropped back to the stone in my hand. "Well, cutting is a distraction, right? And when the cut is made, that's the sensation the mind is focused on." When I looked around, most of the others averted their eyes. Tobias didn't. He nodded at me, understanding all over his face.

"We're ordering pizza. Do you want any?" I stuck my head into the door of my room to hear the reply.

"Uh, sure," Tobias called from the bathroom. He came out with a towel wrapped around his waist. Immediately, I glanced toward the window, but the blinds were shut. "Thought of that already," he said with a smirk.

"Just checking. Made that mistake my first week."

His laugh echoed in the mostly empty room.

I stepped inside, shutting the door. "What kind of pizza do you want?" Grabbing a puzzle cube from my drawer, I started to lay on my bed. Tobias picked up his shirt, the grin fading. "Grab one from my shelf," I said. "We're probably about the same size.

From the corner of my eye, I could see him stare at me. "You sure?" His voice was oddly small, like he wasn't used to having someone do him a favor.

"Yeah. Just wash it before you give it back," I grinned. I turned away to give him some privacy. "Is anyone coming to bring you clothes?"

"My cousin." The words were slightly muffled, and I

figured he was putting the shirt on. "She's supposed to be coming by tonight. Or tomorrow," he added with a touch of uncertainty.

When I was sure Tobias was fully clothed, I got up from the bed and put the cube away. "Time to show you around then," I said lightly. "Darla's been dying to meet you." I held open the door for him, offering an exaggerated bow.

"Ciro, Remington, meet Tobias," I said as we approached the two boys. Ciro's legs were tucked underneath him on the chair while Remington was sprawled out as much as possible, his lanky frame still not taking up much space.

Remington lifted one of his tan hands in greeting but otherwise didn't move. Ciro flashed a bright smile that didn't quite reach his eyes. It was his "faking it" smile. "We're going to talk later," I told Ciro, and his smile wilted. He nodded without saying anything.

Tobias shifted on his feet but also remained silent until we walked away. "What's the age range here?" he finally asked.

"Thirteen to seventeen officially. Though if someone's still in high school at eighteen or nineteen, they sometimes stay here too. Ciro is sixteen. Remington and Renee, the redhead over by the bookshelf, are the youngest at fourteen." We rounded the corner to the dining area/movie room. "Kate and James are the ones working on the puzzle."

At hearing their names, they looked up. Kate waved and called out, "Hi!" while James gave a tiny wave.

"Can we get let outside please?" I asked Kal who was sitting at the desk playing on his phone.

Kal gave an exaggerated sigh and stood. "I suppose." He walked around the desk to the lock on the wall near the courtyard door.

A click sounded in the door, and I pushed it open. "Thanks."

"Wait for me," Kate said, dropping the piece she was holding onto the table.

DARLA

I heard Kate's voice and sighed before plastering a sweet smile on my face. When I looked up, she wasn't alone. Matthew grinned as she started yammering on about something, but the new guy looked around like he had never been outside before. I remembered that feeling.

Before he caught me staring, I turned my attention back to my notebook where I was supposed to be working on my therapy assignment but was instead writing a note. I turned the page so the others wouldn't see if they came over.

"This is Darla." I lifted my head after Matthew said my name and smiled.

"Hi. Tobias, right?" I stood from the bench and offered my hand.

Tobias narrowed his eyes a little.

"Your name was on the board," I explained.

His expression softened, and he shook my hand.

Kal poked his head out of the door and called out, "Matthew, Kate, the doctor wants to see you." He didn't wait for a reply before retreating inside.

They groaned in unison. "Can you finish showing him around?" Matthew hooked his thumb at Tobias. "Sorry," Matthew said to Tobias with a grin.

Kate waved as she walked away. "Hurry up or I'm leaving you behind," she teased Matthew.

"So," I said brightly, "let's continue." Gesturing to the far side of the courtyard where a figure sat at the lone metal table, I continued, "That's Bullfrog over there."

Tobias quirked an eyebrow, and it was the cutest expression ever. "Bullfrog?" he repeated as though he didn't believe me.

I dropped my voice lower, though I doubted Bullfrog could hear me anyway. "His vocal chords were permanently damaged in the fire that scarred him, so it sounds like croaking when he talks."

Tobias stared at me like I was crazy. "You're messing with me, right?"

I put a hand on my hip. "Don't believe me? Go talk to him."

He took a step but turned around instead. "Thanks, Darla. I think I'll figure out my way around from here." With that, he returned inside.

My lips pursed, but, deciding it wasn't worth the effort to follow him, I dropped back to the bench. "He's lucky he's cute," I murmured.

"Pool days are the best days." I skipped a few steps then paused to wait for Kate and Ciro.

"You're only saying that because you have the body for it," Ciro said, snapping his fingers.

I pretended to look offended while a blush heated my face. "Don't you sass me!"

Ciro rolled his eyes, but he was smiling. "Don't try to tell us that you don't enjoy pool time too," Kate teased and nudged him.

"Me?" he squeaked.

Behind us, the rest of the boys hollered at each other. Kate and I rolled our eyes. We stepped aside as Tobias, Matthew, and Remington raced past us. James followed on their heels.

By the time Kate, Ciro, and I reached the pool, the four boys had already jumped in. They weren't alone. "Oak is here," I squealed, watching a blonde boy from the other ward pull off his shirt.

"Careful, you're drooling," Kate snickered.

"Okay, I'll admit it," Ciro chimed in. "I enjoy pool time." He eyed a boy with bronze skin and short dark hair.

Ciro chose to sit on the side of the pool, but Kate and I pulled off our shirts. My shorts also came off, but she kept hers on. Feeling self-conscious, I slightly adjusted the blue bikini top before stepping onto the steps that led into the pool.

"Hey, Darla," Tobias said casually as he moved towards the nearest wall. "Kate, you want to race?"

"Boy, don't you know I can't swim?" she laughed.

"Neither can I. That's what makes this interesting," he

smirked.

Kate scrunched up her nose then stepped past me to stand next to Tobias. "Fine," she said, drawing out the word.

"Ready," Tobias said. They both tensed. "Set." He paused then shouted, "Go!" They took off, Kate's arms and legs awkwardly chopping the water. Tobias flipped onto his back, kicking hard. They were evenly matched for all of two seconds before Kate veered off course into Tobias.

"Cheater," Tobias laughed as they both stood up, abandoning the race.

Kate blew water out of her mouth. "I tried to warn you."

Giggling at their sorry attempt at a race, I ran my hands gently over the water with my back to the wall.

"Hey," a voice said behind me.

A small scream escaped my lips and I clasped my hands over my mouth. My heart sped up, and I knew I'd begin sobbing if I didn't calm down.

"I'm sorry." The speaker came into view. The blonde boy I had admired earlier sat on the edge of the pool and put his legs in the water. "I didn't mean to scare you." He sounded genuinely remorseful, and I took a deep, steadying breath.

I'm safe, I reminded myself. *I'm not going to be hurt here.* It took a few moments longer for my heart to slow, but I forced a sunny smile at the newcomer. "It's all right," I said. "You didn't know."

He chewed on his lip, and it made him appear very attractive. He seemed to realize what he was doing and stopped, but his brow remained furrowed. "I just wanted to say hi. I'm new here, so I've been trying to meet everyone."

"I'm Darla," I said, lifting a slightly wet hand towards him.

"Eric." The worried expression cleared when he realized I didn't hold the scare against him. "You're not in Oak, are you?" He sounded hopeful.

I shook my head. "Maple." Eric nodded and didn't bother to hide his disappointment. "But we have groups together sometimes," I amended.

"Hey, Eric," one of the other guys in Oak said, "Cornhole board is coming out. You still want to play?"

Eric turned back to me. "Guess I'll see you around." He smiled warmly and stood up, the water dripping from his swim trunks. I gave him a tiny wave.

I waited a few minutes while the game was set up. Without looking in their direction, I walked back up the steps of the pool, letting the water run off of me. I reached for a couple of towels then walked to the other end of the pool. Renee and Derek sat at a table under an umbrella. I smiled at them as I passed, but they didn't notice me, deep in conversation about some kind of mysticism. I shook out one of the towels and put it on the ground then carefully lay down on my stomach, using the other towel as a pillow.

The sun's warmth dried my body almost immediately. A deep breath brought fresh air tinged with the scent of chlorine to my nose and lungs. I forgot that I was trying to get Eric's attention again and just enjoyed the beauty of the day.

I'm safe, I repeated in my head.

"Darla, time to go," Kate said, barely reaching me through the fog in my brain.

I mentally groaned. Sleep had taken me. My back was probably fried and my body felt stiff from not moving. Of all the embarrassments. With a nod to show Kate I heard her, I carefully started moving, bracing myself for the surge of pain from a sunburn. It didn't come. A towel fell as Kate helped me to my feet. "Wha—?" I stared at the white fabric.

"Tobias covered you half an hour ago. We figured you needed the rest, so we didn't wake you until now. It's lunch time," Kate said, smiling at my confusion.

"Oh," I said. Master of words, that was me. I gathered up the towels and put them in the basket before donning my shirt and following Kate to the cafeteria. Only a few days before Tobias acted like he wanted nothing to do with me. I smiled to myself while my legs moved automatically.

When I retrieved my tray of food and walked by where Tobias sat with Matthew and James, I paused. All three of them turned toward me, but I kept my eyes on Tobias. "Thanks for the towel," I said, my voice soft and sugary. "It was really nice of you."

His face clouded with confusion. James and Matthew smirked.

"At the pool," I prompted.

"Oh." Tobias shrugged, returning his attention to his food. "Not a big deal. I just didn't want to hear you complain about a sunburn."

Matthew held a fist to his mouth to stifle a laugh.

My cheeks grew hot. "Thanks anyway," I said quickly before heading to a table on the opposite side of the room. Sneaking glances back to their table didn't help. I rested my arms on my table and dropped my head onto them. I could just imagine the check-in for the next group and saying that I felt like a fool. I bet Kate was getting a real laugh out of it. Maybe I could pretend to be sick, then I wouldn't have to face them for the rest of the day. The hope that fluttered in me quickly vanished as I remembered that they could easily take my temperature.

"Are you okay?" a hand gently tapped my shoulder. "Do you have a headache?"

Oh, bless you, Renee! I mentally cheered. Aloud, I said, "The lights are hurting my eyes. I think it might be a migraine."

Her sweet little voice was filled with concern as she said, "Let me go talk to the nurse. I'll be back in a moment."

True to her word, her footsteps receded then came back. "She fell asleep at the pool too," Renee said. "She said it's a migraine."

"Darla," I heard Kal say. "Are you feeling okay?"

I shook my head.

"I'm done with my food. I can take her back to the unit," Renee offered.

"Can you stand and walk?" Kal asked. It could have been my imagination, but it sounded like he didn't believe me.

I nodded and made a show of getting slowly to my feet and holding my head, squinting at the lights. Renee appeared at my side and held my arm as though to steady me.

"Go straight to the unit," Kal told her then he looked at me. "Troy can give you something for it there."

"Okay," I replied, keeping my voice pained.

He stepped aside to let us pass. "I hope you feel better," he added.

Renee waited until we were outside and a decent distance from the cafeteria before she dropped my arm. "I don't blame you for wanting to get out of there," she said.

I moved my hand to shield my eyes from the sun. "Thanks for helping me," I said.

She shrugged. "I want to finish my book. I didn't get a chance to read at the pool because I was talking with Derek."

We walked the rest of the way in silence. A tall iron fence stood to our left after we rounded the corner of the cafeteria. The top of each post had a tipped barb, and I wondered if its design was meant to keep others out or to keep us in. When we reached the door to our ward, Renee pushed an intercom button on the wall. Without an answer, the door clicked, a signal that it was unlocked. I resumed holding my head.

"Everything okay?" Iesha asked, her voice full of concern.

"She has a migraine," Renee answered for me. "Head hurting and light sensitivity," she reported dutifully.

I felt a twinge of guilt for lying to Iesha, especially when I could feel her scrutinizing gaze. "Okay, do you want anything for it?"

"Just some ibuprofen, please," I said while pretending to wince in pain.

She went into the medication room and came back a moment later with a couple of white pills in a small plastic cup in one hand and another plastic cup of water in the other. "Take these and go lie down in your room."

I grabbed both cups and downed their contents. With a weak smile, I turned and went to my room. It was mercifully dark. I lay down on the bed and pulled my blanket over me. Tears started to well in my eyes and I didn't bother trying to stop them.

RENEE

The surrounding chatter broke my concentration again. I really wanted to finish the book I was reading, but the others made it super difficult. Not for the first time, I wished the staff would let us stay in our rooms during the day. But no, they considered that self-isolation. Darla's trick from the other day was not a terrible idea, but I figured Iesha at least would catch on. Maybe a panic attack would get me into the room behind the desk. At least then I could get some peace and quiet.

With a sigh, I closed my book and my head leaned back against the chair. My eyes had barely closed when I heard a sing-song voice call out.

"I'm baaaack!"

I jumped out of the chair and whirled to face the

entrance to the ward. A girl with dark golden skin and shiny, long black hair stood by the desk with her signature smirk twisting the side of her full mouth. Her face looked a little gaunt and there was a discoloration around her eyes, but she otherwise looked the same as last I had seen her two weeks prior.

Everyone fell silent at her announcement. I felt the familiar awestruckness come over me at her ability to command a room.

"Liz!" I hardly recognized the squeal that came from my own mouth.

She held out her arms, and I rushed over to hug her. The top of my head barely reached her chin. My breathing started to catch at the relief of seeing her. "Shh," she said gently, stroking my hair. "It's okay, Ray." The use of her nickname for me put me over the edge and I started crying.

"I thought you were gone," I whimpered, partly hating the whine in my voice and partly not caring.

"You're not supposed to touch each other," Iesha said as a gentle reminder.

Reluctantly, I stepped back. "Not yet," Liz said with a wink.

Iesha raised her voice so everyone could hear. "Go on. You all head to the group room for CPT while I get her situated."

"You're coming to CPT, aren't you?" I looked up at Liz who frowned. "I'm reading today."

Her expression relaxed. "Then of course I'll be there." She reached out and squeezed my hand before turning to Iesha.

I practically skipped away. Reading my story was something I seriously dreaded, but I felt I could actually go through with it while Liz was there. I grabbed my book and notebook before following the others to the group room.

"What's CPT?" Tobias asked. "And who was that?"

"Cognitive Processing Therapy," Matthew answered. "It's for working through the shit that landed us here." He glanced back at me, looking sheepish. "Sorry for the language."

I waved his apology aside. Nothing was going to dampen my spirits with Liz back, and I said as much. We filed into the group therapy room, which was really just a room with a bunch of chairs, a white board, and a window. I settled into my usual seat in the corner opposite from the door, my back against the window. I generally spent the hour staring out at the courtyard watching for birds or bugs, but that would be impossible for this session.

"What happened to her?" Tobias asked, looking at me. He sat a few chairs down from me. Matthew sat on his other side.

Ciro, James, and Kate all turned to look at me, though they all knew just as well as I did. Well, maybe not quite as well. I bit my lip and stared at my fingers, moving each one against its counterpart one, two, three times. "It's not my place to tell," I finally answered.

"Oh, I don't mind, Ray." Liz's voice once again drew everyone's attention. "Tried to off myself," she said, speaking like she'd only taken a trip to the store. "And that little stunt landed me back in Sequoia for a while." She took the chair next to me and patted my knee.

My fingers and the entire rest of my body suddenly went very still. Her touch was like ice.

Liz leaned back, removing her hand. "Where are Bullfrog and Six? Don't tell me they kept me penned up and let those two clowns out."

I couldn't help but smirk at the nicknames she had coined. A sign that we were part of her family.

Derek strolled into the room, hands deep in his black cargo pants. "I thought I heard your dulcet tones, Lizard." Bullfrog, on his heels, said nothing.

Liz stuck out her tongue but welcomed Derek's hug. When he sat next to her, Liz held up her hand to Bullfrog for a high five without even flinching at the scars that covered half of his face and both hands.

Riley was the last to enter, shutting the door behind her. "Liz, how nice to see you again!" I liked that about Riley. Most of the staff seemed annoyed by Liz, but Riley saw what I saw. She looked around the rest of the room and greeted us with a sunny smile as she settled into the chair and kicked off one of her shoes. "Group rules. Be respectful when someone is sharing. Today, that's Renee."

I squirmed in my seat.

"No hijacking, and what is said here stays here. Renee is allowed to use whatever language she wants to tell her story. At the end, we'll have a chance to give her feedback. If you have to leave, go immediately to the desk and talk to a staff member. Any questions before we start?"

"What do you mean by 'it stays here'? Don't you have to keep records or something?" Tobias's question startled me. Judging from the looks of the others, they'd never considered that either.

Riley smiled a little broader. "I do note that you attended group and if you participated or if you had to leave. But I do *not* include the contents of the session. That is what stays here."

Tobias looked skeptical. "Is it legit confidential or is it

the kind of confidential where you tell our guardians or the cops?"

Her smile disappeared. "This is where you are supposed to be safe. If it has already happened, you can speak freely about it and it won't leave this room. If you indicate intentions to hurt yourself or others in the immediate future, I am obligated to report that."

Tobias seemed satisfied with that answer. He nodded and resumed his slouched position.

Riley looked around at each of us once more. "I understand that some of you probably felt betrayed at some point by certain reporting obligations, so I'm glad you brought that up. You do not have to say anything in here if you don't want. It's part of treatment, but treatment isn't one size fits all." Her brown eyes found me and the reassuring smile returned. "Are you ready, Renee?"

I swallowed and gave the tiniest nod, opening my notebook to where I wrote everything. Everything. I forced it out of myself while writing but my voice sounded surprisingly clear when I spoke.

"I was born in Red River, the youngest of four. My brothers were eight and ten years older but my sister was only four years older, so we were best friends. Rachel took me everywhere if she could. My dad said she cried on her first day of kindergarten because I couldn't go with her. When she got into soccer, I did too. If she went to the movies with friends, she made sure it was one I could go to. We were inseparable." I felt a smile tug at my mouth at the same time the knot of dread started building.

"I was nine, Rachel thirteen. She was texting her friends, and I begged her to take me to the park so we could play soccer." The familiar guilt hit me, but I kept going. "She finally agreed and grabbed my green and white ball. We went to the park and she ran me through some drills." For a moment, my eyes closed as I recalled the grassy scent of the field and the grayness of the sky. She hadn't wanted to go because she was sure it would rain.

I refocused on the paper in front of me. "I got really mad because she kept blocking my shots. So I kicked the ball extra hard but I missed the goal and it went into a woody section of the park. Rachel told me to go get it because she wasn't. She was teasing me but I glared at her and ran over to get the ball. Only I couldn't find it. It was bright green, I should have been able to see it, but I didn't at first. Rachel yelled at me to hurry up, and I turned around to see her leaning against the goal."

I knew the next portion by heart, having replayed it over and over during the days that followed the incident. "I crawled into the space between the bushes and trees. I finally found the ball wedged against some rocks. It was deflating and I remember being so angry at Rachel. By the time I crawled back out, she was gone. I was madder at first, thinking she was hiding from me. I started crying. When she still didn't come out, I got scared. I screamed her name, but no one answered."

I expected tears to come as they had when I was writing it, but it seemed I was all cried out. The only sign my body gave was a dryness in my throat. "I ran home. She wasn't there. My brother had come home from practice by then and said he hadn't seen Rachel. I started freaking out. I told him to call our parents, the police, her friends. But I already knew that she was gone.

"Eventually my brother did call our parents. When Rachel didn't come home that evening, which wasn't like her anyway, they called the police. I had to tell them all what happened, that it was my fault we were there at all."

"At first, the rest of the family tried to tell me it wasn't my fault, that it was the fault of whoever took her. But my mom couldn't look at me after a few weeks. As I got older, my dad would call me Rachel if he wasn't careful. So I started acting out. Rachel was such a great student and everyone loved her, so I became the opposite. I barely scraped by in class and quit soccer. I stayed in my room as much as I could."

I took a deep breath, the air catching in my throat. "One time, my mom and I were screaming at each other. I don't remember why. She said, 'Why couldn't you be more like Rachel?' and I told my mom I hated her. I was thirteen, the same age Rachel had been when she disappeared. I left the house and went to stay with my oldest brother."

Everything I had felt when writing refused to come up. It was like reading someone else's story.

"My brother let me stay for a while. Even though we were never super close, it started to feel like it did with Rachel. His friends would come over to the apartment, and they never treated me like a kid. I don't know if they ever knew how old I was. They let me drink with them and sometimes I'd smoke with them. On the anniversary of Rachel's disappearance, it was pretty bad. I wanted to forget her, forget my parents, forget everything. I got drunk and high with one of my brother's friends while we waited for him to come home. We were playing a video game, and I must have passed out."

My voice turned to stone as I continued, "When I woke up, I hurt. My pants were down, and my brother was yelling at his friend to get out. He had a pistol in his hand and was aiming at the friend. The guy left and my brother took me to the hospital. When my parents found out, they sent me here."

Closing the notebook, I leaned back and let a slow breath out. There was silence in the room. No one moved or spoke for what felt like an eternity. I finally felt brave enough to look around. Liz was smoldering but she reached out and took my hand. James met my eyes, his full of sympathy while Bullfrog stared at the floor.

Riley cleared her throat. "Does anyone have anything to say?"

"Oh, there's a lot I'd like to say to that guy," Derek said vehemently. His fists clenched and unclenched over and over.

"I meant, to Renee," Riley reminded him gently.

I curled up, feeling exposed yet oddly relieved.

Derek's expression cleared as he focused on me, and I recognized a subtle switch behind his eyes. "Thank you for sharing," he began. He took a deep breath and let it out through his mouth. "First of all, your sister's disappearance isn't your fault. It isn't," he repeated more forcefully as I looked away. "In fact, none of it is your fault. You reacted out of grief. All of it comes from grief, and no one should blame you for any of it. Including yourself."

"Thank you," I murmured.

There was a brief silence before Matthew spoke. "I can't imagine what any of that must have been like." His voice wavered and he trailed off.

"I want to echo Derek," Tobias said when it seemed Matthew couldn't keep going, "on all of what he said." The intensity of his stare caught me. "It's not your fault. And you do not have to be the daughter your parents lost."

I nodded, my throat closing more than it had during my reading.

"Also, I really want to kill-" he cut himself off, tossing a glance at Riley. "I mean, hurt that guy."

A few of us laughed. That kind of nervous but grateful for breaking the tension laugh. I glanced over at Liz who squeezed my hand and smiled sadly but said nothing.

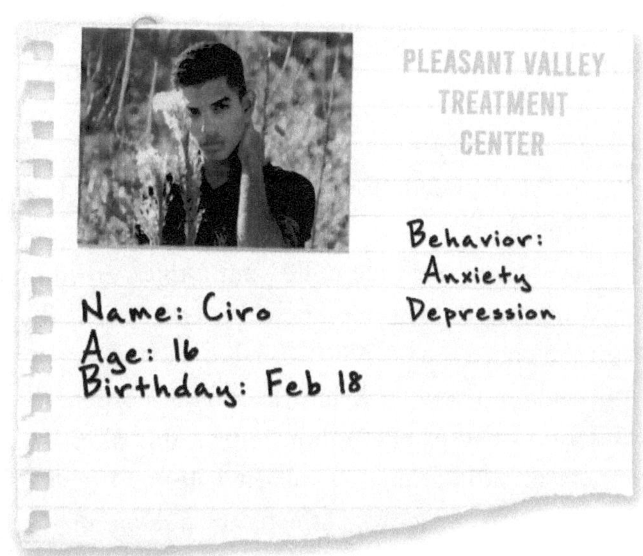

CIRO

No matter how many times I sat outside Dr. Larson's office, it still scared the hell out of me. I tapped my pen against my leg as it bounced until I bounced it too hard with my grip too loose and the pen fell to the ground. It spun around on the tile but I made no move to pick it up even though the heat from embarrassment crept up my neck.

I stared at the pen for a second before reaching out with my foot to kick it closer. The door to the doctor's office opened, and I jumped to my feet.

"Ready, Ciro?" He was careful to pronounce my name correctly after I had pointed out that it sounded like he was calling me "Zero."

I nodded and entered the door he held open for me.

"How are you?" Dr. Larson asked, somehow sounding both sincere and bored.

"Good," I answered too quickly.

He quirked an eyebrow and waited.

"Okay," I amended. When he still didn't speak, I heaved a sigh. "Not okay."

"What's going on?" He pulled out a thick green binder that had my name on it. He opened it and started flipping through the pages.

I thought I should tell him about the conference call with my mom and Michelle, but he probably already knew the important parts of that. "I still can't sleep," I replied.

"Falling asleep, staying asleep, or waking up early?" Stopping at a page, he found a pen and started to note something.

"All three. I dread going to sleep because the dreams wake me up and then I can't go back to sleep."

Dr. Larson's dark hair was streaked with gray, an effect that made him seem almost skunk-like. He studied me intently. "Is the medication working at all?"

I chewed on my lip before admitting, "I haven't been taking it at night. It doesn't stop the dreams, just keeps me down, and that was worse."

The doctor scratched a couple of notes down then tapped his chin. "There is something else we could try. If we give you a lesser dose but pair it with an anxiety medication, that might help you get to sleep and stay asleep. Without the dreams."

A desk clock with a metal frame sat tilted towards me. I watched the tiny silver second hand tic around the gray face. A minute felt a lot longer when you were paying attention to it. "Okay," I said, not that it would matter. My mom wouldn't care any which way so long as it sounded like they were curing me.

"If you don't want to adjust, or if you'd rather come off the night meds, we can make those changes instead." The gentleness of the doctor's voice startled me into looking at him.

"No, it's okay. Whatever will help." Inside, I groaned. I wanted to tell him that whatever they gave me didn't help. I wanted to yell that there was nothing wrong with me, that I just wanted to be me. Except, I didn't know which me I wanted to be.

My head started to ache, and, not for the first time, I wished I could have a cigarette. The doctor looked skeptical but didn't push the issue.

I left the office probably too quickly to seem natural. The more I thought about how weak I felt, the more irritated I became. Why shouldn't I speak up for myself and say I was tired of the meds? I blew past the common room, ignoring the waves from Renee and Kate. There was no way I could handle being around them at the moment. They'd want to talk and make sure I was okay and I just couldn't right then.

Our bedroom was mostly off-white with brown half-wall trim. Derek and I had decorated the shelves and desk with the artwork we made, and it usually made me feel a lot better to get lost inside the colors. But no amount of artwork could distract me from the view I had when I walked in the door.

It wasn't quite crimson. More like an apple red. And it was staining through the tissue pressed against Derek's thigh. His eyes were closed and he had a dreamy half smile on his face.

The increasingly familiar heat hit my neck again, and I quickly shut the door behind me, wishing we had a lock. The staff usually didn't open the door in between groups in case we were changing clothes, but there was never a guarantee.

Derek's eyes snapped open, suddenly filled with fear and suspicion. He tugged the leg of his baggy black pants down to cover up the mark, but the guilt on his face told me he knew I'd seen.

"What are you doing?" I hissed. "If one of them catches you, they'll send you back to Sequoia."

At first he shrugged. "They'll only send us to Sequoia if they think we're going to attempt to kill ourself." His voice sounded strange, a little higher than normal.

I slowly moved away from the door and sat on the bed. Something similar had happened over a month ago where it was like he was someone else. "Who are you?" I tried to sound curious, like we were meeting at a party and not like we had been roommates for weeks. Part of me wanted to run from the room and get a staff member. I would have kept the cutting quiet, but if Derek had stopped taking the meds that suppressed his psychosis, that was something else altogether.

Derek-that-wasn't-Derek blinked but didn't answer. A cloud of confusion crossed his face. He held a hand to his head and said in that same voice, "I don't feel so good. Do be a dear and keep it down please? I'd like to take a rest." With that, he lay down and curled up like a child. A plastic spoon with the concave side busted fell to the floor with a small clatter.

I sighed and grabbed the spoon by its handle, took it to the bathroom, and rinsed off the remnant of skin and blood, crinkling my nose. When it looked clean, I held it up, admiring the jagged section. It didn't look like it could do the job of a knife but enough pressure would tear open the skin. The temptation was there.

Shaking my head, I grabbed some toilet paper, wrapped up the spoon, and stuck it in my jacket pocket, intending to throw it out next chance I got.

Then I sighed and grabbed a sketchpad from my shelf before settling on my own bed. By the time I outlined the shape of the girl I was drawing, I felt a little calmer. A sneaky look at Derek told me his breathing was the even rhythm that came from sleep. Maybe he'd be back to himself when he woke up. Then we'd have a serious conversation.

"Ciro, you have a visitor," Iesha called.

I paused with a chip halfway to my mouth and turned to look at her from my chair near the TV. I liked Iesha. She was a lot of fun to talk about shoes with. I never thought I would hate anything she said, but there it was.

"Cheer up, maybe it's your boyfriend," Tobias said from the seat next to mine. When he first arrived, I thought Tobias would be the type to make fun of people like me. But he and Matthew turned out to be almost more supportive than the girls. That didn't prevent me from shooting a glare at him.

"Call me crazy, but is that a note of jealousy I hear?" Matthew teased with a smirk.

I was so glad my face didn't turn red from the amount of blushing that was happening.

Tobias winked then leaned over and plucked the

chip from my frozen fingers, popping it in his mouth. "Nah," he countered after he swallowed, "Ciro's too young for me."

"Oh, my," I said, fanning myself. The other two laughed, but it was cut short by a voice I knew all too well.

"Where's my darling boy?"

I cringed involuntarily. "I thought I had more time," I muttered. I caught sight of Tobias and Matthew barely containing themselves. "Oh, shut up," I said with as much sass as I could muster.

"You better go, *darling.*" Tobias stuck his tongue out of the corner of his mouth.

I grimaced but stood up, gathering what little mental strength I possessed. *Time to put the mask back on,* I thought. Plastering a pleasant smile on my face, I turned and walked to the desk where my mother was signing in.

She pulled me into an embrace, her bony arms wrapping around me. She somehow seemed more frail than I remembered, even though it had only been a few weeks since her last visit. "How are you, Ma?" My voice sounded sickly sweet to my own ears, but Ma didn't bat an eye.

Iesha used her key to open the visitor room for us. Two chairs and a small couch were crammed in the tiny room around a wide circular table.

My mom put a plastic bag on the table next to a black leather purse. "Oh, I'm fine, don't you worry about me." She peered at me, her eyes appraising my clothes as we sat on the couch. I remembered too late that I had let Darla paint my nails and put eyeliner on me. Ma pursed her lips. "Is this," she paused, searching for the right word, "look part of your new lifestyle?"

Even though I saw it coming, my heart still twinged.

I forced out a laugh. "Ah, no, my friend Darla was practicing."

Ma made the sign of the cross over her chest. "You had me worried."

I tucked my hands under my legs to prevent myself from digging my nails into my palm. "About what?"

"About you, my silly boy." She looked down at her own nails, picking at some of the peeling paint. In all my years, I had never seen my mother without professional-grade nails. She couldn't go a day without fixing them up. But her natural color showed beneath the flecks of gold. "Your last phone call, the one with your therapist, it made me wonder..."

"Ma, would you look at me please?"

The bright blue eyes I inherited from her stood out against her dark skin. Instead of the braids I was used to her wearing, her hair hung in natural kinks. Something was really wrong.

"You're just so young," she whispered. She suddenly placed one of her hands on my knee and looked intensely at me. "How can you be sure this is who you really are?"

My whole body froze, and I could feel my jaw clenching. "I'm sure," I said, trying and failing to keep the ice out of the words.

"But have you tried not being gay?"

"What?"

"Remember when you were little and you insisted that you hated mofongo?"

"What?" I repeated. Her change in subject threw me off.

"You did. You would tell everyone that you would never eat the 'mofungus.'" She smiled at the memory. "But then you tried it finally and you liked it."

Mofongo had actually become one of my favorite dishes, especially when Aunt Sara made it. "Yeah, I remember." Saliva started to pool in my mouth at the thought.

"Is there any way that this is like that time? That you just haven't tried being with a girl?" The emotion choking her voice brought up the usual flood of thoughts.

I closed my eyes tightly, struggling to control my temper. "You think I didn't try?" When I looked again, my mother's eyebrows were knitted. "Do you think I wanted to be different like that? That I *wanted* to be laughed at, bullied, almost killed for being gay?"

Ma flinched at the word and signed the cross again. She started to make shushing noises.

"Are you afraid of it?" I challenged. Then a darker realization hit me. "Are you afraid of me?"

"Of course not, baby," she said. "I'm afraid FOR you. Your soul is in danger." I scoffed. "Your vessel and spirit and everything about you is in danger if you stay on this heathen path," she continued. Her hand wrapped around my arm, gripping tight but not painfully so.

"You say that like I don't know what it's like when I've been living it." My blood felt like it was boiling. All the words I kept buried inside for years erupted from me.

Something in her expression snapped. "Do you realize what it's like to get a phone call in the middle of the night saying a body of a teenage boy was found when your boy hasn't come home?"

Guilt started to gnaw away at my anger.

"It's one of God's miracles that you even made it through that night. So do you understand how terrifyingly painful it is to watch your child willingly throw himself back down the path that led to that night?"

"At least I don't have to hide," I said, my voice so low that I wasn't sure Ma heard me. It sounded like a pathetic low blow, even to me.

"Sometimes hiding is the best chance of surviving." We exchanged glares until she finally rolled her eyes. "You just don't understand."

I got to my feet and shoved my hands in the pockets of my jacket. "Yeah, I'm sure I don't understand what it's like to hide from him." My voice was laced with sarcasm as I turned to step around the table. I made sure the scar running from my hairline in front of my ear down to the lobe faced her as I yanked open the door.

"Ciro," she called in anguish, but I didn't turn back.

I wanted to be alone, but there was literally nowhere I could think of to go. Iesha reached out as I started to pass. At first I pulled my arm away but then she gestured behind the desk to the isolation room. Shooting her a grateful look, I followed her and ducked inside before my mother even managed to leave the visitation room.

The door clicked shut behind me. I left the light off and walked over to the mattress on the floor in the corner. My back hit the wall, and I slid down to land on the mattress.

A memory rose to the surface, one that I had relived hundreds of times before even though it was less than a year ago.

"Hey, anyone fixin' to help me with the groceries?" Ma yelled from the kitchen.

I set my cell phone down on the table and slipped on a pair of chanclas. "On the way!" I called, happy for an excuse to procrastinate on my homework.

When the bags were all inside, I started emptying them so Ma could put the food away. "How was school?" she asked over the rustling of plastic.

I turned away enough so that she couldn't see my grimace. "Fine." There was no way I could tell her my lab partner asked me out. Or maybe I could. "I, uh, might have a date next weekend." I rubbed the back of my neck.

My mother went quiet. When I finally looked at her, she had the goofiest grin on her face which made me laugh. "Oh, my little boy is growing up," she cooked, pulling me into her arms.

"So I can go?" I asked when she released me.

"Make sure to tell me when and where beforehand."

I assured her I would before reluctantly returning to the table where algebra awaited me. My dad stood next to where I had been seated. To my horror, he held my phone in his hand and, judging from the expression on his face, had seen my recent messages.

"What do you think you're doing?" he growled, his eyes narrowed to slits.

"With what?" I asked while fighting the urge to gulp.

"Are you trying to break your mother's heart?"

"No, are you?" I said before I could stop myself.

In a few short strides, he crossed the room then backhanded me across the face. I backed up against the wall. After years of watching his temper get the better of him, I should have known it would eventually turn on me.

"No son of mine is going to be a mariposa," he said, raising his arm again, this time into a fist.

I tried to defend myself, curling up to avoid blows to the stomach, but it didn't take long before I was on the ground and covering my head with my hands as he wailed on me. Eventually the noise must have gotten my mom's attention because her screaming was the only thing that stopped him.

"Get out!" she screeched over and over, shoving him to the door. "Push me around all you want but don't you dare lay a hand on him! Get out and don't come back until you calm the fuck down!"

That was how I knew she was serious. Ma didn't curse.

She was breathing hard when she came back to me. I barely saw the handle of a pistol as she put it on the ground and kneeled. She dragged my hand away from my face and cursed again. "Ciro, what happened?"

I just shook my head, my father's words resounding in my ears.

A scream out in the hall jerked me from the past.

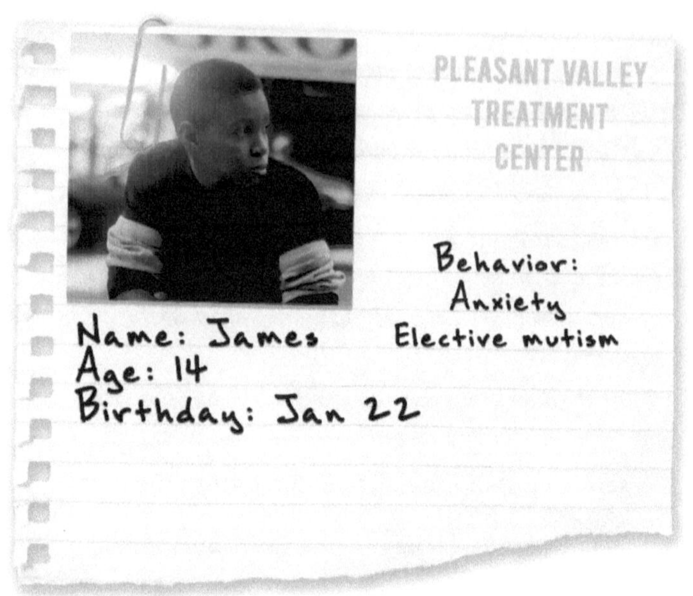

JAMES

A train whistle. That's what Liz's scream sounded like. I covered my ears when it echoed through the halls. For Renee's sake, I hoped Liz wasn't trying to kill herself again.

Kal and another male nurse I knew on sight but not by name ran past mine and Remington's room where I was putting the finishing touches on a model car. Curiosity drove me to peek out of my door where I saw the two nurses stand on either side of Liz, struggling to lift her.

My uncle had a ranch with a herd of wild horses that used to run across his land. I helped him round some of them up last summer. One of them, a real beauty of a stallion, was so vicious that he was kicking and biting any of the ranch hands who came near him. That was what Liz reminded me of.

Her legs lashed out and caught Kal in the knee. "Get the hell off me, you assholes!" she screamed. She threw her head back, her dark hair falling back from her face. From my vantage point, I could see the fear in her eyes as she kept trying to throw her weight away from the two men. They continued to drag her up the hallway to the one confinement room with its reinforced door. Liz braced herself against the frame, thrashing wildly.

Marie hurried towards the small group looking determined with a syringe in her hand. The corral scene flashed through my head again.

"No!" came a shout nearby. Tobias launched himself at the group. The nurses seemed so startled that they lost their grip on Liz as she and Tobias tumbled into the room. Kal recovered quickly and yanked Tobias out, slamming the door shut.

Marie glared at Tobias, but he didn't seem to notice. His eyes were on the door as the pounding started. When the nurses went back to the desk, I sidled out of the room and stood next to him.

Tobias didn't look at me. "She didn't deserve to be sedated," he said. "She probably would hate us all for staring. Either way, she's going to hate me now." He made an effort to sound casual, but I saw the pained expression before he walked back to his room. He rubbed his shoulder where Kal had grabbed him.

Liz continued to pound on the door. Her screams were muffled.

I rubbed my arm and looked around. Derek and Matthew stood at the end of the hall near the common room and kept glancing at me. It was more likely they were talking about Tobias than me, but I made myself scarce anyway. The room that had been Liz's was only a couple of doors away. It took a full minute of me staring at it before I knocked. Renee didn't answer, and I hoped she was somewhere else. She would have hated to see Liz that way.

"If you're going to the cafeteria for dinner, line up," Marie called.

I glanced at Renee's door again before joining the others at the other end of the hall. Tobias reemerged from his room and followed me. Marie walked away to gather the rest of the patients from the other wing.

"That took a lot of guts," Derek said as Tobias and I approached. "She was going wild. And not in the good way."

Tobias half-shrugged. "It was either that or listen to her complain about the sedatives whenever she got out."

Derek nodded sagely. "Still, I don't know if I would have tried that." He started flailing his arms and mimicked her in a high-pitch voice. "Get off, you assholes."

Iesha's concerned face appeared from behind the desk counter. "Did you get your meds today, Derek?"

We stared blankly at her for a moment.

"I'm not crazy, you fucking whore!" he yelled suddenly. His arms dropped to his sides.

I flinched at his harsh words, but Iesha didn't even blink. "Do you need some time to calm down?" Her voice was stern but not cruel.

"Forget this." Derek threw his hands up again and stalked towards his room.

I watched him go.

"I'll go talk to him," Ciro said quietly, squeezing past

Iesha and Tobias.

Tobias and Derek exchanged glances before they both burst into laughter. "'I'm not crazy.' This is just a vacation," Tobias mocked.

"We all just needed a change of pace," Matthew said, holding his side.

When we returned from the cafeteria, I went straight to the desk with a hopeful look directed at Iesha. Her round face lit up in a smile, and she handed over the remote control. I nodded my head in thanks then made a beeline for my favorite chair which I dragged out of the group line to sit in front of the TV. My leg jiggled as I flipped through the channels to land on the show I wanted.

"That's clever," Tobias deadpanned from behind me. "A cat, mouse, and dog fighting over a piece of meat. How original." He settled down on a chair nearby all the same.

From the corner of my eye, I could see Bullfrog glaring at Tobias.

I tried to ignore them, keeping my gaze fixed on the cartoon. Most of the time, the characters didn't talk. Like me. Mercifully, no one in the room spoke for several minutes. Derek entered the room with Ciro at his side. Neither sat down.

Without looking at them, Tobias smirked and asked, "Are you sane now?"

"Shut up," came the deadened reply.

"They made him take a sedative," Ciro explained. He chewed on his lip as Derek's head turned towards him.

I jammed the up-volume button on the remote a little harder than needed. The others took the hint and lapsed into silence again.

"That's convenient," a girl's voice said dryly as the cartoon cat stepped on a rake which swung up to hit him in the face.

I scowled at Liz who dropped onto the floor rather than a chair. Her dark hair hung limp around her shoulders. Her eyelids half-closed over her reddened eyes as she leaned her head back onto the seat of the chair. She didn't say anything else for a while, but the rest of us exchanged uneasy glances. Still, no one spoke, and I turned my attention back to the cartoon.

"Are you okay?" Matthew asked tentatively.

I heaved a sigh and turned off the TV. Matthew sent me a questioning look, but I gestured for him to continue. His attention, and that of everyone else in the room, turned to Liz.

She shrugged without moving her head. Her arm raised up a little to show us the bandage wrapped around her wrist.

"Again?" Renee's voice was tight with emotion. I thought I saw a flicker of regret cross Liz's face, but it was gone before I could be sure. Renee gently lifted Liz's head and slid into the seat before letting the older girl's head settle on Renee's lap.

"It gets to be an addiction," Liz whispered. Renee took a lock of Liz's hair and used the brush in her other hand to start detangling it. Liz moved her head to the other side to give Renee easier access.

"I know what you mean," Matthew said. His eyes were downcast, and he fiddled with the zipper of his jacket.

She let out a snort of bitter laughter. "How could you understand?"

"I'm in here for a reason."

Liz raised her head, a spark of familiar curiosity in her eyes. Noticing the sudden swivel of attention, Matthew coughed.

"I mean, technically we're all here for a reason," Tobias interjected.

"Fair point," said Bullfrog's scratchy voice. He lay with his legs over the side of the chair. The hood of a gray sweatshirt hid most of his face, and he didn't look at any of us.

Putting his hand halfway in the air, Derek asked, "How many of us here tried hurting or killing themselves?"

Laying her head down again, Liz's hand rose. Matthew and Tobias followed suit. Wide-eyed, Ciro's hand went up too.

"How many of us have thought about it?"

Renee and Bullfrog put their hands up.

"Same," Kate and Darla said from behind me.

"Yup," Remington agreed and shot me a quick grin as he sat down.

Derek looked around, a satisfied smile on his face. "That's what I thought." Our hands dropped. "Everyone on the ward."

"Not everyone," Kate pointed out.

I shook my head then grabbed the small whiteboard and marker I carried around when something required more than a 'yes' or 'no'. I held it up for Kate to grab it. She read aloud, "I'm here because I don't talk."

Tobias's lazy smirk returned. "Can't or won't?"

I shrugged in response.

"You're not just faking it?"

"So?" Liz rolled her head around to look at him.

"Everything is fake anyway. Literally everything in society is a thing because someone decided to make it a thing. Therefore, it's all fake."

"That makes a weird kind of sense," Matthew admitted, looking unnerved.

"It really does," Darla agreed.

Liz looked around at everyone. Her eyes landed on me, and I felt my lips quirk up in a smile as I nodded. Laughter bubbled up out of her. Everyone else exchanged mystified looks, but her giggling was contagious and we soon joined in.

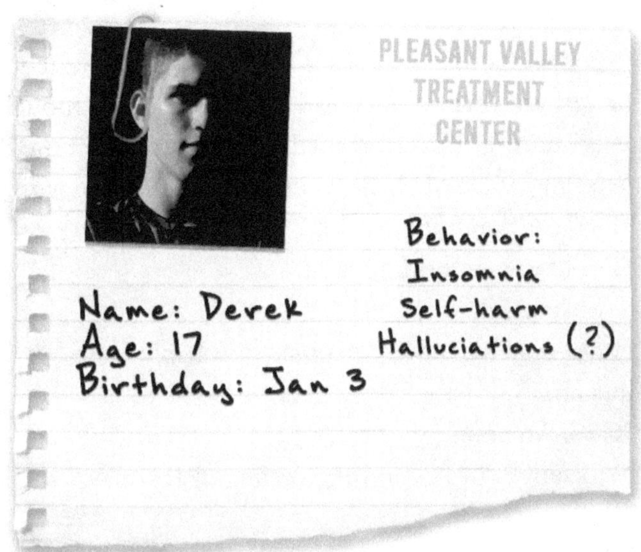

DEREK

It took a few days for the latest dose of medication to stop working. The nurses noted every time I refused to take it, but that didn't bother me. There were things I needed to remember that I couldn't when under the effect of it. It meant that I would lose control sometimes, but that was okay too. Though I probably should have warned Ciro that it could happen. He was pretty freaked out after his run-in with Trish.

"Hey there, Six," Liz said as I walked into the group room, the last to arrive.

I grunted.

"Hmm, is this a new personality emerging? Do I need to call you Seven instead?" I knew she was teasing, but I couldn't keep the hostility off my face. It was way too early for her crap.

I took a chair in the corner and dropped my notebooks on the ground then let my head hit the wall loud enough to make a sound. The door opened. I started to count the dots in the ceiling while Michelle went through check-in with us.

"Darla. Good but anxious."

"I'm Matthew. Feeling tired."

"Tobias. Meh."

James, in his usual manner, probably only gave a thumbs up.

"Ciro. Anxious."

"Morning! I'm Liz and I'm feeling okay today," she said brightly.

I lifted a hand without looking at Michelle. "Derek. Meh."

The door opened again. "Sorry!" I heard Renee apologize.

"We're just doing check-in," Michelle replied with only the slightest rebuke.

"Oh! Uh, I'm Renee, and I'm...worried." I heard her sit down in the chair between Liz and me as the check-in continued. "Here," she whispered, tapping my hand. I glanced down to see her offering me a steaming cup of tea with a slice of lemon in it. "I didn't know how you like your coffee, so I thought maybe some green tea might help you wake up a little."

"Thanks," I said, taking the cup from her. "That's really nice of you."

A sidelong glance while blowing on the hot liquid showed me she was settling into her chair and turning her attention to Michelle.

"Today we're going to be talking about boundaries,"

Michelle began. She unfolded her long legs and walked to the whiteboard on the other side of the room. On it, she drew three badly formed pairs of circles. "Don't be jealous of how well I draw," she commented as she stepped back. Some of the group chuckled.

"This," she continued, indicating the first pair—two circles with their sides touching but not overlapping, "represents a relationship between two people in which they are very conscious of their boundaries. They come in contact now and then but are otherwise not going to overlap." She moved on to the second pair, which had been drawn so that the two circles were almost entirely on top of each other. "And this is what it looks like when two people are extremely dependent on each other.

"This one here, can anyone guess?" Michelle pointed to the final pair, where the circles overlapped a little bit, like one of those Venn diagrams.

"Just the right amount of co-dependency," Tobias called out, sounding bored.

"Sort of," Michelle replied. "The second one is more of a co-dependent relationship where neither person can really function without the other. And the first one is that both are very limited in what they share. But the third is where boundaries are set and respected by both people."

I took a sip of the tea, closing my eyes to really enjoy the slightly lemony scent.

"So what are boundaries?" Michelle asked. "Derek?"

"Physical," I replied.

"Like what?"

A small sigh escaped me. I just wanted to enjoy my tea in peace. "I don't know, like not wanting to be touched."

Renee squirmed. "Sorry," she whispered.

I shook my head. "Not you."

"Touch can be a really important barrier to set, especially after a trauma or when dealing with trauma," Michelle was saying. "People aren't going to know what you are or aren't okay with unless you say something. If you're okay with a tap on the arm but not a hug, it's important to communicate that to the other person. And this isn't just limited to significant others. It can apply to family, friends, and coworkers."

This was so dumb. We were just a bunch of kids, and no adult in our lives was likely to respect any boundaries we wanted to put down. Most of us were here involuntarily. Kate caught my eye across the room and smirked. I returned it automatically and wondered if she was thinking the same thing.

Ciro cleared his throat. "What if," he started to say then paused. "Never mind."

"Go ahead," Michelle coaxed. "You can say whatever you like in these rooms."

"Well, what if you tried putting your foot down about some boundary, but the other person keeps ignoring it?" Ciro bit his lip when he finished the question as though trying to stop himself from saying more.

Michelle studied him for a moment. She was his therapist, so I wondered if she was thinking about what the question could be referring to. She returned to her chair and looked around the room. "You have to ask yourself 'How much bullshit am I willing to tolerate?'"

That caught my attention. The staff members were supposed to be careful about the way they spoke to us, and that included no cussing. I never understood why since they didn't seem to care what language we used.

"If the answer to that question is that you can't tolerate any more, it's probably time to reevaluate the importance of that relationship." Michelle's gaze continued to move between each of us, making eye contact with any who could tolerate it. "Just because someone is family," she said, her voice pitched low even though the room contained sound pretty well, "does not mean you are obligated to keep a relationship with them."

No one spoke for what felt like forever as we all took that in.

"I've always been taught that family comes before all else," Darla finally said. I found myself nodding along with most everyone else.

A pained look crept into Michelle's face. She took a deep breath and slowly let it out. "Your personal safety and well-being come before all else. It doesn't matter if it's a cousin, sibling, parent, or whoever." There was a growing urgency in her tone. "If they are crossing a boundary that violates your safety, it is absolutely within your power to discontinue that relationship. Sometimes it has to be permanent, and sometimes it's temporary." Her eyes came to rest on Renee.

I hadn't noticed before but Renee's shoulders were starting to shake. Without warning, she leapt to her feet and half ran to the door. It only took a moment for Kate and me to exchange a look before following.

Rather than go to the nurse's station, Renee stopped a few steps shy and slumped against the wall. She slid down until she sat on the floor, wrapping her arms around her knees with her head down. Kate and I posted up on either side of Renee and squatted.

Without hesitation, Kate started rubbing Renee's back.

"It's okay to be not okay," she murmured, her voice low and soothing.

There was no warning as Renee started full on sobbing. The sound seemed almost animalistic in nature, and I realized I had never seen her lose control. She had cried before, of course, but nothing so heartbreaking.

My arm went around her shoulders before I realized what was happening. Kate smiled gratefully at me, readjusted her stance, and wrapped one of her own arms around Renee. It felt like we were literally holding her together until she could do it herself again.

We stayed that way for several minutes until the younger girl's sobs subsided and her shoulders slumped in exhaustion. She made no effort to move, though, and neither did we.

"I don't know how to do this." Renee's voice was muffled with her head still in her arms.

"Which part?" Kate asked.

"All of it." Renee's head came up ever so slightly. "I don't know how to set boundaries that my parents will...or can listen to. I don't know how to not be like...her." She started crying again, but it was softer than before. "I don't know how to keep living like this, not knowing what happened to her, with my parents still hoping she'll come home and being stuck with me instead."

I felt helpless. My heart ached for Renee, but I had little frame of reference for taking care of someone other than myself. A tingle went down my spine. A wave of exhaustion crashed into me, and an irresistible urge to sleep followed. The last thing I remembered was my head dropping onto Renee's shoulder.

His arm tightened around Renee's shoulders while, at the same time, that hand gripped Kate's arm, not so hard that it hurt, but enough to reassure them both that he wouldn't leave them. He couldn't.

Renee finally stopped crying. Kate slipped away and returned a moment later with some tissues in hand. "So what if you don't know how? We'll figure it out, and we'll lay those boundaries in a type of concrete that only you can move." Kate put her head against Renee's, her gold hair complimenting Renee's red ringlets.

He nodded in agreement. "You're not alone. We've got your back." His voice came out rough and forceful.

Wiping at her eyes, Renee began to apologize.

"Stop," he commanded. "You have no reason to be sorry. We wouldn't be here if we didn't want to be." He met Renee's eyes and nodded again to emphasize his words.

"Well," Kate said slowly, "not *here* here." She gestured around at the ward's walls.

Renee snorted then hiccupped. "Thank you," she whispered.

I woke with a start, feeling a warmth in my hands that I hadn't had in a long while. Looking down, I almost jerked back out of reflex. One handheld Renee's, and her head lay against my arm. It looked like she was sleeping. In my other hand lay Kate's, her fingers entangled with mine. She too had fallen asleep. The stiffness in my back indicated we'd been like that for a while.

A quick look around revealed most of the ward sitting

around watching a movie on the TV. Some, like us, were settled on the ground leaning against the chairs. Others were sprawled out on the floor. Liz sat in one chair while using another as leg support, creating a makeshift bed. She caught my eye and smiled warmer than I'd ever seen, her eyes shifting to Renee. "Thank you," she mouthed.

I had no idea what she was thanking me for, but I nodded anyway. A dull throb started in the back of my head as I tried to recall. What time was it? How long had I been out, and how did I get from the nurse's station to the common room without waking up?

"Derek?" someone called from behind us. It sounded like Kal.

"He's over here," Liz said, keeping her voice low enough to not startle the others.

Disentangling myself from Kate and Renee, making sure neither would topple over, I stood up. The creaks and pops in my body made me wince, and I had to stretch a little before I could move.

As suspected, Kal waited for me by the desk. We nodded at each other. "Doc wants to see you."

I shook my head slightly then glanced at the clock and gaped. "Six hours?" I must have looked like an idiot with my mouth hanging open and eyes wide, but I couldn't believe I had been out that long. It wasn't the first time I had blacked out but never for so long.

Kal seemed puzzled. "Are you okay?"

I regained control of my mouth. "Uh, yeah. Who moved me while I was out?"

The nurse's eyebrows raised. "What are you talking about?"

"I was over there about six hours ago." I gestured to the

spot where Kate and I found Renee earlier. "And I must have passed out or something because I woke up over there," I continued, pointing toward the common room.

"Let me take your vitals." Kal pointed to a normal dining chair next to a mobile vitals set. "You were up and walking around most of the day."

I huffed and rolled my eyes, more because it was expected of me than out of actual annoyance, but I took the seat. Kal strapped the blood pressure cuff around me and swept a hand-held thermometer across my forehead. The cuff swelled around my bicep a couple of times then deflated. The machine beeped.

"BP is a little elevated, but you don't have a fever." Kal peered into my eyes, but whatever he was looking for must not have been present because he said, "Seems like you're okay. Better get going to the Doc's office."

"Thanks," I said and took off without waiting for a reply. I reached the end of the ward and waited for Kal to push the button that would let me through. When the door clicked, I pushed it open. "Why can't I remember anything?" I wondered aloud, tapping my head with the palm of my hand as if that would jar my memory.

Lost in thought, I reached the opposite end of the hallway without realizing I had bypassed Dr. Larson's office. I doubled back and knocked on the heavy wooden door. I was wondering if he heard the knock and if I should try again when the door swung open, allowing me to pass through.

Much of the hospital made me cringe, but I actually liked Dr. Larson's office. Though it wasn't painted any differently, bookshelves covered most of the walls except for a tiny section where he hung a couple of diplomas or certificates. I never bothered to read what exactly they were.

"How are you, Derek?" Dr. Larson asked, enunciating each word. Our conversations usually started out that way. As the time progressed, he'd slowly fall back into his normal rhythm. He admitted at one point that he spoke slowly because some patients had a hard time understanding his accent. But I had spent enough time on the streets with immigrants that the accent rarely bothered me. Still, it was a habit for him.

"Okay, you?" I replied automatically. The chair on the opposite side of the desk looked like it should have been comfortable, but it definitely wasn't. I preferred the loveseat that cornered the desk.

His pleasant smile remained until he took his seat and saw my face. "What happened?"

I grimaced and rubbed my head. "Is it that obvious?"

Dr. Larson allowed half of a shrug that seemed too youthful of a gesture for a man on the far side of 50.

When he didn't say anything more, I stared at my feet and grumbled, "I had another blackout today."

Even without looking, I knew the doctor's face would display that weird combination of concern and intrigue. "How long did it last?"

"About six hours." The carpet below my feet grabbed my attention with its red and brown pattern. Not really, but I pretended it did.

"It's never been that long before, has it?"

It was my turn to shrug. "Not that I know of." I peeked up to see him jotting something down in my binder. Clearing my throat, I added, "Trish made an appearance again too."

Dr. Larson paused immediately. "Today?" When I

shook my head, he added, "It's been a busy week for you, hasn't it?"

"It's not really me, though," I replied. "I mean, it is, but it's not. Ciro was the one who told me about Trish. It was during a blackout."

"Will you tell me about it?"

I relayed what Ciro had told me, how he'd said it was like briefly talking to a completely different person.

"How long ago did you stop taking your medication?"

Indignation rose in me for a second then evaporated just as quickly. "Other than one dose the nurse made me take, about a week."

Dr. Larson nodded, his mouth pressing into a thin line. "Why did you stop?"

My eyes found the floor again. "I don't like how it feels on them. Everything seems muted. Or dull, or something."

"Like you're tired?"

"Kind of, but more like everything I felt was cut in half. And I still had the blackouts, even if it was only for a few minutes." It had been among some of the worst weeks of my life, and I had lived through some pretty rough times.

Dr. Larson leaned back in his chair, making it creak. He crossed his arms as he studied me. After a few minutes of his staring, it started to make me uncomfortable so I stared right back at him. One of his hands moved up to tap his chin as though he was looking at some kind of puzzle. Which, I guess, he was.

Finally, he moved. He bent over my chart and started flipping through the pages, pausing every now and then to read something. Watching him started to bore me, and I turned my attention to the books on the shelves behind his desk. I expected to see the psychology textbooks and pharmaceutical guides, but another shelf held what looked to be memoirs about living with certain disorders.

"Derek." My head jerked up. Dr. Larson's gaze had turned thoughtful. "What do you recall about the night you were brought to the hospital?"

The question caught me off guard, but I shrugged. Leaning back, I looked up at the ceiling and thought back to a couple of months prior. "I woke up in the emergency room. My stomach had been pumped. When it was safe, they brought me here."

"And before that?"

"Well, I took a bunch of pills, right? Because why else would they pump my stomach?" I looked at him and smirked.

"Do you remember doing it, though?"

No longer grinning, I thought about it again. I couldn't remember it. I had no idea what pills I had taken, where I'd gotten them, or even why I was doing it, though it wasn't hard for me to guess at the last two. My latest foster home had tons of pills around for the different issues we kids had.

My expression must have communicated as much because Dr. Larson nodded. "Why did your previous doctor diagnose you with schizophrenia?"

Shrugging, I replied, "Hell if I know. Another kid at one of the group homes told everyone I was crazy and seeing things that weren't there. The doctor asked me a bunch of questions about make-believe and stuff, and suddenly I was being medicated."

"What did they think you were seeing?" It was a question that normally would make me seethe, but Dr. Larson sounded almost skeptical. And, stupidly, that gave me hope. Hope enough to answer plainly.

"My mom, but I..." I chewed on my lip for a moment, debating on how much I wanted to reveal.

"Derek," Dr. Larson said again, this time gentler. He made sure he had my attention. "I believe they may have made a mistake in your diagnosis and that's why the medication hasn't been working. We cannot help you if you are not honest. Before you can be honest with us, you must be honest with yourself."

I twisted the band around my wrist and didn't answer right away. My jaw tightened while my heart started to beat faster until it was so loud that I thought the doctor must have heard it. "I don't remember her," I said in a rush. "I can barely remember anything before the first home. Foster home," I corrected.

While it felt like a giant weight had been lifted just a tiny bit, it simultaneously seemed as though I was watching someone else. The sensations in my body were still very present, but I had no control. I tried to yell then scream, but nothing came out of my mouth. Dr. Larson continued to peer at me, and I wondered if he could see what was happening. But if he could, then why didn't he stop it?

"It's not very nice to upset him," I found myself saying, but it wasn't really my voice. "I will do anything to protect Dery." My head lifted, almost defiantly.

Trish was the only one who ever called me that. When she was learning to talk, she couldn't say my name, so that's how she said it. It slowly dawned on me what was happening. I was hallucinating. Blacked out and hallucinating. Except I never knew what happened when I blacked out, so this was different.

"I am quite sorry to have done so. Are you Trish?"

She/I scoffed. "Well, yeah," she said as though it were

the most obvious thing in the world. My head started to ache.

"Why don't you want me speaking to Derek?" Dr. Larson asked, giving no indication of his surprise that he was speaking to a girl who died seven years ago.

She crossed my arms and pouted. "He doesn't need to know what happened. He doesn't need to remember. It'll make him sad. And if Derek cries, *HE* might try to stop it." A shudder ran up my body at her inflection. Did she know I could still hear everything?

The doctor nodded sagely like that explanation made perfect sense. "But you remember what happened." It wasn't a question.

Trish used my head to nod.

"Could you tell me?"

She squinted at him the way she used to do to me when she couldn't decide if I was teasing her or not. Like the time I held my hands behind my back and told her one hand held a jellybean and the other held a snail and she'd have to eat whichever one she picked.

One of my shoulders lifted into a shrug. "Maybe another time. But you," she pointed at the doctor, "have to promise not to get my brother mad." My body wriggled in the seat, and I wished I could groan from embarrassment.

"I promise not to anger your brother," Dr. Larson agreed with complete solemnity.

With a satisfied nod, she leaned my body back against the seat. The pounding in my head intensified until I could no longer stand it. *No,* I yelled at myself, *don't let go.* Either my brain and body couldn't obey or they didn't care. I was pretty sure it wasn't entirely up to me anymore. I passed out.

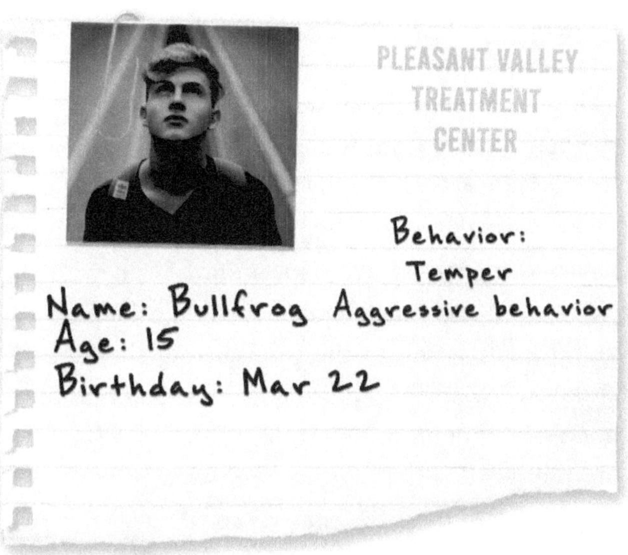

BULLFROG

Everyone was down at the pool except for me when Derek came back. Kal brought Derek onto the ward in a wheelchair, and it looked like he might have been sedated. *Must be nice*, I thought then immediately hated myself for it. Derek and Liz were the only ones who were consistently nice to me. Besides Renee, but she was nice to everyone.

I suddenly didn't feel like playing solitaire anymore. I cleaned up the cards and put them back on the game shelf. Grabbing a chair, I set it by the window that looked out at the courtyard and dreamed about going outside. Only when the skies were gray would the staff let me venture out of the ward, and that was for maybe ten minutes if I was really lucky or if it was barely starting to snow. The cold would sting any part of my exposed skin, but the smell of trees and flowers made up for it.

The sun, though, that was a different thing entirely. Even when I wore protective gear and sunscreen, it still felt like my skin was on fire if I even came close to direct sunlight. Every therapist I had for the past year tried to tell me it was a mental block, association of sun with the fire that destroyed my skin, but I couldn't help it. Which obviously made going to the pool absolutely impossible. I didn't know what the chlorine would do, but the sun's presence was enough to deter me. Which was how I ended up on the ward alone except for Iesha, who was busy refilling medications in the back room.

I should have been practicing reading my trauma story, but it was a struggle to write anything past the first fire, let alone the second. I guess it was lucky I wrote left-handed since my right was barely starting to regain functionality. Continuing to ignore my notebook abandoned on a nearby chair, I watched a bird hop its way along the ground outside and thought of the foxes I used to see by the ranch house. They'd chase chickens around until one of Gran's dogs came around barking. Gran rarely lost a chicken because of those dogs. I focused on how the dogs would jump and play with me, no matter how wet or cold or hot it was outside.

If Gran had been able to handle looking at me after my mom died, maybe that was where I would have ended up. My entire life could have turned out differently. With a sigh, I fought against the tidal wave of emotions that never failed to show up. I needed a distraction. A table nearby had the outline of a puzzle on it, something each of us worked on bit by bit. Puzzles worked wonders for me. There was a thrill of exhilaration at joining pieces together, and there was visible progress with each new connection.

The others eventually returned, laughing and throwing towels at each other before retreating to their respective rooms to change before our next group. Some of them would manage to sneak in a quick shower, but they were supposed to wait until lunch or after dinner. James always joined them at the pool, but he rarely went swimming. Which was just as well since I didn't want our bathroom getting messy in the middle of the day, but it wasn't like I could get mad at him for it. Not again, anyway. It was his first week on the ward when I yelled at James for messing up the bathroom. James had cowered like a kicked puppy, and I hated that. So I stayed quiet about it because there was no way I was going to treat that kid like my dad treated me.

I kept working on the puzzle. It was a big one, some kind of forest or cabin scene judging by the amount of wood pieces. I never liked looking at the picture, preferring instead to figure out what it was along the way.

"Hey, Bullfrog," Liz said as she sidled up beside me.

I grunted without looking up. The name had grated on my nerves at first, but we met when I was still like James and wouldn't talk. My throat hurt a lot when I tried, and I hated everyone. Unlike him, I refused to carry around a dumb board to talk to people. Liz decided that, if I wasn't going to give her a name to use, she'd come up with one for me. I wasn't sure how she came up with Bullfrog, but it's what she called me ever since. The others followed suit, tentatively at first, but when I didn't argue, it stuck. After a while, I decided it was better than my real name anyway.

Liz reached out and plucked a piece from the pile,

placing it within the puzzle to create a couple of spindly deer legs. It always amazed me how quickly she could put things together, whether it was a puzzle or a person.

We moved at the same time, her dark arm brushing against the sleeve of my shirt. I jerked my hand back. Even though the fabric covered the burn scars on that arm, I hated the idea of Liz's flawless skin having to come into contact with my hideousness.

"Sorry," she said, taking a step to the side and giving me a sad smile.

I started to shake my head and even opened my mouth to apologize, but Renee's voice called out to us. "Time for group!"

A cringe came over me before I could stifle it.

"It's your turn today, isn't it?" Liz asked as I gathered my notebook. It was rare to see Liz anything but sarcastic or screaming. The softness in her voice both unnerved and soothed me.

I nodded, and we continued walking to the group room in silence. I paused to let Liz enter first. She suddenly stopped in her tracks, turned to me, and said, "It'll be okay. You can do it."

Surprise prevented me from breaking eye contact from her soft brown eyes. "Thank you," I said. The roughness in my voice wasn't from the scar tissue alone.

We took our seats, Liz next to Renee and me near the door. Riley was facilitating again, thankfully. I didn't mind Michelle because her no-nonsense way of approaching things made, well, it made sense. That day, though, when it was my turn to read, Riley's maternal presence offered a tiny bit of comfort.

She ran through the group rules and the check-in. Only

Derek and Darla were absent. My finger tapped my notebook as I waited, not even bothering to steal glances around the group. My reading was almost guaranteed to alter their opinions about me forever, and there was a high chance it wouldn't be in a good way. Even Liz would probably avoid me after.

Her last words to me echoed in my head, calming me enough to take a couple of shallow breaths before my mind started running wild. If I ever got out of treatment, I would start making tee-shirts that read Anxiety Sucks and wouldn't even care if they didn't sell. Or I would, but I'd be too anxious to sell them anyway.

"Are you ready?" Riley asked, and I realized she was looking at me.

I pulled my hood up over my head, opened my notebook, and nodded. Iesha had let me take a throat spray earlier to ease the pain while I read. The numbness felt strange but good.

"My mom was an angel," I said, my voice croaking a little. Clearing my throat, I went on. "Her family immigrated from Ireland and ended up with some land outside of town. She went away to college and came back pregnant and married to the devil in disguise. I was born on my Gran's ranch, and it became my favorite place in the world because it was my mom's favorite place."

Surprisingly, my voice grew stronger, shaking off the rust with an ease I hadn't felt in a long time. "She got sick when I was eight. I still don't know what it was, but it was bad. My father was gone a lot, traveling for work, so he didn't see how bad it was. But I did. She kept getting weaker and losing hair, but she rarely complained and never lost her smile." I had to pause for a breath before continuing. "I got sick, too. My mom was really worried. She wore a mask when she took me to the emergency room, but it didn't matter. I had pneumonia, and she caught it from me. I guess her immune system was already too compromised to fight it because she died from it. I still wish it had been me that died if she could have lived." My fingers tightened around the edges of the notebook until they turned pink and white.

"My father blamed me too. He took me from Gran's ranch after my mom died, and we moved. I think he hated me after that. Any time something went wrong, it was my fault. At first he'd scream and yell at me, but that didn't seem to get out enough of his anger, so he'd sometimes throw me onto a couch or bed. Then he stopped caring whether or not I landed on something soft. He broke my arm one time and told me he'd kill me if I said anything other than I had fallen out of a tree. I believed he would."

My mouth started to feel dry, dread building in the pit of my stomach as each word I read brought me closer to the recent past.

"A few months after that was when my father brought his girlfriend home. She wasn't much better, though she never laid a hand on me. Instead she'd constantly say I was no good and just a drag on my father and that her own twins were smarter than I could ever hope to be. When I finally met her kids, I thought I would hate them. But Davy and Daisy were actually everything their mother wasn't.

"My father and I left our apartment and moved in with them by the end of the year, something my soon-to-be stepmother never let me forget. The twins almost made it worth it, though. It was Davy who helped me with ice baths when my father's beatings left me sore, and it was Daisy who brought me food when her mother sent me away without eating. With those two, it was like some spark of my own mom was back." Even I could recognize the wistfulness in my voice. I took a moment to compose myself.

"To blow off steam, I started getting destructive. It started off with just taking broken electronics and smashing them in the garage when no one was home, but it eventually turned into me playing with fire. I found it beautiful in ways no one could understand. After a particularly brutal beating from my father, I swiped pictures of my father and his new wife, set them on fire and left the remnants in random places around the house where one of them would find it. Davy tried to say he did it, but they knew. I ended up in the hospital again after that one, and the only thing that kept me from going to the cops was the thought that my father might turn to the twins if I wasn't around to take it. So I went home."

Standing on the sidewalk in front of the house made me sick. My face was still swollen near one of my eyes, so it was hard to make out the house number. My good eye could make out the blue of the paint under the porch lights, the paint I had put on last week because she threatened to tell my father about my box of matchbooks if I didn't do it. I would have clenched both hands into fists, but one of the fingers on my right hand was broken.

I had stayed away from the house all evening to prepare and to prevent the twins from finding out about my plan and subsequently try to dissuade me. It was well past when I knew my father and stepmother would be in bed, but they wouldn't have stayed up waiting for me. They didn't care.

Using the key on the back door, it swung open silently thanks to another chore of mine. I hooked my shirt over my nose, adjusted the cloth bag on my shoulder, and grabbed the gas can. I wasn't going to give my tormentors any chance to escape. The gas came out easily, splashing across the tile of the kitchen and soaking into the carpet in the living room and playroom. All of the bedrooms were upstairs, and I was confident that neither of them would smell the fuel. I felt a twinge of guilt for the destruction that was about to consume Davy and Daisy's toys, but it passed quickly enough. They'd be safe from my father forever after I finished.

I took my time with coating the stairs and the area just below it. When the gas can was nearly empty, I went to my bedroom and grabbed a stack of paper from my printer then tossed them down the stairs a few at a time. The sheets fluttered down noiselessly, stark white against the soaked carpet. Halfway up the stairs, I pulled the bag from my shoulder and withdrew the bottle I prepared earlier. In the dim glow of the night light plugged in the hallway, the liquid inside looked like something from one of those Italian restaurants that they serve with bread. The rag wrapping around the bottom of the glass hid most of the lower half.

I held the bottle carefully and poured out the remainder of the gas onto part of the rag. Then I pulled a lighter from the bag and used it to catch the rag on fire before throwing the bottle across to the other side of the house where it smashed into the corner of the living room, hopefully far enough away where the assholes known as my guardians wouldn't hear.

If it didn't work, I'd need to run before my father woke up. It wouldn't be hard to run back down through the house if needed but going out my window would be faster and make it less likely for him to follow. But I didn't need to worry about that.

The effect was immediate, a ball of orange flames exploding from where the glass hit the wall accompanied by a soft whooshing sound. Though I had not doused that corner, I expected it wouldn't take long for the fire to reach the trail of gas and engulf the house. A smile played on the corner of my mouth as I turned back to my bedroom at the end of the hallway.

I had long since pried the nails out of the window that my dear old dad put in to keep me from sneaking out of the house. The window slid open smoothly, and I sat on the ledge, ready to drop down to the garage roof a few feet below. Something held me back, though. Curiosity, maybe? A need to know they would die?

It took less time than I thought for the heat and smoke to make its way upstairs, stinging at my nose and eyes. It was time to go. A high-pitched scream, too high to be my stepmother's, froze me.

"No," I hissed, praying my mind was playing some sick trick on me. I cursed and pulled myself out of the window. Stumbling into the hall, I could hear pounding and coughing at the door across from mine. "No," I said again, and the panic set in as another scream cut through the air, piercing my very heart.

The cloth bag still hung from my shoulder, empty. I pulled it off and wrapped it around the doorknob to Davy's room. "Get back from the door," I yelled. The handle still burned like hell when I opened it.

Davy sat on the floor a few paces away and looked up at me. His eyes were reddened and his face blotchy. Snot leaked out of his nose which he tried to wipe away with the sleeve of his pajamas. Still, he tried to smile when he saw me, but he dissolved into a coughing fit.

"You're not supposed to be here," I coughed then pulled my shirt over my nose and mouth again. Snagging a blanket off of his bed, I wrapped it around him after pulling him to his feet.

"Dai-Dais" Davy, unable to speak through the coughing, pointed at the bathroom door that connected his and Daisy's rooms.

The pit in my stomach grew. The twins were supposed to be staying over at friends' houses. Why were they home?

"Go to the window in my room," I told him, yanking an abandoned shirt off the floor. The bag lay by Davy's door. "And stay

low," I added then coughed.

The screaming stopped by the time I made it through the bathroom door on Davy's side. My hand started to throb, but I couldn't use the broken one to turn the handle. "Daisy," I yelled, crouching by her bathroom door. No one answered. Again, I wrapped the shirt that was even flimsier protection than the bag around the handle and pushed. It met resistance. I pushed a little harder and saw Daisy's form slump over to the side.

"Stay with me, Dais," I said. I hooked my arms under hers and pulled her around the door into the bathroom. When we were clear, I scooped her into my arms and headed into Davy's room, half-crouched to keep away from the smoke as much as possible. My shirt had fallen from my mouth when I picked up my step-sister, but it hadn't been that protective anyway. I focused on how I would make the twins laugh after all of this was over by telling them how I scuttled like a crab.

Every breath felt like a stab in the lungs, and the thick smoke made it hard to see anything. A cough escaped Daisy's mouth. It felt like an inferno raged at the other end of the hall.

When I reached my room, I put Daisy down and dropped to the floor, dragging her across the carpet on my knees. Davy lay against the wall, his face turned up toward the window where black smoke was escaping.

Throbbing started in my head. All I wanted was to lay down and sleep. I shook my head and pulled Daisy closer to the window. Despair hit me like a train when I realized there was no way to get them both out while they were unconscious. Jump out with one and come back for the other? How much time before the smoke killed us?

I stripped my bed of its comforter, blanket, and pillows. The comforter went out the window onto the shingled roof. I threw out a couple of pillows, hoping they wouldn't fall to the ground, but I didn't bother to check. Sitting on the ledge again, I hauled Davy up and out of the window, dropping him onto the makeshift landing zone below.

People were shouting, and sirens were nearby. I wanted to yell for someone to get Davy, but my throat felt coated in ash and the sound came out too raspy to hear. I ducked back inside, dropping to the floor again. The blanket was within arm's reach, and I used it to wrap up Daisy's still form. She didn't make a sound. When I lifted her again, she felt a hundred times heavier than before.

A single thought ran through my head. Get her out. I staggered to my feet, going to the ledge again. If I dropped her, I couldn't be sure she wouldn't hit Davy. If she stayed in the house, she'd die for sure. I held her close for a moment.

Unwrapping the blanket a little, I grabbed either side to make sure Daisy wouldn't fall out. Lying on my stomach, I lowered the blanket until I couldn't reach any further. My arms gave out, and she fell away from me. I didn't even see her land before my legs gave out and darkness claimed me.

"I woke up in the hospital with a good chunk of my face and arms burned and some internal scarring from the smoke. Apparently the fire department showed up in time to save my sorry ass. My father and stepmother supposedly never woke up, not even to Daisy's screams."

Swallowing the lump in my throat, I kept my eyes on the page in front of me, though I couldn't see the words anymore. My voice took on a roughness that had little to do with the damage to my body. "They rescued the twins from the garage roof, but their little bodies couldn't handle the smoke on top of a viral infection which was apparently why they were home. Neither of them made it."

I wanted to curl up and die by the time I finished. The words sounded monstrous as I read them. Closing the notebook, I sat back in the chair and let out a shaky breath, finally daring to look around.

Renee sat with her legs pulled up to her chin, one hand swiping at the tears on her face while Liz held her head in her hands. James curled up in his chair, chewing on his lip. Ciro and Kate wore matching hardened expressions and held each other's hands. I drew in another breath as my eyes traveled to Matthew staring at the floor in front of him. His body shook, though I couldn't begin to figure out why.

Tobias was the only one who met my gaze. Though tears streaked from his eyes, they were focused intently on me, his jaw set. He opened his mouth like he was about to say something, but he paused before any sound came out. I started to look away, but Tobias cleared his throat, drawing my attention back to him.

"I get what that's like, man, growing up with someone like that. The one who is supposed to protect and guide you turning on you that way..." He paused, and another tear fell. "It's not your fault your mom got sick or that your dad was so pathetic that he couldn't be the parent you needed or deserved. And it's not your fault those kids died." My gaze dropped, and my throat felt tight again.

Tobias kept going. "I get that you think it is because you started the fire, but you were reacting to your shitty home life, and you had every intention of protecting those kids. From your dad and from the fire." He lapsed into silence.

The tiniest glimmer of hope crept into my thoughts. Someone understood. "Thanks," I managed to get out. I didn't think that word could convey everything I was thinking, but Tobias nodded.

"I agree," Renee said in almost a whisper. I met her gaze, and my gut twisted at seeing her cry. She sniffled and tried to say more but didn't seem to be able to get the words.

Liz wrapped an arm around Renee's shoulders but lifted her head to look at me and offered a soft smile. "I do too. After all you went through, I don't blame you one bit for it. I probably would have set fire to my house too." The smile faded, but she held my gaze. "You did everything in your power to keep the kids safe. The fire was your fault, sure, but you know that. The twins, though, that's not on you. You tried to save them. If you really were the monster you think you are, you wouldn't have done that."

"I'd trade my life for theirs in a heartbeat," I choked out. "I wish I could." Saying it out loud, I realized it was true, that it was completely unfair how Davy and Daisy were so good and kind and dead while I lived, ugly and vicious.

Riley's voice cut through before I could completely spiral into the darkness in my head. "I do agree with everything the others said." Her voice had that sweet, soothing sound to it that reminded me of my mother. "You are not to blame for what happened to you as a child or how you were treated growing up. You are responsible for your own actions, and you tried to do the right thing in the end. You can still use your life to do right by them if that's the way you're feeling. It's absolutely awful what happened, but I am glad that you're still here."

Murmurs of assent followed. I couldn't speak, but something in my chest released, like a breath I'd been holding since the night of the fire. I doubted the guilt would ever fade. But their words hit me unexpectedly hard. Something to think about, at least.

KATE

"Bring me some cake please!" I called out as the group left for the cafeteria.

"Who?" Matthew asked.

"Anyone," I said with a grin. He rolled his eyes and looked at Tobias with a "Can you believe this chick?" expression.

As soon as the others walked away, my smile disappeared. It was a relief to stop pretending for a minute. I had my notebook in my hand, intending to rewrite my story, but I couldn't muster up the energy to do it. That would require more strength than I had.

I scowled at the notebook, wishing I could skip it. I knew I had to do it some time. Later.

Tossing it onto one of the tables, I headed over to the

puzzle in the corner. I used to make fun of the people who spent their little free time poring over the stupid cut pieces, but I tried it out with Renee and actually found it relaxing. Not that I'd admit that to anyone but her. Or maybe Derek.

Just for a little while, I didn't want to worry about spilling tea with anyone or trying to help someone come out of their emotional turmoil. I needed time to decompress.

The problem with that was how easy it would be to fall into my own memories, thereby spurring me to focus on others as a distraction and causing a vicious cycle where I'd be emotionally drained as hell. It was exhausting being me. The puzzle, though, drew enough concentration where I could just sort of exist without anxiety for a minute. A few if I was lucky. Because then I would grow restless.

I sighed and stared at the piece in my hand, glancing from it to the partly-formed puzzle, trying to find its place. There was probably some kind of metaphor to that.

"Door handle," a voice said from behind me.

I whirled around, dropping the piece in the process.

Derek stepped back just in time to avoid the swing of my arm. "Easy, girl," he said with a grin.

I rolled my eyes and dramatically clutched at my heart. "Are you trying to send me to an early grave?"

"No more so than you are," he retorted, earning a wry smile from me. After retrieving the dropped puzzle piece, he put it in its spot as the handle to a cabin door.

"Ah, door handle," I said, nodding sagely.

"Brought you some cake." Derek pointed to a couple of plastic containers on the table next to my notebook. Each one held a thick slice, one pink and one green, of what was barely passable as cake, but it was sweet and had frosting that didn't suck.

"You're the best!" Unable to contain myself, I threw my hands around Derek's neck. I cringed and slowly stepped back. "Sorry, I got excited."

He raised an eyebrow. "I couldn't tell."

I stuck my tongue out at him as my face flushed. "Want to eat outside? I could use some fresh air."

Derek picked up the containers and headed to the door while I snagged two cartons of milk from the small fridge. "Can you let us outside?" I called over to Iesha.

"Sure, I can." Her bright smile always brought one out of me too. She put the key into the lock on the wall and turned it, waiting for the click of the door. Derek bumped it open with his hip and held it with a foot while I passed.

The courtyard was one of my favorite places. It was usually quiet at lunch, even though the wall separated us from the ward that held the younger kids. Our lunch meant their nap time, as far as I could tell. The breeze still came through the triangular area, rustling the trees and blowing fallen leaves around. Sometimes we'd play a bizarre game where you could only step on one of those leaves in order to get anywhere else in the courtyard.

Two long stone picnic tables sat at the end opposite from the door, one under an awning and one in the sunlight. A few canvases lay in the sun, drying from that morning's art session, so we took our seats at the shaded table.

"Crap," Derek blurted out, making me jump. Again.

"What?"

"I forgot the forks." He looked so forlorn that I couldn't help but snort in laughter.

I popped open a container. "Have you ever had the cake here? It doesn't require forks." As if to prove it, I picked up the irregularly cut square and bit into it. The green frosting covered my lip promptly before I made a face. I somehow always managed to forget the intense lack of sugar in the cake itself.

"Have *you* ever had the cake here?" Derek laughed.

I turned the cake over so the frosting faced down, careful not to get any on my hands, and took another bite. The sugar hit my tongue before the dryness of the so-called "cake" could hit it. I gave a satisfied nod. "Better."

Derek eyed the other piece dubiously. He opened the container. "This looks sketch as hell."

"If you don't want it, I'll eat it," I said, putting the last of my slice into my mouth.

He barely glanced at me before bursting out laughing. "Nice mustache," he chortled.

"You wear chains and a collar, and you're going to make fun of me for some frosting?" I teased.

Derek pushed his container towards me. "If it makes you happy, have all the cake you want."

"Oh, I would love to, but I'd get fat." With that snakey thought, I suddenly lost my craving.

"Bet you'd still be beautiful," Derek said, his voice pitched so low that I figured he hadn't actually wanted me to hear even though the flush creeping its way back into my face said plainly that I heard.

"How are you feeling?" I asked while resisting the urge to squirm. I focused intently on the remaining cake piece.

"Oh, good," he said. It could have been my imagination, but the relief at the change of subject seemed to exude from Derek as he blew out a breath. "Well, not good. I mean, kind of okay, I guess." He ran a hand through his dark hair, and his leg started bouncing.

I propped my elbow on the table and head in my hand, giving him a scrutinizing look. "Pretend I'm pushing a cup of tea over to you. Now spill it."

Derek didn't bother to cast a withering look in my direction, a sure sign that something had to be really wrong. Instead, he started tapping the table.

I put a hand on his arm, and everything about him froze. "Hey, what's going on, Six?"

His bright eyes found mine with an intensity to them that I hadn't seen before. "You know why Liz calls me that, right?"

I shrugged. "Figured it was just one of her things, like with naming Bullfrog."

"You're not entirely wrong. She was here when I first got here, and I told her that I sometimes had other versions of me around. Schizophrenia," he spat like it was a curse. "There were six by the time I got here."

"Hence the name," I said.

"Hence the name," he agreed. "But, I don't know, maybe I described it wrong or something, but the doc is saying I'm not schizo."

"Multiple personalities?" I guessed. "Like in *Fight Club*?"

Derek shrugged and looked away, resuming his tap rhythm on the table. "Never seen it, but Dissociative Identity is what it's called."

"Hang on. Back up. You've never seen *Fight Club*?" I asked incredulously.

He gave a derisive snort. "I'm telling you I'm legitimately crazy and you're focused on the movies I haven't seen."

I waved his concern aside. "First of all, it's not just any movie. And secondly, get in line for the crazy throne because we're all heirs to it."

For a brief moment, Derek paused again and smiled at me in a way that sent shivers up my spine. Not the way EJ had, which was almost predatory at times, but Derek's was more intimate and vulnerable and comforting all at once. It was all very confusing.

When Derek spoke again, he sounded defeated. "I'm trying to remember something that I can't remember." His closer hand drifted to the side of his head, and he smacked it a couple of times.

"Whoa, hey!" I grabbed his arm and pulled it away. "That trick generally only works on vending machines and video games." My fingers could feel the criss-cross of raised skin on his arm, grazing over the bumps as Derek's arm fell. My gaze dropped when neither of us pulled away. Some of the scars were old, long healed and faded while some still had the pink tinge of healing. Those were just the ones I could see. "When was the last time?"

"For which me?" Derek tried to pull away, but I held him still.

"Aren't they all you?" I dared to look at his face. He was one of the few boys I had to tilt my head up to see. Without warning, my heart started pounding as I felt my eyes go wide. My brain chose that moment to remind me of the awful things that had previously followed a similar moment. I squeezed my eyes shut, desperate to keep myself from crying.

My body was pulled forward until my head bumped into something soft. Derek's arm slid out of my grasp then wrapped around me, pulling me closer as my body started to shake with uncontrollable sobs. I couldn't tell if his embrace helped or made me cry more as memories took control of my brain.

The sobs gradually ebbed away leaving me hiccupping until the sound of his heartbeat slowed mine. Too late, I realized my snot covered Derek's hooded sweatshirt. "I should have warned you," I managed to whisper, "I'm not a pretty crier."

His chest seemed to rumble as he said, "No one really is."

Taking in a deep breath, I steeled myself for moving away, not even completely sure what happened. I grimaced at the snot streaks left on his sweatshirt, but he didn't seem fazed. Without saying anything, he pulled it off and tossed it onto the bench. Derek's jaw was set like he was ready to do serious damage to someone.

"Who did that to you?" His voice sounded deeper, more strained. Though he wouldn't look at me, his brow furrowed.

I fiddled with a bracelet that I sometimes wore, a silver bangle a friend gave me, while working to keep my breathing under control. A quick battle waged in my head to determine if I should play it off or not. No one knew everything about what happened to me, not even my therapist. No matter how hard I tried, I could never bring myself to say the words.

"It's okay if you don't want to talk about it," Derek amended when I didn't reply.

"N-no," I spluttered, "I can." Could I?

From the corner of my eye, I saw his leg start bouncing again. Was he nervous? His expression looked cloudy, his mouth opening then closing as though debating on saying something else.

Swallowing the lump already forming in my throat, I

picked at my nails and started talking. "I met him at the beginning of sophomore year. He was on the basketball team, and I thought I was so cool for catching his attention," I scoffed at my own idiocy. "He, uhm..." I tried to say his name, but it wouldn't come out. Instead, I said, "He was really sweet for a long time. Well, it felt like a long time but was really only, like, six months that we were dating."

The first time he kissed me had felt like fireworks. It was everything a first kiss was hyped up to be—awkward and a little sloppy but sweet. The memory made me shudder.

"We broke up. Well actually, he broke up with me with some crap story about how he couldn't trust himself to stop his playboy ways." His voice still echoed in my head, the fake sad smile plastered to his face as he said it. He had asked if we could still be friends while I nodded, biting my cheeks so that I wouldn't cry. Then he told me to give him a goodbye kiss, which I did. "Later that day, I saw him with his arm around a freshman girl, and I think I cried for a week." One of my hands curled into a fist as I berated myself for the millionth time about how dumb I had been.

"But that's not all, is it?" Derek remarked, more of a statement than an actual question.

Another deep, clearing breath later, I found a small thread of strength to continue. "I pretended I wasn't as devastated as I was, and I changed that summer. Where before I was the quiet, nerdy girl, I became the one at every party just to get him out of my mind. But I steered clear of the parties I knew his team would be at," I added hastily, not wanting Derek to think I was that type of ex, the kind who tried to get revenge by screwing around with a buddy. I wasn't really sure why I wanted Derek to know that, but it felt like an important distinction.

"There was a back to school party at a friend's house. I actually didn't want to go to that one, afraid I'd run into him, but my friend begged me."

"Come on," Leila whined, "It's been months since you and EJ-"

I held up a hand to stop her. "Four months." I wriggled four fingers for emphasis. "And your mom is the one who said it takes twice the length of the relationship to get over it," I reminded her.

Leila stuck her tongue out at me then returned to her closet. The clothes muffled her voice slightly. "I know, but it's my first time hosting and everyone knows you." My best friend since second grade meant it as a compliment but guilt prodded at me for lying to my mom, who didn't care if I went to parties so long as I had a way to get home before midnight. Cinderella had nothing on me.

That night, though, I told my mom I was staying at Leila's for a movie night. While not unusual, my mom was surprised, which probably should have said something about my social habits.

Flopping backwards onto Leila's bed, I heaved a sigh. "Fiiiine."

She squealed in excitement. "This is going to be the best party of the year!"

"It's only the first one," I said, but her enthusiasm was contagious.

I found myself being dragged into preparations after Leila's mom and brother left for a weekend of college visits. I managed to convince Leila that a piñata was too extra for a high school party, though it actually might have been fun. But the last thing we needed was a bunch of drunk kids trying to hit anything and I was not trying to start out junior year being questioned by the police.

I was dumping ice into a bowl when a thought hit me. "Lei, people are gonna start showing up soon and all I see is soda. A sober party?"

"No," she scoffed, rolling her eyes. "We'll have more than pop." She enunciated the last word to tease me. "Some of the guys are taking care of it. They'll be here in a minute." Her cell phone chimed and her hazel eyes lit up. She picked it up, her manicured nails clicking against the granite counter. "Yup, they're almost here," she said, bouncing with giddiness.

I couldn't help but share her smile. Leila bounded into the front hall when a car door slammed, leaving me to finish getting out the plastic cups and chips. Grunts and groans came from the front of the house as Leila directed the boys presumably carrying a keg to the back porch. I shifted my attention to the refrigerator to clear out space for anyone bringing their own drinks. They wouldn't care about the temperature later on, but the kids at our school could be ridiculously particular about their drinks before the buzz hit them.

Carrots, tomatoes, and avocados went into the crisper. I could hear my mother's playful exasperation as she chastised Leila's mom for wondering why her food expired so much faster than ours. I pulled out a carton of eggs and put them in the fridge door, piling butter on top. The milk went where the eggs had been, next to a jug that only had a little bit of orange juice left. I frowned and grabbed the jug by the handle, replacing it with the brand new one on the counter.

"Hey, kid."

I jumped, dropping the orange juice in the process. The flimsy plastic lid popped off and skittered across the floor, but only a few splatters of juice hit the white tile, the curve of the plastic jug preventing a bigger catastrophe. I cursed and grabbed a paper towel from the kitchen island as a rich laugh rang in my ears. My cheeks grew hotter while I cleaned up the mess.

"Glad to know I still make you jumpy," said the same voice.

"Leave it to you, EJ." I tried to sound lighthearted, I really did, but it came across pained to my own ears. I stayed on the floor a

moment longer than necessary and reminded myself that everything between us ended months ago while I also silently yelled at Leila for not warning me.

Planting a smile on my face, I straightened and set the jug on the counter, minus its cap. "Hi."

EJ looked better than I remembered. His brown hair was combed in a wavy style that stopped just shy of his ears, and his bright blue eyes sparkled with mischief as he smirked at me. He leaned sideways on the kitchen island, accentuating the toned muscles of his bronzed arm. Even his shoulders seemed broader. He seemed to be appraising me in much the same way.

I wondered if he could tell I had gone up a bra size or if he could see the shapeliness of my legs from running all summer. My chosen outfit of a black halter top and dark denim shorts suddenly felt very wrong since EJ always preferred when I dressed up a little and "showed some class." A moment too late, I remembered that I wasn't supposed to be feeling any of that. "Well, this is awkward," I said, my hand crossing over to hold my arm.

EJ grinned, showing a flash of his teeth in that way that used to make me swoon like an idiot. Before he could say anything, another guy walked in, looking like he pre-gamed before arriving. "Come on, bro, you gotta come see this." He put a hand on EJ's shoulder then followed his gaze to me. "Hey, Katie," he said, almost as an afterthought.

"Can't you see I'm busy, Will?" EJ said, winking at me.

I attempted a playful smile. "It's fine. He's free to go," I said, addressing Will. A long, slow breath escaped me after they left. Leila seriously owed me.

More people started to show up and, as expected, continued to bring drinks. I helped Leila play hostess in the kitchen for a while before a couple of her friends from the dance team offered to swap out. "We're driving, so it's pop only tonight!" Jessi yelled to make herself *heard over the music.*

"Go mingle," Whitney agreed, pushing a couple of empty plastic cups in our hands.

Leila grabbed my free hand and started weaving through the throng of people to the table where most of the drinks and chips were laid out. Her body, dressed in a cute baby blue crop top and jean shorts, moved with the beat of the music that I had no hope of recognizing, and I followed suit. We snagged some vodka and punch before navigating to the back deck.

The deck was the best feature of the house with three levels descending toward the yard and a hot tub at the far corner of the lowest level. Immediately outside the back door quite a few of the guys from the football and basketball teams were playing beer pong. More people hung out on the second level, talking or dancing to some country music. With a sigh of relief, I didn't see EJ anywhere.

The air was still too warm for anyone to attempt going in the hot tub, which I think Leila was particularly thankful for.

We perched on the railing and watched the guys play beer pong, changing who we were cheering for with every round. I nursed my drink, wanting enough to relax but not so much that I'd regret my life in the morning. By the time it was gone, we were dragged into a game of flip cup.

"All my years of button mashing boil down to this," I called out, somehow designated as the first player.

Squared off against a tall football player who I thought was named Jack, or maybe Jake, I readied for the call to start. A cup barely a quarter full sat in front of each person on either side of the table, six of us in total. I downed the remainder of my own drink and put the cup off to the side to toss later.

"Go!"

I drained the cup in one gulp and placed it on the edge of the table. I flicked my finger under it, causing the cup to arc perfectly and land upside down. My hands shot into the air in victory while the guy next to me worked on his. Across the table, Jack struggled a few times to land the cup. The slow start cost his team the win.

We played a few more times, yelling and laughing at each other as it became progressively more difficult to land the cup. At one point, Leila accidentally hit hers so hard that it flipped all the way over to land inside her opponent's cup, spurring shrieks of, "That totally counts!" and "One in a million shot!" The girl whose cup it was dissolved into giggles, and we lost that round.

I backed away from the group, out of breath and in dire need of water and chips. Squeezing my way back into the house, I saw a line in front of the downstairs bathroom and rolled my eyes. A few couples dotted the stairs, only one not down each other's throats. I slipped and stumbled past them to use the bathroom near Leila's bedroom.

When I finished, a wave of nausea hit me as I stood up, and I had to lean against the wall for a moment, breathing deeply. I really needed some water. Splashing some on my face didn't help as much as I hoped. When I thought I was steady enough to make it back downstairs, I opened the door and walked right into someone.

"Sorry!" I cried out, holding my head while my vision swam from the sudden motion of trying to get out of the way.

"Are you all right, Katie?" EJ's voice managed to reach me through the fog in my brain.

I nodded and started to pull my hand away, but that didn't feel very good.

"Come on, you need to sit down." His voice held a level of concern I couldn't remember hearing before. Before I could protest, his arms were around me, guiding me to sit near the top of the staircase and lean against the railing.

I let my head fall back to rest between two of the posts and closed my eyes, grateful for the lack of motion. "Thanks," I mumbled.

"Anything for you," he said quietly. His hand still held mine, his

thumb occasionally gliding over my fingers.

I wanted to withdraw, to get away before his charm hooked me again. At the same time, I wanted nothing more than to nestle against his shoulder and go to sleep. He didn't say anything for a while, and I started to drift, letting my thoughts dance to the beat of the music downstairs.

"I love you, Kate," EJ said, squeezing my hand. "I was an idiot, and I'm sorry. I never should have pushed you away." He raised my hand to his mouth and brushed a kiss along the back of it. "Can we get back together?

I longed to hear those words for months, to have him hold me and kiss me again. Moving slowly so as to not bring on a wave of nausea, I brought my head to be level with his. A touch of pity coursed through me at meeting his hopeful gaze. I never saw him so serious, and I took another moment.

My eyes stung with unshed tears, but I shook my head. "No," I whispered, wanting to recoil from his crestfallen expression. He had hurt me, made a fool of me, then expected me to take him back because he was done fooling around with other girls? No, I wouldn't take him back, even though part of me wanted to.

"Please," he begged. The sound grated on my ears as it took on a strange whine. EJ wasn't used to not getting what he wanted. I dimly wondered if anyone had ever denied him anything. "You're all I have, Katie."

A sour taste hit my mouth, and I felt like I was going to throw up. I grabbed at the railing above my head and pulled myself to my feet, still shaking my head. "That's not true," I protested. There was no light other than what spilled from the staircase, but I headed away from it toward Leila's room. I just needed to lie down for a while. Maybe get some water. What was that saying, something about not mixing beer and liquor?

I reached Leila's door and became dimly aware that EJ was still with me. It hit me that he could be getting the exact wrong idea from my actions, so I tried to step back but stumbled.

He caught me, and I could smell the alcohol on his breath as he drew me closer. I got my feet under me and pushed EJ away. "Can we talk about this?" I started to say no again, but something in his expression stopped me. He wiped at his eyes. "I might as well go kill myself if even the girl I love doesn't want me." There was something dark about the way he said it.

My conscience screamed at me. "Talk then." My mouth felt dry, and I wished again for some water.

EJ opened the door to Leila's room. I waited for him to enter before I followed, leaving the door open. He sat on the edge of her bed. Leila would freak if he threw up on it. Or if I did.

I elected to sit in her desk chair instead, latching the swivel so it wouldn't spin. When I looked up, EJ was staring at me intently. Out of habit, I ran my hand over my hair, making sure it wasn't messed up. I cleared my throat. "So, what do you want to say?"

"I love you," he repeated. "And I miss you. I miss us."

"You were the one who ended it," I pointed out, dropping my gaze to the floor.

"I know, and I'm an idiot. But when I saw you tonight, I realized that you were always the one and the others were just stand-ins for you."

I bit the inside of my cheek to hold back a laugh. Did he actually think that line would work on me? I looked at him again, expecting the same thrill from before summer or even a shadow of it like what happened when I first saw him that night, but there was nothing there. I smiled then said as gently as I could, "I'm sorry, EJ, but no. We're done."

Since I wasn't feeling as lightheaded as before, I stood up to go, but EJ jumped up from the bed and blocked the path to the door. "Wait, Katie, don't do this," he begged.

I swallowed a flash of anger at his persistence, reminding myself that I was just as bad when he broke up with me. "I told you my answer, now let me go please." My voice was quiet but firm. My mom, a single woman for 13 years, had taught me how to stand my ground.

I tried to move past EJ again. He took a couple of hurried steps backwards, shutting the door with his back so that his body blocked it. Panic started to bubble in my chest. Even with a ton of people in the house, it wasn't likely anyone would hear me scream. If they did, who would take it seriously?

For his part, EJ's face filled with desperation. "Why? Why won't you give us another chance?" he demanded.

A shaky breath came in and out of my chest before I answered. "I don't want to be with you anymore. Now please move, or I'll scream."

He took a step closer to me, but not far enough from the door to give me a chance to escape. "Are you fucking someone else?"

I glanced down at his clenched fists and felt the panic rise again. "No," I said truthfully. "No one." One of my legs took an involuntary step backwards. So much for standing my ground. I took another step back away from the door, and EJ followed.

An angry dog, that's what he was. Except dogs usually didn't get angry. Just scared. And I was scared. My thoughts raced along as I tried to think of what to do, how to keep him calm, how to get out of this.

"There was never anyone but you," I offered, trying to make my voice soothing and hating the shakiness of it.

EJ's face softened a little. He raised a hand, and I flinched. He brushed a strand of hair away from my face. Another step back for me and another forward for him. I forced myself to look into his eyes. He leaned toward me and closed his eyes.

I sidestepped and ran for the door. Hope rose up in me as I pulled the door open before it was slammed shut again. EJ's right hand shoved it closed while his left grabbed my arm and yanked me away from it. I stumbled, lost my footing, and fell. My other arm tried to cushion the landing, but EJ's grip held for a second too long.

Pain blossomed at the side of my head before everything went dark.

I regained consciousness to the sound of EJ alternating between cursing and apologizing. My head thudded loudly, worse than before, and it took a moment to remember what happened. Still on the floor, I managed to resist the urge to get up, to get away from EJ, not wanting to risk another blow like that.

EJ realized I was awake, and I heard a sigh of relief. "I'm so sorry, Katie. I didn't mean to." His words blurred together while I tried to pick them out piece by piece to understand the meaning of each one individually, then altogether.

My eyes shot open when I felt his lips on my cheek. He pulled away for a moment and looked down at me, his face inches from mine. "I love you, and I'm so sorry." His mouth found mine.

I tried to move, to push him off. "No." I struggled to get the word out with his mouth pressed tightly on me. He grabbed both of my wrists in one hand and held them above my head. His other hand slid under my shirt, his fingers tracing my hip, I squirmed. In my head I was screaming at myself.

The hand that didn't have my arms pinned continued to move down until he pushed it in between my stomach and the button of my shorts. I froze. EJ started kissing my neck as his fingers went lower.

I opened my mouth, but nothing came out. Why couldn't I scream? Why was I just laying there? Tears started pooling in my eyes, and I turned my head away, seething with hate for the body that betrayed me.

"I must have passed out again because I woke to Leila screaming and crying, asking if I was okay. She asked who did it, but I couldn't say anything at the time. I just wanted to go home. Leila helped me get dressed in a pair of her sweats and took me to the hospital where they did a rape kit. I lied and said I was 18 and that I didn't want the police called.

"Leila already called my mom, and she showed up, but she didn't force me to do anything. She said it was my choice, but it made me wonder if she even believed me. A few days later, I decided to tell Leila it was EJ." My eyes started to water again, but I continued. "She said that he would never do anything like that. Even after she was the one who found me, she didn't believe me." My breath hitched again.

Derek reminded me to breathe. His hand rested on my shoulder. He kept the touch light, a reminder of where we were but that he was not going to hurt me.

I hesitated for a moment. Telling Derek was unlike any other time I tried saying anything before. I kept my head down, unable to look Derek in the eye as I revealed the part no one else knew. "I got pregnant from it. I had a miscarriage at eight weeks, but for two weeks, I knew I was pregnant and didn't want it. But when it was gone, I felt so much guilt and shame and self-hatred. And people at school started calling me a slut and a whore and a liar."

I felt the need for a snack, something to keep my mouth occupied and prevent me talking, even though the cake sat heavy in my stomach. "I ended up here after my track coach saw the scars on my legs which made my mom take my phone where she saw my diary app. Either the password stuff is garbage on e-Diary or my mother is a hacker for the FBI."

I tried to smile, but my eyes burned with the tears I withheld. Derek looked at me, not with sympathy, but with understanding. It made me want to cry more.

"It's not your fault," he said, wrapping one of his arms around my shoulders again. He left enough space between us for me to move if I needed or wanted to.

"I know, and I've heard that a million times."

"But you don't believe it." He nodded and gave my shoulder a quick squeeze before letting go.

I opened my mouth to protest like I had so many times before, but I paused and thought about it. "I guess I don't. I figure that if I hadn't stayed for the party, if I hadn't told him it was okay to talk, maybe it wouldn't have..." I sniffed in a very unladylike manner. "...happened."

"Maybe. Maybe not. Remember *The Lion King?*" When I nodded, he continued with a childlike grin. "Hakuna matata. It's in the past. And you can't change the past, only your future."

Rolling my eyes, I slugged his arm. "Someone's been paying attention in group. Take some of your own advice."

His smile faded. "It only works if you actually remember your past." He must have seen the doubt on my face because he quickly added, "I remember the more recent stuff, obviously, like the crappy foster group homes and being pushed around at school." There was no bitterness in his voice, just matter-of-factness.

"At least now you can tell them your friend Kate will come beat them up," I said cheerfully.

He laughed, an actual laugh that made his eyes crinkle. "Yeah, because that will go over *so* well."

"Worth it." I made a fist and shook it at an imaginary foe.

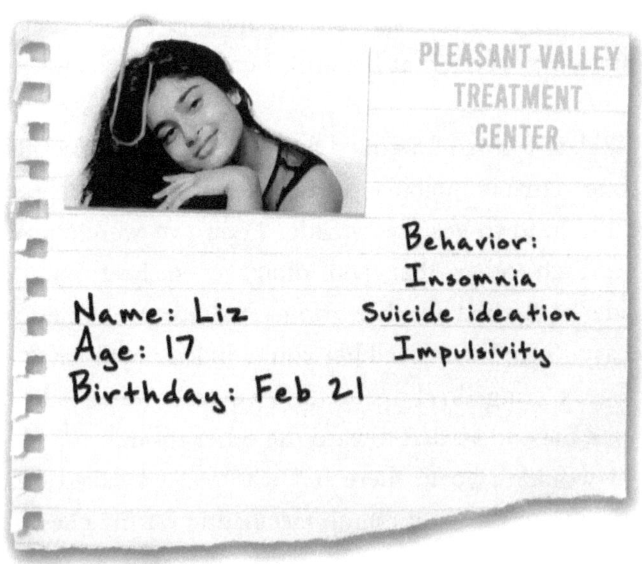

LIZ

"Either you've been crying or smoking. So where's the stash?" I said, tapping Derek on the shoulder.

He spun to face me, brow furrowed. "What?"

I gestured to his face, tilting my head up with a playful grin. "Your eyes are red."

Understanding dawned on him. As it did, his shoulders dropped. "What do you want, Liz?"

Pretending to pout, I hopped in front of him to block his path. "So she finally told you what happened."

"I'm not going to answer that."

"I wasn't asking."

Again, he looked confused. I just loved doing that to people, but he made it way too easy. "How do you know?

Did she tell you? She said she hasn't told anyone before." He started to scratch at his arm, but I put my hand out to stop him.

"Relax, Romeo." I rolled my eyes. "Your perfect image of Kate remains intact. I overheard you two out there." I used my head to gesture outside. "You two were so caught up in each other that you didn't even hear me come outside." I flashed another grin as his face paled. Seriously, too easy. "No, I won't tell her you're in love with her."

Derek cringed. "I'm not in love with Kate." He sidestepped me and started toward the other room.

"I wouldn't go in there if I was you," I called quietly, pretending to find something fascinating on my chewed-up fingernails.

"Why?"

"Yoga's going on in there."

He groaned and took a seat at the puzzle table.

"So, DID, huh?" I asked, pulling up another chair.

"What?"

"Your new diagnosis. Dissociative Identity Disorder." I scanned the pieces for one with a splash of red on it.

I could see him staring at me incredulously. "How long were you out there?"

When I found the piece I wanted, I leaned over and snapped it to two others, completing a cardinal. "I always thought that schizo diagnosis was a load of crap."

Derek wasn't even trying to ignore me anymore. "You've known this whole time?"

I laid a hand on his arm, mine being several shades darker. "You told me it was other versions of you. If you were schizo, you'd be talking to people no one else could see. Or hearing things."

"How do you know?" he challenged.

It was a valid question. I removed my hand and returned my attention to the puzzle. "I've been in and out of here a lot. So I've met quite a few people. One of them actually was schizophrenic, and it was surreal. Which, I guess, is kind of the point." I laughed weakly. "Anyway, you are very much real when you're not Derek."

Seeing the return of his confusion, I sighed and faced him. His eyes shifted almost immediately to look away then back at me. My *daadee ma* used to say that the eyes speak more than the mouth, which I think was her version of the eyes being the windows to the soul. I held up a finger. "That day with Renee, you weren't you. I mean, you were, but different. You held yourself differently, spoke differently, and, as Derek, you had no idea where you were even though you'd been moving and speaking the entire time. And that wasn't the first time."

I held up a second finger. "Before that, there was the time where Ciro walked into your room and found Trish. Yes, he told me," I cut him off before he could get the question out. "And he said that you weren't talking to someone else but more like *as* someone else."

My third finger went up. "There was the time you told me about what landed you here, the suicide attempt." I held up a fourth finger. "Plus the other one you mentioned that got you in trouble at one of your foster homes—where they locked you in your room because you wouldn't stop acting like a cat." I grinned at him and added, "I'd like to see that one, actually."

For the first time since I stopped him, I saw the ghost of a smile flit across his face. "Don't count on it."

"Okay, Neko," I said with a shrug and held up my

pinky. "Fifth, the one that terrifies you." All traces of playfulness left my voice as I said it. An art session during one of Derek's first few weeks here had revealed a demonic image of a face that had made Derek tremble. He refused to pick up a paint brush for three weeks after.

Derek nodded thoughtfully. "Six, counting this me."

I winked at him. "Give the boy a prize."

"So you really suspected it this whole time. Why didn't you say something?" He had long since stopped pretending to work on the puzzle.

I leaned back in the chair, looking at him. "Really? The only thing that changed between then and now is that you've heard it from a doctor." Derek met my gaze, his forehead creased in confusion. Something clicked in my own head. "Do you not ever remember what happens when you switch?"

Derek shook his head and looked away. "Most of the time, no. I get flashes from Trish sometimes, which is how I've known about her for so long, but not the others. It never really occurred to me that there were others. There was always some other explanation." He looked like a dog abandoned by its owner, hurt and confused. Except he was both the dog and the owner.

Well, damn. I hadn't meant for that to happen. "Hey, look, you're not the first one to ever be diagnosed with this, okay?" I said, trying in vain to cheer him up.

He mumbled something but didn't look up.

"Six," I said sternly. That got his attention. "This doesn't change anything about who you are. A diagnosis is just words, okay? You are still you." I stared at him, willing him to believe me.

"Kate said something similar."

A quiet laugh escaped me. "If you don't believe me, at least listen to her."

He took a deep breath in and let it out slowly, the epitome of mindfulness. "I guess you guys are right."

"That's the spirit," I said cheerfully, clapping a hand on his shoulder.

A tiny smile broke through the cloud of gloom surroundding him. "Thanks, Liz."

I tossed my hair over my shoulder and said, "It's what I'm here for."

"If you weren't crazy, you'd make a good therapist," Derek teased.

"The best therapists studied psychology to figure out what was wrong with themselves," I retorted with another grin. I pointed to the fridge. "There's more cake in there for your girl if she wants it."

The best thing about being bipolar is that you get to act however the hell you want and can blame it on either mania or depression. The worst part about being bipolar is that it actually makes you do crazy shit that you would never even think to do otherwise. Like stealing something like a pen and thinking you got away with a huge heist. Brains are weird like that.

"Who took my pen?" Matthew picked up his notebook and shook it out.

"Did you bring it out here?" Tobias asked. He stood up and started helping Matthew look for it.

The weight of the pen sat on my ear, hidden behind a lock of my dark hair that was surprisingly shiny for once. My latest bout of overwhelming depression had given way to a mild ecstasy that the therapists liked to call hypomania. The boys continued to search for it, bringing a smirk to my lips as I leaned against the counter sipping my coffee.

I watched them for a minute until Matthew went down the hallway to the room he shared with Tobias. Then I knelt down and grabbed a granola bar from the cabinet. I took the pen out, set my face straight, and stood up, granola bar in one hand, the pen in the other. "Is this it?" I asked when I heard footsteps coming back up the hall.

Tobias squinted at it then closed the gap between us in a few long strides. "Hey, Matt," he called, grabbing the pen from my hand. "It's in here."

"You're welcome," I said sweetly.

"I would thank you," Tobias said, lowering his voice, "if you hadn't taken it in the first place." He winked and turned away.

The smile froze on my face.

"Liz found it," Tobias explained as Matthew returned.

I waved and turned around to hide my confusion. Why would Tobias confront me then not tell Matthew? I was spared further speculation by Michelle calling for group.

Darla flounced in, more chipper than usual. I raised an eyebrow and remarked, "Someone looks happy."

"Ganx," she said, throwing up two fingers and grinning.

Ciro appeared behind her and asked the obvious. "What's that mean?"

"Good but anxious." Darla flopped into a chair and started bouncing a foot.

"What, are you leaving or something?" Ciro sat next to her and balanced his notebook in his lap. His dark curly hair sat in waves that even I couldn't dare replicate. Though his mouth smiled, there was something about his eyes that seemed stony.

Darla didn't notice. "Yup!" She shimmied in her seat, sending her hair tumbling from its clip. A scowl cut across her pretty face as she twisted the uncooperative hair back up and resecured it.

"Congrats," Ciro and I said together.

"Jinx," I called out. Ciro and Renee were the only ones who played jinx with me, but Ciro stayed silent this time. I studied him as he stared resolutely ahead.

Michelle walked to the front of the room, greeting some of the latecomers.

I put my arms on the back of Ciro's chair and leaned forward to whisper, "You're leaving too, aren't you?"

His head whipped around to look at me, his stoic expression momentarily replaced with a flash of fear and wonder. "How do you do that?"

"Magic," I said.

Shaking his head in disbelief, Ciro admitted, "Yeah, on Thursday."

"Ready for it?" One of my hands went down to his shoulder and rubbed gently.

He shook his head. "Not even close."

Michelle clapped her hands for attention, and the room's chatter slowly died down. I didn't know how the woman did it, but she always managed to look elegant and casual with her natural hair and beautifully colored clothes that seemed to highlight the best of her ebony features. A headband pulled her hair back away from her face to give the perception of openness, a trick I normally hated, but it worked for her.

"Today we're going to be discussing self-esteem and identity," she began, her voice clear and upbeat.

"It should be a crime to sound so happy when talking about such a crap topic," I muttered. Ciro snorted with laughter, which caught us both a warning look from Michelle.

"I'm going to pass out this quiz for you all to take and see where your self-esteem lies at the moment."

"Oh, it lies all right," Derek said, not bothering to keep his voice down.

Rather than chastise him, Michelle nodded. "It does," she said. "Especially when it's low." She moved to one side of the room then the other, distributing several sheets of paper. "Take one, pass it down," she said, keeping one for herself. "This is not a definitive test, but it may give you an idea of where your self esteem currently sits. Go ahead and take a few minutes to answer the questions."

I looked down at the sheet that Ciro handed to me. The test was scale-based. Fill in the bubble that most accurately reflects the thoughts or beliefs. The left side had the description while the right had the bubbles.

First question read, <u>I have to make an effort to socialize</u>. The options on the right were five bubbles ranging from strongly agree to strongly disagree. I grabbed an extra pen from the counter behind me and circled the agree bubble. The questions went on in a similar fashion.

The challenging part for me was answering honestly. I knew what the answers should be for a supposedly normal person, and I was so used to choosing those instead of what I actually thought that I had to go back through several of the questions and cross out my original answers.

"This is a self-reflection test. You know yourselves better than anyone," Michelle said. She took a seat at the front of the room and folded her hands while waiting for us to finish. "What are some of the things you noticed?" she asked after another few minutes.

No one spoke for several seconds. If the others were anything like me, we were all considering how shitty our self-esteem really was compared to where it ought to be. Finally, Renee spoke. "It's not just about how we see ourselves," she said. She kept her head bent over the paper so that only the top of her red hair could be seen.

"That's true," Michelle affirmed. "Self-esteem is also about how we think others perceive us."

Tobias lazily raised a hand. "What is the point of this exercise?" he asked.

Her smile reminded me of a lioness. She turned the question back on him. "What do you think the point is?"

"To remind us how depressing we are?"

I found myself nodding along with several others.

"That's one way to look at it," Michelle conceded. "What are some things that contribute to self-esteem?" She addressed the question to the group at large.

This time, the answers came immediately from all around the room.

"Parents."

"Friends."

"Siblings."

"Guardians." I was pretty sure that one came from Derek.

"Yourself."

"People at school."

"Magazines," Darla added.

"Society," I threw out there.

"Oh, good one," Ciro said over his shoulder to me.

Michelle nodded as we spoke over each other. "All valid

answers. The way we value ourselves has several factors to it, both internal and external. That includes praise and criticism from others or from ourselves. Self-esteem can have a big influence on our identity."

"So are you saying that we should let what others say about us influence us?" Matthew asked, speaking up for the first time.

Michelle shook her head. "I don't like the word 'should' because it involves imposed expectations. So I'm not saying it should, but that it can. If you hear that you are useless over and over again, you may start to believe it, contributing to lower self-esteem. This could also make you less likely to believe it when someone says that you are valued, and that's the trap we as humans fall into."

I raised my hand and waited for Michelle to gesture for me to speak. "How does that end up playing into societal norms? Like sexuality, for instance. If we're constantly told that being anything but straight is wrong, then wouldn't our way of thinking be distorted?"

"I think that's exactly what she's saying, though," Ciro said. "It wasn't that long ago that people were really worked up about anyone who wasn't straight." His voice dropped as he added, "Sometimes they still are."

Tobias nodded in agreement. "It took a few years to accept that I was bi because people kept telling me it was wrong."

"Same," I said, meeting his gaze.

Ciro lifted his head. "I was jumped by some of the guys at school, people I grew up with, and beat so badly that I was sent to the hospital, all because I came out as gay."

Darla put her hand on Ciro's arm and said, "There's still so much hatred out there, but that doesn't mean it has to stay that way."

"I," Matthew started to say. He paused and cleared his throat. "I've had a lot of, um reservations about coming out because of those exact reasons. Actually, I've never said anything about it before." His face reddened and he ducked his head.

"I've just gotta say, I love how this started out being about self-esteem and turned into a huge coming out party," Kate said, clapping her hands. Several of us joined her until Matt was beet red and all of us were grinning.

"And that," Michelle called out even as she clapped with us, "is an example of how to change self-esteem."

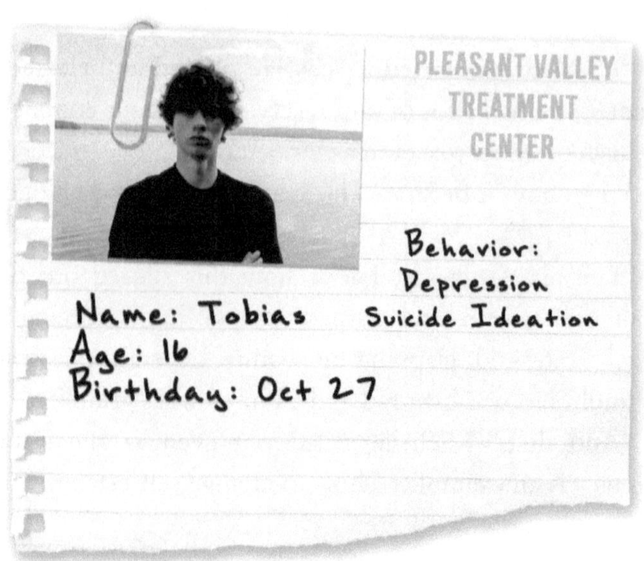

TOBIAS

Darla wasn't ready to go, no matter how much she said she was. Ciro wasn't ready either, but he was smart enough to admit it. It was weird to consider how worried I was about both of them. I hadn't known either one of them before getting sent to treatment, but it still felt like a part of the family was leaving. Not that I'd let them know that.

The driver, a thick woman with bronzed skin and dark hair that swooped over her head, stood near the desk, tossing her keys into the air and catching them while she waited. "Come on, girl, we don't got forever. Traffic's gonna get bad."

Darla started to hug those of us who were in the common room. Ciro was in a therapy session, his last before he left later that afternoon. Darla hesitated when she reached me. She bit her lip, her bright hair falling around her shoulders in subtle waves. If she wasn't so damn desperate for attention, she would have been really cute.

I closed the space between us, reaching out. "Good luck out there," I said. And I meant it. When we pulled apart, she flashed a grateful smile, which I didn't return. "Listen, I don't think you understand how awesome you can be on your own. You don't need some guy around to tell you that."

Her smile faltered. "Why are you saying this?"

I shrugged. "You deserve to know it. You deserve better than to live based on what you think your body can get you. You *are* better than that." I finally grinned. "But if you tell anyone I said so, I'll deny it."

Darla laughed, her shoulders falling just a hair, but it was enough for her to relax a little. She stepped away and waved at everyone before grabbing her duffel bag and a backpack. With a final look back at us, she was gone out the door.

Renee let out a small sob, and James put an arm around her. The sadness made me uncomfortable, so I went back to the room and flopped onto the mattress.

I wasn't sure what to think about. I didn't want to focus on the people leaving because that would bring up emotions. And that was a bad idea just on principle. I wanted to hit or throw something, but I wasn't sure why. Restlessness did not suit me. Times like that made me wish I could have my cell phone, not for calling anyone, but just to play some mindless game for a while so that I wouldn't have to think.

The thing I missed most about life on the outside was

being able to listen to music whenever I wanted. Especially when in a mood like that. I just needed something to be able to get out of my own head. I didn't want to talk to anyone, but I didn't want to be alone either.

There was a knock on the door. Derek poked his head in and said, "Riley is looking for you."

I groaned and rolled off the bed to my feet.

"Don't sound so excited about it," Derek teased.

Without thinking, I retorted, "I'll give you something to be excited about."

A grin danced along his face. "Don't threaten me with a good time."

I smirked as I followed him out into the hallway. "Who says it's a threat?" I asked then joined when he laughed. Nothing like some fake flirting to get out of a funk.

Riley waved as we approached. The tight feeling in my stomach returned as I waved back.

"Look at it this way," Derek said, slowing slightly, "you're skipping Emotional Regulation group and you'll be done in time for volleyball."

I flashed him a grateful, if half-hearted smile. "Yeah, I can look forward to kicking your ass, you mean."

"Yeah, okay," he scoffed and headed toward the group room.

Riley greeted me brightly as I approached. "How are you, Tobias?" She motioned for me toward the room set aside for visitors or sessions.

My shoulders lifted in a shrug. "Fine, I guess." I took a seat in one of the lounge chairs and leaned back.

Riley settled in across from me. She slipped out of her flats and crossed her legs on the couch, propping the binder with my name on top of her leg. She looked at me without opening it and said, "Isn't your cousin coming today?"

I nodded and stared at the short table in front of us. "She's supposed to, but I wouldn't blame her if she canceled."

Riley's head shifted to one side. "Why is that?"

A heavy sigh escaped me, somehow not surprised we were jumping into a heavy topic so soon. "My own parents don't want to see me, so why should she?" It was a thought that had been circulating in my head for a while, unvoiced. Once I said it, it rang true.

"That's not your fault, though. You know that, right?" Riley's round face was creased in worry but thankfully not pity.

"Yeah, I know," I reluctantly admitted. "It's not my fault they'd rather drink rubbing alcohol than spend time with their kid. Doesn't make it any easier to deal with." I reached into my pocket and pulled out a stone Matthew had given me. Its smooth edges slid around in my hand. "I just don't get why," I muttered, keeping my eyes on the hand that held the stone.

"I can't answer that," she said softly. "Are they the reason for your own self-destructive behaviors?"

The question hit me like a roundhouse kick to the face. "No," I blurted out. At her raised eyebrow, I realized how loud I sounded. I took in a breath, counted to three, and let it out. "No," I repeated less harshly. "I never want to be anything like them. Ever since I can remember, it's been a toss-up on whether or not even one of them would be home, sometimes for days."

My arms crossed over my chest, but I continued to hang onto the stone. "I don't know if my parents ever even showed up to a parent-teacher conference. Not that it would have made a difference, I guess. Apparently I'm destined to be just like them anyway."

"Where did you get that idea?" The leather of the couch squeaked as she adjusted her position, leaving her hands resting on the binder that remained closed. "After a certain age, we all get to make our own choices. Your thoughts influence your emotions, but do they control your behavior? Your actions?"

I started to nod then stopped. Something in what she said sounded familiar. "I guess technically not."

Riley bit back a smile and motioned for me to elaborate.

"I mean, if I get mad, I can throw a punch or I can walk away," I explained. "But sometimes it's impossible to stop that immediate reaction."

"Not impossible. Your brain is just wired to connect that emotion with that reaction currently, but that doesn't mean it can't be rewired. If you practice noticing the way those thoughts and reactions are related, you can start to interrupt them. You said yourself that you could walk away."

I didn't answer while I processed Riley's words. She wasn't wrong. If animals could cut new trails through forests, why couldn't a brain rewire itself? "But what's the point?" I asked aloud. "People suck, so why bother trying to be better than them. Not to mention that just sounds pretentious."

She laughed, and it made me smile a little. "Is it trying to be better than others or better for yourself?"

Again, I kept my silence. My foot started tapping the floor.

Riley spoke again after a while, "So if you've been dealing with your parents' issues for so long, what was it that sparked the jump to attempting suicide?"

The knot in my stomach moved to my throat and made it difficult to breathe. I licked my lips but didn't say anything.

"Did it have to do with what you mentioned in group the other day? About your sexuality?"

I blinked, thinking about it, and finally said, "Not really. Not directly, anyway." She waited patiently for me to continue. My head fell back to distract me from her piercing, all too knowing gaze. "I fought myself on that for a long time, especially being in a shit neighborhood where any sign of weakness makes you prey."

"Do you consider being bi or gay a weakness?" she interrupted.

"No," I huffed. "I don't. Anymore. But others did, and I had enough going on than to deal with the perverts trying to jump me. Only place I would have been even remotely safe would be school and even that was iffy most of the time.

"But, yeah, eventually I figured out that it wasn't a phase or whatever. I had a couple friends who helped me with that, including my girlfriend." I closed my eyes. "Ex-girlfriend," I corrected. The tightness in my throat returned. I clenched my fist around the stone, letting my nails dig into my palms so that I wouldn't start tearing up. Though Riley had assured me it was safe and encouraged me to not hold back, I still tried to keep myself from crying. Old habits and all.

After a few moments, the knot dissipated a little, enough for me to breathe again. The pain of the memories sitting at the edge of my consciousness were enough to make me wish all over again that the suicide attempt had succeeded. The hand not holding the stone automatically reached for my arm to scratch.

I felt the need to explain without really understanding why. There was nothing I needed to defend myself from. Riley was one of the least judgmental people I had ever known. But, still, the need was there.

"I lived in the same neighborhood my entire life, and so did a few other kids. A few of us stuck together, for protection at first, but eventually we actually became friends. Or as close to friends as we've ever known, I guess. We looked out for each other, could be, I don't know...real?" I struggled to find the word I was looking for.

"Vulnerable?" Riley supplied.

I made a face. "Yeah, I guess. Anyway, there were five of us, but I was closer with Tori and Miles than any of the others. Tori, Mary, and Milo sometimes made food for us when our parents didn't show up because they were out on a bender. Mary, Milo, and Miles were siblings, I think. Or cousins. It was hard to tell with that family. So, yeah, we took care of each other.

"Then we grew up some. Mary started whoring, but Miles and I made sure Tori wouldn't have to. Tori and I started hooking up last year. And, uh, there was one night where I made out with Miles when we were drunk, but he doesn't remember that, I don't think." Despite my insistence of accepting my bisexuality, my face still started to heat up and I sunk a little in the seat. "But Tori became my girlfriend eventually. I loved her." I hated the way my heart still ached, even after all that happened. I tried to maintain some nonchalance as I said, "Then she cheated on me with Miles. So I guess I figured that, if the two people I loved best obviously didn't care about me and the two who were supposed to love me didn't, well, that was it." I shrugged and kept my eyes averted.

"Tobias," she said and waited until I looked up again. "It seems like you're looking for love and acceptance from others as a replacement for your parents. I'm not saying you're wrong for doing it. Given what you've had to go through, it makes total sense."

I slowly let out my breath and made myself unclench the fist I didn't realize I held. The longer I was in the ward, the more aware I became of tension and anxiety in my body, which was both a blessing and a curse. It helped to know why my jaw or shoulders hurt the way they did, but knowing why didn't mean it stopped hurting.

A pang of guilt hit me as I sat there, whining about my cheating girlfriend and drunk parents when some of the others in the ward actually had really shitty things going on. Who was I to be taking up resources that could be going to help Renee deal with her missing sister? Or to Liz's mania or even Bullfrog's grief. I was an idiot kid who just didn't know how to deal.

It took a second for me to realize Riley had asked me a question. "What?"

She smiled with all the patience in the world. "What are you thinking about there?"

"That I'm an idiot," I said without reservation. I launched into a tirade detailing just how stupid I was for being there. When I was done, I settled back into the chair and stared ahead. "I never realized being totally honest could be so damn exhausting."

"Yeah," Riley laughed, "but honesty with yourself is pretty important. You could say all the right things to everyone else while pretending you're fine, but you know when you're lying to yourself."

It was a bizarre feeling to put everything out there like that. I had seen some of the others do it and maybe that's what helped me do it too, but it still seemed strange to not be guarding my words, always watching what I say in case someone tried to use it against me. I didn't have to do that there, though. There were no consequences to being honest.

"Why does this feel weird?" I finally asked.

"Didn't the first time you rode a bike feel weird?" When I nodded she gestured and said, "Well, this is like riding a bike. It's going to be strange and awkward for a little while, but you'll be flying down the street in no time, I think." She set the binder on the table and grabbed some papers out of her bag. "Here," she said, handing me a small stack. "This is your homework for the week. I want you to write down your biography. Include anything you like, but you need to also include the things that made you want to die. The first couple pages there are just a guideline for things to think about as you write."

"Is this how the others ended up telling their stories in group?"

"Yup," she nodded for extra emphasis. "You don't have to share in group if you don't want to, but if you do, I ask that you share with me first. The other papers are about core mindfulness skills. This is part of something called dialectical behavior therapy, and I think this will be a good approach for you."

"That's meditation and crap, right?" I looked down at the packet and put the top two sheets at the bottom.

"It can be. But this first part is more about noticing and starting to change ineffective thoughts through challenging things that I heard you say such as, 'I should have known better.' But why? Is that thought realistic or helpful?" Riley leaned forward to lift the top sheet and point at a worksheet beneath about describing thoughts. "Read through this and try out the exercise. If you don't understand or you don't like it, we can figure out another approach." She let go of the paper and sat back.

I skimmed the page then looked up at her. She had picked up the binder and was jotting notes in it finally. "So what's wrong with me?" I finally managed to say.

Riley's head tilted in confusion, reminding me of a dog I saw roaming the neighborhood a few years ago. "Nothing. You're human, that's all. Depression isn't wrong, it just is what it is."

"I could be wrong, but I'm pretty sure cutting your wrists and trying to hang yourself aren't normal reactions to a cheating girlfriend." I meant for it to come out wry and humorous, but it just sounded bitter.

Riley didn't flinch, though. The woman was made of butter and steel, but I guessed that was needed for a job like hers. "Under usual circumstances, you're right. That would be pretty extreme." She started to reach out then hesitated for a moment before her hand stretched further towards me. An awkward second passed, but I took her hand. Her four fingers cupped around the side of my hand, and she kept eye contact with me as she said, "You haven't had the easiest time of things, and I believe the situation with Tori and Miles was the catalyst of a lifetime of feeling unwanted, and that's what drove you to the breaking point."

I sat in stunned silence, unable to refute anything she said.

"That doesn't make you weak," she continued as

though my world wasn't tilting on its head all over again. "It doesn't make you an idiot either. There is so much strength inside of you already, Tobias, and I think you know that, deep down. We just need to figure out a way to tap into it again and give you the tools to do more than survive." She squeezed my hand then withdrew hers, leaving me to wonder what just happened and why the hell I wanted to curl up and bawl like a child.

"Thanks," I managed to get out while fighting a lump in my throat the size of Texas.

She gave me an almost maternal smile. "So does this sound like a workable plan for this week?" Riley asked as she resumed writing in the binder.

I cleared my throat and said it was. When she was done writing her notes, she gathered her things to stand, and I stood with her. I crossed the small room before her and opened the door so she wouldn't have to juggle everything. The rooms didn't lock from the inside.

"I'll be around if you need me for anything," she said as we walked back to the desk. She put the binder down on the counter and faced me. When standing, I towered over her by several inches. She patted my arm twice. "Are you all right to go to the next group?"

"It's volleyball. I have a score to settle with Derek," I said with a smile.

"Good, get to it then. And good luck! Oh, here, I'll let you out," she added as I started walking toward the door that would lead down to the gym where the volleyball net was set up. "See you soon."

Outside, the air was warm and breezy. I inhaled deeply then found myself yawning. A nap would have felt great around then, but it would have to wait until after the game. It was kind of surprising how much I looked forward to it.

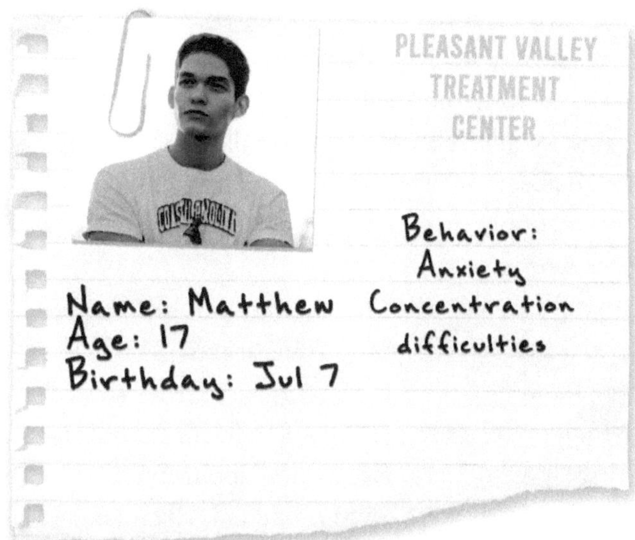

MATTHEW

I leaned backward, put my arms on the back of the bench, and lifted my head up and closed my eyes, letting the sun warm my face. Mindfulness practice, I had told myself. Which wasn't all that far from the truth. I could hear the kids from the other ward on the other side of the wall, but their shouts and laughter didn't bother me. There were a couple of birds sitting in the tree at the far side of the courtyard. But the sun was the best part, especially after the cold air in the unit.

"I don't know how I didn't see it before. There is no way you aren't at least a little gay," Ciro teased. I felt the bench shift a little beneath me and figured he had sat down.

"What makes you say that?" I cracked open one eye to look at him.

He gave me a coy smile, "I'm just saying my gaydar was way off with you. And Tobias, actually. Being in here is throwing me off," he laughed.

"Well, you're about to get recalibrated. When do you leave?" I closed my eyes again.

"In a couple of hours." There was a distinct lack of joy in those words.

I straightened up. He chewed on his fingernail but stopped when he saw me looking at him. "You don't want to go?" I asked.

"Being here is the first time in my life I didn't feel like I had to hide who I am. Everything about me was fair game for people to tear apart, but no one did. Even Natalia, when she was still here. She was super religious but actually supportive."

"Yeah. Is that why you want to stay?"

Ciro let out a sigh and started toying with a turquoise cord bracelet that stood out sharply against his dark skin. "I just don't think I'm ready. I was willing to kill myself after those guys jumped me. Why would I want to live the rest of my life in fear?"

I swallowed hard. I had heard about the attack on Ciro long before I ever met him, and all I had thought at the time was how glad I was that it hadn't been me. Because it could have been. People at our school were notorious for hating anything that was outside of their predetermined norms. "I'm sorry," I said, partly because I didn't know what else to say.

His shoe scuffed against the ground. "I don't think it's going to get any easier for me. I told Michelle the other day that I thought I might want to be a woman." He shot a sidelong glance at me while somehow making himself seem smaller, like he was afraid I would flip out on him or something. That hurt.

Ciro's smile could light up the room, and it sucked knowing the guy struggled with such heavy problems, all the while keeping the mask on so no one knew.

I used my hand closest to him to clap him on the shoulder. "Man, woman, you're still the person we've come to know and love. Just, don't cry because the others will think I'm rejecting you, and you know I'll never hear the end of that."

Ciro quickly wiped at his eyes and gave a nervous giggle. "Thanks."

I leaned back again and added, "You know, if anyone gives you shit at school again, just let me know. Okay? You're not alone anymore, man." I paused. "Er, woman?" I threw out awkwardly.

Ciro, who had brought his water bottle up to his mouth, spewed water out onto the cement ground at my comment. I smirked as Ciro coughed out a laugh and used his sleeve to wipe his mouth. "Thanks for the support," he finally said when the coughing subsided. We sat in silence for a little while. Not uncomfortably, just both being, well, mindful.

"I better go pack," Ciro finally said, though he made no effort to actually move.

"I meant it, you know," I said. "You're not alone. If you need somewhere to go or someone to talk to, I got your back."

"Same goes for you," he said. "Especially with you still pretty much buried in the closet." He nudged me with his elbow.

"Yeah, yeah," I groaned. When he finally stood, I got to my feet and hugged him. "I'll see you around," I said as we broke apart.

Ciro flashed one of his famous dazzling smiles and headed inside. I genuinely hoped he would be okay. Even though I had barely noticed his existence until arriving on the ward, I found myself missing him already.

I waited a few minutes before I went inside. Renee stood at the bookcase, with stacks of books on the three tables surrounding her. "You know the books are supposed to go on the shelves, right?" I leaned on one of the chairs and watched her sort through a stack, placing a book with a blue cover on one pile and one with a darker blue cover on a different pile.

When she finally looked up, I could see her eyes were red-rimmed and kind of puffy.

"Sorry," I lamented softly. "What happened?"

She shrugged and returned her attention to the books. "This helps calm me down," she explained, but I could barely hear her over the noise coming from the other common room.

"So what are you doing with them?"

"Sorting by genre and author."

"You're alphabetizing the ward's bookshelf?" I stared at her.

Renee kept up her work, glancing at the back of a book before moving it to a pile. "It's distracting."

"Okay," I said slowly. Then, "Do you want help?"

She shrugged again. "If you want."

"What do you want me to do?" I picked up one of the books from the table. It had a picture of a cowboy kissing a girl on the cover. "And why is this in a teen ward?" I laughed, holding it up for Renee to see. It got a small smile out of her. Considering that a win, I took the small pile of what was apparently romance novels and started putting them in order by author's last name.

"So you do know how to read," Renee teased.

"Yeah, but don't tell anyone," I replied, slipping the cowboy book behind a flowery red one. "I worked in the school library sometimes, so I do know how to shelve books."

"Can you put those ones on the top shelf? I don't think there are many here who would actually want to read romance novels." She wrinkled her nose at the thought.

"I mean, it's like porn for women, right? So if a guy gets desperate enough while locked up in here..." I trailed off, grinning at Renee's immediate deep blush. The books were light but kind of awkward in my hands as I transferred the small stack to the top shelf, tucking them in the back corner.

"That's something I'd expect out of Derek or maybe Tobias," Renee said, carefully placing another book on an already high stack.

I watched the books sway a little then steady. Renee, meanwhile, paid it no attention, continuing to sort through her pile. "I've probably been hanging out with them too long."

"With who?" Tobias and Derek asked together as they walked in, pausing to take in the scene. Kate followed behind them, her arms stretched overhead.

"Whoa, did an earthquake hit while we were at volleyball?" she asked, lowering her hands.

"Speak of the devils," I said with a wink to Renee, who smiled briefly again.

"Nah, man, I already have one inside me. I don't need another." Derek stepped closer and put a hand on top of a wavering stack.

Kate laughed and put her arm on his shoulder to lean on it.

I sent a questioning look to Renee, and she pointed to a stack of what looked like science fiction books that was about three times the size of the romance pile. I grabbed the top few and started putting them in order, setting them in another stack with the spines facing me so I could make sure they were staying in order. Derek handed the next one to me. Pretty soon Kate and Tobias started doing the same to the largest sorted group, which was full of books featuring vampires and magic.

Renee directed us on what order to restock the shelves, putting the least popular genre towards the top and the more popular ones at the middle and bottom where they would be more easily accessible. Working together, we burned through the piles quickly, and Renee was smiling more broadly by the end.

"That was surprisingly therapeutic," Kate remarked, stepping back to admire our handiwork.

"Yeah, I almost forgot what it was like to be productive," I agreed.

Derek snorted with laughter. "All this therapy and healing is supposed to be productive, remember?" He turned one of the chairs around and sat with his chest facing the back of the chair.

"Productive?" Kate sneered. "Most of these groups have us going over the same stuff over and over. It's not exactly the most productive thing in the world."

Tobias rolled his eyes, "That's what he means. Don't you know sarcasm?"

She stuck her tongue out at him. "I happen to be fluent

in sarcasm."

"Maybe it's time for a refresher course then."

Kate pretended to glare in return.

A sound came from where Renee stood. I thought she was laughing, but when she pulled her hands away from her face, there were tears. "Hey," I called softly, "what's going on?" I started to move towards her but Kate beat me to it.

Kate pulled the younger girl to her and stroked her hair. "It's okay, you're allowed to feel," she murmured.

I looked around to Derek and Tobias who seemed just as bewildered as me. "Did we say something wrong?" I asked.

"N-no," Renee stammered, her words muffled against Kate. "I'm sorry." She pulled away from Kate and wrapped her arms around herself, still sniffling.

"It's fine," Derek said. "You don't need to be sorry for feeling something."

Renee lifted her head to look at Derek for a moment. "I'm going to miss you guys," she said then looked quickly away before she started crying again.

"Whoa, what's with the danger words?" Kate asked, taking a hold of Renee's shoulder. Renee couldn't respond.

Derek's head lowered as he mumbled something.

"What?" Tobias asked him. "What did you say?"

Instead of addressing Tobias, Derek glanced at Renee. "The thing from the news the other day?"

Renee nodded then sank to the floor with her head in her hands.

"Will someone please explain what the hell is going on? Kate asked, looking between Renee and Derek.

"Do you mind?" Derek asked, again speaking to Renee. She shook her head. He took a breath then rested his chin on his palm. "The other day, the news said a body turned up down by the strip." The strip was a section of town known for drugs, homeless, and shootings. Next to me, Tobias visibly tensed. "When they showed the footage of the body being taken away, Renee thought it might have been her sister."

Our gazes shifted back to the girl who was struggling to hold herself together. "Was it?" I asked, praying that, for her sake, it was some other poor girl who got mixed up with the wrong crowd.

We waited for what felt like forever for her to calm down enough to answer. The longer she took, the more drawn Tobias's face became. It occurred to me that Tobias probably lived near there, and maybe he thought the body was someone he knew. His hands curled into fists so tightly that the knuckles started to turn white.

I leaned over to him and whispered, "Breathe."

A second later, his chest rose and fell slowly, and his stance loosened by a fraction.

"It was a girl who would have been the same age as Rachel," Renee said slowly. She kept her hands on her head but moved her arms far enough away from her mouth so that we could hear her. "My parents have to go in to see if it's her, but they've already decided that we're moving as soon as possible. They can't handle it here anymore. Just when," she paused and tried to maintain control. "Just when I finally found friends," she said quickly, burying her head again.

A little more of the tension seemed to fall away from Tobias as he regarded Renee with Kate hovering protectively nearby.

"Why does it have to change?" I squatted in front of

Renee and put a hand on her arm. "We have cell phones when we're not in this place. We can still be there for each other from wherever we are."

"Matthew's not wrong," Tobias said. "Whether we're next to you or not, we're with you."

"Even though I'm pretty sure Tobias is sick because he'd never say something that nice, he's dead accurate with it," Kate said.

Renee let out a strangled laugh while she still cried.

"Matthew," Iesha called out, "the doctor wants to see you." She walked over to us from the desk and noticed Renee on the ground. "Is she okay? Are you okay?" Iesha asked and knelt next to her. Tobias stood and moved away.

"She's having a hard day," Kate explained.

"Come on." Iesha guided Renee to stand up, "Let's see if we can find something to help you out."

"I don't want medication," Renee whispered. "I have to feel what I'm feeling."

Iesha looked confused. "Of course, sweetie. I meant tea or ice cream."

Renee's tear-streaked face burned red, and she ducked her head apologetically. "Ice cream?" she asked after a moment.

Assured Renee would be okay for the immediate moment, we dispersed. I started the walk down the hall to Dr. Larson's, waiting for one of the nurses to let me through the door that divided the ward from the offices. I had not even tried to sit down when the door to Dr. Larson's office opened.

James walked out, his face strangely relaxed and making me wonder how he even conducted his sessions. He gave me a tiny wave and held the door for me.

"Thanks." I passed through the doorway and nodded at Dr. Larson sitting behind the desk. "What's up, Doc?"

A grin creased his features. "You must be in a good mood today." He gestured for me to take a seat and I did.

Almost nodding, I thought about Renee and decided to go with a shrug instead. "Volleyball helped, but I'm worried about Renee."

Dr. Larson allowed a solemn nod. "How are you, though?"

"Could be worse. Saw Ciro before he got ready to go. He doesn't seem ready to go back and face school."

The doctor tapped his chin with a pen. "What makes you say that?"

"Our school—we go to the same one—isn't all that nice to people who are different." I started thinking about the things some of the people at school said about anyone who dared to live outside of their realm of normalcy. "Matter of fact, I think Renee's supposed to start there next year. Or she would be..." I trailed off, feeling the sadness hang over my head like a gray cloud. I looked up to see the doctor's intense gaze on me. "What?"

"You talk much about others but not so much about yourself," he remarked.

"It's not like I do it on purpose," I defended. He waited for me to continue. I squirmed under his scrutiny and hated myself for it. One of my hands headed for my leg to scratch at an old wound, but I caught myself and took a breath. "Okay, maybe I do. I don't like the focus being on me, but how is that a bad thing?"

"How is it a good thing?"

"I put others before myself. Humility, selflessness, all that." I reached into my pocket for one of my rocks and let it sit in my hand.

"So it is good, but to an extent, yes?"

My eyes dropped to the rock. "Yeah, I guess."

"Which means it can also be bad. You can be considerate and still speak up for yourself and your needs. What do you need?"

To be gone, I thought. My body stilled as I asked myself, *Where the hell did that come from?*

"Matthew?" Dr. Larson said. "What are you thinking?"

There was a heaviness in my chest that I couldn't explain even if I wanted to tell him about it. "I could be having a completely normal day and all of a sudden, something pops up in me saying that I shouldn't be here anymore. Alive. Like, that I'm just worthless and it's better if I disappear somehow. It happened just then, when you asked what I needed. And I don't know what's wrong with me. I didn't have a crap childhood or some traumatic event. I don't have any plans or intent or whatever either. They're just thoughts, but I can't control them."

"But you did have some sort of intent at one point, right?"

Again, my hand drifted to my leg. I didn't need to feel the raised skin to remember the stupid knife. All I did was cause pain to people, and I needed it to stop.

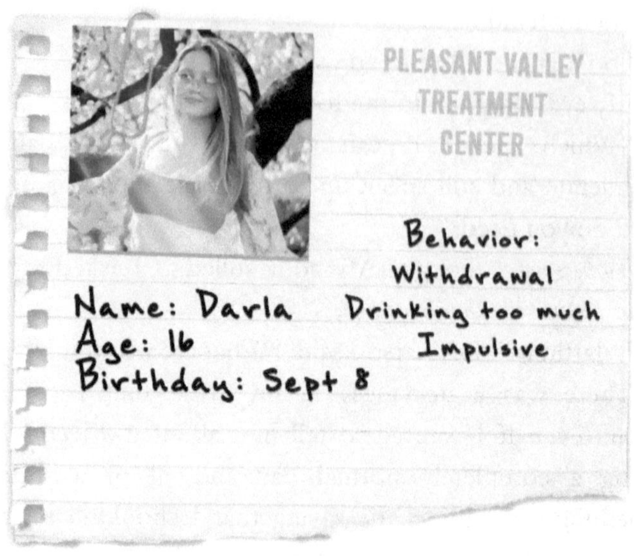

DARLA

After three months of being told what to do and where to go and how to change the way I thought, the sudden blast of freedom felt awesome!

No, no it didn't. Not at all. I cringed at the sight and sounds of traffic on the highway back into the main part of town, and it wasn't even all that bad. It was just too much. I curled up into my seat, holding onto my blanket, and tried to make myself as small as possible while not throwing up. When Pleasant Valley's van finally stopped, I had to force myself to sit up and look around.

The van pulled up in front of a red-brick duplex with white trim and practically no front yard. "This isn't my house," I said to the driver. "Where are we?" I tried to swallow the immediate rise of bile in my throat.

The woman gave me a sad smile. "Pleasant Valley Group Home," she said, turning off the car. "Come on, child, let's get your things."

"That can't be right," I said, refusing to move. "My dad would never let this happen." I knew I sounded like a spoiled child and not someone who just went through months of detox and treatment, but I didn't care. There was just no way he'd throw me in a group home.

"Do you want to see the paperwork?" she offered, not sounding the least bit perturbed by my attitude. She held out a folder that read DISCHARGE across the top. I opened it to find several sheets of paper with my name on them. The top one was discharge instructions from the treatment center.

I skimmed over it quickly, stopping about three-fourths of the way down, where aftercare instructions were listed. A box was checked for transfer to Pleasant Valley Group Home, and the bottom signed by Devonte Radison. Tears blurred my eyes, and I slammed the folder shut. I slammed my head back against the headrest of the seat, silently cursing.

How could he do that to me? I kept his secrets safe, I protected our family and our reputation. Why would he discard me like that?

I took a deep breath, closing my eyes and tried to recall the good things. I could go outside without going through a locked door. I would be going back to school. I had access to my cell phone again.

I almost wanted to tell the driver to take me back. It was too much, all too much.

I grabbed the handle of the door and opened it then slid down to the ground, taking my blanket and backpack with me. The driver grabbed my other bags and hauled them out of the vehicle. She headed up the narrow sidewalk of the left house which was riddled with the attempts of weeds growing in the cracks. Closer up, the paint on the trim was peeling.

"Do me a favor and knock on the door, shug," the driver requested. I obliged, rapping the door three times with my knuckles. A bit of paint, jostled by the movement, peeled and fell to the ground.

I made a face just as the door knob twisted and the door opened to reveal an older dark-skinned woman with a slightly wrinkled face and graying coffee-color kinked hair. She was dressed in a purple jogging suit and held a tabby cat in one arm. The woman sighed as she looked from me to the driver to my bags.

"I told them I don't have room for another right now." Her voice was scratchy as if she was sick or had been smoking for 50 years. I seriously hoped it wasn't the latter.

I bit my lip and tried not to start bawling immediately. I felt homeless.

Seeing my expression, the woman softened. "Come on in," she relented and stepped aside, holding the door further open. "I'm sure we can figure something out."

The house was quiet except for the motorized purring of the cat. The front entrance opened immediately into a staircase ahead with a small room off to the left which the woman gestured for us to enter. It had a fireplace on the far end with an old wooden mantle. At the front window was a bench while a loveseat and couch were crammed in near the fireplace, but not so close as to be at risk of catching on fire. The tan rug looked like it maybe had once been white, but there was a pleasant smell in the air, like gardenias.

I sat on the loveseat, shrugging off my backpack and setting it on the floor. I kept my blanket on my lap so I could hide my shaking hands. The driver chose the couch, and the hostess settled into a rocking chair at the other end of the loveseat, displacing a black and white cat who almost fell off the chair.

"My name is Mrs. Croden, and if you are to stay here, you must abide by the rules." She held up a finger with each rule. "One, no drugs, alcohol, or smoking. You've been given a second chance, don't waste it. Two, you must be back by curfew each day. For the first week, that is four o'clock. Yes, right after school. Three, no boys, especially not the ones next door. Four, you must either help around the house or work, but you may not get a job until at least three weeks have passed. Five, no cell phones except between seven and nine o'clock. Ten on weekends. Any questions?"

"I guess not," I said. Mrs. Croden held out her hand, and I stared at it in confusion for a moment. "Oh," I finally realized, putting my phone in her hand.

Ms. Croden finally smiled. "Don't worry, sweetie, if you stick to your sobriety, you'll be out of here soon."

"Where should I put her bags?" the driver asked.

Mrs. Croden used the momentum of the rocking chair to stand, and the tabby finally leapt out of her arms. "This way," she said, going to the staircase. She climbed steadily to the second landing. A separate staircase continued further up, but Mrs. Croden took a left and stopped at a door to the right. She opened it, pulled out a rolled up sleeping bag, and closed the door again before continuing to the door at the end of the hallway.

A sense of dread filled me as I followed, the driver

behind me. Each step down my treatment path seemed to put me in a worse place than where I started.

The old woman knocked briefly before entering. "The other two girls are at school, but it's expected to knock just in case someone is undressing."

The room was relatively bare, much like the ones on the ward. A closet sat off to the left with a bed along the same wall. A blanket and a few stuffed animals decorated it. Opposite was a bunk bed with another blanket on the bottom bunk. Behind the bunk bed stood a large armoire, complete with mirror.

"You can put your stuff in the closet," Mrs. Croden said, and the driver obliged by putting my bags next to the closet door. She exited soon after, giving me an encouraging smile on the way out that I tried in vain to return. Mrs. Croden offered the sleeping bag to me. "You can take the top bunk. I don't have any extra sheets right now. Laundry will be done tonight, so you can get some clean sheets tomorrow, but you can use this in the meantime so you aren't forced to sleep on the bare mattress."

I never thought I would have been so relieved to receive a sleeping bag. I almost started crying.

"I'll let you get unpacked and settled in. You don't have to go back to school tomorrow if you want a day to adjust, but the next day you ought to go." She said it with a stern look that clearly meant I would have to go.

"Yes, ma'am," I said, because she seemed to be expecting it.

After she left, I tossed the sleeping bag on the top bunk along with my backpack. I used my foot to shove my bags into the closet and closed the door then climbed up the awkward wooden ladder. I landed on my stomach on the bed and lay there until my arms fell asleep.

A slamming door jolted me awake. My limbs felt leaden. It hurt to move and it hurt to stay still. I groaned and shifted onto my side.

"What the hell?" a voice said from below. A face popped up over the railing next to me. "Who- Darla!" The voice squealed and the head bobbed as she jumped up and down on the lower bunk. "It *is* you! Where have you been?"

I blinked and slowly pushed myself to a sitting position with one hand while rubbing my eyes with the other. I took in the girl with bouncy blonde hair and pale skin who finally stopped jumping. "Hannah?" I threw myself over the rail to land on the floor, wincing as my feet hit the wood. But I didn't have time to feel it as I was practically tackled by the rail-thin girl who hit harder than I would have expected.

We both laughed, trying and failing to keep our balance then tumbled to the floor. "Did you just get here?" Hannah asked, rolling so that her body stopped pinning my arm to the ground. She hopped to her feet and held out a hand to pull me up.

"Today, yeah. I didn't know you were here." I took her hand and used it to stand.

"Well, you wouldn't, would you?" Her voice took on a slight chill as she turned away.

I grabbed her hand before she could move too far away. "Han, I've been in treatment at Pleasant Valley for, like, three months. Without my cell. I only just got it back today. Except Mrs. Croden just took it again."

Hannah's expression seemed to soften, but she looked more gaunt than I remembered. A green sundress hung off her shoulders with black leggings covering her long legs. "I guess that'll pass for an excuse," she sighed, but she looked slightly abashed. The moment passed, and she smiled brightly, looking a little more like her normal self. "So, what do you want to do tonight?"

"What time is it?" I glanced at the window on the far wall.

"Like, five," Hannah shrugged. "Dinner will be in about half an hour."

"So what is there to do then? My curfew already passed." I rolled my eyes.

"What Mrs. C doesn't know won't hurt her," Hannah replied with an exaggerated wink. "Come on, May will be here soon, and you want to give her about twenty minutes to herself when she comes home." Hannah flounced away down the hall, leaving me not much choice but to follow her.

I chased her down the stairs, and she giggled, skipping through the living room around the couch and out the other door which led into a small kitchen. Two girls were there preparing dinner—spaghetti and meatballs from the smell of it. "Coming through," Hannah called out as she squeezed past the girls and bounded through another door.

The mudroom was neatly laid out with backpacks and shoes stowed on hooks and in cubbies. Hannah blew past that, not bothering to pause to put her shoes on, and went out through the screen door. She let it slam shut behind her. More slowly, I continued to follow.

My jaw dropped as I exited the house. The backyard was full of beautiful plants and flowers, with trees along the fence, some of which had fruit hanging from branches and scattered around the ground nearby. Hannah stood at a garden plot, making sure I was still coming, then dropped to her knees into the dirt. The girl I knew would have never risked dirtying her clothes, but she seemed happy to be checking the ripeness of the tomatoes.

"Come help me," she urged, waving a hand. When I reached her, she grabbed my arm and pulled me down. "This is the only way to escape Mrs. C's hearing, I swear," she said, bringing her voice to a whisper. A mischievous grin that was much more familiar played at the corners of her mouth. "She doesn't care if we're breaking curfew so long as we're in the yard," Hannah explained at my bemused expression.

"Okay," I said slowly, picking at a weed.

"So, the other side of the house is the boys' home, right? There are a few of us who hop the fence at night and go hang out. You want to come?"

Mrs. Croden's words echoed in my head, battling against my desire to reconnect with Hannah. *It couldn't hurt to go check it out and make sure she's safe*, I reasoned with myself. "Yeah, I'll go," I said, sharing her smile.

We stayed out for several more minutes to make it look like Hannah was actually showing me what she did in the garden. Someone called through the screen door, "Dinner," so we stood up and brushed ourselves off. I led the way back into the house, pausing at the sink to wash my hands.

"I didn't see a dining room earlier, so where do we eat?" I used a nearby towel to dry my hands.

Hannah did the same then said, "It's one of the crossrooms—er, a room that goes across both sides of the house."

"Wait, this is all one house?" I followed Hannah through the kitchen and living room.

"Yeah, Mr. Croden runs the boys' side. The dining room and their bedroom, I think, are the two crossrooms that connect both sides. We aren't allowed to go into the boys' side." She rolled her eyes.

There was another hallway that led around the staircase to a large room that housed a very long dining table. One chair was positioned at either end with several more chairs on either side. Girls sat on the side nearest the door we entered while the boys took the chairs on the opposite end. Another door led out on their side, presumably to the rest of the house.

The two girls from the kitchen doled out plates of spaghetti and meatballs while a couple of boys did the same with vegetables and breadsticks. The room should have been loud with so many people, but apparently the Crodens ran a tight ship because the chatter was kept to a minimum, at least in volume.

I took a seat next to Hannah about midway down the table, across from a dark-haired guy who was probably my age and had a smile to die for. His shy grin accentuated his dimples, and I couldn't help but return it.

The simple dinner tasted divine after the less than savory cafeteria food I'd been subjected to for the past few months. The sauce had a hint of spiciness to it that burned my mouth. I loved it. When the meal concluded, those of us who didn't cook cleared the table. It was Hannah's turn to do the dishes, and I volunteered to help. Together, we made short work of the task, and it felt like we were never parted.

After the dishes were washed, dried, and put away, Hannah and I returned to our room where I met May. She had gorgeous dark skin and eyes to match with curves in all the right places. Her hair, in contrast, was a bright reddish color.

"Hi," she said brightly as we walked in. She sat on the edge of her bed, peeling off orange socks. "I'm May. Mrs. C. said we had a new roommate."

"Yup." Hannah said, putting her arm around my shoulder. "My bestie has finally returned to me!"

May smiled, but I couldn't manage anything other than a meek hello.

"Well, I have homework and a test tomorrow, so don't stay out too late, Hannah." She winked then settled back on her bed, drawing her backpack closer and unzipping it.

I glanced between May and Hannah, but neither seemed ready to offer an explanation. Hannah went to the closet and started pulling clothes out of a dresser inside. She moved an armful of clothes to the drawer below. "You can have that one," she said, shoving the other drawer closed. Then she grabbed a leopard print toiletry bag and stepped away from the closet.

I started unpacking and was nearly finished by the time Hannah returned. I took out my own plain black bag with my toothbrush and makeup in it, along with a pair of black leggings and a loose gray top.

I returned from the bathroom feeling refreshed and just the tiniest bit hopeful about life in the group home. I hugged Hannah and waved at May who grunted in response, nose deep in a calculus textbook. Then I climbed up the ladder again and settled onto the rolled out sleeping bag. It had a built-in pillow so my neck wouldn't hurt too badly in the morning. I still used my blanket to pad it. I thought I'd lie awake for hours, but I felt myself nodding off, not even bothering to go get my phone for the allotted hours.

"Darla, wake up," Hannah whispered, intruding on a very nice dream about a pony in a meadow. Or something equally pleasant.

"What?" I groaned, wanting to roll over.

"Did you still want to go?" she asked, shaking my shoulder.

Go? Go where? My mind struggled to put the pieces together. The sleeping bag rustled as I shifted. Slowly, things started to click. "Oh," I said, "yeah."

"Then come on." She started dragging my legs over the edge of the bed.

"Okay, okay," I conceded and sat up, letting my eyes adjust to the darkness of the room. I pushed off from my hands and slid onto the lower bunk with a soft thud.

Hannah shushed me, and I stepped carefully down from her bunk. She handed me a jacket and then a brush when I had the jacket on and partly zipped. "You don't want to look like you just rolled out of bed," she said matter-of-factly.

"But I *did* just roll out of bed," I argued, but I took the brush anyway and ran it through my hair a few times to get the worst of the tangles out. When I was satisfied that it was as good as it was going to get in that state of delirium, Hannah took a look at me. She brushed a strand of hair away from my eyes.

"Grab your shoes, but don't put them on yet," Hannah instructed under her breath.

Glancing around, I saw May lumped under her blanket, the edges of a book sticking out under one hand. Hannah moved to the door, and gestured for me to follow after a moment. She moved forward carefully, choosing each step deliberately as though avoiding setting off some kind of trap.

Everything in the house was still, no sounds coming from any of the rooms we passed. I couldn't help but smile, thinking of all the times Hannah and I had snuck out before. We stalked through the house like prowling cats until we reached the back door. Hannah slid on her shoes, grabbing my shoulder for balance.

She placed one hand on the door and the other on the knob and slowly started to open it while I pushed my feet into my sneakers. The door opened with a whisper of air.

Outside, the cool air was crisp and carried the perfumed scent of flowers from the garden. Scattered clouds provided some cover from the nearly full moon above. I dimly wondered what time it was. Hannah skipped into the yard, twirling as she went then paused to catch her balance. We crossed to the fence at the back, a surprisingly flimsy chain link one, and climbed over it easily. A few yards behind the fence lay a small forest. Hannah grabbed my hand and started jogging to the forest.

My heart started pounding like it did on the verge of an anxiety attack but not in a bad way. I'd forgotten what it felt like to be excited, but it was exhilarating. It felt like true freedom.

We had only gone a little ways into the woods when I saw a light ahead. I slowed my pace until Hannah was a step ahead of me. "What's wrong?" she asked.

"I think I hear voices," I said.

I couldn't see her face clearly, but I could hear the smile in her voice as she said, "So that's why they locked you up, huh?"

"Oh, shut up," I laughed.

"Come on, it's fine." She pulled me forward into a small clearing where several bodies surrounded a barrel. Yellow-orange flames flickered inside, occasionally dancing at the top for a second before dropping inside again. "Heeey," Hannah called as we approached. She let go of my hand and sauntered toward the gathering with her hands outstretched.

A couple of people stood up and hugged her in greeting. I walked up, using my hands to warm my arms until the fire reached me. Standing near the barrel and feeling awkward, I waited for Hannah to finish saying hello to everyone.

She turned and grinned at me. "Everyone, this is my girl, Darla." The others turned their heads to me and nodded, smiled, or waved then went back to their previous conversations.

"Don't worry, they'll come around soon," a smooth voice said beside me. It was the boy I had sat across from at dinner. He held out a hand, which I took. "I'm Rocky."

We shook hands. "Darla," I said then let go.

"I heard." He grinned, dimples and all, and I hoped the fire's glow didn't reveal my blush.

"So, uh, Rocky, huh?"

His sigh was barely audible over the crackling of the fire. "Yeah, my mom says I was named for the mountain range, but my dad got drunk one time and admitted it was for Rocky Road ice cream my mom craved when she was pregnant."

I scoffed and said, "No way."

"True story. I asked him about it the next day and he got all bothered, saying he couldn't remember anything about that." He had a silky chuckle and the slightest hint of an accent to his words.

I bounced on my feet a little, casting around my mind for something to talk about. It was my first time in months talking about something other than mental health. "Did you have to sneak out too?"

Rocky scoffed and said, "Mr. Croden's sleep apnea machine knocks him out, and the Missus won't stop us. You girls are her responsibility, not us." He indicated a couple of the others who I vaguely recognized from dinner.

"All right, here we go," someone whooped as two more people came into the clearing from a different angle. One carried a brown paper bag in their arms, the top obscuring their face, while the other, a woman, held a plastic grocery bag. Her dark hair was pulled back into a ponytail, and she had bright eyes that sunk into her pale face. Her thin mouth smiled as she looked around the group, taking in the sight of all of us staring at her.

She stepped over a fallen log near the fire barrel and set her bag down. Reaching back, she took the paper bag from the other person, and I could hear bottles clinking together inside. The woman's companion was a sandy-haired guy who was probably only a little older than me. His rounded face was reddened from walking through the chilled air.

"Hope we didn't keep you waiting too long," the guy chuckled as he glanced around. His eyes fell on me, and his grin broadened. "We have a newbie."

My cheeks started to heat up for a reason that had little to do with how close I stood to the fire. I smiled and waved slightly.

Before he could react, another boy from the group home grabbed the edge of the paper bag, tearing it and causing the newcomer to step back. "Hey, watch it," he said with another laugh.

The woman's hand shot out to grab the boy's arm. "Wait," she commanded. At first, it seemed like the boy would ignore her, but he finally relented and withdrew.

Hannah came over and grabbed my arm. "Let me introduce you," she said with such a huge smile on her face that I couldn't resist.

"Sorry," I called back to Rocky as she guided me to the other side. He shrugged, but his expression was unreadable.

Hannah pushed her way past the four others who were standing nearby until we stood directly in front of the two new arrivals. "This is Darla," she announced. "Darla, these are Mary and Kelly, our saviors in this hellhole."

The guy grinned and rubbed the back of his neck. "Shucks, Hannah, you're always so sweet. Yeah, I'm Kelly."

Mary's thin mouth smiled again, but it didn't reach her eyes. "I guess she's with you?" she asked, looking at Hannah.

"She's from the home too," my friend clarified. She turned to me to explain, "Mary and Kelly were in the home up until a couple of months ago."

"Aged out," Mary said with a small shrug of her thin shoulders.

I blinked and said stupidly, "Oh." I had thought Mary to at least be in her 20s, but from what I understood, the house only supported kids up to 18. I rubbed my hands together to cover up my embarrassment.

"Shall we get started?" Mary asked, once again ignoring me.

Hannah and I backed away as Kelly squatted down to retrieve a bottle from the bag. The bottle was clear, revealing an amber liquid inside. I pulled Hannah a little further back and hissed, "What are they doing? Isn't the whole point of the group home to help us stay sober?" I could picture Mrs. Croden's lined face in a mask of disapproval. I hardly even knew her, but this felt like a major violation of trust. Sneaking out was one thing. Still, I recalled all too easily the burning of alcohol as it went down my throat, numbing everything for a little while. What I hated most was how much I missed it, and there it was, sitting in front of me again for the first time in ages. Even as I spoke, my eyes drifted back to the bottle in Kelly's hand.

"Sobriety? You think that's why I'm in that place?" Hannah's incredulous tone drew my gaze back to her. Her pretty face was wrinkled in distaste. "I was too much for my parents to handle, so they dumped me there to focus on my little brother, the heir to the family company." She spat out the words like they'd been bottled up for a long time.

"Mav?" I asked, unable to reconcile this version of my friend with the one who had doted on her preschool-aged brother.

Hannah looked away. "You can go back to the house if you want." The sharpness in her voice had dulled, but she pulled away all the same.

I watched her walk up to Kelly and hold out her hand for the bottle. He had another in his other hand, a white smokey one with a tall neck, but he gave her the clear one. She unstoppered it, glanced at me, then took a long drink from it. I lost sight of her soon after as the others started crowding around, each taking a swig from the bottles. Tears blurred my eyes, and I simultaneously wanted to stay and wanted to run.

Three months of forced sobriety was still sobriety. I

could have walked away and kept it. I caught Rocky looking at me, sympathy in his eyes, and it angered me for some reason. Peering over to where I had last seen Hannah, I saw Kelly step away from the group, a dark brown bottle in his hand.

He saw me watching and smiled. In a couple of strides, he stood beside me and held out the bottle of rum. "You look cold," he said, keeping several inches between us.

I stared at the bottle for a long moment. The words "I can't" formed in my mouth, but I couldn't say them. I reached out for the bottle, instead saying, "I am."

RENEE

Two days. That's how long it took for my parents to come to see me after Dad said they were going to see the body.

My oldest brother arrived first, but I didn't recognize him right away. His muddy brown hair was growing out and disheveled, and he had patches of hair on his chin, brown mixed with red. The most startling thing, though, was how exhausted he looked. There were dark circles under his eyes like he hadn't slept in a week.

"Reed?" I asked even though I knew it was him.

He'd been leaning on the nurses' desk but straightened when he heard me. Without even responding, he walked up and gathered me into his arms, squeezing me tightly. I couldn't explain why, but I started crying right there, wrapping my arms as far as they could go around my brother's chest. We stood there for several moments, and I could feel my brother's heartbeat, steady but not slow.

Reed finally let go and reluctantly withdrew. I had to crane my neck up a little to look at his face. His voice was rough as he said, "I'm sorry, Renee. I'm so sorry I didn't come, that I wasn't here for you."

"It's okay," I said, surprised to find that to be true. There had been so many days that I longed for my family, but I never asked any of them to come, and none of them had. "Did they... Was it her?"

Reed shook his head. "I don't know. They haven't told me or Rob anything."

"Rob or me," I corrected automatically then cringed.

He let out a rough laugh, so very different from the easy one I remembered. "Do you know how many times I heard your voice in my head this year while I was writing papers?" He hugged me again, a half armed one like he used to when he was too cool to show much affection to his little sister.

I smiled and leaned into his embrace. Kal walked up from the other side of the desk and asked if we wanted to go to one of the visitation rooms. I nodded, and Kal let us into the larger one so there would be enough room for all of us.

"Is Rob coming?" I asked as we settled onto the large couch, Reed at one end and me at the other. I slipped out of my sandals and pulled my feet up under my skirt. The leather of the couch squeaked in protest.

Reed's head lowered. "I don't think so."

"Oh." I waited for about thirty seconds before asking, "Why?"

He swallowed then sighed. "He said she's been dead to

him for years, what would it matter now?"

"Oh," I repeated. I had always held out hope that someday my sister would come home, but I couldn't be upset with Rob's outlook. "Did Mom and Dad tell you about the move?"

Suddenly, Reed looked uncomfortable and shifted in his seat. He refused to look at me, his fingers picking at the peeling leather at the edge of the armrest. He mumbled something that I couldn't hear.

"What?"

"It was my idea," he said, louder.

I stared at him in disbelief. "Why?" I whispered. "Do you know what it's like to start all over again?"

Reed's eyebrows raised, "Really, Renee? I'd have no idea what that's like. It's not as though I'm about to graduate or anything."

"College is different!" I insisted, my voice growing louder. "Everyone is starting over there."

"Okay, I'll give you that," he conceded, "But you need to get out of here, away from all of the..." he trailed off.

"Memories?" I asked bitterly.

"Drama." He glared at me.

I scoffed and crossed my arms.

Reed sighed again and relented. "I got a great opportunity through one of my professors. His friend is opening a veterinary practice in Grand Junction and agreed to take me on. I suggested to Mom and Dad that you guys come with, get you and them out of here and maybe start again, a little differently."

It was my turn to look down. I didn't think it would matter where we went because Rachel would never be there. But maybe he had a point. Without the constant reminders of her absence, would my parents be able to let go a little? Would I?

We sat in awkward silence for a few minutes. The door opened again, revealing our parents. Mom entered first, her face just as drawn as Reed's. For the first time in my short life, I could see the wear and tear of raising four kids in the lines on her face. Rachel missing, Rob getting into fights all of the time, finding out Reed sometimes did drugs and drank underage, and then all the hell I put them through. Before Rachel's disappearance, Dad used to call us his Irish princesses and Mom the Queen. I got my red hair and narrow nose from her, but everything else about me more closely resembled Dad. In that moment, more than ever before, I wished everything had turned out so very different.

Mom gave me a small smile and sat in a chair next to me while Dad continued talking with someone behind him. Mom reached out, laying her hand palm up on the armrest of the couch. I put my hand in hers, letting her fingers curl around my hand.

Dad came in and stepped aside to hold the door open for my therapist. Riley entered, nodded her thanks to my father, and took a chair in the corner near me. Since I had asked her to be there with me during my family's visit, I wasn't surprised. I smiled faintly at her as she sat, which she returned, the usual twinkle of kindness in her eyes.

The door closed behind Dad, leaving him to take the only remaining seat, the chair by Reed. His face revealed nothing, the stone mask in place again. He didn't look at anyone and kept his eyes on the ground. A strained silence filled the room for several moments. Mom glanced from Dad to Riley and back. When it was obvious that Dad wouldn't say anything, Mom cleared her throat.

"A few days ago," she began, "they found a body down by the strip, but you know that part." She took a breath and continued. "The girl they found was an adolescent." I sucked in some air and held it. "But she wasn't our Rachel."

I let the air in my chest out slowly and wondered why they still looked so forlorn if it wasn't her. I bit my lip to keep from saying anything, but Riley noticed.

"Renee." Several things were communicated in Riley's tone, even though she only said my name. It was both an encouragement and a warning.

I gulped but nodded. "So, does that mean she's still out there?" My voice sounded weak, and I was afraid they'd have me repeat myself.

Dad stirred, and, when he spoke, it was with such a lack of expression, it was as though he was reading from cue cards. "The girl was from a nearby town. Apparently the killer was sloppy because they found DNA. Yesterday, the police raided the house of the person whose DNA it was." He coughed, trying to cover up a sob.

"They found two more bodies in the basement," Mom picked up. "Both teenage girls. One of them was a DNA match for Rachel."

I squeezed her hand, and she squeezed back. The little balloon of hope that had been sitting in my stomach immediately deflated. I reached out with my other hand, searching for Reed's without looking. He grabbed it and held tight.

Reed wiped at his eyes with his other sleeve. "How long?" he asked. "How long ago did she die?"

Mom looked at Riley, who nodded. Then Mom met Reed's eyes and said, "About seven months."

I gasped and stared at her, open-mouthed. "Wh-where?" I stammered.

Her face took on a pained expression as she looked at me. "Across the street from us," she said in a hushed voice.

My lip started trembling, but the tears wouldn't come. I pulled my hands from my brother's and mother's and wrapped them around my knees instead. All that time, all those years, Rachel had been just across the street, and none of us knew. None of us even guessed.

"They arrested the man who lived there, confirmed the DNA samples on all three girls," Dad continued, almost choking on the words. His hands were clenched in fists so tightly that his knuckles started to turn white.

Reed put a hand on my shoulder and asked, "Did he say why-why he killed her?"

Dad's face twisted again, and he dropped his head into his hands. My father, the super cop, the man everyone knew to rely on in an emergency, could no longer contain his grief. Mom refused to look at us. Her eyes glistened with tears. She knew, of course she knew. And I had a sneaking suspicion starting to form in my head.

"What was it?" I asked, surprised at how firm my voice sounded despite the deadness I felt inside.

"When he was questioned, he said that he thought you were gone," my mother replied dully. She fiddled with the ring on her finger. "He wanted the pair of you but wouldn't take a child. So he waited until you were old enough, but then you ran away to Reed's, and he thought you were gone. Rachel was getting to be too old, so..." she trailed off. "He's a sick monster," my mother said with disgust, shaking her head.

I barely heard her. It was my fault. Rachel was dead

because of me, because I had acted like a petulant teenager. If I had stayed in the house, maybe I could have found her. Maybe he'd have taken me too, but we would have escaped together. If, if, if... My fault...

A scream ripped through me and out into the world, an anguished scream that went on and on and on.

CIRO

My mother didn't make me go back to school right away. For that much, at least, I was grateful. She did make me start looking for a new job, though. We didn't go back to the house, even though I caught Ma looking wistfully at the house key. She brushed off my concern when I asked about it, but the guilt remained anyway.

I suspected she missed the house more than she missed my father. The apartment she rented for us to live in wasn't slummy, but it wasn't the clean sleekness she was used to. The tile in the kitchen and bathroom was cracked in places, and there was a suspicious looking water stain on the ceiling in my room, but otherwise, it wasn't terrible. All the appliances worked and there was mercifully a coffee maker.

That's where I was the morning I had to return to

school, sipping on my coffee from a thermos and leaning against the kitchen counter while watching Ma tear through the apartment looking for her sunglasses. My backpack lay on the floor next to the door. I glanced at the counter and saw Ma's sunglasses sitting on the side table. I waved with one hand to get her attention and pointed at the table.

She blew out an exasperated sigh, gathered her purse and keys, and opened the door. I grabbed my backpack and another thermos from the counter and followed her out, down the stairs, and to the parking garage that housed our building's cars. We got into the silver sedan, and I waited for her to buckle her seatbelt before handing her thermos over then placed my own in my lap while I put on my seatbelt. It was only a ten minute drive to the high school, but the building tension in my neck made it feel so much longer.

Ma pulled the car to a stop at the end of the block near the football field. I still had fifteen minutes before the first bell, and it would take less than that to walk inside and find my first classroom for the semester. I closed my eyes and took a deep breath, feeling the air fill up my lungs, then slowly let it out.

My hand was on the door handle when my mother said, "Ciro." I paused and looked at her. She smiled at me and touched my cheek with the back of her fingers. "I do love you, and you will always come first."

She had said that a hundred times before when we were still in the house, but this time felt different. Maybe it was because she proved it by leaving her husband and home and giving up a solidly decent life for a crappy apartment with her gay son. "I love you too, Ma," I said, wrapping one arm around her as best I could in the tight confines of the car.

She leaned her head against mine for a moment before saying, "Go on, you're going to be late."

I slid out of the car, backpack and thermos in hand, then shut the door and waved as she drove off. When I looked at the school again, it looked a little bit less intimidating.

After the front office gave me my new schedule, I set off in the direction of my first class, which was algebra. About halfway down the hall, a few guys stepped in front of me, blocking my path. I couldn't believe it was happening already. I had hoped to get through at least one class before being recognized and turned into a punching bag.

"Hey, are you Ciro?" asked a tall boy with tan muscles and dark, shiny hair.

"Only if you're cute," I said flippantly. If I was going to go down again, I wouldn't go down cowering like last time.

To my surprise, the boy laughed. "Matthew said you were funny."

Some of the tension drained from my shoulders. "You know Matthew?"

"He's my cousin. He asked me to look out for you until he gets out of treatment. So consider us your own personal guards. I'm Mark." He gestured to his right where a tall white boy stood. "This here is Brandon." Mark indicated the one on his left who was the spitting image of him but taller. "And my little brother Miguel."

"Mhm, 'little,'" I said, looking Miguel up and down. He smiled, and it almost looked like blushing.

"Yeah," Mark laughed again. "So don't worry. No one's going to mess with you while we're around."

"They'd be crazy to try," I said appreciatively. When Matthew had said he would look out for me, he meant it. A few months prior, I would have been skeptical of anyone other than my mother actually keeping their word. Resuming my walk down the hall with Mark beside me, though, it felt like maybe my world could expand a little bit.

Staring at the textbook didn't get me any closer to understanding what it said. I wasn't a great student before, but at least I had understood it. The page in front of me looked like gibberish, just a bunch of letters squeezed together that I couldn't seem to read. I glanced at the clock and groaned at the idea of trying to make it through another forty-five minutes of the class. Not even two days before, I would have been in class at Pleasant Valley, or maybe yoga. When I first ended up in there, I wanted out immediately. Now, though, I missed it. Even though the group didn't know everything about me, there was a freedom to being with them. Not freedom, necessarily. But safety, definitely safety.

I tried and failed to stifle a yawn but didn't get my hand over my mouth in time.

"Practicing for your next blowjob?" A kid snickered nearby.

The back of my neck heated up, but I didn't bother to look at who said it. "Why? Do you want one?" I muttered but refused to look at him. The teacher looked up briefly from writing something on the board but went back to it. Either he didn't hear or pretended not to. I wished I could disappear. My heart started beating faster and my shoulders tensed.

I tuned out the room around me and took a breath. Then another. By the fifth deep breath, I was in control of my body again. I clenched my toes as much as I could in my sneakers for a moment and let them go, pairing it with my steady breathing. *They can't hurt me if I don't let them,* I repeated in my head as I did it. By the time the teacher started the lesson, I was focused and ready.

A bubble of giddiness hit me, and I had to bite my lip from laughing out loud. *I did it,* I thought in triumph.

There was a clicking sound as a pen dropped to the tile floor on my left. "Can you get that?" the guy behind me asked.

I leaned over, the desk creaking a little as I did, and grabbed the pen. A loud thud on the opposite side caused me to jump, knocking my knee painfully into the metal underside of the desk. The jolt shot through me like an electrical current. I winced, twisting to put the pen back on the guy's desk then realized it was my book that was on the ground. The class stared at me, and I could literally feel that bubble inside me squeeze. It felt like all eyes were on me as I stood up and scooched between my desk and the one behind me. The teacher's attention went back to the board. A small sigh of relief went through me when his back turned.

I bent over to get my book and felt something hit my ass, almost hard enough to knock me over. "That's what you like, right, fag?" the guy hissed. I didn't even know his name. I had to blink several times and hurried back to my seat, tears stinging my eyes. My jaw clenched, pulling at the muscles in my head as I fought with myself not to give a reaction. More laughter and whispers spouted around from the others.

What was I thinking, coming back here? I wanted to bury my head but knew that'd just make it worse, so I sat there, wishing I was anywhere else.

The bell rang out mercifully not long after. I gathered my stuff and made a beeline for the door. I could go to the bathroom and hide until lunch was over. I could skip school and go back to the apartment. The choices whirled in my head until I reached my locker. When I opened it, I hid my head inside for a minute and let the shame wash over me.

Of course, my stomach chose that moment to announce its starvation. Maybe I could sneak into the cafeteria and grab some food before anyone saw. Then I could figure out what to do next. The idea had just enough merit to make it worthwhile. Another steadying breath, then I closed my locker, twisting the combination. I used to never bother, but I found out the hard way that people can be cruel and that the ones I thought were friends wouldn't stand by me if it meant they could get popular by tearing me down.

The cafeteria was packed by the time I arrived. I managed to get through the line without any problems, but, as I headed past the first couple of lunch tables, Mark waved me over to one where he sat with Brandon. *Matthew and Derek would remind me that I'm not alone.* I nodded at them and wove through the throng to get to the empty seat next to Mark.

"Hey, what's up?" he greeted as I sat. "Guys, this is Ciro, one of Matthew's friends. These here are Jon, Josh, and Jeffrey. Don't call him Jeff." He was tall and solemn, but he gave me a friendly enough smile and a nod.

Josh was deep in conversation with the guy on his left and barely looked up to give a slight wave. There was a bizarre combination of intense and casual to his air with his backwards cap and slouched posture. The last guy had jet black hair, wore a lazy grin, and didn't take his eyes off me, even as Josh kept talking to him. I looked down at my tray, suddenly losing my appetite.

"Not even going to say hi?" Jon asked, cutting Josh off mid-sentence. "Though I guess that makes sense, since we already met in class."

"Yeah," I mumbled.

Brandon nudged me. "Are you feeling okay?" I nodded, but I guess he didn't believe me because he said, "It's gotta be strange coming back, huh?"

"You have no idea," I agreed, pushing some mashed potatoes around on my plate.

"What's happened since this morning?" Mark asked. "Someone give you a hard time? Just let us know and we'll get on it."

"Yeah, tell us," Jon said. He knew how this game was played. If I said something, I'd be a drama-starting *mariposa*, and the others probably wouldn't believe me anyway. I had no choice but to play it off.

Forcing myself to look up at Mark, I gave what I hoped was a reassuring smile, but even I could tell was weak. "Just first day jitters, I guess."

His eyes narrowed in scrutiny and shifted from me to Jon. "What did you do to him?" Jon scoffed in response. Mark repeated the question more slowly, his tone that of someone who expects an answer.

"Nothing he didn't enjoy." Jon winked at me, and I wanted to vomit.

"I'm gonna go," I said. "Not my place to get between buddies."

"Unless they're butt buddies." Jon made that weird snickering sound like he had in class.

I wanted to punch him. I wanted to leave. I wanted to go back to Pleasant Valley, and that's how I know he got to me. I made to walk away, but Brandon took a light hold on my arm. When I shot him a questioning look, he nodded over my head to Mark, who stood, chair scraping against the floor.

Jon stood too, shoulders tensed, but he looked ready to fight. "The only reason you're defending the fairy is because of your cousin."

Mark looked like stone. Nothing in his expression wavered. "You're wrong. I'm defending him because it's the right thing to do. So let me slap you with some facts. The only reason you're even on the football team is because of my cousin. The only reason why you're not scraping at the bottom of the totem pole here is because of us." He gestured around at the rest of the guys.

For a moment, I thought I saw rage flicker across Jon's face. But it disappeared behind a smirk. "Don't kid yourself. I'm the most popular guy in school, the star of the team."

Jeffrey didn't bother to get up, but he did spare a glance and said, "When Matthew asked me about bringing you on to fill Tony's spot because he said you were half decent at blocking, I had to ask who the fuck you were."

Suddenly, I noticed there was a lot less noise in the cafeteria. I glanced around, and a bunch of people from the nearby tables stared back.

"All I gotta do is go tell the coach you were stealing equipment to sell online, and you're out of the starting job," Jon sneered.

"Let me get this straight." A grin appeared on Mark's face as held up a finger with each point made. His voice became loud enough for the nearby tables to listen. "You plan to lie to the coach to kick the star QB off the team. You're using hate speech. And you sexually harassed someone who needs support in their life more than ever. And that's just today."

I didn't imagine it this time. Jon's face twisted in fury. "You're lying." He looked around at the others watching. "He's lying."

"No he's not," a girl piped up. I recognized her from the class but not as one of the laughing ones. "I saw you harass Ciro in class. I already filed a complaint with the principal."

Jon forced a laugh out and waved his hand dismissively. "No one cares what you have to say." He feigned comprehension as he looked between Mark and me. "Oh, I get it. You're his new boy toy, aren't you?" His gaze landed on me again. "First one cousin, then the other, right?"

"We're not hooking up, but, even if we were, who cares? You're trying to deflect from the fact that everything I said is true." Mark leaned over the table and lowered his voice so only we could hear. "And you're the one who set up the jump that landed Ciro in the hospital." My eyes widened as I took in that bit of information. "Come near him again, and you'll find out just exactly how we take the trash out."

Jon sputtered for a few moments, his face turning redder. "You will be nothing by the time I'm done!" he finally screamed before grabbing his bag and storming out. There was a weird silence that followed as Mark took his seat again.

"You know," Josh finally said, "he has done some good things for the team too."

Brandon pinched his forehead. "Just go," he groaned.

Josh went.

"Um" I said, as the noise picked up again and people went back to their meal. "I'm sorry, but thanks."

Jeffrey shrugged, "Guy's had it coming for weeks. Moved from JV to Varsity only because Tony broke his leg and the second string guy failed Chemistry."

"Once coach finds out about that complaint, he'll be off the team anyway," Brandon added.

"Don't even sweat it," Mark said, giving me a nod. His hands were clenched on the chair, and his leg bounced like crazy. The adrenaline of the confrontation had him amped up and ready to fight. Now he was all psyched but had nothing to spend the energy on.

I chewed on my lip, wondering if I should say something. "Breathe," I finally said.

"What?"

"Your body's in flight or fight mode. Blood flow is redirected from your heart to the other parts of you needed to survive an encounter. It's the animal brain kicking in." My voice had a note of confidence to it that had been missing most of the day. "So, breathe. Breathe deep and let it out slowly. Keep doing that, and it'll signal to the brain that the need for adrenaline is over." Mark gave me a weird look, so I shrugged. "I just spent the last few months learning all about this crap. What's the worse that can happen by breathing?"

While Mark did that, Jeffrey caught my eye. "You know," he said, sizing me up, "You ever consider playing football? I hear there's going to be a spot on the team opening up."

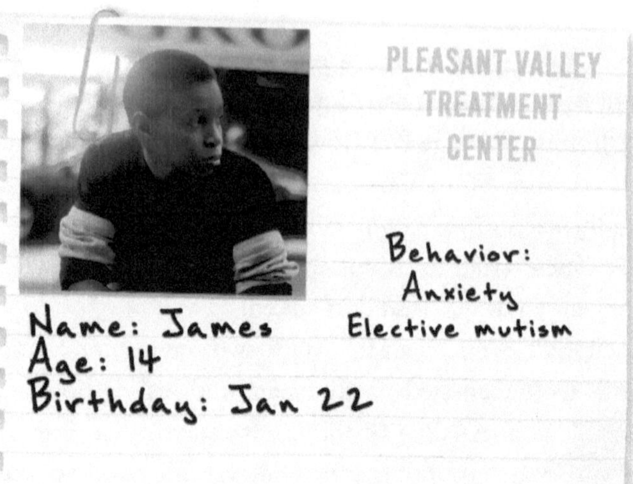

JAMES

My shoes squeaked on the newly cleaned tile as I walked to Dr. Larson's office. The week before, the nurse outside the doctor's office had said it was the only way she could hear me coming. That made me smile, even as I continued to squeak my way down the hall.

The door to the office was closed, and I couldn't decide if I was supposed to knock or not. I figured not was better and sat in one of the chairs next to the door. It wasn't like I had anywhere pressing to be. Though, we were supposed to do art later, and I always enjoyed that. I hadn't known there was such a thing as an art doctor before, but she was nice and never pressured me to speak.

The door opened, and Liz walked out. She always

managed to look casually cool, even in the ward. At the moment, she wore black and white leggings, an oversized shirt, and a woven white shawl that swirled about her knees as she walked. She glanced over and held her hand up when she saw me. I stood and gave her a high five.

"You're it," she said with a smirk and continued in the direction of the ward.

"Come on in," Dr. Larson called from inside.

His office smelled distinctly of sandalwood. It served as a reminder that I wasn't at home. There would never be something as luxurious as that scent in my parents' house.

The doctor smiled kindly as I went to my usual chair and sat down. I inhaled the soothing mixture of sandalwood and leather and started to relax a little.

"Good morning, James," Dr. Larson said.

I couldn't help it. My cheeks immediately heated up, though I knew it would be hard for the doctor to tell I was blushing. I looked down at my knees. "Hello," I whispered. As usual, my voice sounded like a stranger's, even to me. It was only in the past couple of weeks that I started speaking in my sessions, and those had been about things like basketball and video games. It surprised me to find out the doctor actually knew a lot about video games.

"Do you prefer that chair?" he asked, and I nodded. "Can you tell me why? Everyone has a different reason for enjoying leather. What is yours?"

Without thinking, I replied, "Because it gets taken care of."

It didn't seem like he was expecting that kind of answer because he tilted his head and seemed to consider it. "You like it when things are taken care of?"

I started to nod but paused. "And animals." Even more

quietly, I added, "And people."

"Do you like to be the caretaker?" The doctor asked, enunciating the words in his strange accent.

To that, I shrugged, so he asked instead, "Do you like to be taken care of?"

I lifted my shoulders again. "I don't know what that feels like." I shifted in the leather chair a little. I hadn't expected the conversation to go that way, especially not so soon.

"What about with animals?" Dr. Larson asked, seeming to sense my discomfort. "Do you like to take care of animals?"

"Cats," I replied. "Lizards." I waited for him to say something else, but he didn't. "I found a cat with kittens once," I admitted.

Dr. Larson smiled, showing some of his teeth. "I like cats too. They make good companions. What happened with the litter you found?"

"The mom wouldn't let me near at first, but she was so hungry, so I started bringing her food and milk so she could keep feeding her babies. She actually let me hold them a couple of times, but she got angry if I kept them for too long." I smiled at the memory, thinking of how the kittens' warm, soft fur felt in my hands. They were so tiny, like little fuzzy motor balls.

"What happened then?"

"I went back one day and they were gone," I whispered. "I hope they found a good home."

"I hope so too," Dr. Larson said. He let me sit for a moment before asking, "Did you tell your family about them?"

If I wasn't so used to hiding my laughter, I would have

snorted. My hand automatically went to my mouth to hide my wry grin. When I saw Dr. Larson's questioning look, my grin faded, and I dropped my hand.

"I tried," I replied, not thrilled with the defeat in my quiet voice.

The doctor prodded gently, "What happened?"

"They told me to shut up and go away." I bit my cheeks to distract myself from the pain in my chest and eyes.

"Did that happen often?"

I nodded, getting that familiar sense of self-hatred for feeling things. I was supposed to be over it, getting better. I was talking, after all. That was progress. Only I didn't feel like talking anymore. It was exhausting and always brought up pain. Listening did that too, though. There was no way to escape it.

Dr. Larson started to write in the binder on his desk that I knew had my charts and notes in it. He looked up after several seconds of silence. "Can you remember the last time you spoke at home?" He kept his voice low and gentle, making it hard to ignore him.

I did, actually, but I wasn't sure I could talk for that long yet. I opened my mouth but hesitated.

"If you'd rather not say, that's all right," Dr. Larson said. He scratched at the shadow of a beard on his chin, looking past me to the paths outside. "Shall we take a walk?" He asked suddenly. "I do enjoy time outside, and we get so little of it."

Mute once more, I nodded. Inside, my stomach stopped flipping around as much. We stood, and I followed him out of the office. He paused to lock the door and told the nurse at the station we'd be outside for a while.

I had spent so much of my time inside that the warm

outside felt like a shock to my skin, like stepping into a hot bath on a cold day. The paths between the units were mostly quiet since it was too late for breakfast and too early for lunch. A few staff members hurried between buildings, but otherwise it was calm. We took a side path down the hill, and I remembered it being the way to the obstacle course we sometimes did for exercise.

Before I could start getting nervous, Dr. Larson turned again. I followed him down the path to the edge of one of the unit buildings. We rounded the corner, and the sight that greeted us amazed me.

Past the fence further down the hill ahead lay a grassy field that butted right up against the Vale River. Trees lined the bank on the other side, extending as far back as I could see. I had no idea there was such a big forest nearby.

"I asked the staff to put a bench here for me," Dr. Larson explained, indicating a wooden bench fastened to the ground next to the building. A ball camera was stationed a few feet away and up near the awning. "I think the staff enjoy seeing the wildlife too," the doctor chuckled when he followed my gaze.

My head tilted in my telltale questioning look.

"Sometimes the deer will come out here to graze. They have figured out that they are safe here."

I turned back to the field eagerly but didn't see anything stirring beyond the fence.

Dr. Larson settled on one side of the bench with a slight groan.

I realized I had left my communication board in my room on the ward and had a moment of panic before I told myself that it would be okay and I didn't have to talk. I sat on the other side of the bench and crossed my legs at my ankles.

Between the building's shadow and a nearby tree, we had plenty of shade to protect us from the day's increasing heat. A couple of birds sang and flitted through the branches, but no other noise reached us, not even the building's generators.

The longer we sat in silence, the more I relaxed. It wasn't often that someone wasn't put off by my mutism, and I found it enjoyable. Renee usually was the only other one, but that was because she would be reading.

I watched the river for a while then started scanning the nearby area. Another fence bordered the treatment center, surrounding what looked like an empty field. A beautiful paint horse wandered into sight, and I sat up a little straighter to watch it move.

"Do you like horses too?" Dr. Larson asked.

I nodded and glanced at him, but his eyes were closed. "Yeah," I whispered. "My uncle has a ranch."

"Ah," he uttered then lapsed into silence again.

I watched the horse walk around the pasture and thought about working on Uncle Dari's ranch, how he never pressured me to talk either so long as I put the work in to take care of the horses and cows. "I'm the youngest of five," I said. "Three different dads among us. Mine stuck around." I didn't look at the doctor, afraid I'd lose my nerve and stop talking. I wasn't even sure he could hear me.

"My parents were always tired. They had to work a lot to take care of us. When I was a little kid, my siblings always talked over me or for me. Even if it wasn't what I actually wanted. When I tried to say something, whoever I was trying to talk to would tell me to be quiet or go away because they were busy. It was kind of the same at school. I only spoke when I had to. And I don't think anyone noticed until I stopped talking altogether."

"Wonder if his dumbness prevents him from screaming. Want to find out?" Tyrell leered at me. His fist was already clenched at his side, and I knew it wouldn't do any good to point out that I wasn't the dumb one even if I wanted to speak. With three older brothers, Tyrell wasn't going to be able to do anything to me they hadn't already.

His flunkies laughed, and one of them grabbed at me to pin my arms. I steeled myself for the first punch. I expected Tyrell's fist to hit my face, but he went for the gut shot instead, and I doubled over. His other fist came up to hit my face, knocking my head back. I probably would have fallen if the other guy wasn't holding me up. Another punch to the side of my head. The pain left my gut but doubled in my face. I took a quick breath in and prepared for the next blow, making sure I didn't cry out. I knew from experience that would just make it worse.

"Hey!" someone shouted, and the next blow didn't come. "Let go!" Mr. Torres, the football coach said. I recognized his voice from my brothers' games. He was a big man, much bigger than Tyrell, and I felt the other kid let go of my arms.

I wanted to straighten, to show they didn't hurt me, but it really, really hurt.

"Get you next time, Anne Frank," Tyrell sneered and started jogging away before Mr. Torres could catch them.

Yeah, and I was the dumb one. He didn't even know the difference between Anne Frank and Helen Keller. The thought amused me so I smiled and regretted it immediately. My face contorted with pain.

By then, the coach reached me. "You ok, Jimmy?"

I held onto my stomach with one hand and rubbed my shoulder with the other while I straightened. Mr. Torres was scowling in the direction Tyrell and company had gone. When he looked at me, I nodded, though I could read in his expression that he didn't believe me.

"Come on, let's get you some ice." He didn't wait for me to protest before turning back the way he had come. "How many times is that now?" he asked quietly.

I shrugged but only because I lost count after a dozen.

"Did they ever bother you when Zeke and Zack were still here?"

I shook my head but had to stop when it felt like my head would explode. My twin oldest brothers were the toughest guys in school and stars of the football team, and they were the only ones allowed to pick on me. But they had graduated in the spring, and Candy and Jamal were nowhere near their status to protect me. Not that they would anyway.

Mr. Torres's office was inside the boys' locker room, making it very awkward for any of the girls from his classes to try to get a hold of him. The locker room was deserted. Practice wouldn't start for probably another twenty minutes. Mr. Torres opened the door to his office and let me in, closing it behind me. I sat in one of the plastic chairs across from the desk while he went to the small freezer in the corner of the room.

He stepped towards me, holding out an ice pack. "That should help keep some of the swelling down."

I took it and pressed it gingerly against my nose which I really hoped wasn't broken. I wasn't sure if my parents could afford a trip to the hospital.

Mr. Torres handed me a washcloth too. "So your hand doesn't get cold," he explained. He sat on the edge of his desk, one leg dangling as he studied me. I wasn't used to anyone paying attention to me. "You sure can take a hit," he said after a minute. He laughed, even though nothing he said was funny. "I guess that's to be expected being the youngest, huh?"

I nodded slowly and moved the ice pack to the side of my jaw.

"I was the youngest too. Only three of us, but my brothers would gang up on me all the time. Does that sound about right?"

He looked at me with piercing dark eyes, so I nodded again.

"You really don't talk, do you?" He leaned forward a little and rested his elbow on his knee to support his head.

I wanted to scoot my chair back but felt that would have been rude after he technically rescued me from the beating before it got any worse.

"Why don't you join the football team? We sure could use another player from your family this year," Mr. Torres grinned. He slid off the desk in favor of the plastic chair next to me.

Something didn't feel right. I wanted to get out of there. I infinitely preferred being ignored to the kind of attention Mr. Torres was giving me. His hand went to my knee and patted it a couple of times then let it rest. I stared at it.

I stood up and put the ice pack and washcloth on the desk, and Mr. Torres let his hand fall. I said, "Thank you," in sign language and started towards the door.

"If you ever need help or want to talk," he said wryly, "you know where to find me."

I waved without looking back and headed out of the locker room. I was shaking by the time I reached the front door of the school, not even bothering to retrieve my backpack from my locker. When my feet hit the pavement, I ran.

I ran the entire way home, which felt like an eternity but I knew was less than five minutes away. Pushing open the front door, I went directly to my room, which actually only recently became my room. Jamal took the twins' room and vacated the one we'd shared for my entire life.

But I didn't know what to do. I paced, trying to think. I felt gross and not from the run since that barely made me sweat. Had that ever happened to Zeke and Zack? Did they know their coach was... What was he? He hadn't actually done anything, had he? Besides give me an ice pack and creep me out.

I heard a door down the hall open and close. My dad would be getting ready for work. Maybe he could tell me what happened.

When I entered the kitchen, I saw my dad at the counter, making coffee. He turned around and looked as tired as ever. "Dad?" I said, walking closer.

"Hmm?" he grunted.

"Something happened at school," I started.

He turned around to get the sugar and examined my face. "Got to stick up for yourself now that your brothers are at college," he said and went back to his coffee.

In my panic, I temporarily forgot how banged up my face probably looked. I started to speak again, but he waved a hand as though brushing me aside, "Can't I have a few minutes of peace before work?"

My shoulders slumped, and I returned to my room. I heard Candy and Jamal come home from soccer, and then Dad leave, but I didn't go out until I heard the front door open again and Mom's voice calling us in for dinner.

"Whoa, looks like you got beat with the ugly stick," Jamal teased as I went into the kitchen again.

"More than usual," Candy agreed.

"Kids," Mom warned, but the word didn't have a lot of strength behind it. She glanced at me and sighed. "Fighting again?"

"No, I-" I started to say, but she cut me off.

"I won't have you lying to me the few times you do decide we're worthy of your words," she snapped. Though she looked like she regretted it immediately, the damage was done.

"Fine," I said, "I won't speak again."

"And I didn't, not to her or Dad or my brothers and sister. I never said a word about the coach or what happened, never said more than a few words ever again until today." The horse, what looked like a stallion, tossed his head. "It took a while for anyone to really notice, I guess, since I was already pretty quiet. My mom used to say I was like her brother, my uncle Dari." My throat felt dry when I finished talking, and I scuffed one of my shoes along the concrete.

Dr. Larson shifted on the bench but didn't say anything right away. *Now you've done it,* I thought to myself. *He won't believe me either.*

"Thank you for sharing that with me," he said finally and cleared his throat. "James." I looked up. "I want you to know that's an entirely normal reaction to have. All of it. None of what you did makes you wrong or broken. You were protecting yourself in the only way you knew how."

I chewed on my lip and on his words. "Everyone says I'm a freak for not talking."

"Everyone?" the doctor challenged.

"Well, not here, I guess. But out there." I gestured back toward the road.

He nodded. "Many people talk. But few listen."

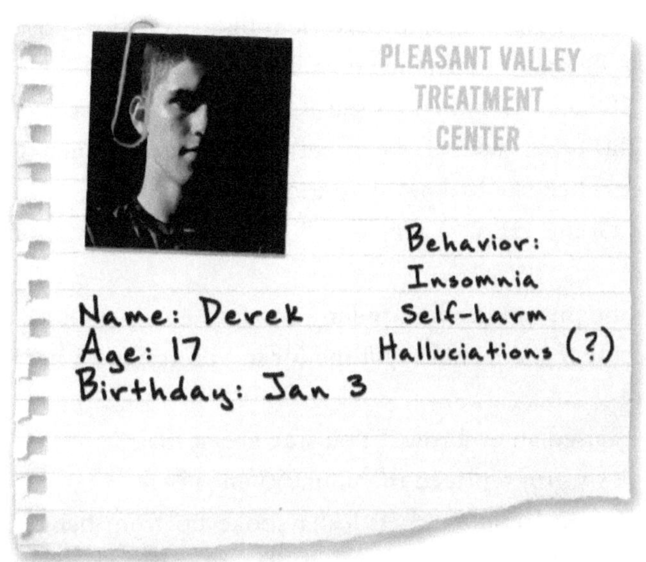

DEREK

"Reduce the Atarax dosage, take off chlorpromazine altogether, and add on sertraline."

I picked at the peeling black polish on my nails while Dr. Larson updated Kal and Iesha with my new medication plan. From the corner of my eye, I could see Kal's jaw drop while Iesha glanced over at me. They were making it really hard to pretend to ignore them even though I was standing at the counter only a few feet away.

"Won't that make the episodes happen more frequently?" Kal almost-whispered.

I grit my teeth and glowered at my hands. *Professional concerns*, I reminded myself. *That's all it is. It's not judgment.*

Dr. Larson's voice cut through my thoughts. "The appearance of the alters seems to be triggered by stress.

Using an SSRI will, in theory, help that stress threshold and allow Derek to remain in control more frequently."

"Derek." I turned to see Kate leaning against the wall on the other side of the partition. "Whatcha doing?" she asked when she had my attention.

"Going crazy, wanna join?" My attempt at humor fell flat.

She pursed her lips, pulling her face into a pout that I'd call cute if she wouldn't hit me for it. "Pretty sure I beat you there."

I raised an eyebrow. "You sure about that?"

A sly grin replaced the pout. "Wanna bet?"

Before I could retort, Iesha spoke up from behind the counter. "Kate, can you back up, sweetie? Patient confidentiality and all." Her bubblegum sweetness couldn't outweigh the severity of the request. She took her job pretty seriously. Kate took a few steps further back to the line on the ground to wait for her own medication while Iesha placed a small plastic cup on the counter in front of me with some orange juice inside.

"And this is?" I eyed the drink suspiciously.

"Sertraline. Did you read the info paperwork the doctor gave you?"

I picked up the cup and swirled the drink. It looked just like orange juice. "Yeah. I just wasn't expecting juice to be the answer to happiness."

"Works for kids, doesn't it?" Tobias called out as he passed and took a spot behind Renee in the ever-growing medication line. With a snort, I lifted the cup towards him in a toast and started walking away.

"At the counter," Iesha said before I took more than two steps. My eyes rolled, but I downed the concoction, which tasted a little sour, and put the cup on the counter for Iesha to throw away. When I turned back around, I collided into someone. "Oof, sorry, James," I said, backing up as he rubbed his forehead.

"It's okay," he murmured, so quiet that I stared at him.

I looked back at Iesha, who was handing Kate a tiny cup with a couple of capsules in it. "What did you give me and how quick does it kick in? Because I think I'm hearing things."

James tugged on my sleeve and allowed a shy smile. "You're not. Or are. But not fake things." It was like listening to a giant mouse. He wasn't a tiny kid, actually was pretty tall for his age, but he was so *quiet.*

"You're talking!" I said stupidly. Looking around, the few others gathered also seemed dumbfounded, reassuring me slightly. Renee ran over from her spot in the medication line and hugged him. After letting go, she nodded at him with a silly grin and practically skipped back to the line while Kate whooped.

James ducked his head, obviously embarrassed. As he walked past the others, Tobias clapped him on the shoulder.

"Now we just gotta make sure he doesn't shut up again," Kate said, appearing beside me after taking her pills.

I nodded but also wondered how in the hell we were supposed to manage that.

"Good afternoon!" Michelle's cheery voice called out as we filed into the group room after lunch.

Various mutterings of returned greetings came with an after-lunch sleepiness. Except for Liz, who practically hollered, "Hey, Michelle!"

"On one of your upswings, huh?" I settled into a chair near the back window and let my head hit the wall.

Liz had her hair up in a half-bun. The sun glinted off it as she crossed the room, practically blinding me. "You know it," she said with a wink and took a chair at the other end of the room. She flipped open a notebook and started writing in it.

It was a small group, with Bullfrog, James, and Kate in their individual sessions. Matthew and Tobias took chairs next to each other on one side of the room, deep in conversation about some football player. A younger girl drifted in, looking lost, but saw Michelle and gave a small smile. Renee came in a moment later, found an empty seat and immediately went back to reading.

I envied her ability to get lost in a story like that. I could do it with video games sometimes, even movies on occasion, but not books.

"There's no way!" Matthew said loudly. My head lazed to one side to look over at him. He was facing me but looking at Tobias in shock.

"Way," I said, not having a clue as to what they're talking about.

Tobias turned and grinned at me.

"All right," Michelle interrupted with a clap of her hands. "Let's get started with check-in. Matthew?"

"Safe. Amazed."

Michelle grinned as she adjusted her headband. "Why?"

"Apparently, we go to the same school." He gestured at Tobias, who still smirked like he was enjoying the show.

"That's assuming I actually go to class, but technically, yeah." Tobias shook his head to get the tousled hair out of his eyes. "I'm relaxed. Safe."

After verifying the rest of the group was safe to proceed, Michelle picked up a dry erase marker, and a few of us groaned. "Hey now, I'm not *that bad*," she said, still smiling. "But don't worry, I'm not drawing today." She turned to the whiteboard and started jotting down some words in neat block letters that only slightly sloped to one side.

GROUNDING

5 STEPS

TIPP

"When our bodies get into heightened emotional states," Michelle began after facing us, "we generally have ways of calming them down. With things like anxiety, those emotions can be more intense and harder to calm, and that's where grounding comes in. This technique is a part of CBT—that cognitive behavior therapy that I'm sure you absolutely love hearing more about."

My eyes closed, but I allowed a smile. This wasn't the first grounding class I'd been to in my time at Pleasant Valley. Due to the ever-rotating roster of patients and therapists, sometimes we repeated classes, and it looked like this would be one of those times.

"Let's start backwards, just to mix it up," Michelle said with a smile. "TIPP is, what?"

"Tip the temperature, intense exercise, paced breathing, paired muscle relaxation." Renee recited the words dutifully like we were in a science class or something. Which, we kind of were.

Michelle clapped her hands once. "Exactly right. You've done some of these parts before as part of the treatment here. So today we're going to focus on the temperature piece. Matthew, can you help me hand these out?"

I opened my eyes, expecting another pamphlet, but instead, Michelle held a small container. That got my attention. Usually we just talked our way through each part by giving examples.

Matthew took the container, what looked like a nylon lunchbox, and walked around. He lifted a limp cloth out of it and placed it in Renee's hands. She immediately shifted it back and forth.

"Try putting these washcloths over your face to lower your temperature," Michelle explained. This will generally activate the parasympathetic nervous system to induce relaxation and lower your heart rate. This is why you often see people in movies or TV splashing cold water on their face, though dunking is actually proven to be more effective."

When it was my turn to take a cloth, the pure freezing sensation almost felt like a burn. Like a brainfreeze on my hand. I leaned forward and let the cloth rest on the back of my neck.

A sidelong glance at Tobias told me he didn't seem too sure about the cloth. He licked his lips, almost like he was nervous. Ordinarily, I'd have averted my gaze, but Tobias wasn't one to get weird about things. His face set in determination, he leaned back and put the cloth on his face. Within seconds, he flung it off, the cloth landing in the middle of the room with a plop.

Tobias stared at it, his breathing fast and shallow, the exact opposite of what the thing was supposed to induce. His face contorted in a way I knew all too well—the kind I felt every time I woke up in the middle of the night. Pure, unadulterated fear.

Tobias was absent from the next group. He missed lunch too. In fact, none of us saw him until dinner. When he showed up in the cafeteria, his face seemed more gaunt and his shoulders hunched over like he was carrying the world. I knew that look.

"Guess you had your breakthrough session, huh?" I said as I took the seat next to him.

He lifted the fork to his mouth absently. "Yeah, guess you could say that."

I didn't want to ask if he was okay, that would have been insulting. But I didn't really know what else to say. We sat in silence for a while and ate the barely edible meal. "You don't have to talk about it if you don't want to. But it's good that you at least maybe got it out with someone. It sucks, but it helps in the end."

Tobias put the fork down and put his head in his hands. "I wasn't even ready for it. It just kind of all came up. Things that I thought I was over but obviously still bother me."

I nodded, though he couldn't see. "Usually how that therapy thing works. Sneaks up on you when you least expect it."

"I mean, I figured this wasn't going to be easy. I'm not exactly in the best of places, obviously." He held up one of his arms, wrapped in a clean bandage. "But I wasn't expecting to have to delve into that depth of my hell like that."

On a whim, I put my hand on his shoulder, and he looked up. The whites of his eyes were red, and he rubbed at them with one hand. "Look, there's no shame in what you're doing here—what any of us are doing. Did Riley tell you about her closet analogy?"

He shook his head. I studied him while I tried to remember what exactly she said and how to phrase it. Tobias actually reminded me of a dog one of the better families I lived with had.

That dog showed up on the street one summer looking shaggy and way too thin. We couldn't figure out what kind he was since he had the face of a Labrador but the fur of something else entirely, maybe Shepherd. One of the other boys tried chasing it off with a stick, but the dog just slunk back when that kid wasn't around. I liked him. Our foster mom did too, and she'd give me scraps to give to the dog to try to coax him to hang around. He started to fill out and would even play fetch with us, but he never came inside. There was one time where we tried giving the dog a bath. He was fine up until the point where we turned the water on. That's when he got really shaky, but we tried to calm him down. As soon as the water hit him though, he yanked away from us and bolted, and we never saw him again.

I didn't want to do that to Tobias.

"She said trauma is like a messy closet. Over the years, more shit gets piled in there and, if we don't do some kind of organizing, it gets so full that the door won't close anymore. And then it's this giant mess we have to clean up, and that's overwhelming as hell. By yourself, you could clean it up eventually, sure, but chances are that it'll be too much and the whole mess will spill back out another time. With someone helping, though, it gets sorted out into boxes, examined, and then put away on the shelf in the closet." I rubbed the back of my neck. "She explains it better, but yeah."

Tobias stared at me for a second before a shadow of his usual grin flitted across his face. "Nah, I get what you mean. Thanks, man. That helped. I'm not weak for not dealing with it on my own. I'm just disorganized."

I let out an unexpected laugh. "Yeah, that's a good way to look at it. We're all just here to pick up some organizational skills."

BULLFROG

Art therapy was a miss for me. Every single time. Even before the fire, I never had an artistic bone in my body. And after, well, the pain was bad enough but worse was having to look at whatever I was making with my messed up hands. To date, I hadn't even finished one of the projects. The first time I tried was a drawing of a cat that looked more like a giant pig, all because I couldn't get the nose to look right. Actually, I'm pretty sure there was more to it than that, but the nose definitely didn't help. Painting wasn't any better either. No matter how I thought it'd look in my head, I could never get that translated to the canvas.

The others didn't seem to have nearly as many issues. Except Renee. She trashed almost every single painting she worked on and had about as much luck as I did with the drawing. There was only one time where she made a painting that she didn't hate, but one of the girls from the other ward mistook it for someone else's and broke it in half. Renee refused to paint after that. She chose to be marked as a non-participant and would sit one of the chairs out of the way and just read. Though she did still help with clean-up, which just made zero sense to me.

That was all running through my head as I stared at the gray misshapen rectangles in front of me. "What is this?" I muttered, poking at one of them. I couldn't feel it because of the nerve damage, but it caved inward like therapy putty.

"It's clay. Try it." The therapist, Tammy, lay out a set of sculpting tools on the table. Tammy reminded me of a horsetail reed. She was tall and willowy, with wild brownish gray hair barely contained by a hair tie. And she was always moving. I heard Kate admit once that Tammy made her anxious just because she never stood still.

Tammy flitted around from table to table, alternating between giving general guidance to the group at large and murmuring encouragement to individuals. Two hours, twice a week, and it was my own living hell.

"You may use whatever medium you like for today. Be it the clay, paint, or good ole fashioned pencil. As you're working..." She paused by Derek's table for a moment and said something about his color usage. "As you're working," she repeated, "I want you all to think about the concept of duality and what it means. What do you think duality is?" She didn't wait for an answer. "It's the idea of two aspects of something—yin and yang, for example. Night and day. What comes to mind with duality inside of yourself? That is what we are creating today."

Through all of that, I didn't take my eyes off the clay in

front of me. What duality was inside me? What a load of crap. I reached out with my less-marred hand and paused, glancing down, first at that one, then the other, and it clicked. Duality.

My hands were covered in gray muck, and I didn't mind it one bit. In front of me sat a pair of hands, my hands. Sort of. One was a decently formed hand, relatively smooth except for the natural creases in the palm. The other appeared the same but entirely different. It was the same general shape and almost the same size, but it was covered in an extra layer of clay, blotched to make it look like my burned hand. I stood back and nodded my approval. They weren't great hands, but they were mine.

"Hey, that's pretty awesome," Derek said as he passed my table.

"Thanks," I managed to say while the normal part of my face flushed. Derek was a natural artist. Any medium he touched turned to something cool, even if he never worked with it before.

Tammy stopped next to me and tilted her head, examining my work. "That's a really interesting interpretation of duality. What brought this out?" It wasn't a critical question, but I still stumbled over the words as I answered.

"I don't really know. I guess, because I have two hands, and one is pretty much normal while the other isn't, and that kind of fit the bill." I glanced back down at the two pieces and suddenly wanted to smash them back to their starting lumpy brick forms.

She shook her head. "I mean, do you see some of

yourself in this work, aside from the obvious? Do you think maybe you have both perfection and flaw inside of you too?"

One of my shoulders lifted in a shrug. If she wanted to read more into it, that was her deal. Sensing I wasn't going to elaborate, she raised her voice. "Let's get the clay ready for the kiln put on the cart over by the door, please."

I carried mine carefully to the cart and put them on top, away from any possible smashing. When Tammy asked if I wanted to help, I shrugged again, though I was actually pretty interested in seeing what a kiln could do. I never even heard the word before.

Tammy had me follow her outside after assuring me that the sky was overcast and that I could go back inside if I felt any pain while the rest of the group cleaned up. She pulled the cart over to a large circular pile of bricks. "Start putting the clay work inside the kiln there."

I followed her instructions, setting each piece a little distance apart in case one toppled. There wasn't enough room for everything, and Tammy held up her arm before I could put the second of my pieces—the burned hand—in the kiln. She bent over the kiln, fiddling with something. When she stepped back, there was a soft glow starting to form around the clay. Before long, a trace of flames could be seen licking along the kiln's surface.

I didn't even realize what was happening until the clay slipped from my fingers and landed with a soft squishy thud on the concrete. My body shook and my heart thudded painfully in my chest as I watched, helpless, while the sculpture of my good hand was changed forever by fire.

KATE

The outside door for the art center slammed shut as Bullfrog entered. No one moved for several seconds as he barreled through the room toward the door back to the ward.

"It's locked," I called out as a reminder, even as he yanked on the handle. "Think he knows it's locked?" I asked Derek as Bullfrog proceeded to push on the other door.

"He seems...scared, almost." Derek and I exchanged a glance then headed over to the door, approaching Bullfrog slowly. "Hey, bud." Instead of that sickening soothing tone the nurses tried using on us when one of us had a freakout, Derek kept his casual, like he was passing Bullfrog in the hallway or something.

We each leaned against opposite walls in the hallway, bodies turned toward the door where Bullfrog was peering through each of the glass windows, still moving from one door to the other.

"Yo," I added, mentally slapping myself for sounding dumb. "What's going on, man? You okay?" Bullfrog ignored me. I put a hand on my hips and sidestepped to get into his direct line of sight without actually getting in his bubble. My other hand came up and waved in between us. "Helloooo?"

He stopped, blinked, and stared at me. With his hood down for once, I could see the piercing stormy blue of his eyes which were wide with panic. His chest rose rapidly with the quick breath that stems from an anxiety attack—a feeling I knew all too well. My sass evaporated.

"Breathe," I reminded him. "Slow and deep."

"Can't," he croaked. His eyes darted back to the door and he pushed on it again in vain, knowing the staff wasn't around to see any of us.

Keeping my eyes on Bullfrog to make sure he didn't start hyperventilating, I asked Derek, "The countdown thing, what's the first one?"

"Oh! Uhmm." Derek cast his eyes around then brought his hand up in a facepalm. "Look"

"Okay right! Bullfrog, can you hear and understand what I'm saying?"

A quick glance and a nod told me to proceed.

"Breathe with me, okay? Just a simple breath, doesn't have to be deep." My lungs filled with air even though my heart was pounding. *Where is the staff? They're supposed to be the ones doing this!* "Look at me," I urged, and this time, Bullfrog held my gaze. I breathed, and watched him mirror me, but he didn't seem at all calmer. His face twisted in remorse and pain, and he ducked his head away to break eye contact.

"Find five things you can see," said a quiet voice from just behind me. The sudden presence startled me, and I clasped a hand to my own chest which was starting to beat irregularly. James stood there, dark eyes focused on Bullfrog, determined. "What do you see?"

"Wall," he managed to get out.

"Color?" James pressed.

"Green. Kind of. Maroon trim."

"What else?"

"Fl-fl-flames." Bullfrog recoiled from us as though we were made of fire.

What is he seeing? My heart ached for the kid who watched the only ones he ever loved die one by one. I reached out, but James stopped my hand.

"He's spooked. Like a horse in a barn fire." It was still so eerie to hear the silent boy say anything, but it sure sounded like he paid attention.

"The kiln," Derek groaned. "Bet he saw the fire heating the clay."

Another twinge of sorrow pinged my heart. "Was that it?" I asked Bullfrog gently. "You saw the pottery in the kiln?" He shook so much that I couldn't tell if it was a yes or a no, but it had to be something like that to give him such a scare. "What else do you see? Inside the room?" I added.

The boy's head swiveled quickly, leaving me wondering if he was still looking for an escape route, but he didn't move. "Book. Gold cover. Black lettering."

"Whose book is it?"

Silence stretched out for a long moment, but then he

whispered a name. "Renee."

"Yes, it belongs to Renee, your friend here. She's been reading it for a day now." Derek picked up where I left off. "How about something else?"

Bullfrog called out the blue acrylic paint bottle and the white unused canvas sitting on a nearby table.

"Four things you can feel," James piped up when we looked at him.

"Cold air." We stood under the air conditioner vent. "My sweatshirt. My skin. And," he reached out to touch the door but didn't push on it.

My own breathing started to slow. "Three things you hear," I said, trying to time the words with my breaths.

A sound came from beside me as Derek pulled something out of his pocket. "That rustling," Bullfrog said. "The sink where they're washing up, and the brushes being put in the jar." Derek handed something over as Bullfrog said, "Two things I can smell are paint and Kate's shampoo." He looked down at the object in his hand, unwrapped it, and popped it into his mouth.

"And one thing you can taste," Derek finished with that small sideways smile at me that conveyed a hundred words at least.

The four of us stood in silence, letting an uneasy calm wash over us. It wasn't over, we all knew that, but it didn't stop us from exchanging a few triumphant grins at overcoming the anxiety attack together.

"I can't believe that actually worked." Derek said. It was after dinner, which meant clean-up for the ward, and we were assigned to the courtyard. "I mean, I've used some of the simpler ones before, but that was just..." He paused with the push broom in his hand and looked up at me. "You know?"

"Surreal?" I supplied. Lifting the lid of the garbage caused me to make a face at the stench. I held my breath while taking out and tying the bag then let my breath go. "That is *not* the kind of paced breathing they have in mind."

Derek leaned on the broom handle and stared at me. No, not at me. Past me. I turned around but nothing and no one was there. A part of me wanted to run, and another part immediately wanted to smack myself for thinking that. I gulped and hated the way I sounded as the words left me. "Derek?"

He blinked and refocused on me. "What? Sorry, I zoned out for a second."

"Are you okay? Do you need to go inside? I can handle this if you need to."

Giving himself a little shake, he said, "No, I'm good. I was just wondering how Bullfrog's doing. Maybe I'll go check on him after clean-up." I nodded and we lapsed into silence. I didn't like it.

"Are you mad at me?" I blurted out.

Derek let out a surprised scoff. "Why would I be mad at you?"

Hearing him repeat it made me burn in embarrassment, and I looked down, not even sure what I could say. "You've just been, I don't know, quiet, I guess." I fumbled through the explanation like the worst juggling clown in the world. I could literally feel my face on fire. "Just, forget it, okay?" I tried to brush it off and turn to head inside, but Derek's hand caught the side of my forearm just enough to bring me around to face him. His grip was loose enough that I could easily slip from it if I wanted, and a surge of gratitude welled up inside of me for it.

I willed myself to not look up into his shining eyes, which would only make me start bawling. "Kate? Talk to me." Those few words had the power to break down the walls I carefully built piece by piece if I would just let them. I could, just lose myself in the warmth of his voice and quiet grin. *Harden your heart and no one gets hurt*, I thought.

"It's not true, what Liz and the others say about you, right?" In an instant, Derek's expression darkened and he dropped his hand from my arm. Already I could feel my heart start to break, but I had to say it before he got any closer to me, before he realized how unworthy I was. "You're not, like, *into* me, right?" I looked up and forced a laugh out into the air that suddenly seemed to drop ten degrees in temperature.

The clouds in his gaze gave way to confusion, and he tilted his head to look at me as if for the first time. "Why do you say it like that?"

I gulped, a ball lodged in my throat. "Like what?"

"Like it's, well, insane." The hurt in his voice damn near broke my resolve.

Another piece of my heart fractured, but it was for his own sake. I was broken, damaged, and Derek deserved someone strong enough to help him hold it together, not fall apart on him when it got hard, not want to run away at the slightest hint of unsettlement. I plastered on a goofy grin and shrugged. "Well, it kind of is, right? I mean, what a pair, right?" I scoffed and gestured across the short distance between him and me.

The doctor's words about stress triggering Derek's episodes resounded in my head. *A little stress now is better than so much worse later when he sees how fucked up I am.* I started to secure the lid on the trash can again before his words hit me. "I don't understand you," he muttered. "You tell me that there's nothing actually wrong with me then turn around and call me insane for wanting to maybe give us a chance at being together. Outside of here, obviously." The longer he spoke, the harder his voice grew. "But all you want is to dangle me on the line like a fish, and when it gets too real for you, you throw me out. You're probably the strongest person I've ever met, but you let your own doubt stand in the way of your happiness. You want to be miserable forever? Fine." He stalked off with the broom, pausing only long enough to put it in the tiny shed next to the door.

I don't know how long I stood there, letting my heart crumble into pieces and knowing it was the right move to make. Derek was wrong. I wasn't strong, far from it. And now he knew that too.

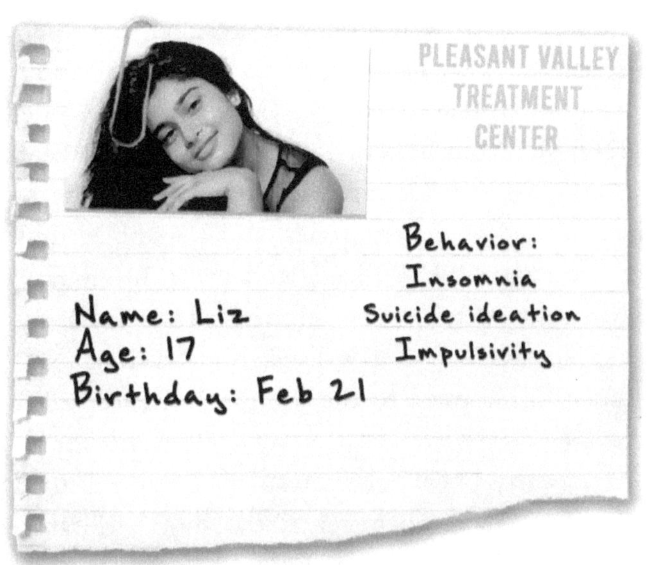

LIZ

"Whoa, there, trouble in paradise?" I quipped, reaching out for Derek's wrist as he passed the table where I was sorting out condiments. He jerked away and kept moving. That was weird. "Yo, Six?" I called after, turning around in my chair to watch him retreat. He didn't even pause. "Ah, hell no." I stalked over to the courtyard door, which was left propped open during cleaning, and pushed it open with more force than was probably necessary, but I didn't care.

"Liz, maybe you shouldn't," Renee started to say, apparently following me, but I held up a hand to stop her.

I couldn't explain why, but white-hot anger coursed through me. *Emotions don't last more than thirty seconds*, I tried reminding myself. But the sight of Kate standing there, not even bothering to turn around to go after Derek, set my blood on fire. "Who in the world do you think you are?"

Kate stiffened at my words. "Go away," she groaned.

"Nuh-uh. Your little sassy princess game may work on everyone else but not on me." In my haste, my sandal caught on one of the flagstones, and I stumbled. If I had been two steps back, I'd have landed flat on my face, but no. My arms stretched out automatically to catch my fall, landing squarely on Kate's back. She cried out and fell forward. We dropped to the ground as Renee yelled our names.

"You crazy bitch!" she screamed. I was still trying to crawl off of Kate when her elbow shot backwards and connected with the side of my head.

"Ow! That's it!" I grabbed a fistful of Kate's hair and pulled hard enough to get her attention away from throwing hands. My head already started throbbing, and I was going to beat her ass if she didn't stop. Her hand clamped over mine, her nails biting into my skin. I let go and scrambled backward.

Kate managed to get to one knee and glared daggers at me through slitted eyes. Her cheeks were the shade of a tomato. "You don't get to attack me after the bullshit you put him through every time you go and do something stupid!"

My mouth opened to retort but no words came out.

"What's going on?" Troy's voice came from the direction of the door. Renee must have called them. Not that I blamed her, but I still had to bite down on the betrayal trying to wind in with my anger.

I got into a crouch and held Kate's gaze. "Difference being, he doesn't love me, so anything I supposedly hurt him with isn't going to do nearly as much damage as anything you do." I swept my hair back and stood, gingerly touching the spot where her elbow hit. "Just an accident, Troy," I said, plastering a placating smirk on my face before I turned to him.

His eyebrows would have disappeared into his hair if he wasn't balding. "Yeah, I believe that like I believe in Santa."

A gasp came from nearby, and we turned to see Renee staring at Troy, horror all over her features.

It was Troy's turn to flush as he stuttered, "You don't really—I mean... You're fourteen."

"So?" Kate challenged. She stepped up and wrapped a hand around Renee's shoulders. "Don't worry, he's just saying that because he was on the naughty list."

"Yeah. Isn't that right, Troy?" I threw in.

For a trained professional, Troy sure looked uncomfortable, and I took perverse pleasure in that. He glanced from Kate to me to Renee again. "Sorry, kid, I was being mean, and that wasn't called for." It wasn't a lie, but he also didn't reassure her. I pursed my lips and looked at Kate, who nodded. "Come on, Ray, I'm in the mood to watch a Christmas movie now, how about you?" I said.

Renee considered it. "Are you two done fighting?" She looked between Kate and me.

"Yeah, we're done."

Troy shook his head and said, "I'm keeping an eye on you," pointing from his eyes to us. He walked away, muttering under his breath something about how impossible girls were.

I followed Renee and Kate inside to the TV and flopped into one of the armchairs. The chairs were insanely comfortable, though it didn't seem like they would be. The backs were super stiff, and the seat curved too deep with a cushion that was too tall. It was a bizarre combination, but it worked. Except for when the cushions would slide out even when sitting on them. That got annoying.

Renee set her book on a chair next to me and left to get the key for the case that held the DVDs. Iesha told me once that the DVDs had to be locked up because someone tried to hurt themselves with one before. I had to admit, that wasn't the dumbest thing I've heard. We crazies can get pretty inventive when we actually want to. Or when the mania tells us to.

Kate cleared her throat. "About earlier, are you, uh, jealous?" She spoke with a hesitation in her voice that I couldn't place. Was *she* jealous? That didn't make sense. Derek was crazy about her and everyone knew it.

"Derek is a sweet guy, but he's not my type, honey." I studied my nails, which I habitually bit to the cuticle. My mom used to scream at me about doing it because it'd ruin my nails, but my therapist said it was a symptom of anxiety. "He's family, though. You all kind of are."

"Oh."

I ran a hand through my hair, grimacing when one of the nails got caught on a tangle. "I didn't mean to shove you earlier. I actually tripped on that stupid piece of -" I snuck a glance over my shoulder to see if any of the staff were nearby. They weren't. "...shit concrete."

"It's okay. I guess I kind of assumed because maybe I deserved it."

A deep breath went in, and a heavy sigh came out of me. "What happened with you two?" I shifted in the chair to face her.

Kate twisted some strands of her hair together, partly

braiding them. "Basically said that I'm too messed up for him."

"Girl, you what?" I held up a hand before she could say anything more. "*All* of us are too messed up. That's what makes our family here functional, better than any of the *dys*functional ones out there. I don't know if you're ever going to find someone else who understands what it's like to feel lost and broken yet still have the capacity to care so much about you." A side of my mouth lifted in a smirk. "I mean, as far as broken goes, you're pretty damn amazing."

Her face turned pink as she smiled. "You are too."

Renee skipped alongside the back of the chairs, a key in her hand. Kate and I exchanged another look. "You're awfully chipper all of a sudden," I said, my voice dripping with skepticism.

"I'm just happy that you worked things out. I don't like it when everyone gets mad." Renee plucked a DVD out of the case and popped it into the player. She spun on her heel to come back to her seat, remote controller in hand.

Kate's eyebrow arched as she studied Renee. "You planned it, didn't you? So, you do know about Santa?"

She scoffed in a manner eerily similar to mine. "Of course I know. I'm fourteen."

I held my hand to my heart dramatically. "We've been scammed!"

"Played!" Kate said.

"Bamboozled!" Renee giggled.

"If you wanted to watch a movie with us, you just had to ask." Kate squeezed Renee's shoulder. "You haven't done something like this before. Is this a side of you we've never seen or are you spending too much time around the Drama Queen here?" She winked at me.

I feigned indignation. "Why, I never! Seriously, Ray, what gives?"

Renee fiddled with the tape on the back of the controller that held the batteries in place. "My family came and they want to move and at first I didn't want to but now we know the police found Rachel's body in the basement of the guy living across the street so I don't want anything to do with that place especially since it's my fault she's gone and I'm scared about leaving and I'm scared of staying-" The words tumbled out of her mouth almost faster than I could keep up. Smart, eloquent Renee, speaking in run-ons. Never thought I'd see the day.

Kate and I, without even thinking, moved to the armrests on either side of Renee and wrapped an arm around her. It did the trick. She broke off mid-sentence and started shaking. We didn't say anything, didn't even try to soothe her. Just let her cry and shake and sniffle. When her tears subsided, she gave a huge sniff. "Thanks, and I'm sorry."

"Stop apologizing for feeling," Kate said, giving her a little jostle.

"Hey, Ray, listen to me." She gave another sniff and looked up at me, tear-streaked face blotchy like it gets with a much-needed cry. "It's not your fault." She opened her mouth to correct me, but I held up a finger. "No, it's not. Don't care what you think, you aren't responsible for anyone but you. What happened to her, all of it, you didn't do to her. That's on the creep who you thankfully managed to avoid."

Kate pushed one of Renee's red curls away from her face. "It's okay to feel sad and to miss her. It's not okay to feel guilty."

Renee nodded slowly and leaned back a little. After a hiccup, she said, "Rachel would have really liked you guys."

I looked up at the sky and said, "Don't worry, Rachel, we'll take care of your little sister."

"*Our* little sister," Kate corrected, patting my arm and smiling.

"Damn straight."

After the movie, Renee wanted to watch another. She turned to Kate and asked, "Can you go get Derek? He's never seen this one and he promised he'd watch it with me."

Kate shifted uncomfortably and noticeably paled. Thankfully, Renee didn't catch it since she was trying to get the tape back onto the controller so the buttons would actually work when she pushed them.

"I'll get him," I offered. "I need to change into my comfy clothes anyway." Renee shrugged while Kate shot me a look that was a mixture of gratitude and relief. No doubt she'd make up some reason to go to her room before I came back with Derek. "Want anything from the room, Ray?"

When she declined, I headed up the hallway to our room. None of the rooms were full of splendor, but ours was pretty homey thanks to my erratic moods and Renee's book obsession. I shed my clothes in favor of some cozy pajamas and went to the door of Derek's room. That made me think of Ciro and hope that he was okay. No one new had come yet to fill that vacancy, and I'd be lying if I said I wanted a new person on the ward.

My knuckles rapped on the wooden door. "Hey, Six, it's

me. Movie night, you in?" The door swung open a sliver. "You decent? Because I'm opening the door." I waited for a couple of seconds before I pushed open the door. "Derek?"

He was perched on the window ledge, watching something outside of the window. When the door bumped against the wall, he turned, a small smile on his lips. A high-pitched, tinny voice that came out of his mouth said, "Derek isn't here right now."

TRISH

Ever since I could remember, I loved it best when my brother laughed. Every time I heard it I'd start giggling in delight. I thought it made Mama happy to hear us that way too. Her smile was almost as good.

Even though I was little, I knew Mama was tired all of the time. She rubbed her eyes a lot and would doze on the couch when she was home from work. I could never remember a daddy. Only Mama, Derek, and me in our little trailer. That is, until we moved in with Grandpa. Then Mama went from tired all the time to scared. She tried to pretend she wasn't, but I knew she was because she didn't doze when we were home from school. Instead, she'd look around and try to keep us quiet. Grandpa didn't bother us, and I couldn't understand why Mama was always so nervous.

It took six months for me to see why. Grandpa started yelling at Derek about little things that Mama would have gently reminded him about. Things like doing the dishes and putting clothes away. But Grandpa screamed at him for it. Mama would run interference, and it would stop for a while.

I didn't get why Grandpa didn't love Derek's laugh as much as Mama and I did. It just seemed to irritate him. He'd call Derek names until he cried then would do it more. Mama started telling us to hide and be as quiet as kittens. I liked that game. I'd pretend to purr and play with string while Derek swatted at my paws.

When we started playing the kitten game, Grandpa got even madder. He'd throw things and yell at Mama instead. He was never that way with me, though. He would always call me "sweet child," and would have me sit on his lap so he could bounce me until I squirmed and giggled.

The longer we lived there, the more attention he paid to me. I thought I was helping because he didn't yell at Derek or throw things at Mama when he was petting my hair, but Derek kept telling me to stay away from him. It did feel kind of weird but at least it was quieter.

The front door opened and the screen door slammed shut. That was what woke me up. Mama stirred next to me so I pretended to still be asleep. She crawled out of the bed to the door. Mama was still dressed in her work outfit, matching faded blue top and bottom that the hospital said she had to wear. She usually fell asleep in it, not wanting to wake us up if she got home from work late.

Someone spoke at the front of the house, but I couldn't hear the words. I opened my eyes and saw Derek staring at me from his cot. He lifted a finger to his mouth to shush me like I was still a dumb kid who needed to be told to be quiet at a time like that. I stuck out my tongue at him. The sliver of light from the door widened as Mama left the room. Derek waited a few moments then crept to the door.

"Dad, are you drunk again?" We could hear Mama's voice from down the hall. Her next words were quieter as she moved further away.

Derek didn't see me walk up behind him, quiet as a mouse. His brown hair was rumpled and sticking up in places from laying in bed. He jumped when I touched his shoulder. "Shh," he hissed. He stuck his head out of the door to see what was happening.

"Don't you talk to me like that, Lucy!" Grandpa's words sounded slurred, but I could have sworn that was what he said.

"Mom's dead," Mama said. She sounded sad. I wanted to give her a hug, so I ducked under Derek's arm and started to walk into the hallway.

"No, Trish," he whispered, grabbing onto my nightgown. I listened and took a step backwards.

"Are they talking about Grandma?" I asked, barely remembering to keep my voice low.

Derek nodded. "Now hush."

"Come on, Dad, let's get you to bed." The floorboard creaked.

"Get off me, you dumb bitch," Grandpa roared. "Trying to keep me from seeing my own kids," he continued loudly. There was a screech of one of the kitchen chairs being dragged.

"Dad," Mama said again, a little stronger. Maybe she figured there was no use keeping her voice down. "I'm not Mom. I'm your daughter. Now let me help you get to your room so that your grandkids don't wake up."

"Too late for that," Derek muttered.

There was another squeal of furniture scraping against wood then a thud against the floor. Derek and I exchanged looks and crept further out to peek around the corner of the hallway to the kitchen.

Mama stood with her hands outstretched towards Grandpa who stood next to a fallen chair.

He had a bottle in one hand. It was one of the big brown ones that usually sat in one of the higher cupboards. I had never seen Grandpa touch it before, but it was nearly empty when he brandished it at Mama.

Mama stepped backwards and turned toward the sink where some of the dishes Derek did earlier were sitting out on a towel to dry. "Here," she said, grabbing one of the cups and turning on the faucet. "Have some water."

Grandpa stepped closer to her. "You were always so beautiful, Lucy." He reached out a hand for her shoulder and Mama froze. "Just like the girls." Grandpa was behind Mama then and wrapped his arms around her.

Derek pushed me back a little so that I couldn't see. "Don't look, Trish," he whispered.

"Why?" I demanded as loudly as I dared, but he turned away and peered around the corner again. I scooted over until I could see just past him.

Mama's voice was like ice when she said, "You get your hands off of me right now."

"Come on, baby girl," Grandpa cooed.

In a flash, Mama pushed him away and held a steak knife up. The bottle crashed to the floor. "Touch me again or either of my kids, and I will end you."

He backed away slowly, his face twisted in rage. "You can't keep me away from them," he snarled. "They can't help it, just like you."

Mama turned toward the hall where we stood. At the same time, Grandpa bent and snatched up the broken bottle and slammed it over Mama's head. She crumpled like a sheet from the washing line. A scream shot through the air, but I couldn't tell if it came from Derek or me. Grandpa's gaze fell on us, and he smiled so sweetly that I almost believed I was having a nightmare.

Then Derek's hand was around my wrist, tugging me back to the bedroom. He slammed the door and grabbed Mama's phone from the nightstand next to the bed. I stood near the closet, unable to think or move. All I could see was Mama's body going down. I could hear Derek's voice nearby, but the room was dark without the door cracked.

"My grandpa just attacked my mom, and my little sister and I are still in the house. I don't know if he's going to come after us."

"Dawn, baby, where are you?" Grandpa's voice was muffled through the wall.

Once again, Derek pulled on my arm. "He's drunk, and I think he's out of it. He kept confusing my mom for his wife and now us for my mom." Derek kept his voice low even as he opened the closet door and pushed me in.

Dark, dark, double dark. Darkness in the room and in the closet and no light to see anything. The closet had horizontal slats that stacked up to form the door. My eyes could just barely see through them to make out Derek's head by the light of the cell phone.

"I have to go, I'm giving the phone to my sister, Trish." He passed it to me then shut the door.

The man on the phone told me to stay calm. He said the police would be there soon. I guess he could hear my breathing because he kept talking.

I couldn't see Derek in the darkness of the room. Everything was quiet except for the footsteps in the hall. I licked my lips, not even listening to the man on the phone anymore. The footsteps stopped. My heart thudded so loudly I was sure hiding in the closet would do absolutely no good because Grandpa was bound to hear my heart as soon as he walked in.

The door opened, letting in the sliver of light again. Derek was nowhere to be seen. Grandpa walked inside, the light casting a long shadow in the room. He walked to the bed and sat down, humming quietly. Then he pulled back the covers.

"Where are you, Dawn?" he called, the words slurring together.

I clamped a hand over my mouth to cover the sound of my breathing.

"You know you can't hide, baby." He laughed and stood up. His body swayed a little, but he managed to stay on his feet. Then he turned and it seemed as though his eyes locked dead onto mine. But he turned to the corner instead and swung his head around as though playing a game of hide and seek.

When I blinked, the light was completely blocked out, Grandpa's form standing right in front of the closet door.

A yell burst out in the room. Grandpa stumbled and it looked like he was going to fall. Instead he rounded on Derek, cursing without any of the words actually making sense. Grandpa threw Derek onto the bed then growled as one of Derek's feet connected with Grandpa's stomach.

"Enough out of you, boy," he spat. He reached out, a hand closing around Derek's neck. My big brother looked so tiny compared to the man. Derek scratched at Grandpa's arms and hands.

The phone fell to the floor as I stood up and pushed open the door. "Stop," I said, barely able to get the word out. "Stop," I said louder, more desperate. "Please, don't hurt him anymore!"

Grandpa paused and straightened, releasing Derek who started coughing. What was left of Grandpa's hair was mussed up, and he was breathing hard. "Shame on you for hiding," he said in a way that was almost teasing even though he frowned.

I ducked my head. "Will you leave Derek alone?" I asked, peeking up towards Grandpa's towering form. Wet streaks fell from my eyes.

His smile finally returned, and he tucked his hand under my chin, lifting my head to look at him. "Let's go play a game," he said. He took my hand and started to lead me out of the room. I looked back to where Derek lay.

He raised an arm and his head and rasped, "No, Trish!" before his head fell. He didn't move. All I wanted was to hear him laugh again.

Even though I didn't make it out alive that night, I still got to watch Derek grow up. He kept me with him. He kept both of us with him... When Derek got too worked up, I took control, preventing *him* from coming out as much as I could.

I couldn't protect Derek from everything, though, as much as I wanted to. He suffered so much after that night, harbored so much guilt and anger. It broke him in ways that no one could make go away. But every time Derek laughed, it made the part of him that was me giggle uncontrollably, just like we used to do.

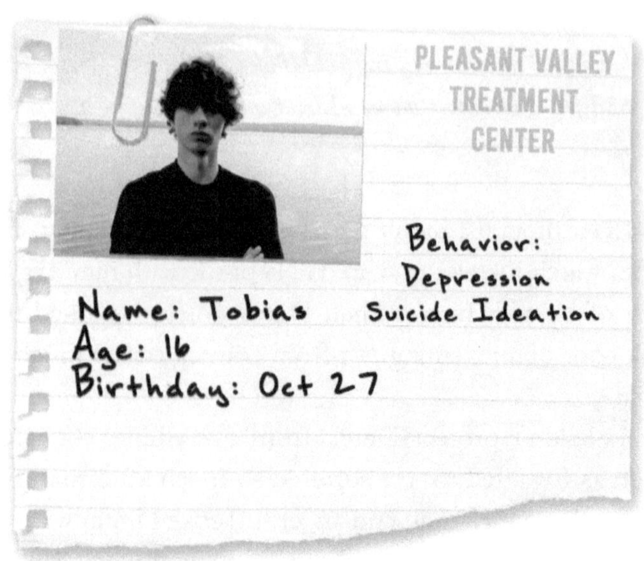

TOBIAS

"It's been two days already. Hasn't he usually, I don't know, recovered by now?" I paced from the window to the door and back again. Matthew lay back on his bed, staring at the ceiling. Two kinds of people, I guess.

Matthew grunted. "Far as I know, I think so. Kate said she overheard Doc telling the staff that stress makes it worse, and she thinks her rejecting Derek's idea that they could get together triggered it."

I stopped pacing and made a sound that was a cross between a laugh and a scoff. "That's pretty egoist, isn't it?"

Sitting up, he shrugged. "I think you mean egotist, but who knows? It's not like any of this comes with a walkthrough." His legs swung off to the side of the bed, and he leaned back, using his arms for support. It was Sunday, which meant group therapies had ended for the day already, leaving the afternoon for us to pass however we wanted. Matthew looked out toward the window. "Think there's anything we can do to help him? Or is it them?"

My mouth twitched in a small grin but it faded quick. "Man, I don't know," I sighed. "I think that whatever could be done to help is what the staff is probably already trying." We lapsed into silence, and I glanced around the room, desperate for any kind of inspiration. My side of the room had filled out some in the few weeks I'd been a patient. Sometimes it felt like so much longer than that. My cousin Miranda had visited a couple of times and brought me some things when I asked, like a duffel bag of clothes. The bag itself had to be kept locked up because of the strap on it, but my clothes sat out on the shelves. A few sets of jeans, some basketball shorts, and a pile of shirts were stacked on one shelf. My favorite hoodie lay over the back of the desk chair. Another shelf held the welcome bag contents with the notebook and a couple of workbooks.

There was a knock on the door, and Kal popped his head. I nodded at him in greeting, which he returned. "You've got a visitor, Tobias."

"What?" I said in surprise. Miranda came last week and hadn't given any indication she'd be coming back. She was older than me by about five years, and, while she didn't ever say she minded bringing me something if I needed it, I knew the hospital made her uncomfortable.

"She's waiting for you in the visitor room," Kal said. "Should I tell her to go away?"

"Uh, no, I'll be there in a second." I turned to Matthew and added, "Well, I guess I better go see what she wants."

He gave me a thumbs up and stood to walk with me out to the common rooms. "I'll see if anyone's learned anything new about Derek," he said, though there was a definite note of doubt in his voice.

I patted his shoulder but said nothing. There wasn't anything I could say that wouldn't either be a bold-faced lie or just fall flat. And we'd already been through too much for either of those to work.

Matthew allowed a grim nod and broke off to join Liz and James outside while I continued on to the small room where my visitor awaited me. My hand hesitated when I reached the door. A feeling of apprehension crawled over my neck, and I halfway considered changing my mind and telling Kal I didn't want to see her after all. But, family was family. Still, even as I thought about it, Michelle's words about not being obligated because of blood echoed in my head.

None of that was helping me get any closer to opening the door, though. So I sighed, steeled myself, pulled down on the lever handle with one hand and pushed with the other.

The door dragged on the carpet some. I knew the room to be crowded with furniture, so I focused on not hitting my foot on anything as I stepped inside. The weighted door started to fall back into its frame by the time I looked up, and if I hadn't been so stunned, I'd have made a grab for it.

A girl who was definitely not my cousin sat on the couch against the opposite wall, one leg crossed over the other and arms folded across her chest. She wore black leggings and a beige sweater that complimented her skin, which reminded me of the toffee Mary used to make for us. The effect was ruined by the heavy makeup surrounding her hazel eyes. She'd always been a natural beauty, and it irked me that someone convinced her to start covering it.

It took a second for me to realize I probably looked stupid the way I was staring. I lifted my head and met her eyes. "You shouldn't be here, Tori," I said then turned to grab the door handle again.

"Tobi, wait," she said. "Please."

Against better judgment, something in her voice stopped me. A heaviness settled over me at the use of my nickname, and I suddenly felt a wave of tiredness hit me like a train. Nothing like having to face one of your demons while mid-treatment.

I turned around. "Five minutes," I said, knowing full well I had no way of telling time in there, "and then I'm out."

Tori nodded, her dark braids shifting with the motion. She watched as I took a seat in the armchair then she dropped her eyes to her lap. Her leg uncrossed and the other crossed over instead. Still, she didn't speak or look at me.

"So... What are you doing here?" I finally said. I almost regretted the coldness of my voice. Almost.

She licked her lips then reached over to pick up her bag. It was a black miniature backpack. Tori unzipped the main pocket and pulled out a couple of folded pieces of paper. She fiddled with them as though she wanted to open the papers but thought better of it. "There's this letter," she said then trailed off. I expected her to hand it to me but she didn't.

"And?" I prompted, starting to feel like her visit was a waste of time. It was all I could do to keep my voice steady. The anger and hurt that drove me past the point of return started bubbling to the surface again. Just the sight of her filled me with longing and pain and so many memories from over the years.

Playing cops and robbers on bikes that Miles, Milo, and I either scrounged up or rebuilt with spare parts from the neighbor's scrap heap. Trying a cigarette for the first time, and last time for me. That first kiss with Tori, back when she was just as tall as me. And the last kiss too, her head tilted up to meet mine.

The balloon of anger inside me deflated. Being mad wasn't going to change the past, the good or the bad parts of it.

"Tor," I said without bothering to conceal the exhaustion I was feeling, "What's going on?" I slumped back in the armchair, the fake leather squeaking as I moved.

She finally looked up, eyes brimming with tears. "I'm so sorry, Tobi," she squeaked before curling over and letting the sobs consume her.

Now that was not what I was expecting. Tori had cried before in front of me. Skinned knees and the cat she took in dying, things like that had set her off before, but not like this. The papers were still in her hand, and I reached out to grab them, all the while fighting the urge to go over and comfort her. I unfolded the first paper which looked like it'd already been opened and refolded a few dozen times and started to read.

Tori -

I'm sorry. Just sorry. I'm a sorry sack of crap who screwed over my two best friends when I thought I was protecting you and Tobias. I messed up and I'm going to try to make things right. There's a decent chunk of change in my spot. You know the one. Take it and get out of here. Get away from this town and be safe. Give Tobias this letter before you go if you can.

There was no signature, but I knew the scratchy scrawl that belonged to Miles. Confused didn't even begin to describe my mental state. I put Tori's letter on the squat coffee table and opened the other paper, ripping some tape off of it. It turned out to be two pieces with the same messy handwriting.

Tobias -

Buddy I owe you the biggest explanation and apology ever. No matter how many times you warned me I didn't listen and it screwed everything up worse than ever. About six months ago I started running for Tori's Uncle Robbie, the one we never really believed was her uncle. It was just to get cash to fix my car but then he kept bugging me to do more jobs for him. When I told him no he said he was going to start making Tori whore to make up for the cash loss, and when I said you and I would never let that happen, he started saying he could make you just disappear. And I believed him man, I'm so sorry but I did.

That night with Tori, it wasn't what you think. Her uncle came to me and said I needed to distract her so he could get some product out of the house. "Fuck her for all I care, unless you want me to," he said. I was scared man. I tried to get Tori to just come with me out of the house, but she wouldn't. So I said we should do a drinking game and we did and I dunno, that party at Leila's came to mind where we uh, you know, and I was freaking out and then I was kissing Tori. I think I told her about the party, maybe out of spite or fear I don't know. She started kissing back and...

The next day I wanted to tell you and I was going to but Robbie found me first. He gave me a cut of cash and told me to keep my mouth shut. I don't know how he knew what I was trying to do. But I was terrified of all of it. Then you found out anyway. When you disappeared, I thought Robbie got to you. I never let Tori out of my sight for three days until we saw your cousin leaving your place and she told us what happened. Tori lost it right there but I wasn't far behind.

I finally realized this was all because of my decisions, and I know what I need to do now to balance the scales. I'm going to the rally in Applewood tomorrow night and letting the judgment of the people figure it out. I'm giving Tori money to get out of here, and I would for you too but I don't know how long they're going to keep you there. When you do get out, don't go home. That place doesn't deserve you.

You're the family I never thought I'd have. I love you both.
Miles Bofant

I stared at the letter and tried to process what I just read. Tori's sobs had quieted to sniffles, and she pulled her legs up on the couch, wrapping her arms around them. When I looked up at her, she seemed so small.

"I didn't read yours," she said so softly that I almost missed it. "He insisted that you needed to see it first and you'd decide if I needed to see it."

I glanced down at the other paper in my hand. It was a list of dates and numbers, but I didn't try to decipher it. I folded the two papers and put them in my hoodie pocket. "You don't want to. Not yet, anyway," I said. "So, where is he? It said he was going to Applewood, but that was it."

Tori closed her eyes for a long minute, and I was afraid she would start bawling again before she answered. When she finally did speak, her voice was quiet and laced with pain. "He did go. You know how it goes with those rallies these days. I think he was counting on it turning into a riot. Milo went with him but said they got separated at one point. He saw Miles make a rush for someone pointing a gun at another kid. Miles got the gun away from the guy, but the police didn't see what happened and they..." She trailed off, face twisted in grief. Tori took a quick breath to continue, but the pit in my stomach told me what she was about to say. "They shot him."

I saw it coming and still couldn't prepare myself for it. Everything suddenly felt distant and echo-y as my brain scrambled to put all the pieces together between the letters and what Tori was saying. Nothing made sense, but all of it did. He was such an idiot! And so was I. If I hadn't been so self-involved, maybe I would have noticed that he was acting strange, especially when it came to money. Though he'd always been weird about money, so I guess maybe I didn't think it was any different. My thoughts raced and all the while, Tori sat curled up on the couch like the little kid she'd been when we met.

She cried again, and I mentally hit myself for being such an asshole. I walked around to sit on the couch next to her and rested my hand on her shoulder carefully. Whatever was or wasn't going on with her and Miles, our best friend was... Was he alive still? I somehow doubted it. After another moment, Tori leaned against me, and I adjusted my arm to fit around her shoulder and just held her.

Her sobs came out harder and she buried her head, choking out the words, "I'm so sorry. I shouldn't have, we shouldn't. I love you, and I'm sorry."

Though my heart still ached, it wouldn't do any good to say something about that. So I didn't. I just held her and let her cry as tears stung my own eyes.

Tori's breathing eventually turned into little hiccups then evened out into shaky recovery breaths. My jaw hurt from clenching, and I tried to force myself to relax, but it didn't work very well.

"I can understand if you don't ever forgive me, but I had to tell you about him. It wasn't something that could wait." She fiddled with the sleeve of her sweater while still leaning up against me.

In that moment, I knew I wouldn't hate her, couldn't hate her. Forgive might be a hard stretch right now, but it was an eventual possibility. For her, not for myself. I'd never forgive myself for being so stupid and selfish that I couldn't see what was going on with Miles. "I know," I said quietly. "Thanks for telling me." It sounded lame and formal after all that we'd gone through together, but it's all I could come up with. "What are you going to do now? Are you going to leave town?"

Tori shifted to the side just enough to be able to look up at me. With a slight hesitation, she took my hand. "Do you think I should?"

I squeezed her hand gently. When I pulled away, she didn't fight, but I could see the hurt in her eyes. "Yeah," I murmured, thinking about her uncle. Without Miles or me there to protect her, there was no telling what he or someone else might try to get her to do. "I don't think home is safe for you anymore right now. Take the money he gave you and get out of here." She started to shake her head, and I knew what she was about to say. "No, don't try to tell me you're not strong or brave enough or what the hell other kind of lame ass excuse you're going to use."

She turned away, withdrawing into herself again.

"Tor," I said and put a little force behind her name so that she would look up again. "You are better than this place. You're stronger than you think. Remember what you told me when we were kids? At the park when that one kid tried taking away your juice and I got it back from him. What did you say to me?"

She allowed just the tiniest shadow of a smile. "I don't need anyone protecting me."

I grinned and nodded. "That's right." Even though I never listened, I knew she could handle herself too, for the most part. My grin faded. "Same holds true now. You don't need Miles or me with you to get started new somewhere else away from all this."

Tori's shoulders straightened a fraction. She took a steadying breath. "You're the best at this, you know," she said. Without warning, she turned back to face me and threw her arms around me in a fierce hug. "I love you," she whispered.

I automatically returned the hug and the words out of reflex and maybe meant it too. There was nothing more to say. She pulled away, grabbed her backpack and her letter and left, only struggling a little with the heavy door.

She'd leave town, I knew that much. Maybe she'd come back someday, but I kind of hoped, for her sake, that she'd never even look back.

My eyes drifted to the two remaining papers. I needed to talk to Riley.

I had to wait to see Riley since she was in a session with someone else. To avoid having to talk about the bomb just dropped on me with anyone else, I asked Kal for some time in the panic room behind the desk. He looked skeptical at first but I guess the expression on my face must have told him I needed it because he relented.

The panic room was just what some of us called it. It was really a small room that was probably once an office or something at one point and was converted by placing a spare mattress on the floor for us to go have a place to chill out if we needed time alone and weren't going to hurt ourselves or someone else. My mind briefly flashed to when the nurses put Liz into the isolation room. Despite the heat of embarrassment on the back of my neck, I was still glad she hadn't been tranquilized like some kind of rabid animal.

Plastic on the mattress peeled in places, but the springs were still decent. I sat down with my back against the wall and tried to stop thinking for a minute. More than ever, I missed having music to lose myself in. There wasn't any helping that, though, and I tried instead to focus on my breathing. It was no use.

I pulled the two papers out of my hoodie pocket. Instead of rereading the letter, I took a look at the second sheet. I couldn't tell for sure, but it seemed like a ledger of some kind. There were dates and locations, and numbers that kind of looked like money but without the dollar sign indicator.

Some of the words were hard to read. I peered at them in the dim light of the panic room and realized the words weren't actually true words. There was a pattern in them, though, that felt vaguely familiar. I reached into my hoodie again, hoping one of my pens was still in there but no luck. "Damn," I muttered, "Of all the times..." I started trying to work it out in my head, but it was still swimming with all that happened during Tori's visit.

Defeated for the moment, I returned the papers to my pocket, leaned my head against the wall and closed my eyes.

"Catch!" I turned around to feel a blast of cold snow hit the front of my shoulder. Miles and Milo laughed from a few feet away. They split up, Miles in his raggy black coat ducking behind his mom's car and Milo taking off across the street.

"You're dead!" I called out, a stupid grin on my face. My bare

hands dug into the powder on the ground, not even caring about the stinging that came with it. I shaped a ball with my hand and took off in a crouch run. I cut across as though I was going to get Milo. He ducked like I had already thrown the snowball, but I waved him down and told him to follow me to get Miles twice over.

Milo's grin was even goofier than mine with a gap between his front teeth where one of them hadn't come in yet. He nodded and grabbed his own ball of snow. We flanked the car Miles was hiding behind. Milo sprung up from the direction I should have come from.

"Traitor!" Miles shrieked and turned only to get a facefull of snow from me. He spluttered from it, and I took off, laughing hard.

My breath came out in puffs as I raced across the snowy ground, not even worried about any ice patches. When I got to the pond, I paused and tried to think quick. A small snowbank, big enough for me to hide behind sat part of the way out. I glanced behind but knew I only had a few moments left before they caught up to me. Shedding my jacket, I tossed it behind the snowbank, just enough to let some of it stick out. I retreated to a nearby tree, careful to choose one large enough to hide behind.

Sure enough, a few moments later, the other two came up. Milo paused a ways away from the pond's start, but Miles kept going a few steps before he turned to Milo. "Come on," he said. I peeked around the tree to see him pointing at the other side of the snowbank, trying to get Milo to flank it like he'd helped me do to Miles at the car.

"No way. That ice is stupid thin. You're an idiot if you think it'll hold both of you."

Miles waved a hand. "Whatever, you're just chicken." He turned back to the snowbank and started trying to tip-toe out there, but his shoes crunched on the clean snow so loudly that I could hear it from my hiding spot. Miles reached down to grab a chunk of snow and took two quick steps to get to my abandoned jacket.

A look of total confusion came over his face. I jumped out from behind the tree and started laughing. "Ha-ha!" I yelled. "Got you!"

Miles looked up in my direction and scowled. "You suck," he called out. He took another few steps and stopped at a cracking sound. Panic hit him. He tried to run and jump clear, but the ice broke beneath one leg and he went down.

"Miles!" I screamed. I think Milo did too. I raced down to the now not-so-frozen pond and couldn't see Miles on the surface. My eyes stayed locked on the hole in the ice as I called out to Milo to go call 911, to get someone to help, anyone. I eased out onto the ice and got to my hands and knees as I neared the hole. I still couldn't see him.

"Miles," I called again, desperation making my voice shrill. The ambulance would take too long to get here and by then Miles might be gone. I took a deep breath and dove in.

The water felt like a hundred bug bites on bruises. Forcing my eyes open, I glanced around the somewhat murky water to see my friend a couple of feet away. I grabbed him by the jacket and yanked as hard as I could back to the opening. It was like moving through molasses. I thought we wouldn't make it. My lungs burned with the need for air as water filled my nostrils.

Then my hand broke the water's surface. I scrambled to get my head out for air. Everything in me screamed to get out of the water, but I couldn't yet. I ducked back in and pulled Miles to the top. His clothes were waterlogged and weighed a million pounds. It was all I could do to tread water and keep Miles from going under again. I tried to lift him up, but my arms screamed in protest. I couldn't even hold him up far enough to hit his back. I had to hold onto the ledge with one arm and the other hooked under his. Cold air blew over the pond, sending stabbing shivers through me.

"Miles! Tobias!" voices called out, and they were the most beautiful sound I've ever heard in my life.

"Here," I tried to say, but it came out like a squeak.

"It was over here," Milo said, his voice getting louder.

A grunt answered him, and the next words almost made me wish I hadn't come out from under the water at all. "Idiot boy," a voice growled. I was facing away from the shoreline, but I knew my father's voice anywhere. His words hit harder than the ice. There was the sound of crunching snow again as my old man carefully made his way out to us. At the first sign of cracking, I knew we'd be on our own again. There it was. I waited for the footsteps to back away, but next thing I knew, the weight on my arm was lifted as Miles was dragged from the water. "You went after him, you get yourself out," my old man said.

Teeth chattering, muscles aching where I could still feel them, I shifted around the hole until I was facing the shore. I tried to lift my body out, but I was spent.

"Help him!" a girl cried. It might have been Mary.

I tried again to lift myself, managing to get my elbows nearly straight, but the rest of my body was too cold to respond. Milo appeared in front of me, reaching out for my hand. When I gave it to him, he pulled hard enough to drag my torso out, scraping along the icy edge through my shirt. When my knee hit the ledge, I propelled forward and almost knocked Milo to the ground. I landed on my stomach, snow mixing with the pond water to form a slush around my body. A freezing slush.

"We need to get to shore," he said, but he didn't leave my side when I couldn't move. I heard a zipping sound then felt the fabric against my body as Miles attempted to put his coat on me. "You're an idiot," Milo said, but in a way as opposite as possible as my old man, full of wonder. "And you saved his life."

"Then you saved mine," I wanted to say, but the fatigue took over.

By the time Riley opened the door, I had cried myself out. My eyes hurt like hell, and my body felt like I ran a marathon even though I never moved from the spot.

Riley left the light off mercifully, leaving the dim afternoon sunlight to come through the long window near the ceiling. "Hey," she said. I lifted a hand to acknowledge her, and she asked, "Mind if I sit with you?"

Even though that was exactly what I wanted, something kept me from verbalizing it. So I shrugged instead.

She settled in on the mattress several inches from me, giving me plenty of space to myself. Her soft eyes studied me, but she didn't push for an explanation. There was pain there, like it hurt her to see me like that, and I turned my head away in shame. When I spoke, my voice was rough and dry, like all the water in my body came out from my eyes earlier and left none for my mouth. "Tori came by. Miles was shot." The dullness of my words didn't remotely convey the world of hurt in my heart.

"I'm so sorry," Riley said, sounding like she meant it. "Is he going to make it?"

Shrugging again, I handed her the papers. She took them and scanned through the letter. I thought she'd set aside the other one like I had, but she studied that one with a strange intensity. When she started chewing on her bottom lip, I knew something was up. In the short time I knew her, Riley had always been cool and collected, sympathetic and empathetic, but never so outright worried.

"What is it?" I asked after a long moment when she didn't offer an explanation.

"Do you know what this is?" Her eyes didn't leave the paper.

"A list," I said in a tone that conveyed how obvious I thought that was.

"No." Riley looked up and gave a little laugh. "Well, yes.

But specifically, I think it's a ledger. I think Miles may have given you something very powerful here that he entrusts to you."

Something stirred in my core, and I felt a little energy return at the curiosity that ran through me. "Do you know what it says?" I asked as I leaned over to look again.

Riley shook her head. "Just the numbers, obviously. But, if you know or can figure out the rest..." She trailed off, conflict raging across her face. "Tobias," she started again, and I looked up at her. "You're still underage, and this could indicate your complicity in a crime. It can also exonerate you, since the letter indicates that you didn't know." Her gaze was intense, and I got the feeling that she was trying to tell me something that my brain wasn't comprehending in my deadened state.

"Oh," I said in that genius way I have.

Riley held out the papers to me. "I'm truly sorry about your friend," she said somberly, the intensity replaced by something gentle.

My throat started closing up again as I fought another wave of grief. I nodded as I grabbed the letter and its ledger. "Thanks," I managed to say. "I've been thinking about the day at the pond again." I studied my fingertips, picking at a hangnail. I told her about it after my freakout with the washcloth during group, so I knew I wouldn't have to go all into it. Not all of it, but the general idea. I was pretty sure my old man would get arrested if I went into detail. Then again, maybe not. Social services was weird that way.

"Do you think that memory is significant to what you learned today about Miles?" Riley asked. She propped one elbow on her knee and held her head to look at me thoughtfully.

"I don't think so. It was years ago, but I guess maybe if I hadn't been so stupidly selfish, he wouldn't have gone to Applewood. If I had thought to look at what he was going through instead of my own drama, maybe he would have told me what was going on and we could have figured something out. Why didn't he say something?" Without thinking, my hand farthest from Riley lashed out to the side and slammed against the wall.

Angry tears welled in my eyes that had nothing to do with the throb starting. "Why couldn't he just have told me before?" I groaned.

Riley, for her part, managed to not even flinch. Maybe she was too surprised. Maybe she was expecting it. But she said, "Can I give you a hug?"

Stupid question. Who asks that? I nodded.

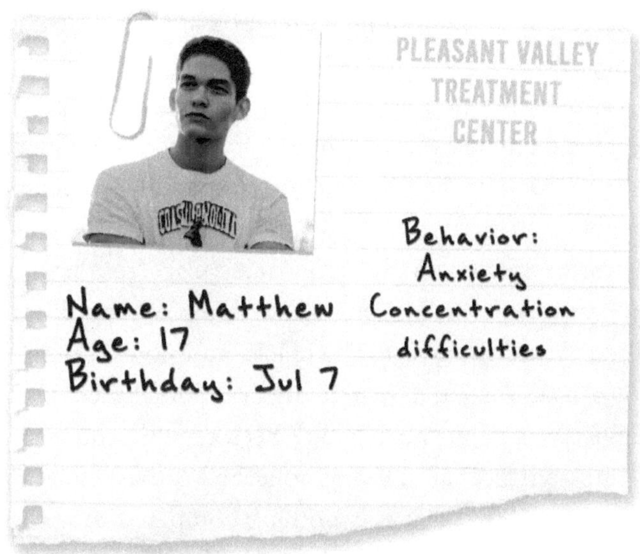

MATTHEW

There's nothing in the world worse than feeling helpless. For all the healing that was supposed to happen in this place, there was a hell of a lot of hurt going on too. We were going on day three of Derek in what the staff was calling his "alter" state, where another personality took over. After seeing it in action, I wondered how in the hell the doctors confused his condition for schizophrenia before.

Then there was Renee who was trying to deal with losing her sister and her childhood home all at once. And Tobias too, with what happened to his buddy. He showed me the letter after he was done talking to Riley that afternoon and relayed what she'd said about the note with the numbers being important. I had my own suspicions about what it meant, but he didn't look at all ready to hear it last night.

Tapping my pen against the notebook in front of me didn't yield any inspiration on how to present my biography without sounding like a total tool, especially compared to the others. With a sigh, I got out of the iron chair in the courtyard, which was the only quiet place to think while yoga was going on. I stretched my arms overhead, leaning to the left and listened to the cracks and pops. After I held it for a little longer, I switched sides. Sometimes my body felt twice its age. Football hadn't been exactly kind to it.

I missed football. Playing volleyball or basketball in the gym wasn't bad, but it was nothing compared to being out on the field, pads on, with the adrenaline pumping. In the ten years of playing, I was pretty lucky. The worst injury I took was a broken clavicle. My mom actually tried telling me not to play any more after that, but I wouldn't listen.

I stared down at the words on the page without actually reading them. Sharing this in group was going to be a disaster.

The door opened, spilling out Kate and Liz who jostled past playfully. "Hey, Stardew!" she called out, waving at me.

My hand lifted up in greeting, but I had no idea what she was talking about. She saw the confusion on my face, traded glances with Kate, and they both burst out in laughter.

"You're the star of the team and your name is Matthew," Kate explained, still smiling. Her hair was loose except for a small section pulled up and fastened at the back. It was a new style for her, and it worked.

I grinned and said to Liz, "Ahh, you're back to doling out the nicknames."

"Never stopped." She winked. I don't know how she did it, but the girl managed to flit between challenger and accessory in moments.

The courtyard door opened again, letting through the sounds of music briefly before Tobias let the door fall shut behind him. He wore a grim, determined smile as he approached. He swiped his hand through the messy mop he called hair and glanced around at the three of us.

"Compared to yesterday, you're looking awfully chipper," Liz said, shifting to allow for Tobias to stand next to her.

"I think I might know of something to try to reach Derek," he said.

That got our attention. Kate reddened, but I think we all pretended not to notice. "How?" I asked.

Tobias withdrew the paper that was now almost falling apart at the side from how many times he must have folded and unfolded it already. "Letters," he said as though it was the most obvious thing in the world.

"You're going to have to explain a little more than that, my guy," Liz said, but there was no trace of her usual snark. "What's the point of writing to Derek when he's not actually, well, fully present?"

"Just that," Tobias said. "You said yourself that he was sometimes aware of when the Trish personality took control. Even if she's the one physically reading them, it's still Derek, and his primary self could process it."

Liz seemed to consider it and started nodding. "I guess that would make sense. If he can actually tell what's going on. It could be kind of like a manic episode where he doesn't even realize what's happening until after it's over, though. And maybe his brain just fills in the holes."

Tobias's smile faltered. "I didn't think of it that way," he said. His gaze dropped to the ground.

"Does it hurt to try?" Kate finally said. She wouldn't look at anyone. "I just, I mean, does it? Whether it's a split of his or not, they're all still actually him, aren't they?" She shrugged and added, "I don't know much about this, so feel free to ignore me." When she finally looked up, it hit me how sunken her eyes were, like she had been sleeping even less than usual.

"Kate's right," I said. "We can still try it." She tossed a grateful smile to me as the other two nodded and agreed.

The door opened for a third time, and Iesha popped her head out. "Come on, ladies and gents. It's time for the next group," she called out in a sing-song voice.

I groaned and picked up my notebook from the table while Liz and Tobias headed inside. Kate lagged behind, waiting for me. "Thanks for backing me up there. I didn't really know what I was talking about but it made sense." She let out a nervous chuckle.

I shrugged and replied. "Made sense to me too. Easy as that." I lowered my voice a notch and said, "Are you okay? Are you sleeping?"

Kate's eyes widened in surprise. Her mouth started to form the words to deny it, but a look of resignation took over instead. "No," she admitted. "I haven't gotten much sleep the last few days." She started chewing on her bottom lip.

We reached the door, and she held it open for me. I stepped over the threshold then to the side. I put my notebook on one of the tables, flipped to the back and ripped out a couple of blank pages as neatly as I could. I turned to Kate and handed the pages to her. "Write your letter. Even if you don't give it to him, maybe it'll help you."

She took the pages from me. "Thanks," she whispered. At normal volume, she said, "Wait, isn't it your turn to read today?"

"Don't remind me," I groaned.

"Don't sweat it," she said with a small smile. "It'll be fine."

"That's why you've read yours, right?" I teased then mentally kicked myself. "That was rude. Sorry."

Kate's expression didn't change, though. "You're stronger than me," she said simply. "I might be ready next week, but who knows? And you're right. It's not fair of me to tell you not to sweat it when I haven't done it yet."

"You're strong too, or you wouldn't still be standing here dealing with my dumb ass," I said. I cracked a grin.

"Yeah, I guess you've got me there, Stardew," she said then stuck her tongue out at me.

We headed to the room where our therapy class would take place. I glanced at the clock as we passed the nurse's station, even though I already knew the time. Two more hours, and then I'd be exposing what a fake I am.

I didn't want to go into the private group room. I didn't want to read. I didn't want to let the people who I'd come to respect and trust know that whatever of the same that they placed in me was fake.

This was going to be the worst. Michelle told me that I didn't have to share in group if I didn't want to, and I kind of wish she hadn't because that gave me an out. Maybe I wouldn't share. Maybe I'd put it off like Kate did. I tried to remind myself to breathe, but it didn't work.

A movement at the corner of my eyes made me turn to see James approaching from the direction of Dr. Larson's office. He gave me a shy smile when he realized I saw him. I couldn't help but return it. I thought he was pretty chill before and now that he started talking, he was proving that assessment right.

"What's up?" he asked. He stopped beside me and crouched to reach into the snack cabinet.

We were in the kitchenette area, and I was stalling. I still had a few minutes of the break before group started. "Not much, how's it going?" I answered automatically.

The cabinet door swung closed as James stood. A crinkling sound told me he found a snack. That was surprising since we wouldn't get our refill cart until tomorrow. Twice a week, a cart of snacks and treats was delivered on the ward for us to put away in our cabinets. The Doritos and Oreos disappeared within a day, leaving the granola bars and generic brand chips to last us until the next refill.

"Want one?" James asked, offering up a blue package as he leaned with his back against the counter like I was.

"Where were you hiding this?" I laughed, taking one of the Oreos.

A sly grin crossed his face, complete with mischief in his eyes.

"Okay, keep your secrets." I crunched into the cookie and gave a happy sigh. "Thanks," I said through a mouthful.

"Looked like you needed it," he said. "You okay?"

"Eh." I held up my notebook, still chewing.

"Ah, you're reading?"

I nodded. James didn't really go to that group. He

wasn't required to and usually opted to find something else to do, and I wished again that I didn't have to either.

"Renee read me hers. You guys are incredible for putting all that down and then telling basically strangers about it. But I think it's probably helpful. Here, anyway. You guys get it, even when you don't." He popped one of his own Oreos in his mouth when I turned to stare at him. He shifted from one foot to the other and looked away.

It took me a moment longer to realize he was uncomfortable and I tore my gaze away from him to look out at the mostly empty room. The staff desk was on the opposite side from where we stood, but Troy was on the phone and not paying attention to us. "You get it, even when you don't," I repeated. I don't know what it was about his words, but the flipping in my stomach settled to some random somersaults. I cast a sidelong glance at James who fidgeted with the Oreos wrapper. "That's some golden wisdom right there, man. Thanks."

He nodded and I think looked a little pleased.

"Yo, Stardew, you ready?" Liz called. She stood at the doorway of the group room, one hand on her silk-swathed hip.

"Stardew?" James asked, grinning again.

"Long story," I muttered to him. "Yeah," I said loud enough for Liz to hear. "I think I am."

I pushed off the counter and headed to the group room. The fear still sat heavy on my heart, but James' words gave me hope that just maybe the people I was about to share with, they might just get it.

Tobias waved as I entered. I took the seat next to him. Kate sat in one corner while Renee and Liz camped out near the window. Bullfrog had the seat next to the door claimed, and Michelle was perched in a chair about halfway along the wall. She gave me an encouraging nod in greeting before asking Bullfrog to close the door then started check-in, beginning with Kate. After Renee and Liz, it was my turn.

"Safe. Nervous," I reported. My leg started bouncing as if to agree.

"Safe," Tobias said. He clasped a hand on my shoulder. I glanced at him but he was looking at Michelle. "Supportive," he added then withdrew.

To my surprise, Bullfrog repeated Tobias. I gave them both a grateful half-smile.

Michelle went over the group rules. I tuned her out, using the time to breathe and mentally ready myself for what was about to come out of my mouth. Palms sweaty, knees weak, arms are heavy. I ran through the lyrics of Eminem's song in my head.

"Ready to start?" Michelle finally asked.

He's nervous but on the surface he looks calm and ready... I licked my lips and nodded.

"I was born in Applewood. Only child to a criminal law attorney and the director of the humane society." The words tasted bitter in my mouth even as I spoke. "My dad likes to say I picked up a football at three and never put it down. He was a star receiver when he played and could have made it pro but a car accident in college destroyed any chance of that. He showed up to every practice and game when I was little, even when he wasn't the coach. My dad took me fishing and hunting too, taught me how to cast a net and everything. When I was little, I got away with everything.

"My mom was often busy but we always had animals in

the house to play with, and she made time to teach me to take care of them. She said you can tell a lot about someone by the way they treat animals. My only worries were about winning the game or getting my homework turned in. My cousins were my best friends. No matter what it was, we'd do it together." I felt a pang of guilt at the thought of Mark and Miguel. I hadn't had the chance to call them since before Ciro left. I'd thought they would have been weird about answering the phone, but it was like nothing ever changed, which was both a relief and confusing.

"I was pretty good at school, never had to really study to get good grades. I wasn't top of the class most of the time, but I never got below a B. Going into high school was like being the heir to the throne, I guess. No one messed with me. I got top picks of seats in class, practically walked onto the football team, and never had an issue getting a date. I started getting calls about scouting prospects late last school year. It was cool at first, knowing these colleges might be interested in scouting me as early as junior year. My dad started pushing for me to practice more and study harder. He even said I needed to go with my mom to volunteer at the shelter. I did it all. My grades rose, my performance improved, and I spent early mornings cleaning out kennels and walking dogs. I even got on the student council.

"There was one girl who worked at the humane society too, and she had awesome taste in music. I started listening to stuff I never even heard of before. A concert was coming up that had a couple of bands that we'd been listening to and I wanted to go, so I got a job. My dad would give me money to go out to the movies or whatever, but there was no way he or my mom would have forked over the cash for those concert tickets. It was fine over the summer. I didn't have football or school, so it was just work and volunteering. I got the money for the concert but I liked having a job too so I just kept working when the pre-season started.

"Then my dad started in with pressuring me to prep for the ACT and SAT and that I needed to have good scores because that's what saved him after the accident took away his scholarship. So I started taking prep classes too."

My breathing felt like it was starting to freeze in my chest, and I had to pause and breathe. "Those couple of months felt like I never got any chance to rest. If I was at home, I had to be studying or practicing. And if I wasn't at home, I better be at the field, school, or work. No more mall trips, no more dates. And then, I just kind of started falling apart. I was going through the motions but couldn't really care. I fell asleep in class a few times and it pissed off my dad when he got a call from my teacher about it. I was just tired, though."

"I couldn't really tell anything was wrong until one day at the shelter, and I was so tired that I didn't latch the gate of one of the dog runs." Self hatred coursed through me as the familiar sense of anger pricked at my flesh. My fingers curled hard around the notebook as I spoke. "The dog in there was a Chow-Shepherd mix. Owner surrendered her for aggression. If you were slow moving, she was fine. Quick movements set her off, though. I didn't even know she got out until I heard her bark and take off across the compound."

"Neesha!" I called as the dog's fluffy form dashed to the fence, barking madly. My sluggish body started to wake up to the situation.

I grabbed a couple of the loop leashes and started jogging after her. Neesha raced up and down the fence, still barking. "What is your deal, dog?" I muttered.

She paused, lowered her head to the ground and started scratching and wiggling. "Oh no," I breathed and picked up the pace. "Neesha!" I said again, but she didn't even turn. I was close enough to see the dirt piling around her before she lunged through the hole under the chain-link fence. There was no way she should have fit, but I guess her fur was more fluff than skin because she slipped through pretty easily. I lunged for her leg, but she was already on the other side by the time I landed.

"Shit, shit, shit," I said, scrambling to my feet. Neesha took off down the street. Going one direction there were a few stores, and the other direction led to a neighborhood. Neesha chose the neighborhood. "Mom's gonna kill me." The gate was on the opposite side of the shelter, and I'd probably lose sight of Neesha if I tried to go out that way. "Over it is," I muttered, shoving the rope-like loop leashes into the pocket of my cargo shorts.

Chain-link fences are not as easy to climb as they look. Trying to get shoes to fit into the nook to gain ground is a struggle in itself, but I managed to get over in one piece and dropped to the ground. I winced from the landing then started running in the direction I last saw Neesha. I started calling her name again and whistling, hoping like hell she'd show up.

When I saw a flash of dark golden blur from the corner of my eye, I turned to see the dog making a beeline for me. Her tongue lolled, and I grinned, opening my arms to try to grab onto her as she approached. At the last second, she juked better than a runningback and scooched past me. I pulled the leashes from my pocket and detangled them as I jogged after Neesha down the street, keeping an eye and ear out for cars. She stopped in a yard and started sniffing around on the ground. I slowed down and started to circle around so that I could get the leash on her without startling her.

I was still several feet away when a little girl came running out from around the side of the house, and my stomach dropped. I tried to make myself run toward her, but a sudden wave of fear froze me in place. The little girl, dark hair in pigtails shrieked in delight at the sight of Neesha. Neesha took off like a runner from the blocks, straight at the kid whose shriek turned into an ear splitting scream.

That set me into action. I ran at the pair of them, and another kid did too. The boy started yelling for his dad while I jumped into the fray. The girl was frantic and screaming and crying, her arms pushing uselessly at the dog. Neesha's teeth snapped and bit and blood was getting everywhere. I shoved one hand in between Neesha and the girl's body and tried yanking the dog back with the other hand. That created enough of a gap that I could get the girl free. I pulled her out of the way of Neesha's jaw and let go to wrap both arms around the dog and push her further away.

By that time, the dad reached us. "Oh my God," I heard him say. My heart pounded so hard I thought it'd burst out of my chest. I looked down at Neesha. Blood discolored the fur around her jaws. She nosed against me, tail wagging a little. I felt sick. I got both of the leashes around her neck and pulled her further away.

"Where the fuck do you think you're going?" the guy yelled at me.

I ignored him and pulled my phone out of my pocket and dialed 9-1-1 while the guy kept cursing at me. I couldn't react to him. That girl needed help.

"9-1-1, what's your emergency?" a man asked. I thought I recognized it as one of my mom's friends.

"Ryan?" I ventured.

"Yeah," the voice replied warily.

"It's Matthew. Maria's kid."

"Oh. Are you okay?" His voice took on a no-nonsense tone like he thought I was trying to play a prank.

"*Yeah. No. One of the dogs got out of the shelter. Attacked a kid. It looks bad.*" The hand I had looped through Neesha's leashes started shaking. I knew what it would mean for the dog.

"*Shit,*" Ryan said. "*All right, hang on, kid. Misty Drive?*"

I confirmed that's where we were and gave him the nearest house number. The dad alternated between screaming at me and freaking out about the girl. The boy stood nearby like he wasn't sure what to do.

"*Sounds rough,*" Ryan said. "*You gonna be all right?*"

I caught a glimpse of the girl's mangled skin and had to close my eyes to fight off a wave of nausea. "*Probably not,*" I whispered.

"*I'm gonna call your mom, but I'll stay on the line with you.*"

"*Okay,*" I whispered. I wanted to throw up.

Neesha whined, sat down, and leaned against my leg. I couldn't help it. I started crying.

"*Matthew, are you still there?*" Ryan's voice came through my phone's earpiece. I sniffled and tried to stop the tears. I guess he heard me because he said, "*Your mom's on the way, bud. She'll be there in a few minutes. It'll be okay.*"

The dad walked over to where I stood and probably would have decked me if Neesha didn't start growling. He stopped where he was, giving the dog an icy glare but didn't try moving any closer. "*Your dog is dead,*" the man growled. "*That thing is a monster and you're going to pay for this!*"

"*Give the phone to him,*" Ryan ordered, and I wordlessly handed it over to the guy, giving Neesha a tug on the leash.

I don't know what Ryan said, but whatever it was made the man's face crumple. I heard sirens and looked up to see an ambulance pull onto the street. Its lights flashed bright as it drew closer. By then, I was able to get a grip on myself.

The man handed back my phone. He had hung up, but I saw my mom's Jeep pull up behind the ambulance. The area became a flurry of activity as the paramedics hopped out and got to work. My mom *stepped out of the Jeep and took only a couple steps towards me before I was running, practically dragging Neesha behind me at first, but the dog caught on and kept pace. I threw myself at my mother and lost control all over again.*

"I'm-so-sorry-Mom-I-don't-know-how-I'm-sorry." The words ran together as her arms wrapped around me. It hit me that the little girl stopped screaming ages ago, and I melted. My mom was pretty strong, but she couldn't support my 6'2" frame, so she just sort of helped guide me to the ground, arms still around me protectively.

"I know," Mom said. "I know, sweetie." She didn't say it was going to be okay. I realized it was because she couldn't say it. She didn't know. And that scared the hell out of me.

Somehow I ended up in the back seat of her Jeep with Neesha in the far back. There was a cargo net just behind the back seat that prevented her from jumping the seat and potentially escaping. One of the paramedics came over to look at my arm which apparently got bit pretty hard.

The paramedic smiled gently at me. She carried a small first aid kit with her which she set onto the rear fender flare and opened. She wiped down my arm. It stung, but I tried not to flinch. While she prepared some kind of cream, she said quietly, "The girl is probably going to be okay. She's in shock but alive. The boy said you jumped in. Smart thinking to make your arm the target instead. Might have saved her life thinking that quick."

Her eyes matched her voice—kind and gentle. I looked away before I started tearing up again. She didn't say anything else as she applied the cream and wrapped up my arm. I remembered to thank her before she left. I couldn't even recognize my own voice from how raw it sounded.

When Mom got into the front seat, I saw her look at me via the rearview mirror, her brow drawn in worry. She drove us the couple of blocks back to the shelter. When her door opened, mine did too. Mom looked at me again but didn't say anything. She walked around to the back of the Jeep while I got out. Neesha sat up panting, tail thumping against the floor. Mom pulled the leash off the hook that she'd installed just for this purpose and let Neesha jump to the pavement.

We headed through the front gate again, latching it behind us. I double checked. I started to walk back to the dog run that Neesha belonged to, but Mom stopped. Pain shone from her eyes when she met my gaze. She turned away from the kennels and toward the building where the treatments and procedures were done.

"Now?" I asked, my voice hitching. "You have to do it now?"

Mom licked her lips before she answered. "Yes. I told him it would be done immediately, and he agreed not to press charges."

Everything in me wanted to scream. It was my fault. My fault the poor girl was going to probably be disfigured if she was lucky and probably be afraid of dogs her entire life. And Neesha had to pay the price for my stupidity. I swallowed hard and nodded resolutely. "Then I'm going with."

Mom looked like she wanted to argue, but she gave a single nod and started to lead the way.

The surgery room was, rightfully, the cleanest room in the entire compound. A giant shiny table sat in the middle. Neesha started to balk and pull back when we entered, but I scooped her fluffy self up and set her on the table. I wrapped my arms around the dog again, holding her in reassurance, and she nervously settled. Mom took a washcloth and drenched it in the sink before using it to wipe the blood off of Neesha's muzzle. The dog squirmed a little, but I kept her still.

Then Mom prepared the sedative shot that would be used to keep Neesha calm so that she wouldn't fight when the next step happened. Neesha whined when the injection went in, and I scratched her behind the ears with one hand, keeping my other arm around her chest so she wouldn't try to hop off the table. She became pretty drowsy quickly and lay down on the table. I didn't have to restrain her anymore so I just stood out of Mom's way near Neesha's head and tried to comfort her.

The intravenous fluid was a weird purplish pink liquid that I knew would kill Neesha within a minute of injection. The dog didn't move while my mom prepped the IV. I leaned over Neesha and choked out, "I'm so sorry, girl."

I stayed right there until Neesha stopped breathing.

Mom put a hand on my shoulder and squeezed gently. I wiped away the tears that leaked from my eyes again and went out of the room to grab the black bag that we'd put Neesha's body in before storing it in the small cold storage room used specifically for this reason. When that was done and the surgery room and table cleaned up, Mom helped me finish the rest of the kennels. We drove home separately.

The homecoming game was that night too, and all I could think about was that little girl's scream and Neesha's tail wagging as she took her last breaths. All because I was too stupid to latch a dumb gate. It wasn't the first time I'd had to assist with a euthanasia. The shelter lost dogs all the time to parvo or malnourishment or some other issue from before they arrived. But that was nothing in comparison. Those hadn't been my fault.

The game should have been a breeze, but it was a disaster. I was distracted, and my arm hurt like hell. I dropped passes that I could have caught in my sleep. Everything felt muted besides the pain. Like watching TV with the subtitles on. I could catch on to what was happening, but it all seemed a couple of seconds too slow. I managed to hang onto one pass the entire game and still lost yards on it.

Dad pulled me aside from the field when the game ended. My teammates filed into the locker room, some of them giving me sidelong glances. Miguel came over. "You okay, man?" he said to me then remembered my dad was there. "Heya, Tio," he said by way of greeting then waved at my mom.

"Maybe you should go," Dad said to him. "You did awesome with those blocks. That interception probably won the game for us."

His voice glowed with approval.

Miguel wasn't used to getting praise from my dad, and he was really pleased with it. "Uh, yeah, thanks! You know, teamwork and all that." He slugged my padded shoulder. "I'll catch you later," he said and started off towards the locker room.

Dad turned to me, and the smile he wore for Miguel disappeared. "What's going on, Mattie?" he asked. I hated when he called me that. Always made me feel like a little kid. "Where were you tonight because you sure as hell weren't on that field." I glanced over to Mom, but Dad stepped in the way. "Look at me when I'm talking to you, son." So I did, feeling exhausted. "Is it a girl?"

I shook my head.

"A guy?" he asked.

I stared at him in surprise. "No, but would you care if it was?"

His dark eyes widened. "Of course not. What in the world would make you think I'd care about whether it's a guy or a girl? What I care about is that you're throwing your life away. Your grades are going down, you're not sleeping. You're lagging on the field like dial-up."

"What's dial-up?"

Dad sighed. "Never mind. Point is, you haven't been working so hard all this time to go and make a mess of it now."

The girl's scream rang in my ears again. There's no way he would understand. If Mom had already told him, he didn't care. And if she hadn't he probably would tell me that death is a part of life and I needed to move on. But it still hurt so much. I felt like I was going to throw up, and my neck started to heat up despite the cooling air.

"I'm not you, okay?" I lashed out. "I'm not the perfect prodigy you keep thinking I am. I can't keep pretending everything is fine because it's not! You have no idea what I've been through today, and you don't even care. You're just mad that I'm ruining your chance to live through me." I started to stalk off to the locker room.

"Boy, don't you walk away!"

I kept going.

"Fine!" he called after me. "You want to waste all these years of training and opportunity, fine! I'm done investing in you."

Instead of the locker room, I pushed my way through the crowd to my car. I threw my helmet into the trunk with more force than necessary. I pulled off my jersey and pads and threw them in too. I didn't even care about the strange looks I was getting from the others who were all heading out of the parking lot or milling around trying to find their friends.

My undershirt was soaked in sweat and I almost wished I would have at least showered, but I was too worked up. There was a tightness in my chest, and I never wanted to hit anything or anyone more in my life. When I got into the driver's seat, I tried to pull my phone out before realizing I left it in the locker room with my gym bag. Wouldn't have mattered, I didn't think there was anyone I could have called. There were a couple of parties going on, but I didn't really want to be around anyone.

I just wanted the pain and anger and guilt to go away.

My throat burned as I fought back the angry tears. I was such an idiot. My stomach flipped around again and my jaw clenched. I could literally feel the tension building in my shoulders as I went on. I came this far. There was nothing for it but to finish it out.

"I ended up driving around for a long time before I finally went home. My parents weren't back yet. I guess at some point I made up my mind because I started looking for my dad's pistol when I got to the house. Usually he kept it locked up, but sometimes he'd leave it out. I couldn't find it, though, so I went to the freezer and got out the bottle of rum. I got down probably half the bottle before I went to the garage. Took a stool and extension cord and tried to hang myself. I guess I screwed it up though because it didn't work. I don't remember what else happened until I woke up in the Emergency Room."

Awkward silence filled the room when I finished. "Um, yeah, that's it.." I said. I closed the notebook and stared at the ground. My leg bounced, shaking so hard that it reminded me of the rabbit from the kid's movie about the deer.

"Can I go?" Tobias asked. He was talking to Michelle. I guess she nodded or something because his hand landed on my shoulder again. "Matthew, bro." He waited until I looked over at him. "Sounds like you were straight up overworked and depressed even before the dog attack, and the guilt from that made whatever else you were going through seem that much worse. You're not an idiot. You jumped in to save the kid, you took responsibility instead of running away from the consequences, and you stood up to your dad. That's not being a coward. That's, like, the opposite of being a coward."

Renee sniffed from the other side of the room. "Tobias is right," she said. "You didn't mean for Neesha to get out. You didn't tell her to attack that girl. She did what dogs sometimes do, and you reacted faster and better than most people would." She sniffed again. "And your dad kind of sounds like a jerk. No offense."

"Well, he is a lawyer," Tobias said, jostling me.

I smiled a little. I didn't really understand why they were giving me the benefit of the doubt. "That girl could have died," I said somberly, no longer smiling.

"Could have, but didn't," Michelle pointed out. "Tobias and Renee have very valid points. You didn't mean for it to happen, right? But you're so used to doing everything right that I think any kind of misstep might have resulted in you spiraling. It could have been a failed test. That it was the dog attack followed by your father's lack of understanding probably only quickened the inevitable for your own mental state. I think that, if you didn't find some kind of way to release the pressure, you would have imploded anyway. Regardless, I am very glad you were unsuccessful in your attempt."

The others all murmured or nodded in agreement.

Liz leaned forward, arms propped on her knees and looked directly at me. "Listen, as someone who has done some pretty stupid and selfish crap because of something feeling just wrong and off, let me tell you that this is not the end of your story. Where it goes from here depends on you fighting that jackass part of your head that tries to tell you that you aren't good enough. And I'll tell you something else. You are good enough. You are loved by your family and friends. You care about people you've never met before. You put damn near every one of us ahead of your own self.

"What happened was freaking awful. Guess what? You're not a superhuman. Sorry, bro. So shut up and listen to your body next time it tells you that you're running on fumes. And if you aren't sure what to do, call me. Or probably any one of us." She leaned back and smiled in a feline way. "We've all felt that low before or we wouldn't be here. So again, if you can't or won't listen to yourself, listen to us."

My eyes started welling up again as I fought against it. *You guys get it, even when you don't,* I thought.

RENEE

I lay the books on my bed, spines up, next to a stack of papers—handouts that I wanted to keep from the different group therapies. Clothes sat in a pile near the pillow, freshly laundered and some of them folded haphazardly.

"You organize books down to the genre and author but you let your clothes wrinkle like that?" Liz teased as she entered our room. She shook her head in wonder, causing the beaded clip holding back part of her hair to slip out of place. Scrunching her nose in annoyance, Liz moved in front of the mirror to fix it.

"I can rewash my clothes. I can't wash books," I said. I liked watching Liz when she did her hair. It looked luxurious and dark as midnight, and she always managed to make her style look effortless while I always felt like a frumpy patch of red peppers. I crossed my arms and rocked on my heels for a moment. A couple of tears leaked out from the corner of my eyes, and I tried to wipe away at them discreetly, turning back towards my bed and the duffle bag that sat there.

"Ray, what's wrong?" Liz asked. Her shoes squeaked on the floor as she approached.

I shook my head and tried to laugh it off. "Nothing," I said, trying to wave her off.

"Ray," she said again, her voice turned stern. "You're supposed to stop doing that, remember? Say what's on your mind, girl." Her hand landed softly on my shoulder then put enough pressure to try to turn me around.

I didn't resist but still wiped at my eyes. Liz kept the one hand where it was and used her other to lift up my chin and look at her. Her eyes were round and bright and full of worry.

"I'm just thinking about how I'm supposed to be happy about leaving, aren't I? Isn't this supposed to mean I'm clear to go rejoin society?" I hated how thin my voice sounded and tried clearing my throat.

Liz arched a perfectly shaped eyebrow. "And you're not happy?"

"No! I mean, I'm glad my family isn't—that we aren't all hating each other. That they don't hate me even after... But I don't want to leave. Does that make me awful?" I lowered my head, feeling the tears start to form again.

To my surprise, Liz laughed and pulled me against her in a tight hug. "Oh, Ray, no. That doesn't make you awful. It just means you're normal."

It was my turn to laugh, but mine sounded far more

bitter. "How do you figure that?" I asked. I let her arms stay wrapped around me, though she'd inadvertently pinned mine.

"Because you like being around people who understand how you're feeling. That's totally normal. Or so I'm told." Liz withdrew just enough to be able to look at my face again.

"I was also thinking about how gorgeous your hair is and how mine's always a rat's nest," I admitted, feeling heat rush to my cheeks.

Her wide mouth smiled mischievously. "Now that is something I can help with. Come with me, child. Let me teach you the ways." She pulled away from me and picked up the hygiene bucket that I hadn't even seen her bring in. She held out her hand to me. I took it, feeling like maybe I'd regret this. But probably not.

Liz sat on the bed and instructed me to sit on the floor in front of her, facing away. She started pulling things out of the bucket as I did. "I have been dying to do your hair for weeks," she said as she pulled the hair tie out of the quick ponytail I usually used. She shielded my eyes with her hand and started spraying something. The air smelled like mangos. Then she used a vanilla-smelling lotion on a part of my hair, using her hands to work it down the strands. "Let me know if I pull too much." Liz used a comb to try to tame the red mane that was usually impossible for me to even attempt.

There was a tug every so often, but it didn't hurt. I was pretty sure I developed a thick skin from my mom's attempts to comb it so often when I was little. "Bristles used to break off in my hair," I said, as Liz's movements became more methodical and rhythmic.

"Really?" Liz asked. "Guess I better be careful then," she teased. Her hands expertly moved through, parting and combing and even massaging where the comb would pull a little so that it wouldn't hurt as much. There was a kind of euphoria to be had, sitting there with Liz silently working.

When she finished detangling my wild curls, my head felt lighter than it had since the last time I cut it. I ran my hand through, marveling at how smooth it felt. She smacked my hand playfully. "Hang on, I'm not done," she said. She chose a portion just above my left ear and used the comb to pull it backwards then did the same with the right side. With a twist, she pinned it on top of my head and pulled another section from back to front of my head. Liz twisted the two parts together, winding them around and around before pinning it in place. She did the same with the other part, this time wrapping it around the smaller part and secured it into place.

"Sit forward," she directed me. I complied, letting her swing her leg over so that she could stand. She crouched in front of me, studying the sides of my face. I stared at her intense focused gaze in wonder. In the couple of months I'd known her, she never looked so self-contained. Liz's fingers reached out to one side of my face. Her short fingernail tugged a series of strands away from the part. She twisted it around her finger, letting it hold for a second then pulled free. Leaning away, she nodded in satisfaction, a slow smile spreading across her face.

"I think you'll like it," she said. She stood again, offering her hands to help me up.

Curiously, I went to the mirror. As soon as my reflection peered back at me, I almost fell in shock. Liz had transformed me. I didn't look like the messy girl I was. I looked older, almost confident even.

"H-how?" I stuttered.

She stepped up beside me and put an arm around my shoulders, looking at my reflection with me. My pale skin contrasted sharply with the rich brown of hers, but, for once, I didn't think I looked so ugly standing next to her. I must have hit a growth spurt while in Sequoia because Liz only had a couple of inches on me now. "Thank you," I breathed.

"All I did is show you how you look to the rest of us—beautiful." She turned and touched her lips to my head gently and briefly.

A red flush appeared in my cheeks so deep that it could have been the same color as my hair, making Liz giggle.

There was a knock on the door, and I quickly sidestepped away from Liz. I thought I saw a look of hurt flash across her face, but, if it was there, it disappeared behind her easy smile before I could verify.

"Wow," came an oddly pitched voice from the hallway. I turned to see Derek lean against the frame. Hope rose up in me at the sight of him at first, but it fell away when I saw the sunken look in his eyes. "You look very pretty," he said in the same weird tone.

I felt rather than saw Liz tense up beside me, but her voice betrayed nothing when she said, "How's it going, Trish?"

The childish smile didn't look right on Derek. I missed his smirk. It occurred to me that I might not get the chance to actually talk directly to him again, not without having to go through this other piece of him. I wanted to read up on what this was so that I knew how to be able to communicate with my friend. Liz tried to tell me that all of

Derek's alters were still him, but it was hard for me to reconcile the guy I knew with the girl trying to stand in his place. The whole thing confused me.

"Liz, can we talk to Renee?" Derek's strange voice said.

Liz looked at me for confirmation and shrugged when I nodded. She left the room without another word. When she was gone, I went to my bedside table and picked up a paper. I hesitated for a moment then whirled on my heel, crossed the room and handed over the letter I wrote to Derek.

His eyes widened, but he took it. He didn't read it yet, just looked up at me. "You're leaving tomorrow." It was a statement.

"Tonight," I corrected. "I mean, we're leaving town tomorrow to I guess go look at some possible houses in Brookhaven, but I'm leaving here tonight." I gestured at the bed that was still covered with my few possessions as if to confirm my story.

"He's going to miss you," said Trish's voice. That caught my attention again.

"You, I mean, can you tell stuff like that? Are you sure?" Torn between curiosity and embarrassment, my eyes looked everywhere but where Derek stood. He was very careful to stand outside of the door.

Trish gave a small laugh that just grated on my nerves, and I hated that it did. "Yes, I can tell. We share most experiences, but not all." His expression sobered. "You have been like a sister to him." The words sounded a little sad.

I gulped and forced myself to look at his face. I hated how normal but off it seemed. Like, he was him, but he also wasn't. "Are you his..." My voice trailed off, leaving the question hanging in the air.

Derek's eyes brightened. "His sister, yes. He thought I was gone after, but I stayed. He kept me with him."

That was something, I guess. Maybe if I kept this part talking, it would bring Derek back. "How old were-are you?" I asked.

"15 next month," Trish answered promptly.

That would make her a little less than two years younger than Tobias. She would have been the same age as me. Maybe we might have been friends.

"Do you still play soccer?" the feminine voice asked.

I shot a glare back. "If you know and share his memories, why would you even ask me that?"

Derek's shoulder lifted slightly. "I always wanted to play. Derek tried it at school a few times, but it didn't work out. Never had a family take enough of an interest to let him really play anything." A note of bitterness lingered in those words in a way that was entirely opposite from Derek's normal matter-of-factness. But Trish forced out a laugh and said, "Sorry, I don't usually talk to others."

"That must be really lonely," I said, taking a step closer to where Derek stood by the door.

"Sometimes, but it's not like I'm trapped. It's a choice for me."

"But not for Derek," I challenged. Anger started chipping away at the mask I wore to bear talking to this imposter.

Derek's chin lifted indignantly. "I protect him," Trish shot back.

"From what? From living his life? From feeling too much? From loving someone else?" I couldn't stop the words even if I wanted to. The fury boiled over and brought tears to my eyes.

His eyes went cold, and Derek slurred, "She's not the only one who survived." Derek took two jerky steps into my room but stopped suddenly.

I matched them in the opposite direction. My heart started pounding. I opened my mouth to scream but nothing came out.

Derek's face twisted as though in pain. When he looked at me again, his eyes were warm and sad and scared all at once. "Renee, I'm sorry," he whispered like it was impossible for him to speak any louder.

A sigh of irritation escaped him as he turned away and started towards the door again.

"Derek," I said in a half sob. I fought through my terror and stumbled the couple of steps between us to grab onto his arm.

His form froze, but when he answered, it was in Trish's voice again, filled with ice. "I protect him from *that monster*."

DARLA

A loud thud pierced my ears like the world's biggest drum. I turned my head ever so slightly to yell at Kate to be quiet, but the pounding in my head intensified ten-fold. "Ughh," I groaned.

"You're such a lightweight now," someone giggled. I squeezed my eyes shut, but every move made the pain worse. "Maybe I should go to treatment if it means I get to have such a low threshold again."

"You shouldn't have let her go so hard," another voice rebuked softly.

"How was I supposed to know?" the first said in defense. "She used to be able to hang." After a moment, she continued, "What do you care anyway? You don't know her." Footsteps hit along the floor away from the bed.

The mattress squeaked, and a hand pushed my hair away from my face a little. There was a quiet thud of something hitting the bed frame. "I'll tell Mrs. C you're still asleep. There's a water bottle here for you when you're ready."

I wanted to thank her, but I still couldn't get my body to respond. Not without risking serious damage. Okay, that was probably not true, but it sure as hell felt like it. The mattress squeaked again as she climbed down. Her footsteps retreated too, and I heard the door close.

My brain felt sluggish, even more so than the rest of me, but it started putting the pieces together. Kate wasn't here. I wasn't in Pleasant Valley anymore. I was in the group home. Hannah took me out back last night. The bourbon was like acid in my throat, and I felt the sudden urge to vomit.

I barely made it to the bathroom before the bile spilled out of my mouth. It landed in the sink with me unable to make it to the toilet. I stood there for what felt like hours, just waiting for another round of nausea to take me out. Eventually, though, I rinsed out my mouth. I retrieved my hygiene stuff then brushed my teeth and scrubbed my face as thoroughly as I could. When I made it back to the bedroom, I wanted to lay down and sleep forever. A neon green water bottle was propped between the mattress and the frame, and I praised May for being so thoughtful. I drained half of it.

Before I could climb back into my bunk, there was a knock at the door. Mrs. Croden barely waited before she opened it and stepped inside. Clearly, she expected us to be dressed at all times. "Oh, good, you're up already," she said, and I could have sworn I heard disappointment in her words. "When you're dressed, there's some cereal downstairs for you. After that, I could use your help with the garden, and then you can go to your meeting before the rest of the girls get home."

I blinked, trying to process everything she just said without making it obvious how fucked up I still felt. "Okay," I managed to say. She lifted an eyebrow in expectation. "I mean, yes, ma'am," I corrected.

She peered at me. I hoped she couldn't see my hand trembling. But her expression softened some. "I know the transition can be difficult, but you'll make it through." My stomach twisted again, and it had nothing to do with the hangover.

Mrs. Croden left, closing the bedroom door behind her to give me some semblance of privacy, though I supposed she and I were the only ones left in the house.

I dug through my bag and pulled out a comfy pair of coral colored pink sweats and a slightly oversized t-shirt. It was my go-to outfit while in Sequoia strictly because of the comfort level. She mentioned the garden, so I didn't want to use any of the clothes I could wear to school since I didn't know when I'd be able to do laundry.

By the time I was done dressing, the world was getting spinny again. I sat down on Hannah's bed with my head in my hands. There seemed to be no helping it. I let my head hang down further, stretching the back of my neck, then twisted to look at the door. When I turned to the window, I saw a little bottle of ibuprofen sitting on the small nightstand.

"Thank God," I whispered. I took two of the oblong orange pills and another swig of water. "With food and orange juice, I might feel human again," I muttered. With that, I made my way downstairs. Mrs. Croden seemed to have gone to the garden already. I saw a box of cereal and an empty bowl on the counter and helped myself, pouring in some milk found in the fridge. The blandness of the cereal would ordinarily have bugged me, but I was grateful for it. Extra sugar might have set me off in search of the bathroom again.

I polished off the food in record time and washed the bowl and spoon with some dish soap. The mudroom was almost completely empty. I found my shoes easily and paused at the door, bracing myself for the brightness that awaited me. I wished I had my sunglasses.

I opened the door and found a relatively overcast sky. It wasn't dim by any means, but it was enough that I could probably put up with it.

Mrs. Croden waved me over to where she was working at a patch of mostly empty dirt. At least, it looked that way until I was closer. When I reached her, I could see there were random bits of green and yellow throughout the soil. "I want you to weed this section here. We're getting ready to plant a crop and I don't want any chance of it being edged out by any weeds. Grab it by the base, right near the soil, and yank it out." She demonstrated on a dandelion, pulling out a small root system along with it. "Understand what to do?"

"Yes, ma'am," I said, keeping my head lowered away from the sun. I knelt in the dirt, glad for the comfy clothes.

The work was simple and gratifying. We worked mostly in quiet, though Mrs. Croden hummed tunes on occasion. Part of me wanted to ask about her life running the group home with her husband, but another part needed the silence. Silence won the argument, and I kept my mouth shut. The head pounding started receding, so I was able to remind myself that it would be a good time for mindfulness practice which would probably also help with keeping the headache at bay.

The dirt crumbled under my hands, some brittle and dry, some moist and oddly soft. Moist was such a weird word to say. I mouthed it under my breath and smiled before I realized I was trying to be mindful of the dirt. Oh well, words counted too, I bet.

Mrs. Croden got to her feet slowly, groaning as she moved. "Getting old sucks," she said as her head rotated slowly, making some audible pops that made me cringe.

"Are you okay?" I asked. I kept an eye on her in case she stumbled.

"Just working out the rust," she said. "I think it's about time to get lunch started. There are only a few of us during the day."

I was sitting on my knees, so I only had to rock back a little to get to my feet, brushing the dirt from my clothes as I did. Mrs. Croden clucked her tongue. "Ah, to be young and energetic," she said wistfully.

Energetic, right. I gave a sheepish smile and ducked my head to hide some of the shame reddening my face. I headed inside and held the door open for her. A cat hopped down from a three tier cat tower and wound its way around my leg. When I reached down to pet the gray fur, the cat leaped away and flicked its tail in indignation.

"Don't mind Petey. He's just a sourpuss." Mrs. Croden waggled a finger in the cat's direction. "You behave yourself, mister." The cat's ears moved but his head turned in the exact opposite direction. "Typical," she muttered and proceeded to ignore the cat.

Lunch turned out to be basic ham and cheese sandwiches with carrots and apples. Mrs. Croden laid out the ingredients for the sandwiches—cheddar cheese, black forest deli ham, mayonnaise, mustard, and lettuce—and told me to make mine however I liked. It was weird making my own food after months of cafeteria. Even before that, Dad had a personal chef who would make my food whenever I wanted. It had been at least a couple of years since I made myself a sandwich. I stared at the food for a moment, feeling a little dizzy.

Everything started spinning more. My mouth went dry. I squeezed my eyes shut, willing the world to stop moving so fast. How could I be so weak to let something so stupidly easy trip me up? What was wrong with me? It was just a dumb sandwich.

"Breathe," a voice said. It took a moment for me to process it as Mrs. Croden. "Open your eyes and take a breath." Her voice was gentle but authoritative.

I tried to listen, I really did. But an increased pounding in my head drowned her out. I held my head and sank to the floor. Angry tears leaked from my eyes. I hated this. There was no damn reason for me to be losing my shit, but I couldn't help it. Can't even make a damn sandwich.

The thoughts whirled around my head over and over, and I couldn't get them to stop. The more I thought about how stupid it was for me to be freaking out, the more freaked out I got. Soon I was full on crying with my breaths coming fast, and the anger flared again at myself for crying. Weak. Pathetic. Stupid. What was the point of any of this? Spoiler alert, there wasn't any.

Mrs. Croden pried my arms away from my body and dropped something soft and sort of heavy into my lap. Grey fur rubbed against my skin as Petey walked in circles, putting pressure on my legs with his paws. That close, I could hear him purr like an engine or like a stuffed animal with a voicebox. Or something in between. His front paws, one of which had a white spot, continued kneading my leg. I rested one of my hands on his back, and he arched, letting my hand slide down his back. He bumped my arm after a moment, demanding more pets. I scooped him into my arms and nuzzled against his body. The cat went limp and purred.

After several more minutes, I felt better. Petey bumped my head with his, and I let him go. He jumped down, shook himself out, and walked off like nothing happened. That made me giggle for some reason.

Mrs. Croden reached a hand down to me and helped me to my feet. I realized it was pretty dumb of me to think she might need help earlier. "I'm sorry," I mumbled. I stole a look at the counter again. The ingredients were still out, but the apples and carrots had been sliced and were waiting on a plate.

"You're not the first to come here with a truckload of baggage, sweetie. And you won't be the last. The transition from the center to here isn't smooth for anyone." She opened a drawer and pulled out a butter knife. "Darla, you're not weak for having that kind of reaction. Look at me." I did. "You came out the other side, and that means you're strong. Understand?"

I nodded, but there was a lingering doubtful whisper in my mind. She handed the butter knife to me.

"We'll take it step by step. You're going to have relapses, and it's going to hurt. But you can make it through if you keep trying."

My eyes widened as I looked at her again. Did she know? Did she know about the sneaking out and the drinking? If she knew, wasn't she supposed to stop it?

I forced myself to look at the knife again. One step at a time. Time to make a sandwich.

It wasn't quite one thirty in the afternoon when Mrs. Croden shuffled me to the front room and outside. Her husband stood in the driveway next to a large gray passenger van. The sliding door was open and waiting.

I glanced at Mrs. Croden, conflicted with hope and despair that she might be sending me back to the treatment center. Reason decided to make an appearance as I realized that if that was the case, I'd have my bags with me.

As though reading my mind, she said, "John's going to be driving you over to the church for your meeting. When it's done, he'll bring you and the others home."

"Others?" I asked.

"Several of the kids here go to meetings at the church too. They get dropped off there by the school, and John picks them up after. The rest come home by bus."

Despite the reassurance, I couldn't get my feet to move. I picked at one of my fingernails. "What - uhm - what is this meeting?"

Confusion clouded her expression for a moment, but she sighed, and it disappeared. "Your treatment doesn't end after leaving the center. You have AA twice a week for a while at the church and group and individual therapy each once a week. Sometimes that'll be here, sometimes the church hosts it."

I closed my eyes and tried to contain the dread that

went through me. Alcoholics Anonymous? I could understand the therapy, but meetings? That seemed excessive. I nodded and said good-bye to Mrs. Croden.

Mr. Croden closed the door for me then climbed into the driver's seat. I leaned my head against the window and looked out at the street passing by. "Do you want to listen to music?" he asked.

"Really?" I said, probably a little too enthusiastically because he gave a low chuckle.

"Sure. What do you like to listen to?"

"Hmm." I thought about it hard for a moment before I realized the longer I thought, the less chance I'd actually be able to listen. "103.7," I said. Mr. Croden hit a button on the radio controls and the numbers came across the screen. A woman's voice came out of the speakers backed by a male vocalist and a steady rock beat. "Yes, I love this one!" I said, happy I hadn't missed so much that one of my favorites wasn't even still on the radio.

I bobbed my head along with the rhythm and mouthed the words along with the singer. The next song was one I didn't know quite as well, but I enjoyed just being able to listen to music again.

The ride to the church didn't take long. The building Mr. Croden pulled up to was large and tan with a reddish brown roof. The sign read Church of St. Dymphna in solid black letters just above the large double doors at the front. We got out of the van, and Mr. Croden escorted me inside.

Immediately upon entering I could see a large beautiful oil painting of a pale girl with lovely red hair that bore a striking resemblance to Renee. Below the painting were the words:

Good Saint Dymphna, great wonder-worker in every affliction of mind and body, I

humbly implore your powerful intercession with Jesus through Mary, the Health of

the Sick, in my present need. Saint Dymphna, martyr of purity, patroness of those

who suffer with nervous and mental afflictions, beloved child of Jesus and Mary,

pray to Them for me and obtain my request. Saint Dymphna, Virgin and Martyr,

pray for us.

The name of the church suddenly made a lot more sense.

A hallway led beneath the painting with rooms on either side. At the far end stood another set of double doors, wooden and red. I guessed that was the way to the cathedral. I looked around and saw lots of reds, yellows, and greens in the decor. To one side of the front doors stood a basket of beads on a pedestal. I peeked in the basket and saw lots of bracelets or necklaces with small silver medallions attached. Before I could get a closer look, a door nearby opened.

I jerked away from the basket and folded my hands together. A woman in a beautiful gray pantsuit with a silky tan shirt stepped into the hall. Her olive complexion looked flawless, and I hoped I could ask her what her skin care routine was like.

She approached us, flipping loose dark hair over her shoulder. "Hi, John," the woman said warmly.

"Viola," Mr. Croden said by way of greeting. They shook hands before the woman glanced at me. "This is

Darla. She's here for the meeting."

"Hello, Darla." Viola offered me her hand to shake also, and I was surprised at her strong but gentle grip.

She would have been only a couple inches taller than me if it wasn't for her gorgeous brown ankle-high boots. "Nice to meet you," I said.

"Viola runs the program here," Mr. Croden said.

"Yes, and I hope you'll find this to be a safe place for your journey." Viola smiled pleasantly. "I don't think the others are here yet if you'd like to go to the room ahead of time. I find it can be helpful to take in new spaces without a bunch of new people around."

"Honestly," I agreed without thinking.

Viola chuckled. "It's the first door on the right. Help yourself to the refreshments if you'd like any."

"Thank you." I glanced at Mr. Croden for confirmation, and he nodded. I left them at the entrance, heading for the room Viola indicated.

It was pretty simple, with chairs lined up in a circle. A table at one side held a platter of cookies and little napkins. Pitchers of lemonade and water stood next to a stack of paper cups. I made a beeline for it. It had been ages since I had decent lemonade.

I closed my eyes in pure bliss as the sweetly sour drink hit my tongue. I wished Kate was there, she would have loved it.

"Enjoying yourself, are you?"

I spun around to see a boy with dark hair, his smirk accentuating a dimple on one side. "Rocky," I breathed. I clutched at my heart like I was having a heart attack. "You sure like to sneak up, don't you?"

"You were facing away, that's not my fault," he pointed

out.

"Noted," I said. "What are you doing here anyway?" I looked down at the yellowish liquid in the cup. My memory from the night before was fuzzy, but I definitely remembered that look he gave me before Kelly gave me the drink.

Rocky approached the table, grabbing a cup but opting for the water. "Meeting, obviously."

I wanted to smack myself. I rolled my eyes instead and retorted, "No kidding."

He flashed a quick grin before downing the cup's contents. A flush started creeping up my neck and face, so I turned away before he noticed. The lemonade went down faster than I wanted, but others were filing into the room and making their way to the refreshments. I stepped away and headed for one of the chairs that faced the door so I could watch. Rocky followed, plopping into the seat beside me. His backpack hit the floor with a soft thud.

We sat in silence, just observing the others. Some were carrying backpacks too and seemed to be around high school age or maybe college. My jaw nearly dropped when I saw May and Kelly enter, talking in the easy way friends do. Kelly's head fell back in a genuine laugh that made May's eyes crinkle in amusement.

Noticing me, May gave me a wave. Kelly followed her gaze to me and smiled, though the expression seemed to grow stony as his eyes fell on Rocky. I snuck a glance at him, but Rocky's face remained impassive.

Before I could ask about it, Viola swept into the room, and the entire energy of the group shifted. I wouldn't have been able to pinpoint it a few months ago, but her presence seemed to have brought a sense of safety. Without prompting, the others all took seats in the chairs. May sat on the other side of me with Kelly taking the seat next to her.

Kelly leaned over May and said to me, "It was so nice meeting you last night." His easy smile was infectious.

"Uh, you too," I murmured, fiddling with a strand of my hair out of habit. One of his mischievous eyes winked as he pulled back.

May swatted his shoulder lightly. "Don't tell me you've corrupted the girl already." She made an effort to appear teasing but there was a definite edge to her voice.

Kelly's shoulders rose in a shrug. "Didn't really have to," he said.

Rocky tensed on my other side. For a moment, I was afraid he'd shoot off some remark to Kelly, but Rocky closed his eyes and soon his chest was rising and falling in steady, deep breaths.

Viola clapped her hands and took one of the last three empty chairs. The noise signaled to everyone to stop chattering. All eyes swiveled to her. "Welcome to today's Alcoholics Anonymous meeting. AA is a fellowship of people who share experiences, strength, and hope with each other that may solve their common problem and help others to recover from alcoholism. The only requirement for membership is a desire to stop drinking. We are self-supporting and not allied with any particular group, denomination, or organization. Our primary purpose is to stay sober and help other alcoholics to achieve sobriety."

She looked around the room as she spoke, and it sounded like something she'd said dozens of times before, but the emphasis stayed with her words. "Let's take a few minutes to check in and say hello. I'm Viola, and I'm an alcoholic. I'm working in particular on steps 10 and 11 this week." Her gaze moved to her left, to where a boy slouched with his hood up.

"I'm Kyle, and I'm here so I don't piss off my probation officer," the boy said without moving.

"Thank you, Kyle," said several people but not in unison.

The introductions moved around the circle until it was Rocky's turn.

"Hey, I'm Rocky, and I'm an alcoholic," he said without shame. "I'm working on step 4 and trying to be completely honest with myself."

Then it was my turn.

My mouth went dry. I had done check-in a dozen times a day in Pleasant Valley, but that somehow felt different. "Uh, my name is Darla. I'm here as part of my aftercare from the hospital." I wanted to sink into the floor and disappear. I hugged myself and looked down.

There was no laughter, though. No snide remarks. May reached out and squeezed my shoulder gently.

"I'm May," she said brightly. "I'm an alcoholic, and I'm working on step 7."

Kelly sat with his arm draped over the side of the chair with an easy smile on his face. "Kelly here and still working on step 1."

I thought about that while the rest of the group finished their introductions. Viola said that this group was for people who wanted to stop drinking, but Kelly certainly didn't seem all that interested in stopping the night before. It made me wonder what the steps were.

I raised my hand after the last girl finished speaking.

"Yes, Darla?" Viola asked with a gentle smile.

"I'm sorry if this is a stupid question, but what are the steps everyone keeps talking about?"

She chuckled and said, "That's not a stupid question at all. AA is a 12-step program. And each of these steps helps us on our journey. Sometimes we have to revisit some of the steps or go in a different order, and that's okay." Viola stood and left the circle, heading for a table at the side of the room that held a rack full of brochures. She picked a couple and came back. Before sitting down, she handed the pamphlets to me.

I glanced at them briefly, but I didn't open them.

"Today, I want us to talk about what addiction is and what it means," Viola said as she returned to her seat. "What is the difference between habit and addiction?"

No one spoke for a moment as we mulled that over. Finally, a girl nearby said, "With an addiction, you can't help yourself. It's like a need."

Viola nodded then said, "Yes and no. Anyone else?" When no one spoke, she continued, "With a habit, you tend to do it without thinking. When you get in the car, you reach for the seatbelt by habit. With addiction, though, it's showing in the most dramatic way possible, that someone is choosing to not make the effort to stop. By that, I mean, you consciously think about the thing, whatever it is. With alcohol addiction, you think about how you're going to get that drink, probably to the point of getting drunk. We could be talking about a concert and your mind is on getting a drink afterwards. Not the socialization, the actual act of drinking."

That made me wonder... I didn't feel the urge to drink right that moment, but I was also still kind of nursing that hangover. And since we were talking about drinking, did that count as habit or addiction?

"You know that drinking can be deadly, yes," Viola continued. "There's the obvious situation where drinking impairs judgment which can lead to dangerous circumstances." She closed her eyes for a moment and took a deep breath. "I lost my twin to one of those."

I gasped and covered my mouth with my hand. Several others started murmuring about how awful that had to be and how sorry they were.

Viola smiled sadly and looked around. "Thank you. We made poor choices and it resulted in the worst thing imaginable. But the other part of deadly drinking is alcohol poisoning. It's not literal poison, but it acts similar. Alcohol slows down body functions, and too much can put the body into a state where the brain slows down so much that it forgets to tell the rest of the body to work at things like breathing and pumping blood."

I glanced to my side where Rocky sat. He wore a sad expression and kept his eyes on the floor.

"May, you look like you want to say something," Viola prompted gently.

May bit her lip but nodded. "I've been to that point before. I didn't think my drinking was a big deal, but I knew my family did. So I would sometimes take an Uber to a hotel and drink as much as I wanted to. Usually I'd go with friends but sometimes I just went by myself. Just to get away. Or so I thought. It took more than a couple close calls to really see what I was doing to myself."

On instinct, I reached out for her hand and squeezed it. She gave me a small smile in return.

"Thank you, May," Viola said sincerely. "It takes so much strength and courage to be honest with yourself and to share that with others. How has your journey been going since then?"

My new roommate's face brightened. "My last relapse was six months ago, and I've been sober since then."

The group started clapping, and May ducked her head in pleased embarrassment.

"So what it comes down to," Viola said when the applause died down, "is choices. Even though we want to drink or may even think we need to, we choose not to do it. And here, especially, we can support each other in that choice. We can help each other limit the potential risks for relapse, and if a relapse occurs, we can be just as supportive in getting back on track. Is there anyone who is having trouble staying sober today?"

To my amazement, Rocky's hand rose, and so did Kelly's. With my heart suddenly pounding, my own arm went into the air just enough that my hand stayed above my head. There were others who raised their hands too. Most of the group, actually. May gave me an encouraging smile.

"Would anyone like to share?"

Half the hands dropped, including mine. I wasn't ready for that yet.

"Rocky?" Viola said. I tried not to look at him.

"Some of my housemates like to go hang out in the evenings, and I go with them sometimes. It was fine the first few times. We'd just chill and talk and maybe play a game. But more often recently, there's alcohol. And the last time, a couple of people drank pretty heavily, to the point that it worried me if they would be okay. But..." Rocky cleared his throat. "It was more than that. I...missed the feeling. I didn't drink," he said quickly, "but I was jealous, I think. Because I know that if I even take one swig, I'm a goner again. I don't want to quit hanging out with this group, but I think I'm going to have to stop anyway. And that sucks, because there's at least one who I wish I could get to know better. Without alcohol." His eyes fell to his hands as he finished talking.

The flood of shame and sadness threatened to overtake me. I wished Mrs. C's cat was around.

"Anyone have anything they'd like to say on that?" Viola asked to the group.

One of the other girls briefly raised her hand before she said, "Rocky, thank you for sharing that. I get what you mean because there's a group of my so-called friends that I had to stop hanging out with because they wouldn't quit drinking around me when I told them I was in recovery. And I think you need to decide if being with that group is worth risking your sobriety over."

"I agree," May said. "I had to make the same choice not too long ago. It's like Viola said, it's up to us to lower the risks or not."

"What's the harm in hanging out with them? If you choose not to drink that's cool, but do you want to throw away your friends because you make a different choice?" Kelly drawled. I peeked over at him, and his head was lifted in a challenge towards Rocky.

"I don't know, man, do you want to throw away your life for making a different choice and enabling others to make bad decisions?" Rocky shot back.

Kelly held his hands up in a mock surrender before Viola could say anything.

"Everyone is at different stages in their journey, and it's not up to us to judge another's progress. Judgment should be left to the Lord—or whatever deity you believe in or don't. With that, I think it's a good stopping place. We will conclude with the Serenity prayer. If you need slips signed, please hang back, but everyone else may enjoy the refreshments and mingle if you'd like."

She bowed her head, and most of us followed suit. As she began speaking, several other voices joined her.

"God grant me the serenity

To accept the things I cannot change;

Courage to change the things I can;

And wisdom to know the difference.

Living one day at a time;

Enjoying one moment at a time;

Accepting hardships as the pathway to peace;

Taking, as He did, this sinful world

As it is, not as I would have it;

Trusting that He will make things right

If I surrender to His Will;

So that I may be reasonably happy in this life

And supremely happy with Him

Forever and ever in the next.

Amen."

As usually happened when I went to church as a kid, a light peace fell over me while listening to the group join together in prayer. That feeling, a togetherness that actually reminded me of being in Sequoia, was right on par with that beginning buzz.

My eyes shot open at catching the thought. Maybe I really was an alcoholic...

CIRO

School became a hell of a lot easier to deal with after Miguel and the others made it clear that anyone who took issue with me, took issue with them. I could go between classes without worrying about being targeted for the first time since coming out. There was a cautious relief that came with that, and I had some optimism that maybe I could enjoy school again.

Of course, this was before I realized just how far behind in class being in treatment had set me. I missed almost the entire first quarter, and, though the school was giving me the chance to try to catch up, they weren't hopeful. I knew I had to show significant progress to be able to even attempt the football team, and that was something I never even considered before either. Me, playing football? But I kind of actually wanted to, and I couldn't begin to figure out why.

I glanced at the time on my cell phone and groaned. Mom had been dropping me off early so I could get extra study time in, but somehow I still ended up rushing to class. Managing to dodge around a couple of seniors on the baseball team, I threw a glance over my shoulder and was stopped cold by the door in front of me. "Oof," I said as I bounced off of it. "Ow."

From around the door I heard a gasp and a girl immediately start apologizing. I rubbed my head and looked at the door just as the girl's blond head popped around it. "Ciro!" she squealed and rushed to pick up my chemistry book. "OMG, I am so sorry!"

I managed a smile despite the throbbing pain forming. "Hey, Darla, I thought you went to school at-"

"I transferred," she interrupted, looking around as though afraid that the others might have heard. Though I didn't know what it would matter since no one knew her.

"Hey," a voice called out down the hall. I felt my stomach drop. "Is this queer bothering you?" Jon asked. His eyes slid up and down Darla like appraising a cut of meat. The intrusiveness of it made my blood boil. For once, I didn't care about my odds. I'd pop him if he so much as tried touching my friend.

So focused was I on my rage that it didn't even register what he said until Darla said, "What did you just call him?" Her voice was smooth and cold at the same time, like someone who was used to dealing with scum and not giving it the time of day.

Jon's eyes narrowed and glanced from her to me. "Don't tell me you're one too." His tongue clicked. "What a shame. Maybe I just need to show you what you're missing."

I would have thrown up if I could. It was one thing to come after me. To try to humiliate me was something I could deal with. The night I was jumped came back to me, how helpless I felt, how I wished for death to escape the pain. But his lecherous gaze turned on Darla, and that was something I couldn't handle.

My fist moved before I even thought out my action. The knuckles connected with Jon's face, and the shock from the impact radiated up my wrist. "Ow," I winced.

Darla gasped again as Jon staggered a step, caught entirely unaware. His fingers gingerly touched his face where a red splotch spread out on his skin. "Asshole," he spat.

He looked like he was about to charge me but glanced just over my shoulder and smirked instead.

"What is going on?" Mr. Rodriguez said, coming out of his classroom where he taught automotive skills. His eyes jumped from Jon, who made a show of cradling his jaw, to me shaking my hand out. The teacher's eyes narrowed. "Fighting, boys?"

"He punched me," Jon said indignantly. By then, others started to stop and gape at us.

"I can see that," Mr. Rodriguez said dryly.

I dropped my gaze to my hand. I never knew punching someone would hurt so much. But another part of me got some satisfaction from it. The next thought nearly caused me to groan out loud. Ma was going to be pissed.

"You," Mr. Rodriguez turned his dark eyes on Darla. "Did you see what happened?" I opened my mouth to say that she didn't, but the teacher held up his hand in a signal to stop. I shut up.

Darla tossed her hair over her shoulder and lifted her chin. "This one," she said, glaring at Jon, "made a lewd and gross comment directed at me." She sent a small but grateful smile in my direction and added, "Then he put a stop to it before it got any worse."

"Hmm." Mr. Rodriguez studied us. "Be that as it may, violence is not the way to resolve things. Jon, go see the nurse and get some ice on your face. You two, come with me. The rest of you, get on to class."

Jon tried to gloat, but it looked like it cost him to do it. He took off down the hall, but I knew better than to hope for that to be the end of it where he was concerned.

Darla and I followed the teacher to his classroom. He shut the door behind us, and the noise from the hallway dropped by half. Mr. Rodriguez put away the protective glasses that sat on his desk and picked up a regular pair. He put them on and leaned against his desk while we stood there in uncomfortable silence. I had him last year for a semester and enjoyed his class, but not enough to take another one.

"Ciro, after what happened to you, I can't say I'm surprised at this change, but I've seen where this road leads."

I blinked. I expected detention or something, not this. How much did he know? How much had gotten around school about me?

"I'm not saying Jon doesn't deserve what's coming to him. I heard a nasty rumor that he was behind the attack on you." I might have imagined it, but I thought I saw a flash of anger cross Mr. Rodriguez's face.

"How...uh...how did you hear about that?" My face flushed for what felt like the millionth time that day.

He smiled and said, "I'm the assistant coach of the football team. Speaking of, word's come about that you might be interested in trying out."

I could feel Darla's stare as I nodded. "Yes, sir."

"Then I need to tell you that fighting is one of the fastest ways to find yourself on the bench." He glanced at Darla then back to me. "I'll let it go this time, but that means I want to see you on the field tomorrow afternoon to work out some of that aggression in a healthier way. Is that understood?"

"Yes, sir," I repeated. A smile tugged at one corner of my face.

He faced Darla directly. "What was your name?"

"Darla," she said quickly with a pleasant smile.

"Was what you said about what happened true, Darla?"

Her smile faded immediately, and the calmly confident girl was replaced by a smaller version of herself. "Yes, sir." Darla practically whispered the words. She cleared her throat and explained the scene in more detail.

No longer needing to pay attention to my own fury, I could observe Darla while she spoke. Her eyes stayed on the ground while she hugged herself. Part of me hoped it was part of an act to get Mr. Rodriguez's sympathy, but somehow I knew she wasn't pretending. Jon's words really had creeped her out.

The teacher's expression grew stonier as he listened. "Thank you," he said when Darla finished speaking. "I'm sorry you had to go through that. I hope you'll believe that his behavior is not encouraged or condoned in this school and it will be dealt with."

I sidled closer and put a hand on her shoulder. "He doesn't even deserve to breathe the same air as you," I muttered.

A tiny laugh escaped her in an exhale. It seemed to prompt her to start breathing again. Her shoulders relaxed a fraction under my hand. "Thanks," she said.

Mr. Rodriguez straightened his shirt. "Okay, you better get going to class. Ciro, tomorrow afternoon. And," he paused to choose his words, "let me know if Jon causes either of you any more problems."

We left the classroom and walked several feet away before Darla sighed heavily and said, "I need a drink."

"You're kidding, right?" I asked with a sidelong glance.

"What? Oh, yeah, of course," she said with a laugh that sounded a little too forced. Her brow creased. She seemed to start putting up a wall between us.

I stepped in front of her and stopped. Darla looked up, blinking in surprise.

"What's the deal, girl?" I put one hand on my hip and pushed out the opposite one. "You're acting all doom and gloom here, and that's just not the Darla I know. So, what's going on?"

She smiled weakly which made her frown lines disappear for a moment. I relaxed a little and grinned. "I don't think I'm ready to talk about it yet," she said.

I considered that and peered at her more closely. She looked tired, more so than she ever had at Pleasant Valley. Not just tired, though. Troubled. My lips pursed, but I nodded. "You'll let me know when you're ready?" I asked.

Darla nodded a little too quickly.

"I'm serious! I don't want any of this secondhand knowledge crap. Gay guys are the best for spilling the tea with, and you're friends with the gayest guy in school." I winked at her, and she laughed.

She held up her hands to stop me. "I promise," she said. Her smile seemed more genuine, so I nodded in approval.

"What class are you headed to?" We paused so that she could fish out her schedule from the stack of books and papers in her hand.

"Uh, pre-calculus," Darla said. She frowned at the paper.

"What's up?"

"I already took pre-calc last year. I'm supposed to be in calculus." She glanced up to see me staring. "What?" she said, reddening.

"Aren't you a junior too?" I asked. "You took pre-calc as a sophomore?"

Darla bit her lip and nodded. "I like math." She practically whispered the words, like she was afraid to say it out loud, and she drew the books closer to her chest. I felt like a jackass for making her embarrassed about it.

"That's incredible. I can barely deal with geometry." I scratched the back of my head and grinned. "If you have some free time, maybe you could help me? I don't know if there's a subject you have a hard time with but I'm not too bad at history if you need help there."

Shifting the books from the front to the side, Darla brushed a strand of her hair back behind her ear. "Yeah, that sounds good. I get dates and names mixed up all the time. It'd be nice to have someone to study with. But I should probably get back to the office to figure out why my schedule's messed up. I'll see you later?" There was a note of hopefulness to her question that made me smile.

"Definitely." I gave her a thumbs-up and headed off to my next class.

"Is there something going on in the coach's life that makes him run us ragged like that?" My head hung down, stretching muscles I didn't even know existed before that afternoon. Football practice, as it turned out, was not just throwing and catching the ball. There were sprints, cut drills, and tackling. Oh my God, the tackling. I rubbed one of my shoulders and winced.

Mark and Jeffrey chuckled. "You get used to it," Mark said.

Jeffrey grabbed a short but large cylindrical piece of styrofoam and handed it to me. "Roll it out. You'll feel better."

"Careful, you won't want that back when he's done with it," muttered one of the other guys as they passed.

I kept my head down, pretending not to hear. I tried to tell myself it was because I didn't care, but really I was just too sore. If Mark or Jeffrey heard, they didn't show it. The two went to their lockers and started pulling off practice pads.

The same voice said in my ear, "What, not gonna go shower with your boyfriends?"

"Oh, so clever," I shot back. "Bet it only took you two hours to come up with that one." Unlike him, I didn't bother keeping my voice down.

A shove hit me on my shoulder, and I fell from the bench, barely catching myself with my hands.

"Ciro," Mark said, crossing the room in a few short strides. "Are you okay? What happened?"

Remembering what Mr. Rodriguez said about fighting, I gritted my teeth. Mark wasn't going to get benched because of me. "I'm fine. Probably dehydrated or something."

He looked like he didn't believe me, but he didn't say anything else. Just held out an arm for me to grab onto to help me up.

"Thanks," I said. I picked up the foam roller and headed out of the locker room to the gym.

What was I thinking, trying out for football? Just because Mark and his brother and Jeffrey were cool didn't mean they all were. Seemed pretty obvious that Jon wasn't the only one with an axe to grind with the gay guy. "Stupid insecure assholes trying to act all big and bad for no damn reason." I kept muttering while I readied the foam roller under my legs. My body weight acted as a pressure for the roller to hit the spots of my muscles that ached. Though it still hurt, I could feel the tension start to ease, both mentally and physically.

When I finished with as much as I could, I returned to the locker room. It was pretty much empty by that point, with everyone either in the showers or heading home. The sweat from practice had dried, but I definitely needed a long soak in some water, preferably warm and with body wash. For the moment, though, I'd swap out my clothes so that I didn't stink up the city bus on the way home.

The shirt peeled off of my skin in a way that made me wrinkle my nose. I would definitely need to invest in some dri-fit clothes if I actually became part of the team. Or if I started working out regularly. I tossed the shirt in my gym bag.

Before I could even reach the clean shirt, the hairs on the back of my neck rose. When I started to turn around, an arm pushed up against my back, pinning me with my face to the lockers. A body pressed against the rest of me to make sure I couldn't move. My jaw hurt where it hit the side of the open one I used.

The same voice as before said, breath hot on my ear, "Think you got what it takes to be part of the team? Or are you just looking to get some fantasizing material, pervert?"

"Says the one all up on me," I said. "If you wanted a date, you just had to ask."

The guy pushed harder, definitely uncomfortable. "Shut up," he snarled. "I'm not one of you."

"Your body's saying you are. Or is that just because you like beating up on others?" My mouth was going to get me in trouble, but damn it, I was tired of being the victim. It wasn't exactly untrue, either. Because of the way the guy pinned me, I could definitely feel something going on.

"You wish, you sick freak." He struck my head with his other arm hard enough to knock me into the locker. He let go. By the time I shook off the dazed feeling, the room was empty again. I reached for my shirt, hands shaking, and didn't bother changing the rest of my clothes.

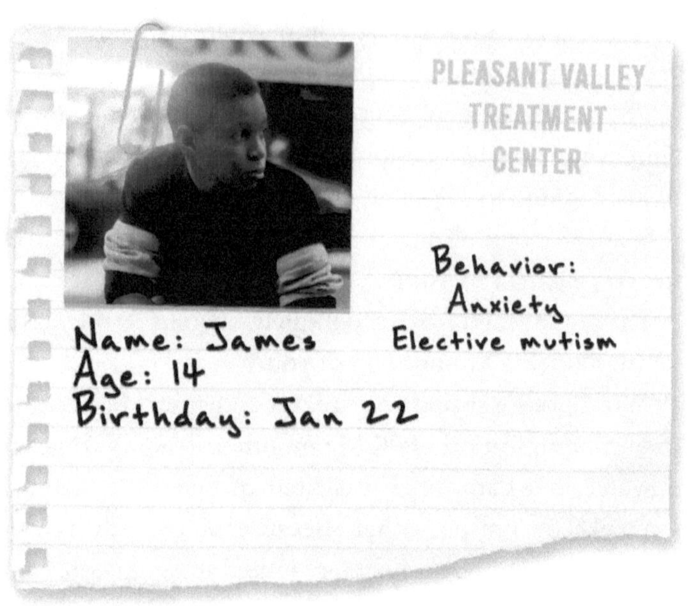

JAMES

Everyone gathered around in the common room like we usually did in the evenings, but the TV wasn't on and no one had any games out. I knew a lot about different kinds of quiet, and this one was definitely sad. With Ciro and Darla, I guess we figured we'd run into them sometime. But there wasn't going to be a chance of running into Renee.

Kate kept hugging her. She'd move away for a little while to let someone else go talk to Renee, but then Kate would find her way back at her side again. Matthew and Tobias kept trying to crack jokes to make Renee laugh. Even Bullfrog gave her an awkward looking handshake. Liz, though, wasn't there. Neither was Derek.

Renee looked completely different than what I was used to. Her hair was piled up in a way that framed her long face elegantly. She wore wide bottom jeans and a black peasant top that made her eyes stand out. It took me several minutes of sneaking glances over before I finally started working up the courage to go up to her. Which was stupid. Just because she looked prettier than usual didn't mean she changed as a person.

Then why did it feel like ankle weights were attached to my legs while I walked over to her?

Renee's head turned to me. She smiled, and I melted.

What was wrong with me? I hadn't exactly talked to her a whole lot, but I'd been around her for over a month and never had this happen.

Tobias and Matthew backed up to let me into the circle they'd formed with Renee and Kate. Matthew clasped my shoulder then was gone.

"Hey," Renee said, tucking a loose strand behind her ear out of habit. "You don't have to say anything if you don't want," she said quickly. "I know you're still kind of getting used to speaking again." Her eyes darted around nervously.

"It's fine," I said. "I just wanted to say, uh, good luck." My mouth felt like sandpaper. "And that, um you look radiant."

Her blush deepened. She bit her lip and checked the nurse's station to make sure they weren't watching. Then she wrapped her arms around me. I hugged her back. "Speak up for yourself. You're worth hearing," she whispered before her lips touched my cheek. When she pulled away, she gave me another shy smile.

Tears stung at my eyes. For the first time, I wanted to

say something but actually couldn't.

Renee went to the desk where her duffle bag waited. The rest of us gathered nearby. Her eyes traveled up the hallway that held her room. She frowned and stared for a few more seconds then turned back to us. "I'll miss you all. I hope when you guys get your phones back that you'll hit me up."

Hurried footsteps echoed in the hall. Liz went straight to Renee and threw her arms around her. She whispered something and held on a moment longer as Renee replied.

"Ahem," Troy said, clearing his throat.

When the girls broke apart, they both had tears coming down their faces.

Renee waved and smiled at all of us again then picked up her bag and followed Troy out of the ward.

Kate walked over to Liz and put an arm around her shoulder. Liz's head dropped, her crying more audible as Kate guided her back to the hall.

Too restless to go to bed, Renee's words lingering in my head, I went to the table that held the puzzle. Most of the pieces were in place. A chunk of the top right was still missing, and that was mostly all the same bluish black color. Other spots had two or three piece chunks missing.

That's what I worked on, finding the pieces that fit in the smaller holes. I lost myself in the methodical searching, flipping over different jigsaw parts to find the ones I needed. By the time I put together a few of the sections, I had an idea of what I needed to do next to be able to move forward.

"Are you sure about this?" Michelle asked.

We sat in one of the smaller therapy rooms. My cell phone lay on the armrest of her chair. She'd had to check it out from the desk for me.

The thing pretty much only was ever used for video games and music before my parents sent me to Pleasant Valley. I didn't text anyone outside of family, and I obviously never talked on the line.

I nodded. My mouth quirked in a slight smile as I reminded myself to speak. "Yeah, I think I need to, but I don't want to do it by myself."

Michelle grinned. "All right then, let's do this." She picked up my phone and hit the call button then the speaker button.

"Hello?" my mother's voice answered. "James?"

"Hi, Ms. Tolin, this is Michelle Gray. I'm one of the therapists at Pleasant Valley Treatment Center."

"Is my boy okay?" Worry filled her voice, pushing out any remnant of the exhaustion that usually took center stage for her. As a nurse, she was always tired.

I wanted to speak, to let her know I was fine. My jaw ached from the tension.

"Yes, he's doing pretty well here, actually. He asked to be able to do a video call with you, if you're able?" Michelle asked.

"Yes, of course," Mom said right away. "Uh, just let me...Oh, forget it." The option for video chat lit up.

Michelle handed the phone to me, and I hit the button to connect. My mother's face filled the screen with a tiny box in the corner where my own face showed. Her hair was pulled up into a bun, and she didn't have any makeup on. Dark circles under her eyes said that she'd probably been dozing when the phone rang. When she smiled, though, some of the tension and years melted from her. "Hey, baby," she said gently.

I grinned back. "Hi, Mom," I said.

Her hand covered her mouth in surprise, and she looked like she was going to start crying. She took a breath instead and asked, "How are you doing? Are you eating okay?"

"Yeah, the food sucks compared to yours, but it's edible."

That seemed to set her over the edge, and she really did cry. My heart twisted from guilt at the pain I must have caused her. "I'm so sorry, Jamie," she managed to say. "I'm sorry we didn't listen when we could. I was afraid we'd never hear you speak again."

While she wiped at her eyes, I peeked over at Michelle, my own eyes searching for some kind of hint on what I should say or do.

Michelle reached over and tapped the mute button. "Are you okay? Do you want to stop?"

I shook my head. "I just wasn't expecting this."

I unmuted the call as my mom regained control. "Is there anything you need?" she asked. "Anything I can bring you? Is it...is it okay to come see you?"

"Yeah." I grinned. "Actually..." I bit my lip and looked at Michelle.

Michelle leaned over enough to be in the frame on the phone and said, "James is interested in going home, and we wanted to talk to you about what that could look like."

My mom closed her eyes and held her other hand to her chest. "Of course," she said, her voice catching with emotion. "I can't wait to hold you again." Her eyes shifted to Michelle. "What do I need to do? When can he come home?"

I studied my mother's face while she listened intently to Michelle explain about follow up treatment. She bit her lip almost in the exact way I had moments earlier at the mention of family counseling. "Does it have to be everyone?" she asked.

"That would probably be most helpful to James so that the family can work through his episodes of silence together," Michelle replied carefully. "But at a minimum you and his father. Siblings aren't always receptive to family therapy, and it shouldn't be a thing James dreads."

My mom nodded, but the tension in her face only slightly lifted.

"It's okay if Dad doesn't go," I said.

"I'll work on it," she said in earnest.

I rubbed at my eye and felt my chest tighten. I always thought I was the forgotten one, the afterthought. But she was willing to go toe-to-toe with my father to try and help me. Maybe I didn't pay attention as much as I thought. "I love you, Mom," I said.

"I love you too, my sweet boy. I'll do whatever it takes to make sure you know that always."

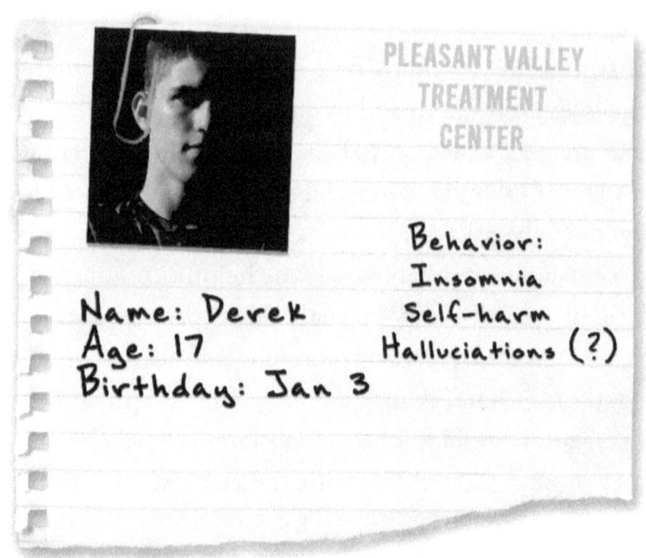

DEREK

Ever been a prisoner of your own mind? I wouldn't recommend it. It sucks. I'd be pacing if I could. It's surreal as hell being actually aware of yourself without being present. I didn't exactly experience everything Trish did. I saw the same things most of the time, but, far as I could tell, my reactions weren't even close to hers.

I wished I could talk to the Doc. I needed to know how to better control myself. I could have hurt Renee... Not that it was really me, I think, but it was close enough for it to be terrifying.

Trish had me sit down at the desk in my room and pick up some folded pieces of paper. I wanted to read them. I tried to step to the forefront of my own mind and regain control, straining against Trish's hold. All it got me was a nudge of my arm.

I wanted to yell. It was my body, so why did she have more control over it than me?

Truth was, I didn't know how any of it worked. She obviously had plenty of practice being in the background, so maybe she knew how to be in tune with me. Because I sure as hell barely ever recalled before when she or any of the other sides took over. This was way different, though. I knew what happened in Renee's room. I knew what Trish chose for breakfast, but I couldn't get any sense of her thoughts. It was like a locked room.

I guess she could still get a sense of mine, though, because my mouth sighed, "Fine," and my arms opened the first letter.

Derek

Man I'm really bad at writing stuff. Renee had to proofread this for me because I apparently spell like "a troll who failed grade school". But ya know she enjoys it.

Tobias says this could maybe help you and who knows? Maybe so. I think we all just really miss having you around. It's like a piece of the family is missing and the rest of it's falling apart without you. Whatever caused you to go away like this has to be really bad I think because you're like one of the strongest guys I ever met. And I don't even care that there's proof I said it, that's how much I mean it. So yeah...

Matthew

I didn't even get a chance to process Matthew's letter before Trish picked up the next one.

Yo Derek,

Where you been? We got a score to settle in volleyball. I'm kidding. Kinda. About where you been, not about the volleyball. So a shit ton has been happening while you have your identity crisis. I don't know how much you know cuz you haven't been at group much but Renee is leaving, leaving town actually. And James is talking more and more. Kid actually tells us to shut up now when he wants to watch cartoons. Can't even be mad at him for it. Kate has been pretty much a shell and Liz is all worked up about Renee even though she won't admit it. My bet is there was something going on there that none of us knew about. And me? Well my world got turned upside down. My best friend basically attempted suicide by cop and I don't even know if he's alive right now. I guess I kind of know what he might have been thinking when I tried slitting my wrists and it sucks. Sorry, I didn't mean to dump all that on you, just kind of needed to get it out I guess. You were right about needing to organize the closet. If you want help with your closet, you don't need to go away. I'll help. And I bet I'm not the only one. Hope to see you soon.

Tobias

I wanted to stare at his words and let them sink in, but Trish just seemed to want to get this over with. She flipped the paper down on top of Matthew's and started to open the next one. Would she just wait a damn minute? There was too much going through me to take stock, and she just kept flooding me (us?) with more.

Hey Six

What's the haps? Wow, that sounds lame. Screw it, it's said.

I kind of get it now—that Trish is there to protect you. It's the part of you that thinks the rest of you needs to be shielded from something. But here's the thing. You can't let her run the show forever. You have to face whatever it is that set you off. Kate thinks it's her fault since her spat with you was right before this major switch. And if it is, dude, you gotta get a grip. She's being stupid because everyone knows she adores you but she thinks she's protecting you. And you're being dumb if you're gonna run whenever your feelings get hurt like that. Right now it feels like you're hiding from all of us and it's not cool.

Trish, let him go. He's going to feel pain in life and that's just a fact. You can't shield him forever or he'll never build healthy relationships.

I miss you, Derek.

Main tumse pyaar kartee hoon

Liz

If I had control of my eyes, I'd probably be tearing up. Liz and I arrived within days of each other. It was her second time in Pleasant Valley, so she already knew the ropes and had zero problems getting me settled. There was a strange energy around her, a sense of buzzing restlessness tempered with eyes that didn't miss a thing. Damn, she'd called it all, like usual.

Trish moved my hands to pull out the next letter. Talk about a living hell.

Derek

It's James. I don't really know what to write. I don't think I ever wrote a letter before. That's another first for the books. I guess it's like a long text? I don't know if you're gonna reply but if you don't it's okay. Matthew asked me to try anyway. Kinda don't really know what's going on beyond what I hear, but if it makes any difference, nothing about you has changed for me. You're the same guy who picked up on my silence practically immediately and never made me feel bad about it. You helped me. You made sure I was respected and heard even when I didn't talk. Nothing can ever change that for me. Wish I could say it to you directly now that I actually use words again but this works too I hope. Thanks for everything Derek. You're like the brother I always wished mine would be.

James (but you knew that already)

Damn... The kid knew how to tug at the heartstrings. Did that even apply in the state I was in? I never really thought that James deserved to be locked up with the rest of us. A smart kid like that who just needed someone to listen to him shouldn't have been made to go through the stuff that the rest of us did. There was an urge in me to tell him that to his face. The feeling in my leg flooded back and it twitched. I swung it back and planted my foot on the ground.

I never thought I'd have to concentrate so hard on doing the basic things like standing. Thinking about that made me lose my grip again, slipping behind Trish's control.

My other foot bounced like Trish used to do when we were little and she was anxious about something. She moved my hand to hover over the next letter and hesitated on picking it up. I got a brief impression from her, almost like she regretted even opening the letters. The next one was from Bullfrog.

Hi
I don't know if you want to hear from me but Tobias said it might help. And you and Liz never treated me any different than the

others so I want to try. Most everyone either avoids me or looks away when talking to me especially at first. But not you. I was still raw from coming from the ICU and felt like a cross between a mummy and a leper. I wanted to die. And you looked straight at me and smirked and said, "You look like you've been through hell, but seems like the afterlife isn't ready for you yet. You've got some living still to do." I thought you were crazy. But you weren't wrong. I got some living to do, and so do you.

Tyron (Bullfrog)

Tyron? That was Bullfrog's real name? Why the hell hadn't he ever told us? I felt like a lion pacing a cage that was way too small. I needed out.

Trish's movement seemed slower as she picked up the letter that had a neat loopy script. There was one more after it. I wasn't sure I could even handle getting through the next ones.

Hi Derek
I wish there was a way I could talk to you before I go. I don't really know what I'd even say except thank you.
No judgment, no hesitation,
you were there without reservation
Giving me tea, making me see
The good inside of me
Even when I thought it was gone
When I thought I was alone.
I owe you more than I know how to say
More than I can ever repay
And all I can think of today
Is how to thank you.

Love to you always,
Renee

Sensation flooded through me as I sort of stepped into the foreground. My body felt weird, like it didn't quite fit right. A series of feelings rushed through me. Throat tightened, stomach clenched, eyes stung. I gasped as the aches and pains coursed in my body.

One hand still held the letter, its papery texture smooth between my fingers. I couldn't remember ever having been conscious for a switch or whatever it was called. It hurt. There was a lingering of doubt and shock in the back of my mind that felt strange. There had to be some way of living with Trish instead of fighting her for control.

I ran my hands over Renee's lettering, regretting a thousand times my last interaction with her. She'd gotten a glimpse of the monster inside, and I would never forgive myself for that. But even after that, she'd still reached for me.

Her letter went on top of the rest. I lifted the last one and held it without opening yet. I wasn't sure I wanted to read it, but I kind of felt like I had to. Liz was right. I needed to try. I lifted the edge.

I'm so sorry, Derek. I was stupid and selfish and scared. I'm not ready for any kind of relationship I don't think but I should have said that instead of trying to make it sound like you were nuts for thinking it was a possibility. I don't think you're crazy. I think you're crazy smart and crazy kind. I feel like I'm broken and not worth any affection but that's my issue. I want to say that your condition doesn't scare me but it does. It scares me to think you—the core you—might be gone. And I'm so sorry for driving you away. If I ever get the chance, I'll try to make it up to you somehow. God just give me the chance.

Kate

I leaned on the desk with my elbows and held my head. I could barely remember the last time anyone actually cared about me for anything beyond the money compensation they got for fostering me. The letters sat as an actual physical representation of that reality. I couldn't help it. Tears started leaking from my eyes, and I had to push the papers away so that they wouldn't get wet.

I supposed they accomplished the mission. Trish was in the backseat again. I needed to go talk to my...to my friends.

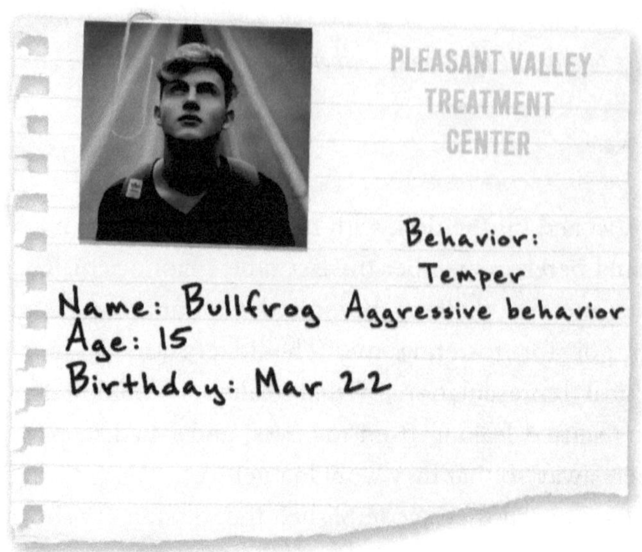

BULLFROG

The paper stared back at me blankly. Literally. It was blank. I was supposed to write some kind of statement on my progress in treatment, but I had no idea what the hell I was supposed to write. Part of me still thought I should have died in the fire. Some days, that voice was pretty strong. Most of the time, I just felt the need to make up for it somehow.

The statement couldn't have made much of a difference, though. I doubted I would be able to ever resume any kind of "normal" life. Maybe I could eventually get a place, especially when I aged out of the system. Maybe I could get a dog. I looked out the window at the courtyard. Most of the others were in the gym, just another thing I couldn't do yet. But the warmth from the autumn sun coming through the window felt good enough to make me sort of sleepy. Definitely not in the mood to write about my progress.

"Hey," said someone behind me.

I jerked out of my dazed state to see Derek standing in front of me. "Hi," I said, shifting in my seat to look at him. He looked like he hadn't slept in a week. Narrowing my eyes, I asked, "Who am I talking to?"

His eyes rolled. "Chill, Frogger."

I cracked a grin. "Good to have you back, bro." I lifted my fist and he bumped it. "The others are at the gym if you want to go see them."

Derek shook his head. "I think I need to talk to Doc before I try to face the group."

"Yeah, I get that. Iesha can probably get him to come by for you," I said, looking outside again.

"Is she here today?"

I nodded.

"Thanks," Derek said. "I'll see you later." His footsteps squeaked as he walked across the room to the nurse's station.

I wondered what it was like for him, living in fractured parts. Even with how much I wished to blame my mistakes on something or someone else, I don't know if I could have handled finding out that parts of myself were locked away.

Iesha escorted Derek to the end of the hall where she unlocked the door for him to go to Dr. Larson's office. On her way back, she paused and said to me, "Are you doing okay?"

I nodded and kept my eyes averted. Iesha was too nice to ever say anything, but I hated the pity that always showed in her eyes when she looked at me. "Just nervous about meeting with the lawyer." I glanced at the clock. "Which he should actually be here soon."

"I can check if you want?" she asked. I shrugged. "Okay, I'll let you know." The brightness of her voice made me smile a little. She was just so damn happy. She headed back to the desk. I could barely make out her voice on the phone calling to the front desk. The receiver thunked against the stand as she called out, "They actually just arrived. They're getting signed in and will be here in a few minutes. Do you want to go wait for them in the visitor room?"

I stood and followed Iesha to the room with too much furniture for the small space. She closed the door, leaving me alone to wait. I tossed the notebook onto the table then flopped onto the couch. There was a stain on the ceiling that looked suspicious as hell. I hoped it was just a leak from the pipes.

My leg started bouncing as I thought about what was coming. The one time I met the lawyer before hadn't really gone so well. The guy was nice-ish, if a little rough around the edges.

Times like this were when I missed having a phone or something to be able to take my mind off things. All I could think about was what the meeting was going to bring. Something told me it wasn't going to be good. I tried the grounding thing that Kate and Derek helped me with but I couldn't get past the first one. My mind kept running off track. I was attempting for the fourth or fifth time when the door handle turned.

I sat up straight and tried to smooth out my shirt, feeling kind of foolish about it.

Mr. Hayes walked in. He was tall with only a little extra

padding around the middle. His head was shaved so the light reflected off his head. He had a slight beard kept neat that was showing signs of graying. And he carried a cane to help him when his leg bothered him.

The social worker followed, and she was his entire opposite. Short, squat, and plump, even her cheery smile seemed to counter Mr. Hayes's own expression. I couldn't remember her name.

"Hello, Tyron," she said, not quite looking at me.

"Hi," I grunted and crossed my arms. Good or bad, at least everyone in the hospital would meet my eyes.

Mr. Hayes watched the exchange. "Ah, Miss Darcy, if you don't mind, could you step outside a minute?"

Darcy didn't hide the confusion on her face. "I have to be here," she said.

"I'm not going to interview him. There are many things in this world you aren't going to understand, chalk it up as one of those." He stood exactly in the spot in the small room where she would be completely incapable of getting by him. I hid a smile. "I will bring you back in, but this is going to be very painful if I have to first get around your discomfort. So, rather than have that battle, I'm asking you to step outside and I will bring you in when I'm legally required."

Darcy huffed and left without another word. Mr. Hayes shut the door behind her, and I breathed out a sigh of relief.

Mr. Hayes turned his calculating eyes on me, but he looked directly at mine, skipping the barely healing burns on my face like they weren't even there. "She's probably calling her supervisor, who will be calling mine, so let's get through this as quickly as possible. Sound good?"

I nodded. "Yes, sir," I said after.

A hint of a smile crossed his stern face then disappeared. "If I'm going to help you, I need to know what happened."

I didn't even know what I was hoping for, but it wasn't that. I slumped back against the seat. "Isn't it in the police report and the news?"

"There isn't a story in the world that doesn't have at least two sides to it. You came out of there mumbling, 'It's my fault' over and over again. Guilt and guilty are not always the same thing." His words were tinged with an earnest that I definitely wasn't imagining.

"Why are you helping me? I'd figure this would be one of those open-shut cases."

Mr. Hayes let out a genuine short bark of laughter. "You watched too much TV. I'm not an assigned defense lawyer. I volunteered for your case as soon as I saw the story on the news."

That made even less sense. Unless he was after the fame that came with high-profile cases. But Mr. Hayes didn't seem like that sort to me. "Why?" I asked again.

His eyes closed as sadness drifted over his face like a cloud on a sunny day. "I served with your mother in the Marines."

"What? My mom wasn't in the military."

Mr. Hayes opened his eyes again. "Tyra di Leon," he said.

I'd seen my mother's birth certificate before my dad hid or threw away all her stuff. That was definitely her name. He even pronounced it right. The smallest bubble of hope rose in my chest. My mother. If nothing else happened in the meeting, I'd learn more about her.

The lawyer smiled at some change in me, I don't even

know what. "Can you tell me what happened?"

"If you tell me more about how you knew my mom," I countered.

Mr. Hayes held out his hand. I shook it. "Deal," he said. He didn't even flinch at my hand. He leaned back and said, "Di Leon was the crew chief on the helo that dropped my platoon in. They were supposed to come back for us, but the area got too hot. They were gonna leave us. Then I guess the pilot got shot trying to turn away from the rendezvous. The other guy on the flight said later that your mom didn't hesitate longer than it took to check for a pulse. She pushed the pilot out of the seat and came in for us." Mr. Hayes held my gaze, but I recognized the feeling behind his eyes. The same one any of us got in the group room during our reading. "She got out seven of my guys and she came back. She made the other Huey follow her in to get out the rest of us. My platoon would have died without her.

We kept in touch from time to time. I think you were still too little to remember, but I was at the funeral." Mr. Hayes clenched his fists, and he definitely fought back some tears. His voice was rough as he said, "I got to watch my kids grow up. My Marines got to go home. If I can help di Leon's son, it still won't even begin to repay my debt to her."

I wiped at my eyes. It sounded like my mom. She was an angel even in a war zone. "Thanks," I said. "I- I didn't know she... Thanks."

Mr. Hayes cleared his own throat and met my gaze again. Waiting.

I inhaled. Held it. Exhaled. And, quickly, quietly, I told him everything.

He sat there and listened to all of it. When I finished, he

didn't say a word at first. My stomach twisted in the way it did when I was afraid. Mr. Hayes held his hand out, palm up. I put mine on top of his, and he held it loosely as he bowed his head. It took me a moment to realize he was praying.

He let go and looked at me after a few moments, studying me as my heart beat a thousand times faster in my chest. "You are your mother's son," he said at last.

Something in me caught. My throat closed up and my chest hurt. I shook my head, unable to speak.

"You are," Mr. Hayes said with enough force in his words to make me meet his eyes. "You could have let those kids die and saved yourself, but you went back and damn near lost your life trying to get them out. That is exactly something your mom would have done."

Something in me broke, and I shook with the sobs and tears that I'd been battling and bottling for what felt like forever. Mr. Hayes didn't say anything, he just let me be, and I never needed anything more in my life.

When I calmed down to the point where I was just crossing my arms and trying to breathe normally, Mr. Hayes asked if it was okay to let Darcy back in. I nodded and he opened the door.

Mr. Hayes rotated to the chair closer to me and let Darcy have the one across the too large table. She was too busy trying not to appear disturbed to notice that I was still trying to compose myself.

The lawyer made a show of getting the paperwork in order and having Darcy sign some things to give me some extra time.

Mr. Hayes, when he spoke, was all business. "The arraignment is set for tomorrow. The charges are first-degree arson and four counts of first-degree murder. I think the arson can get changed to criminal mischief, and there's no way the murder charges will stick."

My stomach twisted in a nasty way. I leaned back and closed my eyes, fighting the tears.

"Usually, a family member's testimony would help reduce or get rid of prison time, but that's impossible in this case. On the other hand, this is a first-time offense and the circumstances surrounding this are highly unlikely to be repeated."

"What does that mean?" Darcy asked.

Mr. Hayes took a moment to compose his face before he said, "Put simply, Tyron was backed into a corner. He was beaten by his father, verbally abused by his stepmother, and he retaliated in a method that made sense to him given the violent circumstances around him. He lashed out, not knowing the house was occupied. And when he found out it was, he tried to save Daisy and David Tuttle. Tyron survived, but no one else in the house did. Therefore, it is extremely unlikely that Tyron would be put in a position where this would happen again. Does that make sense now, Miss Darcy?"

Her cheeks tinged with embarrassment, Miss Darcy nodded meekly.

The mention of the twins' names hit me like a sledgehammer. I buried my head in my hands and wept for them all over again. My arms could still feel Daisy's weight. The look of Davy's head slumped against the wall under the window was burned in my memory forever. It was my fault they were dead, and I deserved whatever I got.

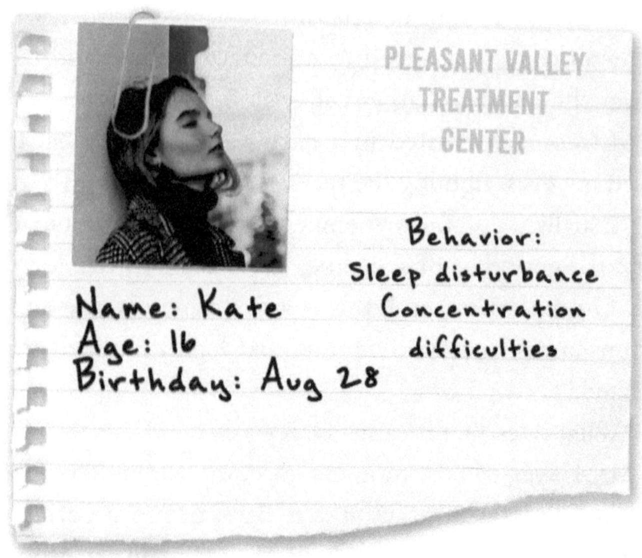

KATE

"Don't you think you're being hard on yourself?" Riley's words sliced through my self-hatred like a bucket of cold water.

"What?" I had just finished a long rant about what an idiotic fool I was and how my stupidity affected ones I cared about.

She smiled patiently. "Were you in Derek's head, controlling his thoughts and reactions?"

I shook my head, but I was pretty sure I knew where she was going with this.

"So you couldn't have possibly known what his reaction was going to be. And it being what it was is not on you."

The chair squeaked a little as I shifted my weight in it. "Yeah, but-"

"But nothing," Riley interrupted. She took the binder from her lap and set it on the small table. Her arms rested on her knees as she looked intently at me, and her words matched her gaze. "You are allowed to say no to someone. That does not mean something is wrong with you or that you're a bitch."

I let my head fall forward. One of the things they taught us was to pay attention to our bodies, and mine started to tense up. "When I said no before, it didn't matter. I still got hurt." I wasn't sure she heard me because she didn't respond for a moment.

"Kate," she finally said. I peeked up at her through a curtain of hair. "I wish there was something I could say to take away your pain. But what I can do is tell you as many times as you need to hear it that it is not your fault." Riley reached a hand across the table, stopping about halfway.

I took her hand with mine, and she squeezed gently. Riley said, "You control your actions and no one else's. No one gets to control yours either."

"I guess," I said. "Derek has all this pain too, and it makes sense as to why he withdrew, I think. I don't know, I just feel like I'm too broken."

"Not that I am encouraging a relationship between patients," Riley chuckled, "but maybe you should give yourself as much of the benefit of the doubt as you're giving him."

"What do you mean?"

Riley raised one of her shoulders in a half-shrug and leaned back in the chair again, stretching out her back. "I mean that you are so wrapped up in giving him a break because of what he's gone through, what he's facing. Why can't you do that for yourself? You've gone through some stuff too. Cut yourself some of that slack."

I sat in stunned silence for a second. "Derek and I aren't the same," I said.

"Of course not. You're different people, with different histories. You and Renee aren't the same either. Nor you and Liz. And none of them are the same as each other either. But you do all have some common threads that tie you together, make you all relate to each other somehow. And if that's the case, can you not give yourself the same forgiveness and grace that you give them?"

I left the session feeling like I just survived a fundamental earthquake. One of the things they tried teaching us in the group sessions was that core beliefs could be the hardest to redefine but that it wasn't impossible. Still felt daunting, though.

"Hey," a voice said.

Apparently I'd been staring at the ground because I lifted my head to see Derek standing in front of me, a plastic carton in his hand. "Hi," I said cautiously.

Derek's cheeks flushed, and he held the carton out. "I got you some cake," he said.

"You're back?" I immediately regretted the words.

But he chuckled a little and said, "Yeah, I guess Tobias's plan actually kind of worked. The letters sort of helped me see that maybe I'm not as pathetically useless as I think."

"I'm sorry-"

"Don't," Derek interrupted. He held up his other hand. "I talked to the doc a while ago and I think I have it worked out. When I was really little, I lost my whole family in one night. I thought I was too little to remember, but really Dr. Larson thinks my brain tried to protect me by splintering, locking away the memories. But I still always felt alone. So I never tried really connecting with someone, which meant I never got rejected. So when it finally happened, I regressed. Or reverted. Or whatever the psycho term is for it. Point being, my anger was entirely misplaced. Especially after what you told me happened to you, I should have never put any kind of pressure or expectation on you. That was entirely unfair of me, and I am so sorry. I can understand if you don't want to, but I would be more than happy just being your friend." He wiggled the cake carton.

I grinned sheepishly and took it. "I think I had some misplaced feelings going on too, which was also unfair. I'm not saying yes to more, not yet anyway. But I don't think my answer will be no forever. Friends?"

"Definitely."

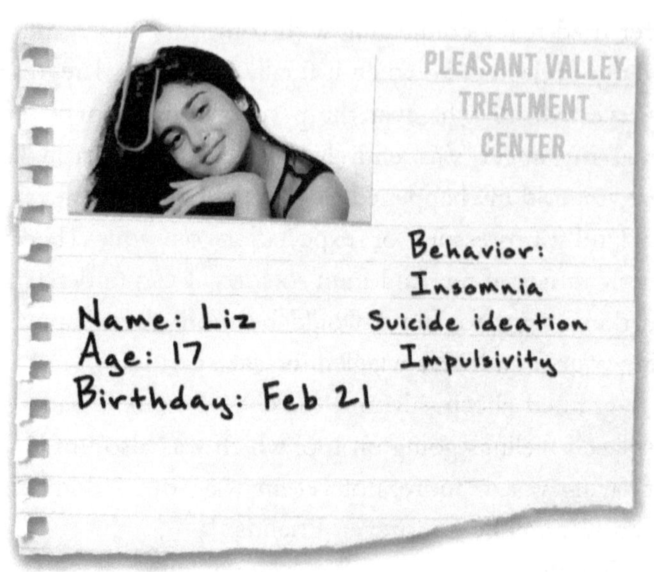

LIZ

*W*ho needed sleep? Not me. There was too much to do, to see, to learn. I spent enough time sleeping and more when I was tired, but I wasn't tired. I could do anything while I was awake. I needed to do as much as I could before the melancholy set back in and I didn't feel like doing anything again.

When was the last time I ate? Maybe I should have cooked something. That sounded like something Mumy would say. She'd also tell me to cover up, though, because "Nice Indian girls don't dress like that."

I looked at myself in the mirror with my faded jeans and red crop top. The more I looked, though, the more I found wrong with it. I tried another shirt—long sleeves, navy blue. Didn't like it. Tried leggings and a peasant blouse. Even worse. What happened to me? I looked gross and exhausted.

My phone buzzed. The message said, "Are you ready?".

All the excited air in me deflated. "I'm not going," I typed back.

"Why??"

I turned my phone over and flopped on the bed. After a moment, I curled up, wondering if it was a mistake and maybe I should go anyway. I wanted to sleep, but I couldn't. The restlessness wouldn't let me. Kicking my legs in a pseudo tantrum, I let out a scream of frustration.

A shower would help. I went to the bathroom and looked in the mirror. My reflection showed deep, dark circles under my eyes.

Why was I so pathetic?

The hottest shower in the world wasn't going to do anything for me. Maybe being around my family would help.

I went downstairs to find Mumy. When I was little, I could just curl up in her lap and let her do my hair, and everything in the world seemed like it would be okay.

Mumy sat in the living room, dressed in her usual sari and choli, looking elegant and humble all at once. I used to watch her put together her outfits and once asked why she still dressed like she was in India. She said that we shouldn't forget where we come from.

She was smiling at something Lena was working on. My younger cousin had come to stay with us while her father was working to bring the rest of Lena's family over from India. Mumy's eyes lifted to see me, tension creasing her brow immediately. "Lanaisha," Mumy said. Her gaze moved to my clothing, and I burned in childish embarrassment.

"Liz!" Lena called out, hearing my mother. She waved enthusiastically, but Mumy pursed her lips at the anglicized form of my name.

"Hey, squirt," I said to Lena. I turned back to my mother. "I was going to ask you something, but I forgot." I ran back upstairs without waiting for a reply, mentally cringing at knowing my mother hated running in the house. Back to the safety of my bed where I

wouldn't be a disappointment.

A short while later, gentle footsteps came from outside my room. With a soft knock, Mumy said, "Lanaisha? We are taking Lena to see her father, okay? We'll be back later. Unless you want to come?"

I couldn't bring myself to say anything.

"Money is on the table if you want food." I heard her walk away.

I waited until I heard the front door close before I got up again. The bathroom seemed even gloomier with the lights off, but I didn't have any energy left to turn them on. I just wanted to sleep. On a whim, I went to my parents' room. My father had sleeping pills in the medicine cabinet in their bathroom. I could just take half of one of those. He would probably notice half suddenly showing up, though.

I opened the bottle and shook one of the pills out. It was a capsule, which meant there was no cutting it in half for a partial dosage. I stared at the little pill then back at the bottle. Maybe I could just get out of my family's way for good. No more disappointing Mumy. No more drama. No more exhaustion. I could just sleep forever.

That sounded too good to be true. Probably I would just get sick. I put the bottle back in the cabinet and washed down the one pill with some water. I just wanted some sleep.

My leg bounced as I read the last few lines. Everywhere ached. My arms itched where I had cut them up a few months prior. I scratched at my neck where a makeshift noose had sat a few months before that. Three attempts in all. But that wasn't even close to how many times I had thought about it. Almost to the point of obsession.

I felt raw, exposed, and I wanted to hide in my room more than ever before. I tucked my legs under myself on the chair and forced my eyes to Michelle. But I didn't look at her face, only her hair. It was expertly done in short braids that cascaded over one side in a beautiful waterfall. My fingers twitched as I thought about the motions for the style.

"Do you think about the future?" Michelle asked.

I tapped on the notebook a little. "Not really."

"Is there anything you'd like to do? See? Would you want to travel?"

Shrugging, I said, "I don't know. I have a hard time just focusing on the day ahead, let alone a week or year or whatever. Sometimes I feel like I can do it all, like I want to see the world. Other times, I just want to be left alone and not deal with anyone or anything."

Michelle studied me and tapped her chin with a manicured finger. "Are there any days where you're kind of in between?"

"Sometimes. Kind of like when I was a lot younger. Where I could just exist and not have to be going all the time or not be moody. But I mean, most teenagers go through this depressed phase, right?" I let my eyes meet my therapist's.

"Yes and no," Michelle answered. Yes, in that lots of teenagers go through emotional changes, but not usually to the point where suicide becomes a daily fixation."

I slumped back in the chair again. "So I'm broken."

"No," she said quickly. "You are not broken."

"I'm outside the range of 'normal variance,' so I'm broken," I countered, air quotes and all.

Michelle snorted, and I allowed a small smile. "Have you ever heard of kintsugi?" she asked.

I blinked and shook my head.

Pulling out her cell phone, she tapped on the screen a bit, carefully avoiding breaking one of her nails. "Kintsugi is a technique used in Japan to repair pottery. Rather than throw something out, they use a precious metal infused lacquer to bind the pieces together again." She held out her phone. Dozens of beautiful pieces laced with gold or silvery lines covered the screen.

I scrolled, finding more and more images of pots, plates, cups, even decor, never with the same pattern. "They're pretty," I said, not really knowing what else I was supposed to say.

"Liz, you said you were feeling broken. Instead of throwing yourself away, could you maybe look at rebuilding yourself to become even more beautiful?"

My first thought, as I caught a glimpse of my scarred arm while handing back Michelle's phone, was to retort that I could never be as beautiful, but for once, I stopped myself. I glanced at the picture again, then back at my arm. The bowl was a rich brown color with two simple lines of gold running all the way through it. The resemblance was uncanny, even to me.

Michelle noticed my pause. "The broken pottery can't repair itself either," she said gently. "With support and staying on medications to control your bipolar swings, you can rebuild. You can live and be generally happy."

I nodded and put the phone on the table. Lifting my head a little, I said, "I want to try."

When I walked out of the room a while later, most everyone was gathered in the main room for the evening check in. My eyes swept over them all, and I smiled, grateful for all of them and for the ones who had already gone on to rebuild their lives. Derek caught me looking and lifted his hand in a wave.

"Hey, Six," I said, leaning on the back of his chair.

"You good?" he asked.

I smiled and said, "Yeah, I'm kintsugi. We all are, and we're gonna be okay."

ACKNOWLEDGMENTS

There are so many people who indirectly or directly helped bring Insanely Sane fully into the world. Without their support, this would have been immensely more difficult.

This story might have never seen the light of day had it not been for Sarah Hawkaluk, who devoured every word in my writing binder in middle school and kept asking for more. Thank you for all your encouragement.

Thanks to Diane Windsor at Motina Books. Without you, this book probably would be collecting virtual dust in my files. Thank you so much for taking a chance on it. Thank you also to my wonderful beta and ARC readers.

Thank you to my parents and grandparents for passing on their love of a good story and appreciation for music. Special thanks to my mom, who somehow convinced me that I was getting away with something when I would stay up late reading, and to my dad—the bravest man in my world.

To my husband Allen, thank you for supporting me through… well, literally everything. Thank you for not abandoning me. Thank you to our three boys for keeping me on my toes (always) and to the extended family who help with them.

Thank you to Captain Baile for sticking with me on my own journey of healing and your wise analogies about closets and kintsugi that have obviously stuck with me. To the ohana from my time in treatment, thank you for showing me what resiliency and support looks and feels like.

Thank you also to the friends who supported me on the journey of making this book a reality: Sara for being an amazingly inspiring D&D Dungeon Master and the best sibling from another dribbling; Blake and Patrick for helping me brainstorm; Ginger for your patience and encouragement while I was sidetracked from Sethi's Song; Mark for standing up against the trolls; Derek, Vince, John, Ryan, Devin, Joe, Alyssa, Tyler, and Josh for helping keep me insanely sane.

My best friend, Tawnie Wallette, thank you for being unapologetically you. You are the strongest woman I know, and I am so grateful for you, always.

Finally, I want to thank you. Yes, you, the person reading this. Thank you for your support, your time, and your energy. Most importantly, thank you for being brave and being enough.

ABOUT THE AUTHOR

Jasmine Shouse was born in Littleton, Colorado, and raised in Billings, Montana. After high school, she joined the U.S. Navy, stowing her uniform for good after nearly 12 years. She lives in northwest Florida with her husband and their three kids and two dogs. She's an avid gamer, a terrible artist who enjoys painting, and an amateur archer who can hit the target (most of the time). Jasmine is the co-author of the military fantasy series *Sethi's Song*. *Insanely Sane* is her first solo novel and first foray into Young Adult fiction. Visit her online at

www.jasmineshousewriting.com.

Mental health awareness is a very important topic that needs to be discussed. It's the goal of the author and the publisher to encourage people to have meaningful conversations surrounding all facets of mental health.

We want to remove the stigma. Your mental health is just as important as your physical health. No one should be ashamed to seek help.

The following section includes discussion questions that can be used in a classroom or book club. We also offer mindfulness exercises and mental health resources.

There is hope—you are not alone.

DISCUSSION QUESTIONS

1. During a group therapy session, Michelle says, "Just because someone is family…does not mean you are obligated to keep a relationship with them." Darla counters that she's been taught family comes first. Do you agree with Michelle or Darla? Why?

2. Liz challenges herself to answer honestly on the self-esteem questionnaire despite knowing the answers that would be considered "normal." Can you relate? How?

3. Do you think Renee blaming herself for her sister's fate is justified? Do you think her family blames her?

4. When Kate tells Derek it's crazy for him to like her, she's trying to push him away before either of them gets hurt. Aside from what Derek goes through next, do you think this strategy was helpful for Kate? Why or why not?

5. What do you think Tobias ought to do with the ledger his friend gave him?

6. While trying to reassure Matthew about his reading, James says, "You guys get it, even when you don't." What do you think he means by that?

7. Ciro thinks things will be worse for him if he lets others know how the harassment bothers him. Why do you think he still feels that way? Is he right?

8. Bullfrog thinks it's his fault the twins died and that he deserved whatever he gets because of it. Do you think he deserves the shame and guilt he piles on himself?

9. Derek and Kate apologize to each other and agree to be friends. What do you think their relationship will look like later on?

10. Liz says, "I'm kintsugi. We all are." Do you think she explains to anyone what she means?

11. Part of the treatment in Pleasant Valley is group therapy in different forms. Do you think it helped any of them? Why or why not?

12. Music is mentioned throughout, particularly lamenting the loss or celebrating the return of it. Do you think music has an impact on thoughts and feelings?

13. What do you think happened to everyone next?

MINDFULNESS EXERCISES

Grounding Stone Mindfulness

Pick up a stone. Usually a smooth or polished stone or rock works best but choose whatever appeals to you.

Take a deep breath in so that your chest expands then let it out slowly.

What does the rock feel like? Is it light? Is it warm? What is the sensation against your skin? What are your thoughts as you hold it?

What does the rock look like? Is it all one color? Are there patterns or streaks?

What is going on around you? What do you hear? Smell? Taste?

Focus again on the rock. Does anything feel different or changed about it? What feels the same?

While this can often be used to counter anxiety, panic, or PTSD episodes, the grounding rock can also be used as an awareness technique to practice mindfulness in a way that isn't about visualization or meditation.

This can also be done with other objects besides rocks.

TIPP
These are often used to help with emotional regulation. Feeling things isn't a bad thing. Sometimes those feelings

are so intense that it blinds us to making solid decisions. TIPP is designed to interrupt that intensity in order to make better choices.

Temperature

HOW: Hold your breath and submerge your face in cold water for at least 30 seconds. You can also use an ice pack or cold cloth, but the bowl has the most intense effectiveness. Keep water above 50 degrees F. Best used when sitting quietly.

WHY: The exposure will begin the mammalian diving reflex which causes the heart rate to drop and blood flow redirected to the brain and heart.

Intense Exercise

HOW: Engage your body in some sort of vigorous exercise, even for a short time. Run, walk quickly, etc.

WHY: Exercise increases your heart rate and gives you an outlet for the intense emotion.

Paced Breathing

HOW: Breathe deeply so that your belly expands. Slowly release it. Repeat so that your exhale is slower than your inhale.

WHY: Deep breathing can help relax tension and stress and provides something to focus on rather than the intensity of the emotion. It increases the supply of oxygen to your brain and stimulates calmness.

Paired Muscle Relaxation

HOW: While breathing into your belly, tense your body's muscles (but not to the point of cramping). Take notice of the tension in your body. While exhaling, mentally say "relax" and let go of the tension. Identify the difference in your body.

WHY: This elicits a relaxation response which lowers the heart rate and reduces tension.

**TIPP exercise taken from *DBT Skills Training Handouts and Worksheets, Second Edition*, by Marsha M. Linehan. Copyright 2015.

RESOURCES

The following is a list of mental health resources. Please reach out to any of them if you need help.

National Suicide Prevention Hotline
1-800-273-8255 *shorthand 988 available July 16, 2022
https://suicidepreventionlifeline.org
Free, 24/7 access to crisis counselors. Available to all, including military.

Boys Town National Hotline
1-800-448-3000 or text VOICE to 20121
 boystown.org
Free, 24/7 access, available in over 100 languages to teens and young adults (20s).

The Trevor Project
1-866-488-7386 or text START to 678-678 or chat online.
https://www.thetrevorproject.org/get-help/
Resources for LGBTQ+ youth under 25.

Crisis Text Line
Text 741741
www.crisistextline.org

Veteran Crisis Line
Text 838255
www.veteranscrisisline.net

Canada Suicide Prevention Service
1-833-456-4566
http://www.crisisservicescanada.ca

Kids Help (Canada)
Text CONNECT to 686868
https://kidshelpphone.ca/need-help-now-text-us/

Lifeline Australia
13 11 14
https://www.lifeline.org.au/

-- Suicide Prevention Resource Sites --

American Association of Suicidology
www.suicidology.org
"Promote understanding and prevention of suicide and support those affected by it."

American Foundation for Suicide Prevention
www.afsp.org
Funds scientific research, educates the public about mental health and suicide prevention, and advocates for public polices

American Psychological Association
www.apa.org/helpcenter
Find a psychologist near you, coping techniques for being affect by suicide, how to find a therapist, etc.

Befrienders Worldwide

www.befrienders.org

Emotional support centers in 32 countries

Depression and Bipolar Support Alliance

www.dbsalliance.org

In-person and online peer support on education and wellness regarding mood disorders.

Guardians Mental Health

www.guardiansmh.org

Promotes mental health awareness and offers resources and peer support.

Jason Foundation, Inc.

www.jasonfoundation.com

Educational and awareness programs to equip youth, educators, and parents to identify and support at-risk youth.

Lite for Life Foundation

www.yellowribbon.org

Education, training, and support for suicide awareness and prevention.

Mentalhealth.org

www.mentalhealth.org

Informational site for veterans, families, and supporters.

National Alliance on Mental Illness

www.nami.org

Educational programs and advocacy for public policy to fight stigma surrounding mental illness.

National Center for PTSD

www.ptsd.va.gov

Research and education on PTSD and trauma.

Mobile apps: PTSD Coach, PTSD Family Coach, Mindfulness Coach, Anger and Irritability Management Skills.

National Organization for People of Color Against Suicide

www.nopcas.org

Outreach and education for people of color at risk of suicide.

Question, Persuade, Refer Institute

www.qprinstitute.com

Learn how to recognize warning signs of a suicide crisis and question, persuade, and refer them to help. Training can be online or with a live instructor.

Suicide Awareness Voices of Education

www.save.org

Suicide prevention through public awareness and education, reduce stigma, and serve as a resource for those affected by suicide.

Center for Suicide Prevention (Canada)

www.suicideinfo.ca

Suicide prevention programs and skills through multicultural trainings. (A fee is required to access online databases)

www.ingramcontent.com/pod-product-compliance
Lightning Source LLC
Chambersburg PA
CBHW030709190726
48286CB00001B/249